Outpost Scotland

ABBOTT A. BRAYTON
Outpost Scotland
A World War II Novel

Celtic Cat Publishing
KNOXVILLE, TENNESSEE

Celtic Cat Publishing
2654 Wild Fern Lane
Knoxville, Tennessee 37931
http://www.celticcatpublishing.com

Manufactured in the United States of America

Book design and production by Dariel Mayer

Cover illustration: An original watercolor by Will Workman

Maps by Jack Brayton

Permission to use the badge of the Royal Highland
Regiment of Scotland, the Black Watch was received
from The Black Watch Museum Trust.

ISBN: 978-0-9847836-7-0

Library of Congress Control Number: 2012943149

To my grandsons: Will, Jack, and Ethan

Peace is neither free nor easy

Acknowledgments

THE CREATION OF THIS BOOK HAS been a labor of joy. The story emerged over decades of travel in Scotland in pursuit of history and family heritage. I'm grateful for the assistance freely offered by Ms. Sarah Dallman of the National Library of Scotland. Dr. Anthony Morton, Curator for the Sandhurst Collection of the Royal Military Academy provided additional assistance regarding The First War, known today as World War I. Colleagues at the Imperial War Museum answered questions on Scotland in World War II. Mr. Ian Abernathy of Ben Nevis Books in Fort William generously answered many questions about the Western Highlands.

As the book progressed it became a family affair. I'm grateful to my wife, Esta, who carefully read the book several times, offering suggestions, and correcting errors. Daughter, Alison Brayton Bullock, provided many editorial comments and, together with Esta, offered a woman's perspective that assisted me enormously. My son, Matthew Brayton, was a close companion on this project, especially during the collection of data which proved essential to the story. Grandson, Jack Brayton, served as my computer consultant and cartographer.

Colonel J. Thomas Hennessey, Ph.D., USA-Ret, a former US Army Attaché to the Court of St. James, provided valuable comments. He was joined by Major John A. Rains, USAF-Ret in a careful critique and analysis of the finished product. Mr. Will Workman painted the cover picture. Mr. Alfie Iannetta, Chief Executive of The Black Watch Museum Trust provided permission for use of The Black Watch logo.

My dear friends, Jean and Michael Hemingway of Barnard Castle, England, gave valuable advice and corrected errors which an American could make when writing about Britain. My publisher, James Johnston, provided guidance on final content as we prepared the book for publication.

To everyone, including the many Scots who assisted me during my research visits, I give my sincerest thanks. For those errors which may have crept into the story, I alone am responsible.

Glossary

Aldershot: British Expeditionary Force headquarters and mobilization base
Argylls: Argyll & Sutherland Highland Regiment, based at Stirling
ARP: Air Raid Precautions
Black Watch: The Royal Highland Regiment, based at Perth
Blitz: German bombing of Britain during World War II
Boys Rifle: Anti-tank rifle, .55 inch bore
Bren Gun: Automatic assault rifle, .303 caliber, 29-round magazine
Browning Automatic Rifle: U.S. assault rifle, .300
       caliber, 20-round magazine
Camberly: British Army Staff College for mid-level officers
Cameron Highlanders: Queen's Own Cameron
       Highland Regiment, Inverness
Chief Constable: Chief of police
Civil Defense: Civilian agencies formed to protect civilians in wartime
Continent, the: Term used by the British when referring to mainland Europe
DCM: Distinguished Conduct Medal, awarded to enlisted men
DSO: Distinguished Service Order, awarded to majors and above
E-boat: Fast attack craft
Fifth Columnist: Civilian loyal to enemy forces
Gordon Highlanders: Gordon Highland Regiment, based at Aberdeen
HLI: Highland Light Infantry Regiment, based in Glasgow
Home Forces Command: HQ for British Army
       units located in the UK, at London
Indian Army: Indian colonial force, largely officered
       by British Army personnel
Jerries: Slang term for German forces
Lewis Gun: WWI light machine gun, .303 caliber
Loo: British reference to toilet
Maginot Line: French fortifications along border with Germany
Mentioned in Dispatches: Recognition for distinguished
       service (below the Military Cross)
Mills Bomb: Mark 36 hand grenade from WWI
MC: Military Cross, awarded to junior officers for heroism
MM: Military Medal, awarded to other ranks for heroism
Molotov Cocktail: Petrol (gasoline) bomb in a glass bottle
Petrol: gasoline

POW: Prisoner of war

Provost: Mayor of small city

Quetta: Army Staff College located in India; equivalent to Camberly

RAF: Royal Air Force

Ross Rifle: Canadian WWI rifle, .303 caliber, used by British Home Guard

Sandhurst: British Army Royal Military Academy, to train new officers

Scottish Command: Territorial HQ for forces
in Scotland, Orkneys, Shetlands

Seaforth Highlanders: Seaforth Highland Regiment, stationed at Ft. George

SOE: Secret espionage force

Sten gun: Light assault machine gun

Subaltern: Newly commissioned officer, term for second lieutenant

Territorial Army: Army organized reserve forces, mobilized in 1939

Tommy gun: Nickname for the Thompson submachine gun

U-boat: German submarine

Vickers: Medium machine gun, .303 caliber

War Office: British Army headquarters, located in London

Webley: Officers' revolver, .455 caliber

Wehrmacht: German Army

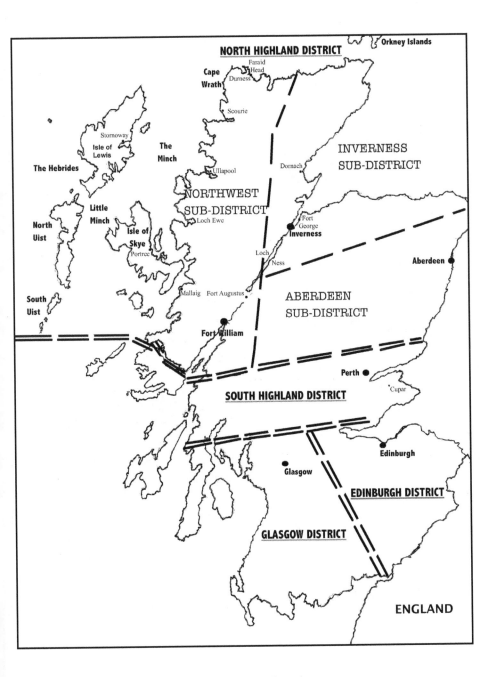

Map of Scotland

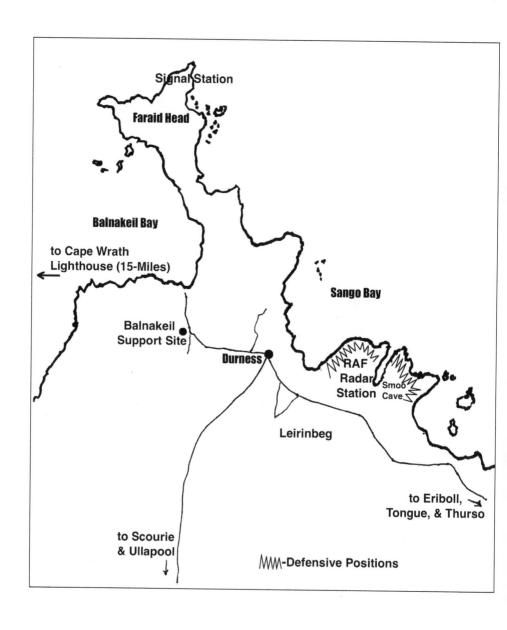

Map of Durness and Sango Bay

Preface

COLONEL DAVID MCKENNA was known to me only through stories, for I was born during the war, in suburban Boston, Massachusetts. I heard a great deal about him from my Aunt Bessie, Elizabeth McColgan, who was born and raised in Dumbarton, Scotland.

When the war broke out in 1939, Bessie applied for a clerical position with the Royal Navy and was assigned to the newly established Coastal Forces Training Base at Fort William, Scotland, named the HMS *St. Christopher*. She soon joined the social circuit at Fort William, enjoying movies and dances with young trainees during the evenings or on weekends.

In early 1944, Bessie met a young U.S. Navy sailor who had been assigned to the training center to learn small craft operations in preparation for the Normandy Invasion. They fell in love and, several months later, were married. Elizabeth McColgan became my Aunt Bessie. In late 1945, the war having ended, Don and Bessie relocated to Pawtucket, Rhode Island where Don established an accounting practice.

Quite often, at family gatherings, Bessie would talk about her years in Scotland. World War II was a defining experience in her life and the lives of many others. Unlike World War I, commonly called the First War in Britain after 1939, World War II directly threatened the entire population of Britain. Bessie frequently would discuss Colonel David McKenna and the impact he had on her life. Although, she never had a formal meeting with him, they often exchanged pleasantries when he visited the Royal Navy Headquarters at Fort William's Highland Hotel for coffee with one of her superiors. She said that people throughout Lochaber often spoke of him and of his many efforts to protect

Scotland against an invasion by the Jerries, common slang for the German forces. Perhaps this was a case of hero-worship, but she would tell how his presence gave everyone a sense of security and confidence.

Many years later, I discovered David McKenna struggled with his own inner demons.

1

June 24, 1940

THE DREARY CHILL from a rain-darkened sky matched the somber mood of foreboding that hung over London. People walked quickly through the streets with a new sense of fear and urgency. The war, just nine months old, had been unwelcome from the beginning, but suddenly loomed ominously over Britain. The previous autumn, unlike 1914, saw neither excitement nor enthusiasm, as battalions marched through the streets to waiting ships. The collapse of France, days earlier, had brought the German armies to the coast of the English Channel, a mere twenty miles from British shores. Not since Napoleon had Britain been so threatened, and not since the Spanish Armada had she felt so defenseless.

A taxi sped through the streets and turned onto Pall Mall, driving a short distance before stopping in front of the United Services Club at Whitehall. David McKenna, a retired Colonel of the Royal Highland Regiment of Scotland, the Black Watch, stepped out and checked the time. It was 11:57 a.m. He paid the driver and bent over to buff the toes of his shoes with his handkerchief. A sharp pain shot down his right leg. Standing erect, he adjusted his tie, snapped straight the seam of his trousers, and dashed up the steps. His limp was barely noticeable. A tall, lean figure with light sandy hair and a thin mustache, he was dressed in a dark brown business suit.

The club was bustling with uniformed officers of the armed services and many retired officers in civilian clothes. A heavy air of gloom hung over the crowd and small clusters of older men huddled together, speaking in hushed tones. The usually lively dining room with white tablecloths, spotless crystal, and sparkling silverware was subdued as diners ate with a deep sense of melancholy. At 11:59, David walked to the desk of the dining room *maitre'd* and asked for General Ismay. Hastings Ismay, a large man in his early fifties, was beginning to show his age with

3

a thickening waistline and receding hairline. He wore the uniform of a serving major-general.

"Good morning, David, right on time as always, good! Have a seat and order the stew. It's quick."

"Thank you for meeting with me, Sir, I know your time is valuable." Although normally comfortable with Ismay, David felt as awkward as a schoolboy. The general had a reputation as a strict and demanding superior who expected precision and perfection in his subordinates' work.

"I wish I could have met with you when you first called last month, David, but we've been working day and night with this mess on the Continent. The last chaps got off the beach at Dunkirk three weeks ago and from Cherbourg last week. No equipment, of course, but they're back in their garrisons or on our beaches waiting for the Jerries."

The British Expeditionary Force, or BEF, under General Jack Gort, was first sent to France on the outbreak of war in September 1939 following the German invasion of Poland, a swift thrust known as the *Blitzkrieg*, or lightening war. As the months passed without fighting, the initial force of five British Army divisions soon grew to almost fourteen divisions. Newspaper pundits called that quiet time the Phony War or the *Sitzkrieg*. The quiet was broken in April 1940 by the German invasion of Denmark and Norway. An Allied force of French and British troops was hastily assembled and shipped to Norway. After some sharp encounters with the Nazi forces, they were soon forced to withdraw, and Norway surrendered to the Germans.

On May 8, the German *Blitzkrieg* was turned on Luxembourg, the Netherlands, Belgium, and France. In four short weeks, the Allied forces were pushed back as each country successively surrendered. British forces were driven into a small perimeter around the port city of Dunkirk. The Miracle of Dunkirk saw a third of a million troops, mostly British, safely evacuated to England by June 4.

A second force of almost three divisions, under Lieutenant-General Alan Brooke, was landed at St. Malo. Their mission was to establish a new defensive line along the Normandy Peninsula in order to retain a toehold on the Continent. During the next few days, the French armies collapsed, forcing the British to withdraw back to England from its second Dunkirk, actually the port of Cherbourg. There, having left most equipment in France and with rifles drawn from stockpiles of old weapons, the BEF was sent to defensive positions along the coast of Britain to await the expected German invasion.

"Things look very bad, General."

4

"It's worse than very bad. If we get through this mess, it will be a second miracle. There will be no opportunity to muddle through this time. It was a gift from above that we got most of the forces out of France at all. You know that we lost most of your old 51st Division, and two battalions of the Black Watch. Captured, dammit, and not their fault! They were separated from the BEF and sent far out to the east in front of the Maginot Line. What was thought to be a good decision, at the time, proved a catastrophe. The Jerries encircled them and wore them down with repeated attacks until they were exhausted and out of ammunition. They had no choice but to surrender at St. Valerie-en-Caux. And now, they're in some damned German POW camp," he spat out.

"The French Army was in tatters, Paris was evacuated, and the French Vichy government surrendered." Ismay paused for a spoonful of stew. "I think I'll keep the rest of my thoughts to myself. Maybe, I'll comment further at another time. Anyway, you look well, David. How's the leg?"

"Much improved, thank you, my hip actually. It was pretty well shattered in the accident, but it gets better each month. I run three miles several times a week, and it holds up quite well."

"David, I was deeply saddened to hear about Anne. Damned stuff, that cancer. How long has it been?"

"Thank you, Sir. Actually, it's been almost fifteen months now. I appreciated the flowers."

"The least I could do. And the girls?"

"They've adjusted very well, under the circumstances. We had some pretty rough weeks after Anne died, especially at night. Last year, the girls moved in with my sister in St. Albans; she has three girls of her own. She has always been a second Mom to them, and the five girls are very close. My brother-in-law has been a prince through all of this. I send money each month and try to see them on weekends. It seems to be working pretty well."

"Good. And your new business, export-import or something?"

"Yes, Sir. I'm with Williamson-Sweeney, good people. It was a bit of an adjustment at first, but it's running smoothly now. We're mainly facilitators, working primarily with the Empire. A businessman in Egypt owns a large cotton farm. When he needs tractors and packaging equipment, he contacts us. We locate a manufacturer for the equipment and a buyer for his cotton. We arrange financing and transportation. He loads his cotton onto trucks we have leased; the cotton goes to port and is loaded on ships we've chartered. A few weeks later his new machinery arrives, probably at the same time the money arrives at his bank for the balance of the transaction. He's happy. The next season becomes more productive, raising even more cotton, and the cycle begins all over again. Multiply that throughout the Empire: jute from Kenya to Dundee, wheat from Canada to Liverpool, tea from Ceylon to Plymouth, and so on."

"Weapons?" Ismay asked without looking up.

"Occasionally. We were busier with weapons two years ago. Now, with the war on, everyone wants to buy and nobody wants to sell. Except for the Americans, of course, but their government has clamped down on the private arms dealing. It's just government-to-government sales under strict Neutrality Laws, leaving little room for our company. We did facilitate the purchase of Ross rifles from Canada. That's still in process."

"Yes. Mr. Churchill is trying to arm the Home Guard. Speak quietly about that subject, David, as the walls have ears. What role did your firm play?"

"We arranged part of the shipping. The War Office came to us because we already had a transportation network in place."

"Hmm. Well, the less said about that, the better." Ismay dug for a piece of mutton in his stew. "So, David, I suspect you didn't ask to meet me just to exchange pleasantries."

"No, sir. I very much appreciate your willingness to speak with me. I guess you know what I'm going to ask."

"Of course." Ismay paused to take another spoonful and sat back silently for a moment. "David, look over there at the bar. All those chaps standing there, glancing occasionally over here, are retired officers. Every one of them would give fifty pounds sterling to be sitting where you are right now. Each would like to be back in uniform. They were all good soldiers once. Almost all fought the Germans in the last war and they'd like another go at them. 'Any assignment, General, no matter how small or insignificant,'" he mimicked. "I'm going to have to stop coming here. I can't eat. Constant interruptions. They line up when I come in, each pleading his case. If you leave the table now, David, they'll be right over here. So, sit still until we leave. I simply don't have time to hear their pleas and gently explain that we cannot find a place for them. I don't wish to hear their secret ideas on how to beat the Germans. Good chaps, but too old and out-of-date.

"The past few weeks have been horrible! Our strategy was wrong, our tactics outdated and our equipment obsolete. Our leadership . . . well, never mind. We need younger men in key positions, men with good experiences, good ideas, tactically sound, and the energy to reorganize, retrain, and lead the forces against the Germans. Those chaps at the bar simply will not do. They're as obsolete as a Lee-Medford rifle and they should best stay retired."

"But you were willing to have lunch with me."

Ismay put down his spoon and leaned back in his chair. "Yes, partly out of loyalty to a former hard-working subordinate at the Defense Ministry, and partly because you retired just over a year ago. You were working on advanced concepts for the coming war and you're not very much out of date. I respect your brains and energy."

"Thank you, Sir. Is there a chance I can return to service?" David began to feel optimistic again.

"I don't know. You have several strikes against you." Ismay paused, searching for the right words. "You're retired . . . out! Getting back in is never easy, as you well know. You have a bad hip. How bad I don't know, but I'll ask the Chief Medical Officer's opinion. And you made a rather large mistake in your go-around with General Haining. Very bad judgment, David, and it cost you heavily. You thought you were right and you may well have been. But, he was a lieutenant-general and you were a colonel. You didn't handle it well and you made a powerful adversary. Now, he's a full general and still in the War Office as Vice Chief. And I'm not."

"But you have enormous influence, Sir."

"It's not what you think, David. I'm Mr. Churchill's Chief Military Staff Officer and Secretary to the War Cabinet. I serve on the Chiefs of Staff Committee, and you might say I'm Mr. Churchill's Chief-of-Staff in the new Ministry of Defense. He's both Prime Minister now and the Minister of Defense. He's the decision-maker. I'm not and I'm very careful not to abuse my role with the service Chiefs. I don't even make recommendations to them for fear of compromising my position. I don't know what I can do for you, if anything. Let me think on it. If something comes up, I'll call you. Now, finish your stew so we can leave together. There's a war on, you know."

June 26

THE PHONE RANG INSISTENTLY as David dashed from his bathroom, lather still on his face.

"Colonel McKenna, is that you? This is Gladys Nichols from General Ismay's office. Do you remember me, Colonel?"

"Yes, Mrs. Nichols, I remember you very well."

"Thank you, Colonel. General Ismay asked me to call and inquire if you could come to his office tomorrow morning at 8:30. He said it's most important."

David's heart skipped two beats. "Yes, Mrs. Nichols, I'll be there at 8:30 sharp."

"Thank you, Colonel. I'll put you on his schedule."

As David began to hang up the phone, she said, "Oh wait, Colonel, the General also wants you to come in full uniform and decorations. Would that be possible?"

"Yes, Mrs. Nichols. Tomorrow at 8:30."

June 27

DAVID ENTERED GENERAL ISMAY'S OFFICE in the Ministry of Defense and greeted Mrs. Nichols. "He's very busy, Colonel, but he asked me to get him out of his meeting when you arrived." David took a seat alongside several officers who carried papers and maps. After a few minutes, Ismay came out of his conference room, nodded at David and went into his office. David followed him in and saluted.

"Sit down, David, and listen carefully. There may be an opportunity for you to return to active service, but it's not what you might think, nor probably want. The Chief Medical Officer reviewed your file and the news isn't good. Your hip has mostly healed, but it is very fragile and will never again be the same. It can break or dislocate quite easily, not that it will, but it could. I'm sorry to say that you're rated as unfit for field duty, and that will not change."

David's heart sank and he felt almost sick. "Yes sir, I knew it never would be one hundred percent, but it has healed quite well, and I can run again, probably farther, and faster than many other soldiers."

"David, you have been rated unfit for field duty and that's final! I can't change it. I'm very sorry to tell you this, but I think you must have known it for some time. It doesn't matter that you can run. We're not fighting a trench war again, as we did in France last time. This war is different. It is fast moving and our leaders must be perfectly fit in every way. This isn't a debating issue, David," he said sharply. The pause was awkward, and David felt his face turn red. After a moment, Ismay's face relaxed. "There may be some other service you could perform."

"Could I work in the Ministry of Defense or the War Office again?"

"No. There's nothing here in the Ministry, and the War Office is definitely out. General Haining is adamantly opposed to your return in any fashion, and he controls appointments there. There's very bad blood between you two. As I told you before, he's now General Dill's Vice Chief and a full general. He's in a position to veto your appointment and he has made it very clear that he will."

"Perhaps I could lead a training or depot command." David felt himself grasping for straws.

"Perhaps, but it's unlikely, given your hip. And that's not a good use of your talents. No, I think something else." Ismay glanced at a paper on his desk, put it aside, and went on. "Now listen carefully, David. There's a job for which I think you would be well suited. It's a command, but not a field command. It's an obscure assignment that has emerged with some prominence over the past few weeks. Mr. Churchill has taken a personal interest in this position."

"Mr. Churchill?"

"Do you know him personally?"

"No, Sir, I've seen the Prime Minister, but I've never met him."

"Let's just say that he's aware an officer is being offered the position today. Once it is filled, he very well may forget about it entirely. David, I may have said too much already. The position is not mine to offer. You've a 9:30 meeting today in the War Office with General Dill, so you had better get along over there. Let me finish with some advice. I believe General Dill will offer you a position in Scotland . . ."

"In Scotland!"

Ismay said slowly, "Let me finish, David. Yes, in Scotland. Beyond that I'll say nothing, except that General Dill over-ruled General Haining's objection since you'll be so far away, and there was no other qualified candidate immediately available for the post. My very strong advice is for you to accept it and give it everything you've got. It will not be an easy job and, frankly, neither Dill's staff nor mine have any idea how you or anyone else can do it. But it's a command, and you will be back in active service. Any questions?"

"No, Sir," David said, fumbling for words, "but thank you for everything you've done for me. My words cannot express my gratitude." He saluted and left. Mrs. Nichols gave him a knowing smile as he passed by her desk.

Sitting in the outer office of the Chief of the Imperial General Staff flooded David's mind with memories. General Dill's position was akin to that of the Commander-in-Chief of the British Army. The many meetings and briefings David had attended here came rushing back, and he began to think about. . . .

"General Dill will see you now, Colonel McKenna."

Startled, he jumped up, regained his composure, and entered the inner office. Dill, a tall and courtly officer extended his hand. "I believe we've met, McKenna."

"Yes Sir, I briefed you several times in Aldershot, and you were a speaker when I was a major in Staff College at Quetta. You dined with several of us that evening."

"Damned fine class you had, McKenna. Yes, well, you've come highly recommended for a position and you fit our model."

"Sir?"

"Several weeks ago, Mr. Churchill directed the War Office to look hard at Northwest Scotland. He thinks it's a soft spot in our defenses and he's right. No forces up there to speak of, a small population, long coastline, rough terrain and not much defense capability. He thinks the Jerries could land parachutists, or a submarine could drop off a raiding party and make mischief. It would discredit the Government and cause a sharp drop in public morale, lower than it already is. We've no military forces to commit up there for the foreseeable future. Everything we have, or what's left of the Army, is focused on Southern and Eastern England. The Jerries are forming up right across the Channel and they're converting river barges to carry troops and tanks. An invasion could begin in days or weeks. We can't divert troops to the Scottish Highlands and weaken our defenses down here. We're practically naked as it is.

"I decided after talking with General Ironside . . . you know he's the new Commander-in-Chief of Home Forces since leaving this office . . . anyway, I decided to find an available colonel or make an acting colonel from a highland regiment and appoint him commander of the new sub-district for the Northwest Highlands. We've been reorganizing the Army districts in Scottish Command. The current commander of the Highlands district . . . oh, what is his name? Grey-Wilson, I think. Well, no matter, he'll command the South Highlands District and Brigadier William 'Jack' Campbell has been appointed commander of the North Highlands District. You know the Highlands were a single district until now, but we found that to be impossible. The area is huge and the threat to the eastern Highlands is much different from the threat to the west. So we're splitting Scotland into four districts for the time being: the North Highlands, the South Highlands,

Edinburgh together with southeast Scotland, finally Glasgow together with southwest Scotland. Each district will have two or three sub-districts. I want you to command the Northwest Sub-District. At least we'll try it this way for a while." Dill paused for a moment and looked out his window.

"So, I suppose you want to know why you were selected." David nodded. "You're a Scot and a Colonel in the Black Watch. That alone will give you credibility in the Highlands. You have several decorations from the last war and from the Punjab, including a Military Cross, and you were three times mentioned in dispatches; plus you have two war wound badges. This all carries great significance with the Scots. You were a successful battalion commander, you have extensive War Office and Ministry of Defense experience and, had you not had your accident, you probably would be moving up to become a brigadier right now. Also, you're available. Frankly, I haven't another Highland colonel to spare at the moment."

"General, I'm honored, but what will I have to work with?"

"Well, not much, Colonel. I guess that's for you to figure out. The new Home Guard is beginning to get organized; you know, the Local Defense Volunteers that were established just this past month, the LDV. The name 'Home Guard' isn't official yet, but I expect it will be soon, as Mr. Churchill likes that name, and LDV will be dropped."

"Yes Sir, I've been helping the London LDV Headquarters after hours these past few weeks."

"Splendid, then you know what we're dealing with: great enthusiasm, fine patriots, but no equipment, no pay and little training, except whatever they're receiving during evenings and on weekends. Not very encouraging, but it's absolutely essential we get them trained and equipped as quickly as possible. Mr. Churchill takes a very personal interest in the LDV. We also have various Civil Defense and Air Raid Precautions formations, mostly untrained as well, to help protect our communities. In any case, your mission will be to command all this effort in the Northwest sector: organize, train, equip as best you can, and make them successful. Technically, you are not the Home Guard commander, but you will become their commander in an emergency and the commander of all active forces within your sector. Unfortunately, there are really no active forces in your sector. You'll have to determine how best to perform this mission, as neither Scottish Command nor the War Office staff has figured this out yet. Do you know Brigadier Campbell?"

"Yes Sir. He and I served together twice."

"Good, as he will be your immediate superior. He commands the North Highlands District with three sub-districts under him, including yours. He will give you a more extensive briefing on the situation in Scotland. How soon can you get up there?"

"I think I should have things wrapped up by Sunday. I can drive up then."

"Will you drive your own motorcar?"

"Yes Sir, I recently bought a fairly new Ford Tudor."

"Excellent. The Army has no spare vehicles to offer you, but you will be reimbursed for expenses. And a weapon?"

"I have a Webley revolver which I bought from Army surplus in India back in the twenties, along with my field kit."

"Good. Now, you probably remember Colonel Trevor Henry in Operations. He's expecting you shortly and will give you further information. I suggest you go to his office now. You may consider yourself to be on active duty again as of this moment. Do whatever paperwork the clerks require before you leave here today. Good luck, McKenna."

"HELLO, OLD CHAP, another fresh victim for the wolves!"

"Good morning, Trevor," David said as they shook hands, "nothing like a cheery welcome."

"Sorry, but it's true. General Dill's assistant told me to prepare a briefing for the new Commander of the Northwest Highlands sub-district. I was quite surprised to learn it was you. I thought you were retired for good."

"Well, I'm back for better or worse. So how have you been?"

"Working my arse off with this bloody mess we're facing. Most nights this past month, I slept right here at my desk. Not conducive to a happy wife and marriage."

"How is Carol? I haven't seen her since Anne's funeral."

"I guess she's fine. She's spending her time helping the Civil Defense effort, doing something to coordinate the rescue services in our neighborhood. I don't see her most days, but she seems to be happy helping the war effort. She's good at those things. I expect she'll rise to become the managing director of London's central relief efforts before long, or something like that."

"Give her my best. So, what is your job here?"

"Officially, I'm the Director of Home Defense Planning and Coordination." In reality, I'm the fellow who answers all the questions for the War Office about home defense of Britain and I'm the liaison officer to the Home Forces Command at St. Paul School."

"It sounds impressive."

"Not really. I'm pretty much the chief gopher for every office in London that wants something from the Home Forces Headquarters. Nevertheless, I get to sit in on the meetings of the big shots as they discuss grand strategy or whatever they discuss."

"At least you received a promotion for this. Congratulations!"

"Thanks. You became a colonel first, but I bet I'll be a brigadier before you."

"Yes, you will. I'll not make brigadier with this hip. I'm rated unfit for field service, you know. I don't even know how long they'll keep me on active service."

"It depends on many things. It could be a few weeks, months, or the duration of the war. I don't know and I suspect nobody else does either. They told me about your hip. Sorry, that stinks. Actually, I'm surprised they even let you return to active service."

"It's because of my blue eyes and winning smile." They laughed.

"Alright, David, I'm supposed to give you a briefing."

"First, tell me why Mr. Churchill's involved with this assignment. I understand from General Dill that he thought the Northwest Highlands was vulnerable to an attack or something."

"Actually, I was at the meeting early last week. Mr. Churchill led the service chiefs in a planning session with their home defense staffs and a few cabinet officials. We reviewed the invasion threat and counter-invasion preparations, studying the coast of the British Isles, sector by sector. Mr. Churchill asked question after question about the defenses. None of the answers were satisfactory, of course, as the Army had gotten its bloody arse kicked by the Germans in Belgium, and the evacuations have taken all the War Office staff's time. When we came to Scotland, the Home Forces staff discussed the Lowlands and the Eastern Highlands. They never even mentioned the Western Highlands, assuming that was not a threatened area."

Then Trevor mimicked Churchill, "'now General Ironside, weakness invites attack, don't you agree?' Ironside agreed. 'And Northwest Scotland and the islands have a longer coastline than all of England. We have parts of twenty-seven divisions defending England. What do we have defending Northwest Scotland?' Of course, the answer was 'nothing.' Admiral Pound suggested that the Royal Navy would do its best to defend the Highlands, maybe with help from the RAF. Churchill would have none of that. He launched into a tirade about the Army's failure to anticipate even the most remote threats, and how could we call ourselves professional soldiers if the Nazis could exploit our weaknesses. When he calmed down, he turned to Ironside, pointed his finger, and said 'let not one foot of Britain go undefended!' Ironside winced and looked at his staff assistant, Mitchell Davis, who was writing all this down. He said, 'I'll commission a full staff study forthwith.' And so, David, my weekend went to hell forthwith!"

"So, what did you decide?"

"Well, being an astute staff officer, I decided that the Home Forces Command should prepare a plan to defend the whole Highlands. Of course, they'll pass the mission down to Scottish Command. Brilliant, right?"

"You passed the buck."

"Certainly. I have enough to do right here and, besides, they should've anticipated this from Mr. Churchill. They had become too complacent with Neville Chamberlain, but they cannot pull the wool over Mr. Churchill's eyes. He knows more about defense matters than the lot of them. Scottish Command has come up with a partial plan and they're studying the remainder."

"What's the plan?"

"The recently revised plan to split the Scottish Command into four districts, with two sub-districts in each district, has been underway for several months, and eight colonels have been appointed to command those eight sub-districts. Because of Mr. Churchill's admonition, the latest version of the plan will create a ninth sub-district— exclusively for the Northwest Highlands. That's why the War Office quickly had to find a colonel from a Highland regiment to be the new commander. That's you!

"Collectively, the commanders will put together a plan to defend their respective coastlines, subject to approval by Scottish Command and the War Office. Brilliant again, and it's so simple, right? Let someone else do it. Now, listen to this, David. After you've put together your plan, you get to go out and find the resources to implement it. Easy, no problem! Actually, problem solved as far as the staff here is concerned. You have no forces to work with; you have a very small population to draw from, and very recalcitrant people who don't like being told what to do. You have no equipment and aren't expected to get any, and your sector has a larger coastline to defend than all of England. Don't you see the beauty of this? It's all on your shoulders, and the Home Forces staff is off the hook, unless the Jerries mount a raid."

"Mr. Churchill accepted this?" David shifted uncomfortably in his chair.

"Not exactly. Mr. Churchill said that this was a good first step. I think the Home Forces staff hopes they all will have new assignments before Mr. Churchill starts asking questions again. If I know Mr. Churchill, he will, and if they don't have good answers, the Home Forces staff will definitely all have new jobs; jobs they won't like!"

"So, I'm the scapegoat?"

"Not necessarily. If all goes well, and the Jerries do nothing up there, you could have a very quiet war doing little or nothing." Trevor's words dripped with sarcasm.

"You know me better than that."

"Yes I do, and here's a good point. You'll probably have some small leverage to get modest amounts of equipment when it becomes available. Scottish Command won't want to give it to you. They think the Southeast Lowlands sector is the most threatened area and it surely is. But, they also know Mr. Churchill will ask questions eventually and they don't want to be caught with their pants down again. Keep that in mind."

"I will. You know, Trevor, just before I retired, the War Office, based on the best intelligence assessments, considered the likelihood of war with Germany to be only a remote possibility. If, however, war did break out, we all were confident that the powerful French Army would stop the Jerries in Eastern France, and that Britain would never face a German invasion threat. Now everything has changed. What happened? What's your assessment of the German threat right now?"

"Frightening. They're extraordinary! They have displayed an uncanny ability to overwhelm everyone. Our lads fought well, but they were outmaneuvered and outfought. The Jerries used better doctrine, better tactics, better training, and better equipment. Understand this, David: they conquered France and the Benelux countries with smaller forces than the Allies had."

"That's not what the newspapers said."

"The newspapers were wrong. The Allies outnumbered the German forces in manpower and numbers of tanks, artillery, and aircraft. But the Jerries concentrated their forces like three huge lances and punched through or outflanked our forces again and again. Nothing seemed to stop them."

"Not even the damned Maginot Line."

"I wish the French had bought tanks and aircraft instead. If they had, they would have stood a better chance of stopping the *blitzkreig*.

15

The Jerries went right around the Maginot Line as if it didn't exist. Of course, the whole purpose of the Maginot Line was that France wouldn't have to spend much money on defense. They certainly are paying the price for that mistake right now."

"But the French Army seemed to just collapse. It wasn't the French Army we fought with in 1918."

"Precisely. Poor leadership. Old, fat generals, lousy morale, disorganization, confusion, no leadership from the government until it was too late, and no real commitment to the war by the people. It was a recipe for disaster. Now, despite what others say, I don't think the Jerries can land Panzer armies on our coast and run them all over Britain. They're converting river barges along North Sea ports right now to land men and even some tanks. I think, however, the Navy and the RAF will sink most of them. I'm more worried about parachute forces seizing a good harbour and the *Wehrmacht*, the German Army, shipping over thousands of infantry with a small number of tanks, all protected by their Air Force, the *Luftwaffe*. They can wear us down, especially since we lost almost all our equipment in France.

"Our intelligence tells us that Hitler has ordered the landing of forty divisions, 500,000 soldiers, over a forty-mile front from Ramsgate to Lyme Bay. How can we defend against that? The soldiers in our brigades and divisions have rifles, some machine guns and damned little else. It will be many months before our factories catch up and replace the lost equipment. My fear, David, is that the public may just give up after a while and force the Government to sue for peace. Public morale is dismal right now."

"I can't believe Britons will surrender, Trevor, and, by God, it will not happen in my sector. Trevor, you said the Scots were recalcitrant. Remember, I'm a Scot and I grew up in the Highlands. Yes, we Scots are recalcitrant and don't like being told what to do. That's true. But we'll fight any hostile outsider, especially the Germans, just as we fought the English many years ago. I'm not worried about that. I just want to make sure they've something to fight with."

"Well that's your job, now isn't it?" David said nothing. "David, how are you getting to Scotland?"

"I'll drive my motorcar. Sounds like I'll need it."

"Will you go near Carlisle?"

"I could, why?"

"Colonel Jim Prescott is being reassigned from our operations department to Western Command. Do you know him?"

"I'm not sure."

"He's from the Border Regiment. I know he would appreciate a ride, if you have room."

"If he can be ready Sunday morning sharp, he can come along. Have him call me at my flat."

Two hours later, after signing numerous forms in the personnel office, David called a taxi. He felt exhausted, but excited by a new challenge. And he felt deeply troubled.

2

June 30, 1940

THE CLOUDS WERE PARTING on a damp Sunday morning as David drove north to meet Colonel Jim Prescott. There had been a tearful farewell with his daughters after spending the night with them in St. Albans. He felt a mixture of excitement toward his new assignment in Scotland and sadness at the prospect of relocating so far from his girls.

People were beginning to stir in the suburbs and small towns north of London, some walking to church, while others were out for a morning stroll. Every few blocks, there were groups of men assembled in marching formations as they learned the rudiments of military drill and ceremonies, known irreverently to the volunteers as "square stomping." The Local Defense Volunteers, soon to become the Home Guard, was taking shape, just a few weeks after inception. Very few wore a military uniform, most of those uniforms having hung in back closets since the end of World War I. A few carried personal rifles or shotguns, but most carried swords, broom handles, or sticks; army rifles being in short supply after the losses in France.

David found himself saying a prayer that the Germans wouldn't attack soon. Presently, Europe's Western Front was quiet, as the Germans swiftly consolidated their hold on France and the Low Countries, and replenished their armies. The War Office estimated there was an 80% likelihood of a German invasion. It could be just a matter of weeks before Britain would be fighting for its very survival.

Jim Prescott was standing in front of his house, surrounded by several suitcases and a large trunk. "Going to Africa for a safari?" David asked jokingly.

"No, just too much stuff that I might need during the next few months." They loaded the bags and were soon on their way north. The sun was quickly drying the roads and traffic was light, being a Sunday morning and with gas rationing having taken effect.

"It should be a nice day for a drive in the country, David. So, what's your new assignment in Scotland?"

"I'm the commander of the new sub-district which covers the Northwest Highlands and all the Western Isles. Some chaps call it the Northwest Sector."

"Do we have troops up there?"

"We probably have very few, if any. The Scots are organizing the Home Guard and various Civil Defense groups, but there are no regular formations in the Northwest Highlands. I'll learn more after I report to Brigadier Jack Campbell in Glasgow tomorrow. He commands the whole North Highlands District, which is headquartered at Cameron Barracks in Inverness. Do you know him?"

"We met at the War Office a few times, but I don't know him personally. Do you?"

"Yes, we served together twice. He was always at least one rank above me and a very decent fellow, but tough as nails when he needed to be. Our families got together occasionally. By the way, I plan to stop for the night in Preston. Tomorrow morning, we'll drive to Carlisle to drop you off, and then on to Glasgow." They spoke pleasantly for the next half hour until they were clear of London's outlying villages.

Jim continued, "Tell me David why you joined the Army and how you earned your two wound stripes."

"Actually, I didn't plan to join the Army. I was going to become a haberdasher like my Dad. He ran a small dry goods shop in Cupar, where I was born. Later, he moved us to Perth to buy a larger shop. After age twelve, I spent summers with relatives on a farm north of Stirling. My uncle persuaded my father to send me to school at Hurst Grange in Stirling. When I matriculated in 1914, the war clouds were gathering. As a young boy, I had watched the Fife & Forfar Yeomanry Regiment drill near Cupar, and the Black Watch in Perth. At Hurst Grange, the Argyll and Sutherland Highland Regiment would march past our school regularly. They were always a grand spectacle. It was exciting to play army when we were young, but I never thought of becoming an officer.

"My father persuaded me to enroll at St. Andrews University. He said a university education would prepare me better to go into any profession, including business. I was nervous at first, but the University is only a few miles from Cupar, where we still had relatives. During the first year, the war got worse and many Brits died. We were bombarded with "support the war" enthusiasm, and the Cadet Corps at St. Andrews regularly held vigils for fallen graduates from the University. In the spring of 1915, I signed up to take the Sandhurst entrance exams, really just a spur of the moment decision. A few weeks after the exam, I received notice I'd passed and could enroll that summer. I told my parents what I'd done. My Dad calmed my Mother down by telling her the war would probably be over before I completed the course. I wish it had been.

"One afternoon, I was called out of class to report to the Adjutant. I was afraid that a relative had been killed. Instead, he asked me how I would like to be commissioned in the Black Watch. I was so excited I almost kissed him! The Watch had lost a number of officers in battle and I would be one of the replacements."

"So you went to France."

"Yes, shortly after leaving Sandhurst and a few days leave with my family, I joined the 51st Division at the front. It was fairly quiet along the front that summer, although I earned my first wound stripe within weeks of arriving."

"What happened?"

"It was nothing serious. I was in the forward trench one morning when the Jerries decided to send some artillery fire our way. I had become accustomed to their periodic harassing fire and I wasn't as careful as I should've been. A shell landed nearby and a splinter grazed me across my buttocks. Nothing too painful at first, but it bled profusely. My commander ordered me taken back to a field dressing station, and the next thing I knew I was on a truck with several other casualties. We were taken to a railhead, put on an ambulance train, and taken to a hospital in the rear. I was held there for almost two weeks until the surgeon was satisfied the wound had healed."

"What about the other wound?"

"That one was more serious. During the Battle of Arras in 1917, our brigade went over the top to attack German positions almost a mile to our front. I was a full lieutenant by then and a platoon commander. As usual, the Jerries were waiting for us, and we were hit by heavy machine gun fire about halfway along. Many of my men were shot and went down. I gathered up as many soldiers as I could, some from other units that had lost their officers. I led them forward along a sunken road and we came out fifty yards from the German lines. We charged forward and seized a piece of their forward line, then rolled up their flank for almost one hundred yards. By now, other units had joined us and we dug in to hold our gains against a counterattack. About a half-hour later, the Jerries struck and we were ordered to fall back to our original trenches."

"Attack, fall back, attack, fall back. Terrible way to fight a war."

"Exactly. I was the last man to leave our position and, shortly after, was hit in the back by a bullet. It broke a rib, went alongside my right lung, and came out the front. I don't remember anything after that, but I was told that several of my men saw me go down. They picked me up and carried me back to our lines. I woke up sometime later in our division collecting post. I was in shock and the pain was awful. A surgeon gave me some morphine, and I soon passed out again. I vaguely remember the long, bumpy, painful ride in the back of a truck. I woke up several times and thought I'd rather die than continue that trip. We finally arrived at a railhead where I was loaded onto an ambulance train, given some more morphine, and taken directly to a general hospital far to the rear. I had two surgeries over the next few days, then a week or so stabilizing before they put me on a boat and took me to England."

"Mercifully!"

"I don't remember much during that time. I guess my body was reacting to the shock of the wound, the truck ride to the railhead, and the surgeries. Also, we were exhausted to begin with."

"And full of morphine."

"Exactly. At least they were generous with the morphine, although I had a tough time when they stopped giving it to me. I can understand very well how addictions get started. It was just the most wonderful feeling, especially when you're in pain. I don't remember much about the voyage or the train ride that followed, but I ended up in Chelsea at the 2nd London General Hospital."

"Did they send you to Scotland to recover?"

"No, I spent the whole time in Chelsea, almost three months. My parents came down from Perth by train. I think it was the only time my father ever closed his shop for a week. It was wonderful seeing them, but it was so hard. You know, tears streaming down their faces, barely able to talk and all that. They stayed several days and didn't go back until they saw I was recovering. I remember my mother telling the chief nurse that I was too seriously injured to ever go back to the army, so would she please arrange to have me discharged, and they would take me back to Scotland."

"That must have gone over well."

"The chief nurse was very experienced, and she was ever so gentle as she explained to my parents that I was a soldier and an officer, and that the army would make its own determination at a much later date, but thank you very much for the advice. I guess she mollified my mother somewhat. I was sad when they departed. In any case, I healed and slowly regained my strength. I had several weeks of convalescence. Several of us would leave the hospital grounds together during the day and see London. That was a whole new world to most of us and we were dazzled by its size. "Now don't forget to come back," a pretty nurse would say each time."

"Did you socialize with the nurses?"

"No, we'd all been seriously wounded and were grateful to be alive. A nurse would bring us tea and stay occasionally to have a cup if the supervisor wasn't watching, but nothing more than that. In any case, I was sent back to France to rejoin my unit in late August. Upon arriving, there was a ceremony, and I was decorated with the Military Cross for my actions that day in April. It was good to be back with my men. They were already involved in the Third Battle of Ypres and the fighting had become quite hot. I was mentioned in dispatches during the battle, almost as good as receiving a medal."

"And, after that?"

"After that, things pretty much settled down until the First Battle of the Somme in March 1918. That battle was bloody hell, and we lost far too many soldiers. My company commander, the major, was killed and our captain was seriously wounded and evacuated. I was named company commander and was promoted to captain shortly after the battle."

"As a company commander? You should have been a major."

"There were many companies commanded by captains then, and I commanded my company until the Armistice. Our division fought continuously for much of the remainder of the war, with battles at Lys, Arras, Aisne, and several battles during the final offensive up to the German border. I was mentioned in dispatches for a second time. When the war finally ended, the only good thing I had to say about it was that we'd won. At least we all thought so at that time, but I'm not so sure now."

"Remember, it was the war to end all wars."

"Oh, sure, the politicians said that, but I don't think any British officer believed it."

"And here we are at war again. So, why didn't you leave the army after the war? You said you wanted to be a merchant or a businessman. What about the university?"

"We stayed in place for some weeks after the Armistice in 1918. Gradually, the army began withdrawing forces. When the time came for the 51st Division to return home, I volunteered to go forward into Germany with a liaison party to help establish the Rhine Army and occupy the German Rhineland. You joined soon after. By now, winter had arrived and other units were being sent to North Russia to support the Whites against the Reds. I wanted no part of that. I'd never traveled outside Scotland before the war and I wanted to see more of the world, but not Russia after the Revolution. Germany, however, was interesting. It had never been bombed or shelled like France, so there was no damage. Nevertheless, the British blockade of German ports led to severe rationing, and starvation had begun. Plus, it was a rough winter and coal supplies were very short. Many Germans were starving, freezing, or both. Then, almost four million German soldiers came home from the war, many carrying their rifles, with no possibility of finding jobs. It was a highly explosive situation. The Allied forces were able to keep order in the Rhineland, but we didn't occupy other parts of Germany."

"When I got there, David, it wasn't pleasant. The Germans were angry about the armistice. They were stunned to learn they hadn't won the war; their propaganda during the war having been very effective at deceiving the public. Conditions were bad, as you said, and allied soldiers were standing guard during the day and going to German pubs or *gasthauses* at night. The Germans hated us and hated having us there." Jim paused. "So, when did you come back to Britain?"

"Our work was done in February 1919 when the last of you chaps got into place. Several of us sailed down the Rhine and booked a passage to Leith. My parents came down to meet the boat, and we spent a merry night in Edinburgh before heading north to Perth. Of course, they were much happier than when I last had seen them. I reported to my regiment at Queen's Barracks in Perth the next week, planning to resign my commission. Colonel Kincaid had come up from Scottish Command and asked me to have a drink with him that afternoon. We talked for over two hours, and I told him my plans to resign and go back to St. Andrews. He said I'd an excellent war record and it would be a shame to leave the army now, especially as peacetime service was much easier. I was unmoved, but interested. Then he asked, 'How will you pay for university study?' I said I'd some savings from the war and may have to borrow from my father. He said 'You know the army will pay for university studies toward a degree and will give you half pay besides.' I didn't know that. All of a sudden everything fell into place. I'd go to St. Andrews at Army expense, take my degree, and then resign from the army. Of course, I never resigned."

The war seemed far away as they drove through the countryside, crossing the many small canals that laced the region. The sun shone brightly on fields filled with crops, and a breeze pushed the trees softly. Neither man spoke for a while. Jim finally broke the silence.

"So, you finally returned to St. Andrews."

"Yes, I enrolled again in 1919 and took my degree in 1921."

"But something changed your mind and you remained in the army."

"Actually, two things changed my mind. A new assignment beckoned and I met Anne."

"Your wife, I presume."

"Yes. In 1920, while I was at St. Andrews, The University of Edinburgh was asked by the City to host a public affair to honor veterans and raise money to help the war wounded. It was to be a grand affair, and each Scottish regiment was asked to send an officer to represent their soldiers. With a battalion of troops in India and the remainder on a lengthy training exercise, the regimental adjutant decided that I would be the perfect representative for the Watch. I was young; war wounded, and wore a few ribbons. We'd wear our dress uniforms for the occasion."

"Kilts?"

"Definitely kilts and all the Highland regalia. I took the train to Edinburgh and secured a room for two nights. The celebration started the next morning with a parade, then displays, concerts by several regimental bands and, of course, speeches. In the evening, we relocated to the auditorium. I, the dashing young officer, strutted around making myself seen by all. At one of the tables, some university students were selling poppies to raise money. As I strolled by one table, a lovely young student caught my eye. She was the most beautiful woman I'd ever seen. I continued on for a few minutes, then turned and went back. As I approached the table, that very same woman quickly came up to me and said, 'Would you like to buy a poppy, Colonel?' I fished out a shilling and explained that I was only a captain. She asked if I'd served in the war."

"Not very observant, was she."

"She didn't know much about the army. Anne had gone to Mary Erskine School. Her Dad was a solicitor in Edinburgh who felt she'd benefit from a university education, and she was only in her first year. She was living at Cavendish House and was expected back promptly after the ceremony ended. At one point, all of the regimental officers lined up and were introduced by the master of ceremony. Of course, everyone applauded. When I stepped forward and was introduced, there were loud cheers and applause for the regiment. Afterwards, Anne came up and almost breathlessly told me how proud she was."

"She was smitten."

"I presume so. We talked for quite a time, then the ceremony ended and people started home. I asked her if I could walk her home."

"Such a gallant officer," he said smirking, "I bet she said 'yes'."

"Indeed. We started back to Cavendish House and talked like we'd known each other for years. I wanted to talk longer and pretended to be confused. We took many wrong turns and arrived later than we should. Mrs. Wilkins was waiting on the porch. Anne mumbled some apologies, and I explained that I was new to Edinburgh, but Mrs. Wilkins just looked at me sternly. Of course, there was nothing she could do. As Anne went inside she whispered, 'Please write to me'."

"And you were hooked."

"I certainly was. We corresponded for weeks, and I found every excuse I could to go to Edinburgh and do research in their library."

"A much better library than at St. Andrews, I'm sure."

"Absolutely. Of course, we saw each other with every visit, and even Mrs. Wilkins seemed to warm to me over time. I asked Anne to marry me, then asked her father's consent and we set the wedding date for right after I took my degree. In 1921, I was then assigned to Scottish Command in Edinburgh and that's where I first met Jack Campbell. He was an impressive figure; I worked for him for almost two years.

"Anne and I enjoyed our time in Edinburgh. Sarah was born in 1925, shortly before I was reassigned to India. That was hard, although we knew it was coming. I sailed to Alexandria and spent three months in Egypt, a brief orientation tour, before going on to India. I was posted to Indian Army Headquarters, but soon was given command of a company. Anne and Sarah were able to join me in 1926, and Jessica was born in 1928. It was hard on Anne at first, but she soon learned to make do. At least, we were together again. In 1927, I was promoted to major and, in 1928, I was posted as a student to the Staff College at Quetta, finishing in 1929. I joined the staff at Western Army headquarters and had been there just a few months when fighting broke out in the Punjab.

"The Viceroy ordered the army to repel the Punjab incursion, and one of the units assigned this task was the Lahore Brigade. The brigadier immediately notified our headquarters that his brigade major was seriously ill and he had no other officer available to replace him. The poor fellow was eventually evacuated to England, and I never heard another thing about him. Being a recent Staff College graduate, I was assigned as a temporary brigade major for the campaign. The fighting was sporadic and lasted but a few short months. I guess I did well, as I was again mentioned in dispatches."

"Very impressive."

"Not really, but it was a good experience for me and taught me quite a bit about irregular warfare. It wasn't at all like France in the First War. I remained as permanent brigade major until my assignment ended in 1931 and I returned to Scotland. In 1933, I was transferred to the War Office in London, where I served under then-Brigadier Hastings Ismay. He was a tough boss, very demanding, but I learned a great deal and was promoted to lieutenant-colonel in 1935."

"That was fast. I guess it helped being right there in the War Office."

"Probably. Or they were trying to get rid of me. Right after my promotion, I was sent back to Scotland to command a battalion."

"That was a very nice way to be kicked out!"

"In early 1937, I was called back to the War Office. Anne was disappointed, as she had enjoyed our brief time in Scotland where she could see her family quite often. I served in the War Office just a few months, and then was reassigned to the new Ministry of Defense at the request of newly-promoted Major-General Ismay. As you know, tension was rising on the Continent and in the Pacific. Hitler had retaken the Rhineland and threatened all of Europe. The Japs had invaded China, and most of us could see war coming. I'd been working long hours in the War Planning Division when General Ismay called me to his office. Several other senior officers had gathered there. He said some nice words about me and then announced I'd been promoted to colonel. Nobody was more surprised than I. He said I was to be given responsibility for the European Section of War Planning. Unfortunately, Anne was diagnosed with breast cancer a month later. We were devastated. The doctors said her prospects weren't good. Anne and I decided to live each day as best we could, but that Christmas was not a joyous one. To add to our troubles, I had an auto accident in January. Anne was injured and my hip was smashed."

"Good Lord! That was bad luck. How did you handle that?"

"I was hospitalized for six weeks. General Ismay brought Peter Woolsey over from another section to substitute for me. The doctors said my hip would never fully recover. That was probably the lowest point in my life. Both my hip and my career were shattered and my beautiful wife was dying. I didn't know what to do. Finally, I decided to retire from the Army and, in April, went on pension. I felt I had completely failed General Ismay who had done so much for me."

"But it was an accident."

"Yes, but it was my fault. Well, enough of that. Anne died two months later. At first, I just stayed home with my girls. It was so hard on them. I started a regular walking program and worked up to 10 miles a day. Then I added some light jogging, very little at first, but I built it up to three miles and walked the rest. In late July, a friend called and suggested I speak with the managing director of Williamson-Sweeney, an import-export company. They were looking for another broker, and he felt that with my background I could learn the ropes quickly, which I did. When the war started, their business declined sharply, and I decided to speak with General Ismay. I thought I might come back into the War Office or the Ministry of Defense, but this is the assignment I was offered."

Both were silent for some time, stopping for lunch, then driving on to Preston for the night. Monday morning they arose early and proceeded north, arriving in Carlisle by mid-morning.

"Thanks for the ride, David, awfully decent of you. I hope we meet up again sometime."

"Sure. Call me the next time you vacation in the Highlands." They laughed and shook hands. As he drove north, David found himself thinking about Jim Prescott's assignment in Western Command. Several divisions of Regular Army troops were stationed there and dozens of battalions of Home Guard were being formed. There were cities, factories and everything needed to establish a strong defense capability. In Scotland's Northwest Sector, there was practically nothing.

"Maybe I'll create something out of nothing or nothing at all."

3

July 1, 1940

"DAVID! WELCOME AND COME IN. YOU must be tired. Did you drive straight through from London?"

"No, I spent the night in Preston. It's good to be here, Sir. You look well."

"Never been fitter."

They entered Brigadier Jack Campbell's spacious home in a comfortable neighborhood not far from the River Clyde. The drive across the rolling hills that separated England from Scotland was marked by scattered showers. Good for the crops, David thought, as he viewed fields coloured a light green and stretching as far as the Cumbrian Hills would allow. By harvest time, the crop fields would turn a deep green and the hay meadows a light russet, bringing a new beauty.

"Betty is fixing lunch, David; you'll spend the night here."

"Sir, I can go to a hotel."

"Nonsense, we want to spend some time with you. Besides, you and I have Army business to discuss."

Jack was not as tall as David. He was a broad-shouldered, stocky man with a growing waistline that revealed a fondness for occasional culinary indulgences. The bald top of his head betrayed beads of sweat in all seasons, but especially in summer. Jack was known as a pusher in the British Army, a powerhouse of energy and ideas who gets things done.

Betty came from the kitchen wiping her hands and gave David a hug. She was short and plump. "Good to see you again, David. We were so sorry about Anne. I just loved her and we wanted to go down for the funeral, but Jack was in the hospital and we couldn't get away." She shook her head, "Awful, just awful."

"Thank you. Your letter meant a great deal to me."

"So, David, sit and let's talk while Betty gets lunch ready. Not a great feast, what with food rationing and all, but more than adequate.

She's a great cook. Let me get some whisky. When was the last time we talked, maybe at the War Office? That was 1937, shortly before I relocated to Scottish Command. You had just been promoted to Colonel and you told me Anne was sick. Anyway, it was just before my little heart event."

"You had a heart attack, Jack," Betty yelled from the kitchen.

"Thank you, Luv," he yelled back. "She's right, of course, good nurse that she is, but it was quite minor."

"That's right," David replied, "I'd forgotten she was a nurse. Isn't that how you first met?"

"Exactly. You may remember I was commissioned in 1910 into the Highland Light Infantry, the HLI. That was my father's regiment, Lieutenant-Colonel William Arthur Campbell. I was named for him, becoming William John Campbell, known in my family as 'Jack.' Our family had lived here in Glasgow for four generations. You frequently reminded me that Glasgow is not in the Highlands and Highland Light Infantry was a misnomer." Jack grinned. "Anyway, I went straight from school here in Glasgow to Sandhurst. I was still a Sub-Lieutenant when the First War broke out in 1914, but was quickly promoted to full lieutenant that September when I was serving at Aldershot and to Captain in early 1915. I served in several units and, like you, wound up in France with the 51st Division which, by the way, is the 'Highland Division,' as you bloody well know!"

"The War Office is not always intelligent and I'm not sure they all can read maps. They probably thought Glasgow was in the Highlands."

"Ah, David, you'll never quit, will you?" he said smiling.

"Why didn't they send you to the 52nd Division with some of the other HLI battalions?"

"I have no idea. In any case, you and I never met then, being in different brigades. I was wounded in September 1917 near Langemarck, during the Ypres battle. I had just been promoted Major and was a company commander."

"As I recall, you were damn near killed."

"Yes, artillery tore big holes in me. I woke up in a General Hospital near Calais. The doctors had performed two or three surgeries on me already, and I was stable enough to be evacuated to London, where they put me on a train to Edinburgh. I don't remember much, going in and out of consciousness. When we arrived, I was taken to the Royal Infirmary, like so many of the wounded. The doctors performed another surgery, as I still had shrapnel in me. I finally regained full consciousness late one night and woke up looking at an angel."

29

"Betty."

"Yes, she had been sent from her usual ward to the post-surgical ward because they had so many casualties coming in from the Ypres battle. Hospitals all over Britain were filled with wounded. The doctors and nurses were working around the clock. She was a beautiful woman, and I really thought I'd died and gone to Heaven with an angel by my side."

"That should have been the first indication you were alive. You'll never get into Heaven."

"Hah! Still at it, I see. No, probably not, but living with Betty is all the Heaven I need."

"Thank you, Luv," she hollered from the kitchen, "but I don't believe a word of it."

"Anyway, I was several months recovering. Betty worked nights quite often and lived at the nurses' residence. She came over almost every night to see me, if she could get by the supervisor. She was pretty resourceful and usually got onto my ward. Well, I fell in love and, during my fourth month there, we had our first date."

"It wasn't a date! Nurses weren't allowed to go out with patients."

"Well, what do you call it?" he yelled back.

"It was a therapy session. I was escorting you outside the hospital grounds to help you regain confidence during your recovery."

"As I said, she was very resourceful." Jack smiled. "After I recovered, almost eight months later, I was sent back to France and assigned to Brigade headquarters for several months. I was promoted to acting Lieutenant-Colonel and briefly commanded a battalion. But, after the war, I reverted back to my permanent rank of Major. I wrote to her daily and she to me. When I got home, I asked her to marry me, and she said yes."

"I foolishly said yes," yelled the voice from the kitchen. Jack smiled again. "We've had five children and a wonderful marriage."

"One man's opinion! Come to the table now," Betty responded, as she brought out a steaming pot of soup.

During lunch, Jack continued the conversation. "David, I think we first met and worked together at Scottish Command in 1919, before you went back to St. Andrews and met Anne, right?"

"Right. You cut quite a dashing figure as a young major with both the Military Cross and the Distinguished Service Order, and a pretty wife. The second time we worked together was at the War Office in 1933."

"Yes. Those were good times, David, despite the Depression and all the problems of the world. I miss those years when we were young and undefeatable. I wish I wasn't stuck in this job now. Hell, I'm a brigadier and I should be commanding a brigade of infantry or maybe a division. The Army needs people like me."

"Darling, you know your heart isn't up to the strain," Betty said quietly. "Lord knows you have enough strain in this job, so I can only imagine what commanding troops would do to you."

"I'd be fine." He winked at her. "After my heart attack, David, the Army surgeons said I was unfit for field duty and should retire, just like you. The War Office actually was processing my paperwork to go on half-pay last August. I guess I should say 'retirement' now, as the Army has done away with the half-pay system. Then, the war broke out. Lord Carrington said he would find a job for me somewhere and here I am."

"It sounds like a perfect fit, Sir, commanding the entire North Highlands District of Scottish Command from your office in Inverness and your home here in Glasgow, surrounded by family and friends."

"Not the whole family, of course. Jonathan is a Subaltern serving at Aldershot. Like me, he was commissioned into the HLI. Stephen is a cadet at Sandhurst. Elizabeth is in nurses training, she takes after her mother, and the other two boys are still in school. My old friend, Brigadier Charles Guthrie, commands the Glasgow District here. He has been a most gracious host in allowing me to reside here and do some work from my house. Of course, I spend most of my time in Inverness, but it's always grand to be able to come back occasionally to see the family."

"Tell me about the North Highlands Area and especially the Northwest Sector."

"Finish your lunch, and we'll go out back to my office."

As THEY WALKED TO HIS OFFICE, Jack said, "I'm not going to sugarcoat this for you. The situation is very grim. The Jerries can come over here at any time and practically walk over us, especially if they can first land two or three Panzer divisions on the ground. Frankly, I'm not sure they can do that, what with the Navy and the RAF picking them off as they come across the Channel. But, if the Jerries can establish air superiority, they can sink our ships and, weather permitting; those river barges can slowly sail over here with one or two tanks each and land on our beaches. They've been seizing all the barges along the coasts and rivers from France up to Denmark. Over a thousand taken so far, I'm told. They're modifying them to carry tanks, troops and other equipment. The RAF has begun attacking them at night. I'm told they've sunk a good number so far. I hope they can sink them all, but I don't know that they can." He poured himself another glass of whisky; David declined his offer.

"We think the prime target for the Jerries would be to sail straight across the Channel and land just south of Dover, or maybe further southwest along the coast towards Portsmouth or north of the Thames in East Anglia. If they seize some airfields along the coast with parachutists, they could land troops by aircraft. They then could move southwest to seize one or more ports and start shipping large Panzer forces over here. If that happens, we'd all better learn to speak German. Of course, they could choose another invasion target or go elsewhere to mount a secondary attack, like Scotland."

"I would expect the Army has some counter-attack plans, if that happens," said David quietly.

"Oh yes, the Army has established stop lines south and east of London, heavily defended trenches running laterally along rivers and other natural barriers, with mobile reserves behind the lines to counter-attack any breakthrough.

"But let's be realistic, David. We lost most of our tanks, artillery, and mobile equipment in France. We have in Britain today maybe 400 to 600 tanks. A few are new ones, including some infantry tanks, but most are the old Mark Six tanks that proved totally ineffective fighting the Panzers in France. We could commandeer civilian vehicles to move our forces, but they wouldn't be as effective as military lorries. Our factories are gearing up to run night and day, but it will be many months before we produce sufficient war material. Our major ammunition reserves were also lost in France, and it'll be at least a year before we can replenish them, and only if the Jerries leave us alone which, of course, they won't. The Expeditionary Force soldiers are now battle-trained, but so are the Germans and they have our equipment as well as their own."

"They also captured all the French Army equipment."

"Yes, David, plus Danish, Belgian, Dutch, Austrian, Czech and Polish equipment, as well as all the overrun countries' factory production. It's not a pretty sight. So, what do we have? Maybe one-and-a-half to two million soldiers under arms in Britain, including the half-million Territorial Army and Army Reservists called up last August. Many are new recruits and, perhaps, only one-fourth of the Army has had any battle experience at all. They are woefully under-equipped and need time to reorganize, retrain, and reequip with the modern weapons that Parliament denied us all during the 1930's. When German bombs begin to fall, and they will, the British public will be subjected to their first real invasion threat since the Norman Conquest nine centuries ago. How will they stand up to that? The Brits have backbone, but will it be enough? Public morale isn't good and, frankly, I'm apprehensive for our future. I'm hopeful we can hold off the Jerries, but I simply don't know."

"What about Scotland?"

"If the Jerries take London and the Midlands, Scotland will fall. I hate saying that, but it's a simple fact. Look, we have perhaps 45 or 46 million people in the UK, of which Scotland has maybe something close to 6 million at best. Germany has over 80 million people. Add Austria, Italy and their other allies plus the conquered countries and they probably have 200-225 million people, plus a very large industrial base."

"And they have the advantage of a very efficient dictatorship to pull it all together."

"Yes, they do and they're extremely well organized. It all will be directed at us. Not a pretty picture at all." Jack poured himself another whisky. "Now let's talk about your mission."

"Before we do that, Sir, could we talk about the plans to defend Scotland?"

"Right. Today, Scottish Command comprises perhaps 75,000 men of the British Army. Three infantry divisions are stationed here now, each with three brigades. The 51st Highland Division is said to be in the Highlands, but is mainly in my district along the eastern coastal region from Inverness to Dundee. The 51st mostly was captured in France. Only the 154th Brigade escaped. The newly activated 9th Division was renamed the 51st with some 154th brigade units added to preserve the lineage. It will take many months of training to regain its battle readiness." David nodded.

"In addition to the 51st in the Eastern Highlands, David, the 5th Division is defending the coastline north of the Firth of Forth and the Edinburgh region. The 46th Division defends the rest of the Lowland coast as far south as the English Border. Placed behind the 46th is the newly-organized 2nd Motor Machine Gun Brigade, which serves as a counterattack reserve. That force is mounted in old armoured cars and lorries that can't possibly stop Panzer forces. These four organizations include a total of 33 infantry battalions, plus their artillery and support forces. They are each positioned to repel the expected invasion.

"Although these are some of Britain's best units, none of them is fit to fight. Their manpower losses are being replaced, but retraining will take many months. Replacement rifles have been issued to the forces, plus a few machine guns and even some artillery, but this has come from old First War stores, not new equipment from the factories. As the factories increase their production, the forces will begin to receive new equipment, but it will be issued first to units in Eastern and Southern England where the invasion threat is greatest. The Highlands may be the last to get new equipment, except possibly Northern Ireland.

"There are another thirty or so infantry battalions in Scotland, mostly home defense and depot training units armed with rifles and a handful of old machine guns. They're composed primarily of new soldiers and will not achieve wartime proficiency for 18-24 months and only then if they receive proper equipment. So, David that's the Army's ground defense situation in Scotland. It's quite tenuous. We need equipment and we need time. We also need the Home Guard and Civil Defense units to become proficient. It's all very discouraging." Both men shifted uncomfortably in their chairs.

"The Navy is totally over-extended trying to cover the Mediterranean, the Indian Ocean, and the Pacific, as well as protecting Britain and the North Atlantic. If the Japanese come into the war, and the War Office expects they will, the jig will really be up. Plus, the Navy has all the sea-lanes to protect, defending against both the German surface ships as well as the U-boats.

"The bulk of Home Fleet is normally based at Scapa Flow, but it has only three or four battleships, an aircraft carrier, and smaller vessels. Most large ships have been moved temporarily to Loch Ewe for safe-keeping, beyond German bomber range. We've the usual other naval bases in Scotland: Cromarty, Leith-Rosyth, Glasgow-Greenock and all the little naval stations, but they host only a handful of cruisers, destroyers and smaller boats.

"Further south, the great Channel Fleet of the First War, with its squadrons of powerful battleships, is today a name only; just a handful of destroyers, minesweepers and an occasional cruiser. The massive Royal Navy and its Grand Fleet was mostly scrapped after the First War and very few ships were built to replace them. We simply don't have the Navy we once had, and the Jerries are determined to sink what's left.

"Now, the RAF is a different story. Sure, we have many older planes, but our new Hurricanes and Spitfires are very effective against the Germans. The problem is that we have so few of them, maybe 500 or so modern fighters to defend the whole British Isles. Even worse, we don't have enough pilots. It takes two years to train a pilot properly and we simply don't have that time. Most of the fighters are stationed in Southern England, of course, and Scotland has only a few squadrons. Is any of this a surprise to you, David?"

"No, Sir. Except for the defeat of the British Expeditionary Force, the situation really hasn't changed much since I left the Ministry of Defense. It's very discouraging. In peacetime, Britain limps along from year to year thinking we somehow can avoid the war by not preparing for it. Meanwhile, the Jerries have been on a wartime footing for several years and have built the forces to roll over most of Europe. Are we really that foolish?"

"No, David, we are a democracy and democracies can be quite naïve at times. People begin to believe that good times will continue forever and that very bad things somehow will be avoided."

After a few moments of silence, David spoke up. "OK, Sir, how about our Home Guard, and Civil Defense organizations?"

"Well, David, the Home Guard has been something of a surprise. Originally, Mr. Churchill envisioned that the Home Guard would serve as an anti-parachutist force and could raise perhaps 250,000 men. That many enrolled in the first 24 hours alone! Last week, Scottish Command reported that there were still lines of volunteers waiting to enroll and it appears these lines are found throughout Britain. They estimate we'll enroll over a million Home Guardsmen before summer ends, over 200,000 in Scotland alone. Those numbers could go much higher. Good men have joined and many are veterans of the First War. But, they're unequipped for the most part and much in need of a few months training. Scotland has over 100 Home Guard battalions forming right now, and more are likely to be formed."

"That's well over 1,000 men per battalion, larger than a Regular Army battalion."

"More than that, David. Many battalions are approaching 1,500 in strength and quite a few have well over 2,000 men. I wouldn't be surprised to see some battalions at 3,000 men before they're fully enrolled."

"That's the size of an infantry brigade. Why are they so large? Why not split them into two or even three battalions?"

"Two reasons, David. First, we simply don't have enough trained leaders to command and staff the battalions as it is. We even have some platoon and company commanders who have no prior military experience. But most positions as platoon commander or above are actually filled by experienced officers, mostly veterans of the First War or later service. Most left the forces at some point for business or personal reasons and, of course, we've numerous retirees. Many of the Home Guard volunteers also were former servicemen who are now serving as corporals or sergeants. Additionally, we have former Navy and RAF servicemen in the Home Guard."

"I worked with the London Home Guard until this past week. We enrolled retired Navy Admirals into the ranks and some into leadership positions. We also had retired Air Marshals from the RAF."

"Exactly. It's all about motivation and experience; even civilian experiences are valuable. These chaps are highly motivated, and I'm well impressed by their enthusiasm. The second reason we have such large battalions is the War Office thinks that, if we are invaded, many Home Guardsmen will disappear, and only 60-70% will report for duty."

"I cannot believe that!" David exclaimed. "If anything, I think many more will show up, if there's an invasion; mostly unarmed, but where else would they go?"

"I agree, David. These men are highly motivated now. Upon invasion alert, I believe most men of all ages will flock to Home Guard recruiting offices. The main problem right now is that so many of them are unarmed. Those that have arms have mainly fowling pieces, or hunting rifles, even a few pistols. There are some Enfield rifles in the ranks, the older First War Mark III model, not the newer Mark IV, and a few older Army rifles.

"The War Office has encouraged the Home Guard to make petrol bombs to throw at the Panzers, so the Home Guardsmen will have at least something with which to fight. These are the 'Molotov Cocktail' bombs in whisky and wine bottles and there are thousands of them now all over Britain."

"I guess those would be better than nothing, Sir, but it's hard to get that close to a Panzer without getting shot."

"Better than nothing, indeed. Do you know that Mr. Churchill is also trying to purchase rifles and other arms from the Dominions and from America?"

"Yes Sir, I had a minor role in the Canadian rifle purchase. I understand that a contract was signed recently to purchase several hundred thousand Canadian Ross rifles for the Home Guard. I remember seeing them in the trenches in 1918. They were a good rifle, but they jammed easily unless perfectly clean."

"The War Office reports that the Americans will sell us over a half-million surplus rifles for the Home Guard, David, mainly P-14s and P-17s from the First War. They fire the American .300 caliber bullet, which is not compatible with our .303 caliber rifles. The Army lost many rifles during the evacuation from France and some older Mark III Enfields have been issued to the Regulars as replacements. New units also are being equipped with the Mark III, so only a few are being issued to the Home Guard at this time, a few to each company to give the men marksmanship training. Also, no mortars, machine guns, or anti-tank rifles are available for the same reason. It will take months for the factories to catch up with the Army requirements before anything begins to flow down to the Home Guard."

"Tea?" Betty Campbell interrupted Jack with a tray carrying the silver tea service and a plate of small wafers.

"Thank you, Luv." Jack reached for a wafer and replenished his whisky. David poured himself some tea. "Let's go onto the porch while we still have some sunshine."

The porch view revealed a handsome garden full of vegetables, not flowers. "I spent many hours last month helping Betty take out her flowers and replant the beds with vegetables. We must be prepared for terrible food shortages . . . and much worse."

Worse was yet to come.

4

July 1, 1940

CONTINUED

As the afternoon lapsed into dusk, the streets of Glasgow became increasingly congested. Busloads of shipyard and factory workers returned home, having been replaced by busloads of workers beginning their evening shifts. Wartime production had increased such that many firms had established round-the-clock operations and increased work tempo, a great improvement from Depression era stoppages, but exhausting for employees working 60 to 80 hours per week.

David's tea was quite cold when he asked Brigadier Jack Campbell, "What's your assessment of the Northwest Sector, Sir?"

"Let's talk about the strategy first, David. Before Mr. Churchill's admonition to General Ironside about defending everywhere, the War Office had determined that your sector was quite unlikely to be attacked. That is mostly true. Ignoring your sector, however, was probably more a matter of expediency. They simply didn't have the forces to commit to defend an area that's less likely to be attacked, and they still don't. 'Unlikely to be attacked,' however, is not to say 'impossible to be attacked.' Mr. Churchill is persistent, and Mr. Eden carries out his instructions to the letter, as do we all. Let me explain what has happened here since Mr. Churchill became Prime Minister, and especially since Dunkirk." Jack was getting worked up and paused to pour himself another whisky. David again declined his gesture and sipped cold tea instead.

"Last month, I worked with a group of senior officers at Scottish Command to rethink our strategy for the actual— not the theoretical— defense of Scotland in the face of invasion. We had some of the best minds in the Army and we worked day and night for several days looking at all our options. None of them is perfect. My immediate superior right now is Major-General Adams. He was recently brought in as Lord Carrington's deputy to command all regular and territorial forces for the ground defense of Scotland. This probably is a temporary assignment until the threat of invasion passes. For many years, we've administered the Highlands as a single army district, with a single commander who reports directly to Scottish Command. The Lowlands was the second Scottish district. The Highland District Commander was responsible for everything in his area and that worked fine as long as nobody actually invaded us. When we restudied the situation, in the face of an actual invasion threat, things looked very different.

"General Adams believes that Scotland has two areas threatened by invasion, not one. Southeast Scotland from the English Border north to Edinburgh is the most threatened coastline and should receive priority for defensive forces. The coastal Highland area along the Angus coast north of Edinburgh up to Dundee, however, also has a very long and vulnerable coastline. For example, if the Jerries were to land along the Angus coast and stage a diversionary attack someplace along the north coast, or against the Western Isles, or even along the west coast, the Highland District commander would be forced to fight on two fronts. He would face the North Sea invasion force, but always would be looking over his shoulder at his flanks and rear. We war-gamed it several ways, but in the end decided that we simply had to split Scotland into four districts, not two, each with two sub-districts. This was just weeks ago.

"The North Highland District, which I command, is based at Cameron Barracks in Inverness and comprises two sub-districts, Inverness and Aberdeen. It encompasses a total of ten counties. The South Highland District, commanded by Brigadier Grey-Wilson, is based at Queens Barracks in Perth, with sub-districts at Perth and Argyll. It encompasses the other seven counties, which were part of the old Highland District. The Edinburgh area, really the East Scotland District, is based at Edinburgh Castle and includes all eastern counties in the Lowlands as far south as the English Border. The Glasgow area, the West Scotland District, is based at Maryhill Barracks and includes all western counties in the Lowlands south to the border. The Orkney Islands garrison and the Shetland Islands garrison have their own defense command reporting directly to Scottish Command.

"I studied this arrangement and determined we still hadn't resolved the possibility of simultaneous attacks on both coasts, which mostly would affect my North Highland District. I asked Major-General Adams to allow me to temporarily establish a third sub-district to deal with the Northwest sector. That would allow me to release my staff to focus on the threat from across the North Sea. He agreed, and Lord

Carrington approved this arrangement just last week. Our recommendation coincided with Mr. Churchill's directive to 'defend everywhere.' This is why the War Office suddenly needed to locate an available colonel from a Highland regiment to command the new sub-district. I had no idea that you would be the nominee, but I'm delighted." He smiled.

David thought for a moment. "So I will face North and West."

"Exactly." Jack got up and went inside to a wall map. "All of our intelligence seems to agree that the Jerries will attack fairly soon. If they attack across the Channel into Southern England, they may very well mount a secondary attack across the North Sea into Scotland's Northeast Coast. If they land at Aberdeen-shire or Nairn-shire, I'll become the operational commander under General Adams. Brigadier Grey-Wilson will become my supporting commander. Colonel Matthew Harris, my Inverness Sub-District commander, will become my subordinate on-site commander if they land at Nairn-shire. You will become his supporting commander. In that capacity, you'll command and defend the North Highland rear area, send forward reinforcements as needed from your sector, provide logistics, and protect the population as best you can. If, on the contrary, the Jerries raid your sector, you'll become my on-site commander. Colonel Harris will become your supporting commander.

"If the Jerries attack further south, say Angus, Brigadier Grey-Wilson of the South Highland District will become the operational commander under General Adams. In that event, both Brigadier Guthrie in Glasgow and I will become his supporting commanders, and so on. Although this sounds confusing, David, it becomes quite simple when you look at the map." He gestured toward the wall map. "This change in districts will avoid the operational commander having to do periodic pirouettes during the battle, which seems easy, but never is."

"This sounds like quite a readjustment, Sir."

"Well, it could be, David, if we had many troops. Sadly, we don't. This new arrangement will remain in place at least until the invasion threat ends. When the threat is over, I expect the districts and sub-districts will revert back as before and the Highlands will become a single district again, as will the Lowlands. This arrangement is strictly for warfighting purposes only.

"Now, David, back to your earlier question: what is your mission? The first mission for every commander in Britain is to build his military and civil defense capabilities to the maximum possible, so as to deter Hitler from even attempting an invasion. We must make him think that we're so powerful Germany could never succeed in conquering

Britain and will not even make the attempt. We want our Civil Defense forces to be strong and capable in every city and town. We want the Home Guard to be so well armed and trained that, together with the Regular Army, German invaders will face a battle-ready force of four million. The Germans probably would never attempt an invasion then because they'd know they could never defeat such a force!" Jack slammed his hand on the table. When he calmed down somewhat, he sat back in his chair and continued.

"Failing that, David, your second mission would be to fight the battle with all your forces, defeat the invaders and throw them back into the sea. All of Britain will be fighting that battle with you. Our casualties would be in the tens of thousands, God forbid, maybe even in the hundreds of thousands. However, in a nation of 46 million, that would be a reasonable price to pay for freedom from Nazi murderers. You know how I hate the thought of casualties, but we would have no choice but to fight hard and maybe die."

"For King and country."

"For Scotland, King and country! Your immediate task, David, will be to insert your headquarters into the new organization as it is being reconstituted. You'll move forward as if our organization had always been this way. Assess your situation in the Northwest Highlands, review your resources, then build and train your forces."

"It sounds like quite a challenge, but I'm excited despite the shortage of forces."

"Your Northwest Highland weaknesses are obvious. You've a large land area with many inshore islands, bays, and river mouths. Put that coastline together with the islands and you have the longest coastline of any sector in Britain. Add to that the small population available to defend that coastline and we would say, in a strictly military sense, your sector isn't defendable.

"Realistically, however, I believe you have only to worry about two or three threats. First, it's possible for the Jerries to land a small parachute raiding force to seize a modest objective. We might even say they could land a larger force of parachutists, seize a somewhat larger target, and hold it for several days or weeks to give Corporal Hitler a propaganda victory. He then could say to the world that he was holding British mainland territory and not just the Channel Islands."

"I agree the latter would be less likely, but not impossible."

"The second threat to your sector, technically your sub-district, would be a raid from the sea, most likely from U-boats. They could do their damage and then withdraw in comparative safety. Or they

41

might send several E-boats at night along the North Coast, or go south through The Minch, and land a small raiding party, perhaps to burn a fishing village like Portree or Mallaig. They would then withdraw after they'd performed their mischief."

"I hope our Navy would prevent that."

"They certainly would like to prevent that, David, but the Navy is stretched thin and has few vessels to patrol the Minch. They rely mainly on aircraft which happen to be flying overhead, plus the ferries and fishing boats, all of which are unarmed."

"And they would become vulnerable targets."

"Precisely. Now, the third threat to your sector is simply a German bombing raid. To me this also is less likely. Frankly, you have no worthwhile targets in your sector, although the Germans might not agree. You have no major cities with large populations or big factories. Your largest city is Fort William and that entire area has only nine or ten thousand souls. I think the Jerries are far more likely to bomb Glasgow and the Clyde Basin, or Edinburgh, or even Aberdeen. Now, we might argue that the aluminum plant just outside of Fort William could be a tempting target, or the torpedo plant at Balloch. But the distances are long, and there are far better targets in Glasgow, Greenock, Clydebank, and so forth. So, I think your bombing threat is slim."

"Do I have anti-aircraft batteries to defend targets in my sector?"

"No, and you probably won't get any, with two exceptions. First, Lord Beaverbrook, our bullying Minister of Aircraft Production, wants to defend your aluminum plant and is determined to get anti-aircraft guns by hook or by crook. He probably will get them by crook; so don't be surprised if guns suddenly appear. Second, Loch Ewe has some new anti-aircraft batteries to protect the battle fleet there. In general, however, we are woefully short of guns and crews. What the Army has is needed elsewhere.

"You also have no harbour defense artillery except for the few guns at Loch Ewe, although Stornoway may get a gun or two from the Emergency Batteries, which are now reinforcing our coastal defenses throughout Britain.

"So, David, as I explained earlier, we have divided our territory and our resources. The Highlands have fewer forces because they have a smaller threat than the Lowlands, or so we think, and a smaller population to draw from. The Lowlands have a much larger population and much more of our industrial base."

"Because I have the smallest population of all nine sub-districts in

Scotland, and commensurate with a lesser threat, I have no regular forces."

"Precisely, David. Your sector has a population of approximately 125,000, as best we can determine. Not a large number, but not insignificant either. If we assume that the Highlanders volunteer for the Home Guard in a larger percentage than elsewhere in Britain, your Home Guard forces eventually should total 7,500 men. It may become larger, but your force will serve Scottish Command well whatever the size, as the Highlanders are good fighters.

"As I said earlier, General Carrington has assigned Major-General Adams, my boss, the responsibility for the land defense of Scotland. That means General Adams supervises the day-to-day operations of all British Army forces in Scotland, including the Home Guard, all foreign armies, the four major district commands, plus the Orkneys and the Shetlands."

"Foreign armies!"

"We have small groups of forces in Britain from France, Poland, and Norway which escaped after their countries were over-run by the Nazis. Plus, we've a few remnants of Belgian and Dutch forces. Not many, but I understand men are still escaping Occupied Europe in some numbers. Some of these are in Scotland. The largest foreign army is 17,000 Polish troops located southeast of Glasgow in Lanark-shire. They'll be transferred to the Eastern Highlands soon to take up anti-invasion defenses. Our job is to form these rather dissimilar groups into useful military formations, then train and equip them for future combat. Unfortunately, many of the French already have asked to return home. We don't know how many will remain under General De Gaulle who, by the way, is not terribly popular in much of France.

"Besides the four Army combat divisions, there are about twenty individual home defense and training battalions under Scottish Command, although they're little more than pools of men at this time. They'll become the next priority to receive training and equipment after the combat divisions are equipped. Half of them are in North Scotland, but none of them are in your sector. They're all located at the regimental headquarters towns of Stirling, Perth, Inverness, Aberdeen, and so on. As I said, my North Highland District is divided into three sectors or sub-districts. You command the Northwest Sub-District, Matthew Harris commands the Inverness Sub-District, and Richard Sinclair commands the Aberdeen Sub-District."

"I don't think I know Sinclair."

"No reason you should. He's had a fairly undistinguished career, but someone in Scottish Command likes him. He's originally from a small town south of Aberdeen, I think Montrose. He was commissioned during the last stages of the First War into the Fife & Forfar Yeomanry and he later moved to the Gordon Highlanders. He likes his food and drink quite well and is developing an expanding girth. He's a decent enough chap and seems to make friends easily, but he hardly inspires confidence. Anyway, he's being made an acting colonel for this assignment.

"Harris was just promoted to colonel after France fell. He came back from Dunkirk pretty well banged up and it was decided to take him out of troop duty until he recovered. He's also a Seaforth Highlander, so he also fits into my district rather well. You are senior to Sinclair and to Matthew Harris, and you rank second to me in the North Highland District."

"What about your deputy commander?"

"I have none. My chief-of-staff is Lieutenant-Colonel Steve Whittaker who is a fine officer, also a Seaforth Highlander, and a really bright fellow. He's too young to have fought in the First War. Six months ago he was a major. He does a mountain of work each day and takes care of all our paperwork, bless his soul.

"Now, let's look at the map again." Jack poured himself another whisky, but David again declined. They walked to a wall map of Scotland. "The map is a gift from the Royal Geographic Society and has no marks on it so that I don't have to keep it locked up. Here's what your sector looks like, David. Essentially we divided your sector at the Great Glen, with modifications.

"Brigadier Guthrie from the Glasgow District and I have established your southernmost boundary south of Loch Linnhe at Loch Leven and east through Glen Coe. We decided that you should command the forces in the northernmost portion of Glasgow's Argyll Sub-District, as that will give you more flexibility. It will also allow you to quickly call on the entire North Argyll Home Guard Battalion in an emergency without waiting for permission from Glasgow. You will command the whole peninsula region to the west of Fort William down to the Sound of Mull. The Glasgow District's Argyll Sub-District will take the Isles of Mull and Coll, and all the islands to the south. All the islands north and west of Mull are yours."

"So, I'll command a small part of Argyll?"

"Right, the very northern portion. Now, your eastern boundary roughly follows the mountains. From Ben Nevis, just south of Fort

44

William, go north to include Fort Augustus in your sector, then further north to Ben Wyvis, Ben Hope and up to Stralhy Point, east of Betty-hill on the North Coast." Jack traced the line with his finger. "Remember, these boundaries are approximate only. Everything west of this line, including the islands, is in your Sub-District. East of here is either the Inverness Sub-District under Colonel Matthew Harris or the Aberdeen Sub-District under Colonel Richard Sinclair. Do you know Harris?"

"Yes, after the war we served together in the 51st Division."

"Excellent. You'll have to work well together to make this whole business function properly. It's vital you both understand that the boundary is for administrative purposes only. It's not an operational boundary and each of you may operate across the boundary at any time as needed. Just coordinate with each other. Don't get your egos involved. There is only one enemy."

"Understood. I think I passed the ego stage some years back and I look forward to working with Matt."

"Good, because you both will be sharing the same Home Guard and Civil Defense forces."

"Because the shires are split between Colonel Harris and me."

"Exactly. If one sub-district is attacked all the forces will be available to that commander and the other sub-districts will become supporting commands. If two sub-districts are simultaneously attacked, Major-General Adams and I will decide who gets what.

"Let's review the shires from north to south, David. Caithness is totally in the Inverness Sub-District and has but one Home Guard battalion. The other shires, however, are like layers of a large cake, one on top of the next one, each stretching from the North Sea across Scotland to the Atlantic. Sutherland also has a single Home Guard battalion, most companies of which are in Harris' sector. If you alone are attacked, however, you get the whole battalion. Next to the south is the shire of Ross and Cromarty, again with a single battalion. Then Inverness-shire, which has two battalions. You have part of the western battalion. Then Argyll-shire with two battalions and you get part of the northernmost battalion. Finally, there's a battalion to be formed soon on the Western Isles, all yours. So, you'll have all or parts of five battalions, a pretty handsome brigade except that the Home Guard has no brigades. It has battalions, groups, zones and areas, but no brigades."

"That's just to confuse everyone, especially the veterans in their ranks."

Jack smiled. "Actually, it was a War Office decision to make sure nobody confused the Home Guard with the Regular Army. And they don't use military ranks, nor will they have army uniforms, nor will they be paid for their service. Doesn't seem fair, does it?"

"How are they taking all that?"

"Actually, rather well, but they would like to have weapons, uniforms and military ranks. Because most of the officers and senior non-commissioned officers are veterans, they want to be called by proper titles of rank. It's who they were and what they know. So, the area commanders and I have unofficially allowed the use of their former military ranks. We think it's only fair and certainly has boosted morale. And the non-veterans seem to understand the rank titles better than whatever they now are supposed to call their leaders. This is certainly not official doctrine, but it works and Scottish Command looks the other way."

"How about the Civil Defense and the Air Raid Precautions services?"

"A hodge-podge, as you might expect, with thousands of untrained volunteers swarming in to recruiting stations in every city and town, but too few trained personnel or equipment to make it all work yet. This should sort itself out in time."

"I know there are women in the Civil Defense and ARP organizations. Are there any women in the Home Guard?"

"That's a very sensitive subject, David. For several years women have been recruited as auxiliaries for the Army, Navy, and RAF. Officially, however, there are no women permitted in the Home Guard, even as auxiliaries, and the War Office is adamant about this. Must protect the delicate things, you know; very Victorian and all that. In reality, yes, there are women in the Home Guard, but they officially have a Civil Defense or ARP status. They serve as clerks, drivers, medical staff and so on. You'll also find some women carrying privately owned weapons. We ask them to give the weapon to a man and they say 'push off!' Will they fight like infantry if we're invaded? I would say a definite 'yes.' Scottish Command also looks the other way with all this and pretends that women are assigned to a nearby Civil Defense unit. I would suggest you do the same."

"I definitely don't want to wage war with women over this. With the population so small in my sector, I need all the help I can get. Do I command the Home Guard units and the other civilian services?"

"Yes and no. The Home Guard was formed originally at the direction of Mr. Chamberlain and now Mr. Churchill. It's supervised by Mr. Eden through the War Office. The Home Guard has their own commanders at every level: Area, Zone, Group, Battalion, Company, and so forth. Actually, the War Office does not officially recognize the zones at this point, but I expect they soon will become official. Each Army District has a Home Guard Area Commander from the Regular Army. Colonel Usher is a regular officer who commands the North Highland Home Guard Area and all Home Guard forces in my district. He reports to me. The vast majority of the other commanders are veteran officers who no longer serve in the Army.

"If an invasion occurs, David, all Home Guard units will come under the command of the British Army so, yes, you will command those units. Until then, we serve as advisors and will assist their development in any way we can. I would simply recommend that you develop a good working relationship with the civil authorities, the Lords Lieutenant, the Provosts, the Town Councils, the Chief Constables and, of course, with the Home Guard commanders themselves. They know you will be their fighting commander and they are looking to you for direction and assistance. I encourage you to be the commander of your sub-district just as if you were a brigade commander. People are frightened and they're looking to you for protection. Be highly visible, lead them, and infuse them with confidence.

"Speaking of being a brigade commander, David, you are more than that. Given your wide range of responsibilities, you are more like a division commander and must form a suitable staff. It's up to you to recruit your own staff, as we have nobody to give you. Your staff will not be part of the Home Guard, but rather part of the Army. Unfortunately, we cannot pay them; they must serve as part-time volunteers. Choose veterans where you can and others who can do the job. You'll have to train them. I'll back you on all your decisions and I leave it to you to give them any rank that's reasonable. At this time, you're authorized to hire only one paid staff person to help you with the administrative work. Choose anyone in whom you have confidence."

"Any recommendations on where I should establish my headquarters, Sir?"

"Actually, that's already been decided. Fort William will be your headquarters and let me explain why. I know it's not central to your sub-district, being along your southern boundary, but it is the largest town in your sector. You'll need a population base from which to recruit your staff. From there, you can travel by road everywhere, weather permitting, or by rail at least as far as Glasgow or Mallaig, or by boat. Should I happen to be here at my home, the railroad is essential if you're to come down to Glasgow in any weather, or at any time of day. There's no rail line from Fort William to Inverness. There was supposed to be one, but only the branch line to Fort Augustus was built. You have a motorcar, but the road from there to here at night or in bad weather can be difficult, sometimes even treacherous. Most roads are narrow, unpaved and a single lane, but passable.

"Fort William also has a central Post Office and a central telephone switching facility, and it has a small airstrip, which might come in handy. I also suggest you find convenient lodgings in other towns where you'll travel throughout your sector: maybe Portree, Ullapool, Durness, and Stornoway, for example. Perhaps a friendly Home Guard officer or local official will accommodate you for the night occasionally, if you cannot locate other lodging. Your travel and other expenses should be submitted to Steve Whitaker's office periodically for reimbursement, and you'll receive a priority gas coupon card to permit regular travel for work.

"Tomorrow, you'll drive to Fort William to start work. Stay in a hotel as needed, but find lodgings as soon as possible. And find a suitable office location for you and your staff. The plan is that we'll take over part of a hotel for the Army sub-district headquarters. This, however, would make you somewhat aloof from the public and you wouldn't be in the center of activity with good visibility. Good public relations are most important and good public morale follows. I suggest you initially lease an office on High Street with a prominent sign saying, 'British Army, Northwest Sub-District Headquarters, Scottish Command,' or something like that. As you know, there are no military forces stationed anywhere near Fort William, with the exception of that tiny Navy station being established on Loch Linnhe.

"Now, I want to give you one vital admonition." David listened carefully. "Throughout your career you've been the very image of the finest of British officers who have led our forces for centuries and loyally served the Crown. You are smart, brave, hardworking, diligent, imaginative, and all the other characteristics we look for in rising young officers. I'm certain those characteristics drove you forward and led to your early promotions." David started to protest.

"Hear me out, David. You also are impeccably dressed at all times and present yourself quite well before the public. A quick glance tells people that you are truly a professional officer of high rank and vast experience. In your new assignment, however, you must add a new dimension. You must become one of the people. You will be the most senior officer in you sub-district, but you really must become the *primus inter alles*, the first among equals. In the Army, we often must push our soldiers to accomplish their mission. In your new assignment, you must lead the public, show them, gain their confidence, and they'll accomplish the mission on their own.

"I cannot emphasize too strongly that in their minds you truly must become one of the people. Soften your image somewhat, be gentler in your dealings where possible, and become one of them. You'll capture their minds, their hearts, their souls and they'll follow you anywhere. You've never been an officer who struts around with your nose in the air, barking orders and demanding the privileges of your rank. I'm confident this is one reason you were given this assignment. Your very presence will give confidence to the people of the Highlands, but your dealings with them must show your humanity. Their perception of you and your plan for their defense against the Nazis will determine the success or failure of your mission.

"We want to tell the people that the Army is here to protect them as best we can, David, but they must contribute to their own survival."

"With one soldier!"

"Ah, but a Colonel of the Black Watch."

5

July 2, 1940

THE MORNING HAD DAWNED with the promise of more sunshine and a hint of passing rain clouds. David said his goodbyes to Jack and Betty early in order to get a jump on Glasgow traffic. As he drove north, Jack Campbell's admonitions swirled through his head . . . "You're in command . . . They're looking to you for leadership and answers . . . You're a Colonel of the Black Watch . . . You have vast responsibilities and very little to work with . . . I've very little to give you . . . Trust your judgment . . . Do whatever you feel needs to be done . . . Pick good people . . . I'll support your decisions. . . . " It almost seemed overwhelming.

As he entered the rolling hills of Argyll, north of Loch Lomond, the beauty of the highlands began to fill his soul. Anne would like to have been here and give him her support. Loneliness for Anne and his children crept into his thoughts and he became increasingly distracted. As he entered Tyndrum, he saw a small hotel beside the road: "Coffee," he thought.

The owner was apologetic. "Nae coffee for months, Colonel, 'tis the rationin' ye know, seven months already. I do ha' some Earl Grey tea."

"Tea will be fine." The steaming tea pushed back his loneliness and he thought again of Fort William. "How's the road going north?"

"Needs repair. No' much ha' been doon for several years and 'tis full of holes." David finished his tea and left a shilling on the table.

"No' much Army around here, Colonel. Ye'll be goin' to set up a camp hereabouts?"

"Not exactly, but the Army's here."

IT WAS MID-AFTERNOON when David drove north on the Achintore Road along the south shore of Loch Linnhe, the longest sea loch in Scotland. It was an unusually warm summer day, but the only boats

50

on the loch were merchant vessels and an occasional naval craft. David admired the splendor of the Grampian Mountains, stretching eastward from Loch Linnhe as far as the eye could see. Ben Nevis, the highest mountain in the British Isles, stood in stately grandeur overlooking the junction of the rivers Nevis and Lochy as they flowed into Loch Linnhe.

David drove past the railway station, down High Street, through the center of town and stopped at the Alexandra Hotel across from the town square, known as The Parade. After taking a room for the night, he bought a newspaper and scanned the advertisements for rental property. A Mrs. Carruthers was soliciting tenants for a vacant storefront on High Street near Lochaber House, and lodgers for several vacant flats. A quick phone call brought the two of them together at the storefront location.

"'Tis ready for occupancy, Colonel. Of course ye'll be responsible for all furnishin' and the cleanin'. The stove works fine, but ye mun buy yer own coal. The last tenant wa' a haberdasher who wa' quite happy here. He moved out one night owin' me several weeks rent, but he left a safe over there against the wall, empty I'm sure. I guess he decided the safe wa' too heavy to move quickly. I also ha' twa vacant flats upstairs, quite convenient to yer work. If these quarters are no' satisfactory, I ha' several others to show ye." Mrs. Carruthers was a thin, severe woman in her 70's who clearly knew her business. She'd been widowed during the First War and had run the business alone ever since. "Mind ye, I expect the rent payments promptly each Friday mornin'." The shop was about 30 by 40 feet, with a small portion boxed off for an inner office near a window; a rear door led upstairs to the flats.

"And how much would the rent be?" he asked.

"T'will is twa pounds sterling per week for the shop, and the flat is one pound, five shillings."

"That sounds a bit too high. I'm willing to pay you nine pounds per month for both the shop and the flat; the government will pay you in advance."

"Ten pounds," she countered.

"I'm sorry, but I'm authorized to spend only nine pounds," he fibbed.

"Weel," she grumbled, "when will I get me money?"

"After we sign the agreement, I'll prepare the authorization through our Inverness headquarters."

They walked upstairs to the flat. "This one faces High Street, the other faces the back. No' too fancy, ye know, but all the essentials are here. The loo is down the hall. Mind ye, the stove needs ashes removed regular' and dumped out back."

"This will do," he responded without enthusiasm. There was a full-size iron frame bed with a doubtful mattress lying on metal springs. A sad-looking overstuffed chair and a small table with two straight back chairs completed the furnishings. "I feel like I'm in a Spartan Army camp," he thought distastefully.

Before returning to the Alexandra for the night, David stopped at another hotel on High Street and entered the almost empty dining room. There was nobody in sight, so he took a seat at a nearby table.

"Not there! Sit over here," said the sharp voice of a thin woman in her early forties, wearing the black uniform and white apron of a waitress. David moved to the proper table. "Ye men think ye can do anythin' ye bloody well please," she continued. "Weel, there's no' much food to offer tonight and precious little drink."

"I'll have whatever the chef recommends tonight and a cup of tea," he replied.

"Twi'll be along soon." She sat down at his table across from him, much to David's surprise, and drew out a cigarette. After lighting it, she asked. "Mind if I smoke?" She went on without waiting for an answer. "Ye married?"

"Widowed." David sat in amazement at her familiarity.

"Humph. I wa' married twice, both bums; both took off and didna' come back. So, ye're in the Army?" she asked as she looked at his uniform. Without waiting for an answer she continued, "I hate the Army. I donna' like wars and I damned well donna' like this war. Twa's all thought up by politicians, rich industrialists, and Army officers. They can all go straight to hell. I didna' ask for this war, I donna' know anyone who did and I refuse to be in it. As far as I'm concerned ye're nobody special."

"I never thought I was."

"Ye soldiers come in here and try to get us girls to go up to yer rooms. Weel, don' ask 'cause I'm no' goin'. I've ha' it with men!"

"I didn't ask and I never would. I'm here on business, that's all."

"Probably funny business, but ye ain't gettin' it from me." She got up quickly, went to the kitchen with the cigarette still in her mouth, and returned shortly with an unappetizing plate of food and a cup of steaming tea. David ate in grateful silence and then left to return to the Alexandra.

July 3

DAVID POSTED A NOTICE on the billboard outside the Town Hall. It read:

Notice of Full time Position
Assistant to Sub-District Commander
Excellent Initiative, Organizational and Office Skills Required
Inquire at Army Headquarters, Granite Building, High Street

Returning to his office, he looked again at the months of accumulated dirt and the years of neglected maintenance. "Must get a cleaning crew in here," he mused. He walked to the window of his box-like office. People were coming down High Street in some numbers now, dodging cars as they hurried to work. David was amused at the variety of clothing, from one gentleman dressed in his best finery to common labourers wearing old work clothes that hadn't been washed for weeks.

His eyes fell on a woman down the street who was walking faster than others. She was taller than most women; her very dark brown shoulder-length hair blew gently in the breeze. She walked purposely with her back straight and her head erect. David's uncle would've called her "a well done package." Her dark cotton dress was simple and without adornment; she needed none. She approached the intersection by the corner of his building, crossed the road, and walked towards his door. David stepped back from the window. Momentarily, there was a firm knock on the door and it opened.

"Good mornin', Sir. My name is Elaine Donaldson Ross and I am lookin' to fill the position of assistant to the sub-district commander."

"Good morning. I'm Colonel McKenna, but I'm not yet ready to interview for the position. I assume you saw the handbill."

"Yes," she replied, as she took the handbill from her purse and began to unfold it. "This looks to be a perfect position for me."

"You took down my handbill?"

"Yes, of course. You wilna' be needin' it anymore. I'm the best qualified for the job and this is just wha' I ha' been lookin' for."

David suppressed a smile at her audacity. "And what makes you the best qualified, Miss?"

"'Tis Mrs. My husband is in the Navy at Devonport on the cruiser HMS *Bonaventure*. I know I'm the best qualified because I won the top scores in school. I am verra' well organized, I work fast, I donna' take days off and I can type 90 words per minute. Mr. McGowan says I'm his best assistant ever because I'm a fast learner, I get my work done quickly and I donna' make mistakes." She spoke so quickly she was out of breath.

"Mr. McGowan?"

She took a breath. "I'm the legal assistant to McGowan and Son, Solicitors, over on Bank Street. Auld Mr. McGowan inherited the firm from his father when he retired in the 1890's. He'd run the firm for many years with his wife as his assistant. He retired almost ten years ago and turned the firm over to his son William, whom I call young Mr. McGowan. I'm young Mr. McGowan's legal assistant, or at least I was until he was called up for the war. He's a captain in the special reserve, you know, and he served in the First War. He finished his law studies at the University of Glasgow soon after the war ended and joined his father in the firm. I wa' hired seven years ago, and young Mr. McGowan trained me to be his legal assistant."

"So, young Mr. McGowan is off to war, and you're out of a job."

"Not exactly. When young Mr. McGowan wa' called up, auld Mr. McGowan came back into the business to keep it goin'. His wife, Mrs. McGowan, came back, too, as it made him feel more comfortable to have her there. She does things his way, and I do things young Mr. McGowan's way. Weel, the business ha' shrunk since the war began, and auld Mr. McGowan canna' afford to keep me on. He was verra' nice about it. He said I should look for another job, but I could stay with them until I find one. Colonel, I want to do my part to help the war effort, but I donna' want to work in an ammunition factory or at the aluminum plant. Things would be fine if young Mr. McGowan wa' here, but he's livin' in a castle someplace in County Durham."

David thought for a moment. "He must be assigned to Barnard Castle. That's the name of a town south of Durham, now just castle ruins, but there's a very large army training center just outside of town."

"I see. Weel, I really am the best person for this job. I know everyone in Fort William and no' one of them can do this job better than me. Please, Colonel, I really want this job." She looked imploringly at him.

"This job will be tough, Mrs. Ross. There is nothing here now and we'll establish this headquarters by ourselves. I need a good organizer and someone whom I can trust to run the office when I'm away. It will take many extra hours, some nights and weekends, and this will affect your family. You do have a family, don't you?"

"Oh, aye. I ha' twa laddies, my only bairn. Aaron is eleven and Timothy nine. We live with my Mum, Julia Donaldson. My father, Edmund Donaldson, died in 1934. Mum watches the boys when they're out of school, if I'm workin'. I can work evenin's and weekends, if needed. I do that now. Mum does sewin' and takes in laundry. She would be verra' happy to wash and mend your clothes, Colonel. She is verra' good with her work."

"Very well, Mrs. Ross, I'll hire you for a trial period, say for one month. The pay is set by the Army at two pounds and fifteen shillings per week. Your first duty will be to prepare your job application and your pay documents. I don't have any forms, I don't have any furniture or equipment, and I don't even have a damn telephone to call Inverness to get the forms. So, maybe you can start work next Monday and we'll work on all this then. I've two meetings set for today and I'll be in Fort Augustus tomorrow."

"No, Colonel, I'll start today even without pay. I'm verra' resourceful and I'll get these things worked out myself. Just tell me who I should call first."

"Call Lieutenant-Colonel Steve Whittaker at Army District Command Headquarters in Inverness."

"Yes, Sir, thank you for this opportunity. I wilna' let you doon." She looked around the room. "This buildin' is owned by ault Mrs. Carruthers, isn't it?"

"Correct. Do you know her?"

"I know everra'one here and she's a witch! Look at the filth in this place. Ha' she no shame? Nae, she doesna'. All she cares about are the precious shillings she makes each week and stuffs in the bank. I could tell you some stories about her, but I willna'. I'll speak to her. You go on to your meetin's, Colonel, and leave all this to me."

As he walked up High Street, he thought, "What a beautiful face and those eyes are magnificent. In another life she could be a model for Harrods." He turned into the entryway of the Royal Bank of Scotland and walked to the office of the Managing Director. The secretary ushered him into the office of William C. Murray.

"To what do I owe the pleasure of this visit, Colonel? May I assume you're looking for banking services for you or your new headquarters?"

"Word of my appointment travels fast, Mr. Murray. No, I'm not setting up my banking services just yet, perhaps next week. I understand you're President of the Northern Bankers Guild."

"Yes, I've been honored to hold that post for the past three years."

"I'm concerned about the fate of all banks in my sub-district in the event of invasion. Do you have instructions on how to safeguard the bank's assets?"

"Invasion? No, I don't think so. The Bank of England has issued its standard War Instructions for Banks. You know, locking the vault in the event of an air raid, safeguarding files and sending the staff home, that sort of thing."

"In the event of invasion, Mr. Murray, that may not be enough. I hope it never happens, but I'm sure you read the newspapers. You certainly know that the 'Honours of Scotland,' our crown jewels, were placed in a vault near Edinburgh Castle last year. You may also know that the Bank of England brought its gold reserves to Scotland last October, and then shipped them on to Halifax, Canada, being a safer storage location. This is a very dangerous situation we're facing and it's quite possible we could be invaded and, God forbid, even conquered." Mr. Murray's face turned an ashen gray. "I'd encourage you to discuss this with other bankers in your Guild on a very private basis, and for each bank to develop an invasion plan. It's important that you not write this down nor share your plan with anyone other than the very top bank officials; for the Germans can read English quite well."

"Yes, well, you've caught me quite unprepared, Colonel. I guess I assumed the Army could hold the Germans at bay."

"We all thought the French Army could hold the Germans at bay, as they did in the First War. But that didn't happen, so it's best to prepare for the worst. Does your bank hold much specie, bar or plate metal?"

"A fair amount, yes. We keep on hand several thousand pounds sterling in coins and bars. The plate metal is privately owned and is held quite safely in a vault for our customers."

"The Germans have very efficient explosives and they've easily opened the bank vaults in Poland, Belgium, Norway, and the Netherlands. I imagine they're doing the same in France right now."

"I see your point. Yes, we had best develop a plan. Have you any suggestions, Colonel?"

"No, not really. I think you might keep petrol available to burn your pound notes . . . "

"Oh, the Bank of England would never permit that," he interrupted.

"Mr. Murray, we're talking about actions during an invasion. The Bank of England may have been bombed away by then. Would you rather have your paper currency burned or given to the Germans? I imagine they could make great mischief with all those notes."

"I see your point, yes, best to destroy it. How about the coinage and plate?"

"It would have to be well hidden. Perhaps you alone should arrange that and tell only one responsible person where it is hidden. Do you have a trustworthy colleague who has a farm in the country?"

"My brother."

"If Scotland is invaded, maybe you should bury all precious metals someplace on your brother's farm; say under a large manure pile."

"That's disgusting. I don't know if I could do that." He grimaced. "Of course, I shall have to speak with my superiors first."

"You may have no choice, Mr. Murray. The Germans are not fools. They will unearth a freshly dug earthen pit. A manure pile would probably disgust them also, and the manure will quickly fill in any traces of digging. In any case, I strongly advise you to prepare for the worst and to pass this on to your fellow bankers. They should each develop their own plan separately and not share the information even within the banking community. I suggest you tell your superiors only that you've an invasion plan and nothing more."

"Yes, there could be a Fifth Columnist even in banking."

David left the bank and walked to the office of the Chief Constable, Angus MacDonald. After a warm greeting, MacDonald explained to David the organization of the Inverness-shire Constabulary, first established in 1840. It was divided into four divisions, each under a chief constable: Inverness itself; Lochaber, which was headquartered in Fort William and included many communities throughout the region; the Isle of Skye and nearby areas headquartered in Portree; and much of the Inner and Outer Hebrides headquartered at Long Island. The Lochaber division was served by almost 40 regular police officers and augmented by another 55 part-time officers.

"More are volunteering every month, Colonel. My biggest concern is getting them trained and equipped. I've one issue on which I need your advice. The Nazis have announced that, when they invade Britain, they'll hang any policemen found shooting at them. Can they do that?"

"If the Nazis conquer Britain, Mr. MacDonald, I expect they'll do whatever they damn well please. You and I probably will be shot early on." MacDonald shifted his seat in discomfort.

"How do your policemen plan to act if we are invaded?"

"They'll kill the Nazis just like any soldier would. They're not intimidated."

Chief MacDonald then walked David to the office of the town Provost, a position akin to that of mayor. Provost Simon MacDonald also served as chairman of the Town Council, the elected officials who governed Fort William. After tea and a long discussion of town affairs, Mr. MacDonald asked David to speak at the next meeting of the Council and, thereafter, to hold several public meetings.

"We can meet in several area churches where people can sit comfortably and ask questions after your talk." David quickly agreed.

It was nearing noon when David stopped in The Argyll, a local pub and hotel on High Street, for a brief lunch. The waitress brought him a copy of the *Oban Times,* the weekly newspaper that also served the Lochaber region with a section called the Fort William News. The newspaper had several stories about local Territorial Army soldiers and other local units also on active service. David made a note to have Elaine subscribe to the paper and also to the *Harbour News,* a small local newsletter.

After lunch, David made a brief visit to Belford Hospital to introduce himself to the director and assess its capabilities. The hospital had fifty-five beds and was the largest hospital north of Oban and west of Inverness. It would serve both civilian and military casualties in the event of invasion. Its capacity would be quickly overwhelmed. They must make plans for alternate medical treatment sites, but where would they find additional medical staff?

"The Navy says they'll bring in one or two surgeons and some medical assistants, Colonel."

David replied that staffing was a pressing issue for every organization in wartime, but he was confident many women and girls would volunteer, if asked. Medical professionals, however, were in short supply.

As he walked back to his office, he wondered if he would soon find staff for his own headquarters to help with this and many other issues. David's military background hadn't prepared him for the many civilian issues facing him in his new assignment.

IT WAS MID-AFTERNOON when David arrived at his new office. As he approached the door, he heard the humdrum of activity inside. Opening the door, he saw seven women cleaning floors, windows and walls. Elaine, who quickly came over to him, was supervising the activity.

"You're a wee bit earlier than I thought, Colonel, but we'll be done in another ha'-hour. Your flat is all cleaned and ready for use. There's a fire in the stove and I took the liberty of checking you out of the hotel.

The manager said he'll ha' your luggage sent over promptly. No sense in runnin' up a bill when you ha' your flat ready."

"Who are these women, Elaine? I must pay them for this work."

"Nonsense, Colonel, they're all my friends and they volunteered to help get your office ready. Mrs. Carruthers is payin' for the cleanin' supplies, reluctantly. She also ha' paid for the three new windowpanes that were broken. Mr. Evans kindly came over earlier and replaced them. I've also arranged to have a coal delivery tomorrow mornin'. Oh, I spoke with Lieutenant-Colonel Whittaker by phone this mornin'. He's such a nice man and he said tha' I will be hired as of tomorrow mornin', if tha's your instruction. I took the liberty of tellin' him that it wa' your decision, but he said to tell you that you can cancel my appointment anytime. He's sendin' my appointment forms immediately, along with a box or two of office supplies and stationery to get us started. He said to send him a list of our requirements whenever we're ready. Do you like your new desk?"

"Desk?" David looked around in amazement. In the smaller office stood a large oak desk and chair. "How much did you pay for those?"

"Nothin'. I convinced auld Mr. McGowan that he didna' need it until young Mr. McGowan returned from the war and that he could help the war effort by loanin' it to you, along with the large conference table with eight chairs. We havna' used the table since young Mr. McGowan left. The table and chairs will be along soon. Mr. Crumley, he's a neighbor who has a truck and two strong sons; he brought the desk first with its chair and my typewriter. Mrs. McGowan has her own very old favorite typewriter and didna' want to use mine, so we're borrowin' that, too. On his next trip, Mr. Crumley will bring the table and chairs. I think I can borrow a file cabinet, as well. As soon as the stationery arrives from Glasgow, I'll prepare a verra' nice thank you note from you to auld Mr. McGowan. I think your office also needs two armchairs, don' you agree?" Without waiting for an answer, she took the arm of one of the women and pulled her over. "Colonel, meet my mum, Julia Donaldson." They shook hands, and Elaine introduced all the other women one by one.

"We'll be finished shortly, Colonel, and I see Mr. Crumley has arrived with the table. Elaine commanded, "Could someone hold the door, please?" The large oak table and its eight chairs were placed in the center of the floor. "I think my desk will fit just outside your office, wouldn't you agree? Oh yes, the telephone men will be here tomorrow to install two phone lines, which Colonel Whittaker said were authorized, with as many extensions as we require. I said three phones on each line, for now. As she glanced at David, the look in her eyes said, "Never underestimate my abilities."

"Doris, is the water ready for tea?" Elaine asked loudly. Doris confirmed that it was and began preparing the cups. "Wasn't it nice of Mrs. Carruthers to purchase mugs for the office?" she said loudly so that Mrs. Carruthers would be sure to hear. Everyone nodded in agreement. "When you've finished, ladies, put your rags up and come have a cup of tea with the Colonel." They began to move toward Doris who was passing out the cups, except Mrs. Carruthers who slipped out the back door. "Sir, you sit here," Elaine said softly, "you're payin' for the tea."

After a half hour of conversation about David's background and a sincere thank you to each woman, the ladies said their goodbyes and left for home. David and Elaine sat quietly. Finally, he said "You are remarkable. I never expected anything like this. I thought it would be two weeks before this office was usable."

"'Tis as I said, Colonel, I'm a good organizer and I get things done."

"I notice you don't have as much Scottish brogue as most people here, Elaine."

"'Tis from workin' for young Mr. McGowan. He tried to teach me to speak like folks further south, 'more professional' he called it. 'Twas quite a game between us. He'd say words and phrases to me each day, which I repeated back to him, like "Good morning to youuu . . . ," emphasing each vowel clearly. I'd say it back and if it wasna' quite right he'd say it again and I'd say it back again."

"Sounds like he did you many favors."

"Oh, indeed." Glancing at her watch, she stood up. "It's late and I need to get along home to my boys and help Mum with supper. If you will draft the wordin' for the outdoor sign tonight, I'll arrange it first thing tomorrow. Ha' a good evenin', Sir, and a good day in Fort Augustus, tomorrow."

6

July 5, 1940

THE DAY BEFORE HAD BEEN A good day at Fort Augustus, twenty miles northeast of Fort William, located at the western end of Loch Ness. David had met all day at the Station Hotel with his Army counterpart, Colonel Matthew Harris, Commander of the Northeast Sub-District, which included all the shires north of the Aberdeen Sub-District. Equally important, Colonel Harris had brought with him to the meeting the Area Commander of the Home Guard for the North Highland District, Colonel Charles M. Usher, a well-decorated officer who had served with the Gordon Highland Regiment of Aberdeen. The Home Guard areas corresponded to the Army districts; Usher reported to Brigadier Jack Campbell. Five other officers also attended, including Colonel Sir Donald Cameron of Lochiel, a retired colonel of the Queen's Own Cameron Highland Regiment and the Lord Lieutenant of Inverness-shire. Lochiel commanded the Home Guard Inverness Group, which included Fort William and all of Lochaber.

The eight officers focused on issues related to the Home Guard, Civil Defense, and plans to defend Scotland and the Highlands in the event of invasion. All shared the same concerns: lack of weapons and training. The Home Guard was just six weeks past its establishment and only a handful of weapons had been found to arm them. They lacked uniforms and other equipment, and they were barely able to keep in step when they marched. "A motley collection of enthusiastic volunteers," said Matthew Harris, "and they would be completely helpless without the large numbers of veterans in their ranks." The Civil Defense units were only somewhat better, most having been established several months before the outbreak of war. Like the Home Guard, untrained volunteers were flooding the Civil Defense ranks and overwhelming the units' training programs and equipment. This would all be worked out in time, if only they had the time to work it out.

Like David, Colonels Harris and Usher had just started their new assignments and were learning about the Home Guard and the Civil Defense structure. Ideas flowed freely, and David felt very comfortable as a member of this council. David found the meeting to be highly productive and his working relationship with these officers very cordial. They encouraged him to visit various Home Guard and Civil Defense units whenever possible without regard for sub-district boundaries; he vowed to himself to be sure to contact these commanders first whenever he did so.

"It couldn't have gone better," he thought to himself as he drove home. "Tomorrow, I'll begin to assemble my staff."

July 6

DAVID WAS AT HIS DESK EARLY on Saturday morning reading from a large packet of papers that Jack Campbell had sent up by train from Glasgow. Each train conductor had a lock box or safe for carrying government documents. The package included numerous Army information documents disseminated to senior commanders to keep them abreast of the war; beyond what was publicly available from newspapers or BBC radio. Jack also enclosed several pamphlets that described different towns in the Northwest Sector, plus yesterday's *Manchester Guardian* newspaper.

There was a sharp knock on the door. Elaine hadn't yet arrived at work so David opened the door. A tall, dark-haired gentleman dressed in golfing clothes held out his hand. "Colonel McKenna? I'm Rear-Admiral Christopher Evans-Cooper, Royal Navy Retired. I wish to introduce myself and see if I might be of help." He entered and looked around at the office. "I retired here to Fort William with my wife in 1935 and I've met many people throughout Lochaber. Until this week, I'd no idea the Army was establishing a headquarters in Fort William, but it is most welcome indeed."

"Admiral, it's my honor and pleasure to meet you." David was interrupted by Elaine Ross' arrival. They exchanged greetings as the Admiral said, "Good Morning, Elaine. I had no idea you worked here."

"You know each other?" David asked.

"Yes, we met at McGowan & Son when I had some legal work done. Elaine was very helpful and even came to our house to help me sort some papers for recording."

"The Admiral has a beautiful home overlooking Loch Linnhe, just west of here," she interjected. "He's a hero from the First War."

The admiral looked at David with a slight grin. "I'm definitely not a hero. I was first lieutenant on the cruiser HMS *Canterbury* during the Battle of Jutland. We were involved in some sharp actions for two nights and our ship was hit by gunfire several times. The Navy decided to give a few minor decorations to our captain, our gunnery officer and me, nothing special."

"It sounds like you've had quite a career."

"My career has stretched over forty wonderful years. We decided to stay in Scotland, but didn't want to live in Edinburgh or Glasgow. Fort William has been a fine home to us."

"I certainly would be grateful for your valuable counsel as I form my staff."

"Maybe I can help with more than just counsel. Yes, I know many people in Fort William, but only some of them have a military background. I've encouraged those veterans to join the Home Guard and most indeed have done so. Your headquarters, however, is a very different story. You need a different level of expertise here, and I may be able to give you some names. One of my retired brethren, Rear-Admiral Bill Elder, commands a Home Guard battalion in Portsmouth. Many Navy retirees are serving at every level of the Home Guard, from ordinary soldiers to senior ranks. Frankly, I never had any interest in joining the Home Guard myself, but I think I could give you valuable service here in your headquarters."

"That's sensible," David replied. "I think we can work out a satisfactory arrangement." They shook hands.

As the admiral started to leave, he turned and said, "Are you free Monday, Colonel, I know it's the start of another busy week."

"Monday is just another day in the week, Admiral, until we've stopped the German invasion."

"I'd like to introduce you to a chap you should meet. CB Foster is a civil engineer just back from India. He's a veteran of the First War and I think he may be helpful to you. I'd like to take you both to lunch."

"I'd be honored."

As the day wore on, David pored over a series of documents given him by Matthew Harris on the state of the Home Guard, Civil Defense, and Air Raid Precautions units then being organized in Northern Scotland. He seemed to be interrupted constantly by visitors, most of whom were well-wishers or curiosity seekers. The war had brought great tension to Britain, and the supreme confidence held by the public in 1914 was absent in 1940. The people of Fort William were fearful of an invasion and pleased there was again an Army presence in their community. There had been no armed forces stationed there for almost a century, with the exception of the recently established small Navy training station.

Elaine was busy greeting visitors and typing letters to provosts and town councils. The letters announced David's appointment, and his willingness to meet with town officials and to hold public meetings at a suitable location in each town. At these meetings, David would make a brief presentation on the war threat and the government's response. He would show how each town, no matter how small, could play an important role in the eventual victory, and then answer questions.

David planned to speak in every village and town in his sector before winter storms made driving difficult or impossible. He and Elaine traced on a map his weekly routes, hoping to speak in two or three villages and towns each day, then return to Fort William Friday evenings so as to work at the office during the weekends.

"'Tis is a gruelin' schedule, Colonel," Elaine remarked halfway through the project.

"It has to be done," he replied.

By late afternoon, they were ready to stop for the day. "Excellent work today, Elaine. May I reward you by taking you to dinner?"

"No, Sir, but thank you. I'm needed at home tonight. Let me fix some tea instead." As they sat sipping their tea, David broke the silence. "Are you originally from Fort William?"

"Yes, Sir. I wa' born here and finished school in 1927."

"You never thought of going on to the university?"

"Oh no, Sir, no one in my family has ever been to a university, nor anyone we knew, save for the teachers, of course. I really never gave it a thought. Besides, Paul and I were courtin' then and we were married in early 1928."

"What was the attraction to Paul?"

"Well, first of all he wanted to be with me, and that's an attraction for any girl. Paul was handsome, athletic, well-liked by the other chaps and he worked well with his hands. He could do carpentry, plumbin', mechanics, and all sorts o' work. I thought he would be a good provider for our family, but he lacked focus. He'd start somethin', but ne'er finish it. Of course I didna' realize tha' at the time. I worked as a secretary to bring in money while he did various jobs, but he ne'er earned very much. He ne'er paid much attention to our lads, or to our family life. Then Paul came home one day and announced tha' he was joinin' the Navy. I didna' know wha' to do. We moved in with Mum and Dad, as Dad wa' quite ill and needed my help. Shortly after Timothy wa' born,

Paul left for the Navy, and Dad died three months later. Paul ne'er came home for the funeral. He said the Navy wouldna' let him, but I ne'er believed him.

"It wa' an awful time, what with losin' my Dad, and it took me many months to get back to a normal life. I canna' say I ever got over losin' Dad. The boys needed most of my attention and Mum wa' a big help. They helped both of us through that time, you know, new life replacin' old life. Timothy soon wa' a toddler and took much of my time for most of another year, but I needed to go back to work. We just couldna' make ends meet with twa bairn to feed. One day I saw an advertisement for the job with McGowan & Son and I went for it. There were quite a few applicants, but young Mr. McGowan said he thought he saw some real potential in me, and I wa' hired. Mum took care of Aaron and Timothy while I worked. Of course, she still sewed and did laundry. We got through it all."

David mumbled a suitable response, and then Elaine suddenly stood up. "Colonel, I must get home. Thank you for listenin'."

"Tomorrow is Sunday. Don't come in until 10 AM, later if you wish."

"I'll be here by nine," she said, flying out the door.

July 8

DAVID WENT DOWNSTAIRS TO HIS OFFICE early Monday morning and checked the safe where he'd stored the documents received from Jack Campbell. A week earlier, Elaine had hired a locksmith who opened the safe and reset the combination. After heating some water for tea, he began working on his talks to town councils and villages. The first one was scheduled for the next day in Fort William. "Nothing like starting at home," he thought. Time passed quickly. When Elaine arrived, she went to work silently on the letters to Provosts and Town Councils. Shortly before noon, she interrupted David to remind him of his lunch appointment with Admiral Evans-Cooper. David went out quickly and walked to The Argyll Hotel.

"Good morning, Colonel, meet CB Foster." Mr. Foster was a short, dark-haired man, stocky with a barrel chest and a fairly muscular body for a man in his forties. He wore steel-rimmed glasses and had an intensity in his piercing black eyes that was rather unnerving. He wore a look of quiet determination. David subsequently would find him to be stubborn and intolerant of slackers, inefficiency, and waste of all kinds.

"'Tis an honor, Colonel McKenna," CB said.

"Gentlemen, let's order lunch and then we can talk," said the Admiral. A few minutes later he began, "CB is a civil engineer and a veteran. I asked him to meet with you because I've been impressed with his work."

"What are you a veteran of, Mr. Foster?"

"Call me CB, Colonel, everyone does. I didna' like my name when I was growin' up in East Glasgow and it caused any number of fights. Of course, I started most of them because the fella's wouldna' stop callin' me by my proper name, Cedric Boutwell Foster. They would call me 'Cedric' in a girly tone o' voice or 'Boutie.' Then we'd have a fistfight because I just couldna' stand it. As I got older I settled on 'CB'."

"East Glasgow is a tough area. Were your parents originally from there?"

"No, they were from Berwick-upon-Tweed, in Northumberland. My Dad was a labourer and work was scarce in Berwick, so he moved us to East Glasgow where his brother had moved several years earlier. I guess the rent wa' cheap in the tenements, and he soon found a job in the steel mills, like my uncle."

"I wouldn't expect to find civil engineers coming out of East Glasgow."

"You'd be right about tha', Colonel, and I would ha' been just another beggar who ran around in street gangs. But I had one verra' special teacher in school. I didna' like school and took every opportunity to skip out. Mrs. Whitehurst made me stay after one day for no special reason, or so I thought. She sat me down and told me that I wa' quite a bright young fellow. Nobody had ever told me that before. She said that, if I really applied myself, I would learn to like studyin' and could even go to the university. I didna' believe her, especially the part about likin' to study, but I listened. Later, I told my mum wha' Mrs. Whitehurst ha' said, and she went straightaway to school the next day. They talked, and I guess they worked out a plan for me to study. Well, I did learn to like school better, but I'm not sure I ever loved studyin'. I studied because I saw that as a way out of the slums. My mum had very little schoolin' herself, but she sat with me most evenin's while I studied. You might say she learned more than I did," he said with a rare grin.

"So you entered the University of Glasgow?"

"Right. I took the exams and did fine. Mrs. Whitehurst ha' already lined up some fundin', and I worked weekends as a labourer on construction projects to earn my keep. I became fascinated with the engineerin' part of construction and studied it at school. Then the war broke out. I was caught up in the volunteerin' madness like everyone else, but my mum wanted me to stay and finish my studies. In late 1914, I enlisted anyway along wi' some of my school chums into the University of Glasgow Company of the Cameron Highlanders' 6th Battalion.

"We were part of the 51st Division, as you know, and we shipped off to France in late-May 1915. The next month we fought in the first Battle of the Somme. We took casualties, of course, but our Pioneers were hit especially hard. Because of my engineerin' schoolin', I was transferred to our Pioneer Battalion, the 9th Gordons, and promoted to lance-corporal. One infantry battalion in each division was given the mission as Pioneers. They became a 'pick and shovel' engineer unit that helped dig trenches and bunkers, install minefields or barbed wire, and breach enemy field fortifications.

"I served the rest of the war in the Pioneers, being promoted to corporal, then sergeant. In 1916, when most of the original group of lads I'd enlisted with were either killed or wounded, especially the officers, I was commissioned a subaltern and I became a 'temporary gentleman' like you." CB grinned mischievously at David.

"I thought I'd be sent back to my infantry battalion, but they kept me in the Pioneers. Later, I was promoted to full Lieutenant and then to Captain, in early 1918. I ended up commandin' a company o' Pioneers by war's end."

"You certainly have an impressive war record," said David, "were you ever wounded?"

"No' like you, Colonel," he said looking at David's uniform sleeve. "Just scratches, cuts and bruises, but no' enough to get any wound stripes like you. I was verra' happy about that."

"Did you go back to university after the war?"

"Yes, Sir, I did. After my wartime experiences, I was unstoppable. I was determined to finish as quick' as possible and I took my degree in civil engineerin' in 1921 and went to work for an engineerin' firm in Glasgow, now known as Alfred McAlpine & Company. They liked Army veterans and I liked them. My parents were verra' proud. I ha' also joined the TA as an engineer officer right after the war to bring in a few extra shillings.

"I was promoted Major in 1928. McAlpine sent me to India several times, where I worked on roads, bridges, and dams. As I gained experience, I became a senior engineer, then later a chief engineer. We worked all over Scotland, Northern Ireland, and the north of England and even had some consultin' jobs on the continent. In 1928, we started a branch of McAlpine in Inverness, called Rutledge, Foster & Davis. Bad timin', as the Depression hit a year later and much of our work in the UK dried up. Thank God for our India work. It's picked up again durin' the past four years. Mr. Rutledge lives in Inverness, Mr. Davis is in Aberdeen, and I'm here in Fort William."

"CB is a lieutenant-colonel now," said the Admiral.

"Well, sorta'. We were so busy with our India work that in 1933 I transferred from the TA to the Reserve of Officers. In 1934, we won a two-year job on a road project near Delhi. I was the chief engineer and, like other Brits living in India, hadda' join the Indian Auxiliary Force, the Indian Army reserve force composed of expatriate British subjects.

"The Indians all addressed me as 'colonel,' even though I was only a major. My IAF work eventually required me to hold the actin' rank of lieutenant-colonel. I spent considerable time at the British Officers Club in Delhi and made many friends there. Pretty soon, they were callin' me 'colonel' as well. When I got back to Scotland in early 1936, I received notice that I had been promoted to lieutenant-colonel in the Special Reserve. It seems that one of the generals at Indian Army Headquarters had corresponded with another general at Scottish Command about my work. Anyway, I guess I'm a lieutenant-colonel, although I've never held an assignment in the British Army above the grade of major."

"I think we need a man of CB's talents in your headquarters, Colonel, and holding the rank of lieutenant-colonel," said the Admiral.

"It certainly is worth considering. CB, you do understand that the positions in my headquarters are unfunded, just like the Home Guard positions. You are paid only for expenses incurred. The Admiral is not paid for his work. Of course, we have not agreed on a position for him yet."

"I earn a good salary, Colonel. I donna' need to be paid to kill Nazi bastards."

"I agree," said the Admiral. "I have a very decent pension and let me just say that I married well. We live quite comfortably."

"Is it possible to meet again Wednesday morning to discuss this further?" Both agreed.

WITH LUNCH ENDED, DAVID WALKED THE short distance up High Street to MacIntyre & Sons, where his motorcar was being serviced. "No' yet ready, Colonel, 'twill be another hour or so." David had planned to visit the British Aluminum plant at Lochaber to meet the plant managing director, Colonel F.E. Laughton. He crossed the street to the bus stop and, a few minutes later, set out for Lochaber, a mile to the northeast.

The Lochaber aluminum smelter, completed in 1929, employed over 700 men and was the largest and newest of three plants. Thirty miles to the northeast, a smaller aluminum smelter had been opened in 1896 at Foyers on the south bank of Loch Ness. Ten miles to the south of Fort William, a second aluminum smelter at Kinlochleven was opened in 1909, turning that sleepy village into a bustling town of almost 1,000 souls. Together with the Lochaber plant, the three smelters provided some 85% of Britain's aluminum, which was vital to the manufacture of armaments, especially aircraft.

The Lochaber plant was located a few hundred yards from the edge of Loch Linnhe, at the bottom of a steep hill behind the plant. Towering above the hill were the largest of the Grampian Mountains, including Ben Nevis. Few homes were located nearby because of the smelter's smokestacks, but a whisky distillery sat nearby. "Must be more than a coincidence for that location," he thought. Bauxite ore was processed into alumina in Larne, Northern Ireland, and then shipped to the Fort William smelter. Five large pipes called penstocks carried water from Loch Treig and a series of interconnected mountain lochs to a power plant. There, the turbines converted the enormous water pressure into electrical power, which melted the ore. Molten aluminum was then drawn off and poured into massive ingots, some weighing 1000-1200 pounds, others much more. The ingots were then shipped to rolling plants in England or Wales, which provided aluminum sheets for aircraft, or to foundries, which provided other aluminum parts. By 1944, Scotland had its own rolling plant.

Colonel Laughton had served as a Territorial Army officer, but hadn't been mobilized for the war because of his vital position with the aluminum plant. He put his military skills to use by also commanding the Lochaber Home Guard Company, part of the 2nd Inverness-shire Battalion, with the Home Guard rank of major. He introduced David to his assistant, Lieutenant Duthie, who also served under Laughton in the Home Guard.

After touring the facility, they returned to Laughton's office and tea. "My Home Guard Company stretches from Lochaber halfway to Fort Augustus to the east, and as far west as the Irish Sea. We have enrolled over 500 men and I expect that more will join before long.

"That's an enormous company, Mr. Laughton, almost a full battalion in size.

"Precisely, but we'll be better prepared for the Jerries when we have more weapons and more time to train. I'm very fortunate to have so many veterans in our ranks, maybe one-quarter to one-third of my force. Of course, without weapons there's precious little we can do against a real invasion force."

"How many weapons do you have?"

"Several dozen Enfield rifles on loan from the Army for rifle training, which I'm told we will be required to return soon. We have over one hundred privately owned weapons that I know of, mainly fowling pieces. I suspect we have more than that, but many of our lads are unwilling to declare publicly their personal weapons. They're afraid the government might seize the guns. Of course, some private weapons probably were acquired under questionable circumstances, so they probably have good reason not to declare them." Laughton smiled broadly. "We also have made several hundred petrol bombs, the 'Molotov cocktails,' but they are of limited use. My company drills at Territorial Hall, vacated by the TA lads of the 51st Division last September. We conduct field training and fire weapons at a rifle range located at the Plantation, just to the west of town. My lads are enthusiastic and eager to learn, Colonel, but it will be some months before they're ready to face any German attackers." David nodded in agreement.

"The men are busy with trainin' and performin' our new missions: guard posts throughout Lochaber, patrollin', ground observers watchin' for aircraft, mine watchin' in case Jerry decides to drop a few in the lochs, guardin' the Caledonia Canal and assistin' the Civil Defense units. They are learnin' mine disposal and a hundred other tasks they might ha' to perform. Like all Home Guard units, we maintain a dusk to dawn guard duty everra'day, watchin' for the enemy. Each volunteer must perform 48 hours per month of patrollin' or guard duty."

The three men talked for another hour, agreeing to work together very closely. They would need each other now as never before.

That evening, David walked to Territorial Hall to witness the training assembly of part of the Lochaber Home Guard Company, Colonel Laughton commanding. Initially, the company gathered into a semblance of a formation, the men trying their best to look like professional soldiers in front of the new sub-district commander. The veterans, almost one-third of the force, stood out with their professional manner and bearing, but the inexperienced volunteers stood out for the opposite reason. There was confusion and considerable movement in the ranks as heads turned to glance at McKenna, hands scratched at backsides and fingers wiped noses. Laughton was unable to control this movement in ranks, despite numerous barked orders and threats by section leaders.

When the Home Guard was first authorized in May 1940, they wore a simple armband. It soon became apparent that some type of uniform was required and, since Army uniforms were in short supply, it was decided to give each Home Guardsman a denim hat, shirt, and trousers. The unattractive and unmilitary denims were greatly disliked by the Home Guard, but they were wearing them in various stages of dishevelment.

Most men carried broom handles or similar clubs. Less than one-fifth carried a firearm. Civilian weapons supplemented the few Enfield rifles on loan from the Army and several men displayed swords. A handful wore old uniforms from the last war, mainly the officers, and those serving as squad or section leaders. The lack of military ranks in the Home Guard caused confusion and sarcasm. David witnessed one incident on the drill floor as a company leader addressed his volunteers.

"This is the Home Guard, mates, no' the bloody Regular Army, so ye'll no' be usin' them fancy ranks. No 'Lance-Corporal' this and 'Sergeant' tha'." He paused for a breath. "McMahon," pointing to one man, "ye lead a platoon and yer a 'Platoon Commander,' no' a 'Lieutenant.' Then, pointing to another, "Fowler, ye lead a section and ye'll be called 'Section Leader,' no' 'Sergeant.'"

"Pub crawler is more like it!" shouted a voice from the back, the younger men joining in the laughter.

"None o' yer lip, Mister!" barked the company leader. "Ye'll be polishin' floors tonight after we're doon here."

David walked away, concealing a slight smile at the Scots' healthy disrespect for authority. He knew it would take many months of training to turn this rowdy group of eager volunteers into an organized military force. "Please, God, don't let the Jerries invade just yet."

July 9

DAVID AROSE EARLY as usual, dressed, and walked down to his office. At noon, he was to address the Town Council and other key officials of Fort William and he wanted to review his notes. It wasn't normal for the Council to meet at noon on Tuesdays, but these weren't normal times and the councilors were eager to hear from the new colonel. The talk must be short, direct and with no equivocation. These are dangerous times and everyone's efforts would be needed to make it through. He would answer all questions from attendees as long as they did not infringe on secret information. The Provost had invited various officials from other towns in the area, and he told David to expect 50-60 officials and key citizens to be in attendance. A shortened version of the talk would be presented later to the public, perhaps several times, mostly in area churches that could hold large groups. He had put on a clean uniform for the occasion and brought down his laundry for Elaine to take home to Julia Donaldson.

Soon after, the door opened. "Good morning, Admiral."

"Colonel, I would like you to call me Christopher. I believe we'll be working closely for some time and I technically will be your subordinate."

"I don't know if I can do that. Will you call me David?"

"If we're alone, otherwise you'll be 'the Colonel'. CB should be along shortly," he said as he poured a cup of tea. "He's really one of a kind, isn't he? I think you'll like him."

As he spoke, CB arrived. "Should I salute this auspicious gatherin'?"

"No, you don't have your uniform on," David responded. "Get some tea if you wish, CB, I'd like to tell you both what I've decided."

They settled into chairs in David's office, and he continued. "CB, I think you have several attributes which have served you well and would also serve this headquarters. First, you grew up in a tough environment and really made something of yourself. All that persistence paid off and you've enjoyed a wonderful career as an engineer. Second, you're a veteran with excellent experience during the war and after. You've only one major drawback."

"Wha's tha', Colonel?"

"You're from Glasgow." CB smiled at the humor and nodded. "And so is my boss, Brigadier Campbell. Despite that, I need you in this headquarters. Engineers pay attention to details, they try to find ways to make things work better, and they don't give up. I suspect you've never given up on anything you wanted. I'd like you to be the Chief of Staff of this sub-district. Of course, we don't have a staff yet and recruiting one will be a top priority. You'll be appointed as a Lieutenant-Colonel and will serve as the third ranking officer in the sub-district."

"Who will be the second rankin' officer?"

"He doesn't know it yet, but I'll ask the Admiral to be my Deputy Commander. All that military training and experience shouldn't go to waste."

The Admiral shifted uncomfortably. "Colonel, I don't know if that's a suitable selection. I know very little about land warfare. You army blokes do that sort of thing. I'm at home on the high seas."

"That won't matter, Admiral," David replied, "I need you for your leadership and organizational skills."

"Canno' we get him one of those denim uniforms the Home Guard is fixin' to wear? I think the Admiral will look good in denim," said CB good-naturedly."

"I'll resign before I wear one of those damned denim things," the Admiral barked at CB. "I'm not in the Home Guard and I'd like to wear my naval uniform, Colonel."

"Maybe we can appoint you also as our Naval Liaison Officer to justify the naval uniform."

"Colonel, maybe you should also appoint him as liaison officer to the various Lords Lieutenant. He would be more impressive in his naval uniform, since the Lords'll be wearin' their army major-general uniforms much of the time. Tha' would also take another burden from your shoulders."

"Excellent idea, CB. Now, we've agreed on each of you filling a key position in this headquarters. I believe Elaine is quite capable of serving as my adjutant, and handling the paperwork and key personnel issues coming from the Home Guard and Civil Defense units, would you agree?" Both men nodded. "I believe we should now focus on the one remaining staff vacancy, a quartermaster. We need an officer who knows the Army supply system and who can help our subordinate units with their equipment. Give this some thought." Both heads nodded again. "I'll be leaving shortly to address the Town Council. When Elaine comes in, you can instruct her how to prepare the appointment documents for each of you."

"Colonel, I've been here for the past twenty minutes," said a voice.

David smiled. "As usual, my staff is a step ahead of me."

7

July 11, 1940

It was mid-morning when David returned from another meeting with Chief Constable Angus MacDonald. He found Elaine and CB hunched over the table looking intently at a map of the Outer Hebrides. On the wall behind them, CB had mounted several Royal Ordinance Survey maps; some smaller ones surrounding a large map of the Highlands.

"Good work, CB, I knew I could trust an engineer to come up with maps."

"These are on loan from my firm, and we expect them to be returned in good order, soon after we whip the Jerries' arses." Although a dour personality, CB occasionally let humor slip out among friends.

"Agreed," said David, "I look forward to that occasion. What are the two of you studying so intently?"

"Your travel schedule to give your talks in everra' village and town in our sub-district," replied Elaine carefully. "But, with all your other responsibilities, I donna' know if you can fit all this in before winter."

"Then I'll travel during the winter as well."

"I'd be careful about winter travel in the West Highlands, Colonel. My firm is reluctant to send an engineer out from December through February. 'Tis no' like where you grew up in the Eastern Highlands, Cupar, Stirling, even Perth. Those areas get snow, but 'tis no' like over here. The storms come up sudden like from the ocean and blanket us wi' snow and ice. 'Tis best to find lodgin' 'til the storm blows over."

"We'll see," he replied. "How many days must I travel?"

"It's more like weeks. Elaine and I estimate all or part of about fifteen weeks on the road to visit 90% of your sector. Look at the wall map, Sir, starting from the south. The Glencoe and Kinlochleven area would take three days of meetings. Going west, Loch Eil, Loch Eilt and the villages to the south would take a full seven days, and the Mallaig area to the northwest another three days. Going further north, the Isles of Skye and Raasay would take at least four days and the Kyle of Lochalsh, Plockton, Lochcarron area another five days. To the northwest, the Gairloch, Loch Torridon, Kinlochewe, and Ullapool regions would take at least ten days, the Lochinver, Scourie, and Kinlochbervie areas another six days, and the Durness and Bettyhill areas along the North Coast would take eight days plus travel time to get there and back. Add to that the inland villages and the Outer Hebrides and you'd be travelin' from now until Christmas, or thereabouts.

"I know you value your public meetin's and, from wha' I hear, the meetin's you held already around Fort William were verra' successful. People are frightened o' the invasion threat. They've been through verra' hard times and the bad years o' the Depression affected everra'one. The war was unexpected and the collapse o' France was just more than they could bear. You were no' here, so you didna' know how bad things were. Now they're just beginnin' to feel a little more confident and better focused on what they can do to help the war effort."

"That's the purpose, CB. My visits with village or town officials and the public meetings are essential to our work. The Home Guard and Civil Defense organizations are vital to Scotland's defense, but it's more than that. Our mission includes public relations and encouraging all people to continue the war effort in every way. Different groups in every community are holding scrap drives: metals, paper, clothing, and cloth, really anything that can be reused is valuable. This saves us shipping space. If we can import fewer of these goods, we will have more shipping space to bring in essential war supplies. One of the ladies last week used the phrase, 'Make do or do without.' That's a good motto. We have little good news from the battlefields and we must do our utmost to keep people from becoming discouraged.

"During my visits, I also meet with Home Guard and Civil Defense officials to get some idea of their readiness status. What the Home Guard reports on paper and what I see myself may be quite different. The visits give me a truer assessment of their capabilities." CB nodded as David continued.

"Elaine, take this plan and start scheduling the trips around my other functions, and then write the letters to notify them of my visits. I'll help you prepare the wording. Schedule the meetings in each village, arrange the locations of the public meetings, and ask to have the local Home Guard commander brief me, even if he's only a corporal. Also, we'll need to notify Colonel Harris and the Lords Lieutenant in each shire of my visits. Colonel Harris can notify his Home Guard Battalion commanders and others, as needed. You and CB can determine where I'll spend each night and you must arrange lodging. In some villages, I'll spend the night with a town official or Home Guard representative, if no other lodging is available. I'll leave it to you to work all that out." As David spoke, the Admiral arrived, uniformed as usual.

"Good morning, Colonel. CB and I have an idea for your consideration. It looks like this is a proper time to bring it up." He glanced at CB, who gave a quick nod of his head. "We think you should add a chaplain to your staff."

"A chaplain? I don't see why we would need one. We won't be conducting church services and the Home Guard units all have their own chaplains. No, Admiral, I think not."

"I really think you should reconsider," he responded. "Right now you're dependent upon the Home Guard commanders for information about each village and town. So far we're getting nothing from them. Of course, this headquarters has just gone into operation, but I'm not optimistic about the flow of information upwards. A well-respected chaplain could be in fairly continuous contact with all the local pastors in the West Highlands and could be an alternative information source. Also, I believe most of your public meetings will be conducted in churches. Wouldn't it make sense to have the pastors of those churches contacted periodically by your staff chaplain, good public relations and so forth?"

"I suppose you and CB have someone in mind, just in case I said 'yes.' I probably won't say 'yes,' because I don't want any overweight staff officers hanging around who have little to do from week to week and don't even know how to salute properly."

"We do have someone in mind and he's fairly trim and athletic. He's also a veteran of the First War and would be a real asset to your headquarters. I'd like for you to meet him and then make your decision."

"A Church of Scotland pastor?"

"Yes, Sir, and he grew up in Cupar."

"Cupar? I wonder if I know him."

"His name is Ben Douglas and I'll invite him to lunch today."

REVEREND BEN DOUGLAS ARRIVED at the Argyll, breathing hard and dressed in athletic clothes. A man of medium height with curly red hair, he had a youthful, almost cherubic look, despite his age of 41 years. Dressed in clerical garb, Ben barely looked like a pastor. Without his garb he looked like an eager young man who'd recently started his first job.

"Sorry if I'm late. I was out having a run when I received your message."

"Quite all right, Reverend, but you don't look like what I expected."

"Call me Ben, Colonel. No, I don't always wear a suit. I coach two football teams for our youth and a cricket team in the spring. We have a practice session after school today."

"The Admiral said you grew up in Cupar and are a veteran. I was born in Cupar and moved to Perth when I was quite young."

"Cupar was a grand town, not much different from Fort William, except it had no mountains or sea loch. Yes, I served in the First War. I think almost all the boys from my class joined up by the end of 1917. I wanted to join the Fife and Forfar Yeomanry, the mounted regiment based in Cupar, but when school was out I was sent on holiday to visit relatives in Aberdeen. I had two cousins there, one my age and the other a year older. We had a grand time and we hiked in the hills almost every day. One day, we came upon a group of soldiers who were undergoing training. They invited us to join them during their lunch break and they told us about the fighting in France. It sounded exciting and the three of us went straightaway to the recruiting depot and joined the Gordon Highlanders. Our parents were appalled!"

"Did you serve in France?"

"Yes. After training and a few weeks of recruiting duty in Montrose, I went to France as a replacement in February 1918 and joined the 8th Battalion of the Gordons."

"But you were not then a chaplain?"

"No, Sir. I was a plain infantryman living in the trenches. I became a chaplain as a result of the war. We saw some minor action at Cambrai and on the Somme that spring, but my first real battle was at Lys in the summer of 1918. The division had moved back and forth along the Ypres and the Lys rivers for several months. We called it 'jousting with Jerry.' One afternoon, the lieutenant told us that the next morning we'd go over the top, my first frontal attack against enemy lines." Although the day was cool, Ben paused to wipe sweat from his face.

"I was frightened and couldn't sleep that night. I knew I'd be killed. The next morning, I was shaking so much I couldn't even buckle my belt. I prayed to God that, if he let me live, I would become a pastor. Suddenly a wave descended on me like a warm blanket. It was like He reached down and put His hand around me to protect me. I felt a great peace and, when the whistle blew, I climbed up and ran with the other chaps toward the Jerries. It was awful. Wave after wave of bullets flew around us. I should've been terrified and frozen up like a stone, but I just kept going until we were ordered to pull back. The attack failed. We took heavy casualties and many of the lads were killed, but I never suffered a scratch. I knew He had protected me. As we retreated back to our lines, I helped drag a wounded man back to safety. He died just as we reached the trench, so I went back and got another. The wounded and dead were everywhere. After that, the fighting died down until the Great Advance began, and that ended the war. On Armistice Day, we were on the River Scheldt, where we stayed until we returned home."

Ben again wiped beads of sweat from his forehead. "I left the Army in the spring of 1919 and entered St. Mary's College in 1920, the Divinity School for St. Andrews University. Kathleen and I were married in 1922, probably the smartest thing I ever did. I took a degree from the Divinity School and was ordained in the Church of Scotland in 1925. For the next ten years, I served a series of small churches and, in 1935, was called to serve the church here in Fort William."

There was a long pause while everyone digested Ben's story. Finally, David spoke up. "Quite a story, Ben, you certainly aren't the typical community vicar."

"I'm probably more typical than you realize, Colonel, but we don't use the term 'vicar.' That's Anglican Church. I'm a minister. Some of my flock calls me 'pastor.' Most pastors are similar in that we're committed to our faith, our families, our congregations, and our communities. Some wear their faiths quite openly, others less so. But, on Sunday mornings, each one of us goes into our pulpit and preaches from the Good Book."

"I respect that, Ben. CB and the Admiral have recommended you for an unpaid position as staff chaplain for the Northwest Sub-District, which we're just now organizing. Based on your background, I would probably recommend your appointment at the rank of Captain. Your job would be primarily to stay in contact with other pastors in our sector and to monitor any emerging problems that could impact on the defense of Scotland. How would you feel about that?"

Ben thought for a minute, and then said "I think I would be honored to serve as a chaplain and especially to hold the rank of Captain. I'll make time in my week to correspond with other pastors and to serve on your staff, as necessary. Will I wear a uniform?"

"For now, only if you own one. We should get uniforms sometime in the future, but not until the regular forces have their requirements filled."

"I think I still have my old uniform someplace. I may have to ask you for the captain's pips."

"I probably have some extra pips in my room," replied David. "I'd be pleased to loan them to a fellow St. Andrews alumnus."

July 27

REAR-ADMIRAL EVANS-COOPER ENTERED the office to find Elaine typing at her usual furious pace. The light was on in David's office and the smell of tea hung in the air. "Good morning, Elaine, has our road warrior returned from his latest excursion?"

Before she could answer, a voice from the inner office said, "Elaine, if that's an unemployed admiral, point him in the direction of the sea loch and send him on his way."

"Retired, Colonel. Not unemployed. During your absence, I'll have you know I worked here every day in my capacity as your distinguished deputy."

"'Tis true, Colonel. While you were gone the Admiral visited as many government officials as you. He just didna' ha' to drive as far as you."

"Did your visits go well, David? Any surprises?"

"No real surprises, Admiral, except the Home Guard units are really taking shape faster than anyone thought possible. In Portree, the Home Guard Skye Company has almost 40% veterans in their ranks, not all First War veterans, of course. Some veterans were Navy, a couple were RAF, some served in the Territorial Army during the 1920's or '30's, but they all seem to have solid military backgrounds. The company has arranged its sections and platoons so that each veteran supervises two new chaps, the inexperienced soldiers. Consequently, there's less fumbling around and the new volunteers are learning much faster. I watched them march and conduct basic section and platoon drills, simple attack and defense maneuvers, and they're coming along well. The public meetings also went well. I visited all of the Isle of Skye, Raasay, the Kyle of Lokalsh, and other villages in that area. The Civil Defense organizations are getting better organized, and there are enough experienced people there to train the new members."

"Did you hear Mr. Churchill's speech on BBC while you were away? It was brilliant. He challenged all Britons directly to fight like soldiers or die like sheep." The admiral mimicked Churchill. *"Should the invader come, there will be no placid lying-down in submission before him as we have seen, alas, in other countries. The vast mass of London itself, fought street by street, could easily devour an entire hostile army and we would rather see London laid in ashes and ruins than it should be tamely and abjectly enslaved."*

"He has a remarkable way with words," David replied, "and he galvanizes the public like no other politician in my memory."

"Nor mine. Oh yes, I wanted to mention the Victory Gardens. They were everywhere I went, even in the downtowns, and it seemed that every square foot of farmland was planted."

"Yes, the villagers were tilling lawns, flower pots, every empty space, and even a few rooftops where they'd spread soil. Some seem to have been recently planted, so I'm not sure they will be able to harvest vegetables before the first frost. Nevertheless, people will be ready for next year's planting, if they can get seed."

As they spoke, the front door opened and a short, thin, middle-aged man entered. As Elaine rose to greet him, the Admiral said, "Frank, come in and meet the commander. Colonel, this is Captain Frank Leslie, Indian Army Supply Corps retired. I met Frank during a visit to our Navy Station several days ago. I was impressed with his background in logistics and I asked him to stop in and meet you on his way to work."

"Welcome, Captain. What's a retired Indian Army officer doing in Fort William working for the Navy?"

"It's a bit of a story, Colonel," he said, as they sat down. "I'm originally from Greenock and worked in the shipyards like my Dad, since I was fifteen. When the First War began, I enlisted in a Pals Battalion with a group of friends and went off to infantry training.

"I'd some experience working with supplies at the shipyards before the war. I injured my shoulder in 1913, and the foreman had me work with a bookkeeper in the storeroom for several months while it healed. Bookkeeping came easy to me. When my army sergeant found out I could do supply bookkeeping, he had me assigned to our battalion quartermaster section. Soon after, I was reassigned to the Quartermaster section of the 15th Division. We completed training in May 1915 and shipped to France soon after.

"Being a supply clerk, I spent a great deal of time in the rear areas and met many quartermaster officers and sergeants. As battles were fought, we moved from sector to sector to bring up ammunition and other supplies. The 3rd (Lahore) Indian Division had taken casualties that summer during the Battle of Neuve Chapelle. I was sent over to help them for a few days and wound up being reassigned to their quartermaster section." As Frank spoke, the phone rang and Elaine answered it.

"Eventually the division was sent to Mesopotamia where, in 1917, I was temporarily commissioned as a subaltern in the Indian Army for the duration of the war. We served under General Maude when he led the offensive that captured Baghdad. When the war ended, I was offered a chance to stay in the Indian Army as a quartermaster officer. My Dad had written to say that, with the war ending, work was stopping in all the shipyards and he didn't know when there'd be work again. So I joined the Indian Army as a full lieutenant and was assigned to Dhaka in the Bengal District. In 1923, I went home on leave and met Jane. She was from Glencoe and had gone to Greenock to find work. We were married and returned to India. I was promoted captain in 1930, retired in 1936, and we moved to Chittagong to take a job with a shipping firm.

"Early last year, I was warned by a friend to get out fast, as the anti-British Indian National Army guerillas were becoming active nearby. We packed up what little we could and boarded a merchant ship that night for Singapore. From there, we sailed west through Suez to Newcastle, then on to Aberdeen. Jane wanted to settle near Glencoe, but when the Royal Navy station here offered me a part-time job, she agreed that Fort William would be a pretty good compromise."

David thought for a moment. "Frank, we're looking for an Adjutant-Quartermaster here. There's no compensation, but Elaine does most of the Adjutant's paperwork. I really need someone who understands the Army's supply system in order to help the Home Guard and Civil Defense units acquire and maintain equipment. Would you be willing to do this? You would be appointed as a captain."

"Colonel, I'd be honored to serve under you and I certainly know the Army supply system. It would be fine to put on the uniform again."

"Excellent. Well, Admiral, you did it again and now we have a complete staff. Elaine will prepare your paperwork, Frank, and you can sign it anytime today or tomorrow."

Elaine came in. "Sir. That was Colonel Whittaker on the phone. Brigadier Campbell is coming for a brief visit and will be here on the first train next Wednesday. He'll arrive from Glasgow mid-morning. He said to tell you he has some guns!"

8

July 31, 1940

IT WAS A DAMP WEDNESDAY MORNING when David walked quickly from his office up High Street toward the train station at Gordon Square. The early morning showers had receded and blue sky was beginning to poke through the puffy clouds. The morning rush of cars and pedestrians had dissipated and buildings were full of activity. Store windows were becoming depleted of inventory as war production supplanted the production of civilian goods. Shopkeepers often were reduced to selling used items purchased from relocating families. The air of tension persisted, as the war dominated people's thoughts and conversations.

At a distance, he saw clouds of smoke as the locomotive churned its way around the valley from Spean Bridge to the north, along Loch Linnhe toward Fort William. The configuration of the valley and city structures precluded the straight in and out of a normal railway station. Trains would pass alongside the center of Fort William to the station and stop at a platform to unload passengers. The train then moved forward a short distance onto a large turnstile which rotated 180 degrees, allowing each train to face forward. Passing through the station again, the train crossed over a switched track and chugged briefly north around the mouth of Loch Linnhe and westward toward Mallaig on the coast.

"Over here, David!" came a familiar shout, as Brigadier Jack Campbell stepped off the train.

"Let me carry your briefcase, Sir."

"Nonsense, I'm not that far gone," he replied, "yet!" They both laughed at the reality of the aging process. "I'm eager to see your office and meet your staff."

"I asked them to assemble at 11 o'clock to brief you, what little there is to say at this point, and to include something of their civilian and military backgrounds. I thought it would give you a chance to make an assessment of their abilities."

"Splendid. I also want to get a sense of how well they'll work together as a team. Will they be up to the task should we actually suffer an invasion or some other emergency? I'll also need some private time with you to bring you up to date on some special issues. I plan to take the late afternoon train back to Glasgow. I relish the five-hour trip as it gives me time to catch up on paperwork. Tomorrow, I'll return to Inverness." David had become used to the occasional stares he received when he went out in public in his uniform, but two senior officers walking up High Street, one a brigadier, elicited glances from every pedestrian plus an occasional tip of the hat or a murmured 'Good day.'

"Friendly folks, David, must make your job a bit easier. Ah, there's your office sign and I can read it a full two blocks away."

Scottish Command Headquarters
Northwest Sub-District

"Good. The people know that the Army is here and they haven't been abandoned after all. The more I think about it, David, the more I agree with Mr. Churchill. If we expect the people to fight, we must show them that we are here fighting alongside them; we will never abandon them." David nodded.

"One quick update before I meet your staff. As of July 19, General Ironside is no longer the Commander-in-Chief of Home Forces. General Alan Brooke has replaced him. Brooke will be responsible for all forces located in Britain and will serve as our 'anti-invasion commander.' He's changing our whole anti-invasion strategy. It will no longer be based on strong beach defenses, Ironside's 'crusts.' Instead, we shall maintain thin forward defenses supported by strong mobile reserves, which shall be positioned behind the invasion beaches to drive an invader back into the sea. I knew Brooke when he was the commander of the Experimental Mechanized Division, back when I was a colonel; he's absolutely brilliant. He will energize Home Forces and I would hate to be the first officer to cross him. He always demands excellent performance and can be ruthless. I understand that one of his first actions was to cancel the 'stop lines,' the network of deep trenches that General Ironside was having dug across southern England to prevent panzers from sweeping into our industrial centers.

"Scottish Command also was working on two 'stop lines' until recently. The main line begins at Dysart in Fife and runs to Loch Tummel in Perthshire. It was to protect Central Scotland from a landing along the beaches of Fife or Angus. A smaller line in my district begins just south of Aberdeen and runs over fifty miles west to the Grampian Mountains, presumably to protect Aberdeen itself. The chaps have been working on these lines for several weeks, but General Brooke ordered work on all stop lines to be, well, stopped. I never thought stop lines made sense. It's just a cheaper version of the Maginot Line in France which, of course, the Jerries easily bypassed.

"The strategy now will be to guard the beaches with Home Guard forces and some Home Defense battalions, while keeping the combat brigades and divisions well back to the rear as a reserve force. This will mean a change of mission for the Home Guard. Those battalions located in the coastal areas will move forward in the event of invasion to man the beach defenses. There will be no more passive village defense for those Home Guardsmen, and I'm confident this will lead to a more active defense role for inland units as well. In the event of an invasion, the Home Guard and other beach defenders will delay and damage the Germans. Then, the mobile reserves will move forward to fall upon the invaders and quickly destroy them." He paused, and then added, "We hope."

Arriving at the office, a hush fell over the crowded room. David went through the introductions and asked everyone to sit at the conference table. After a few introductory comments, David turned the meeting over to Jack, who made a series of remarks about the value of everyone's service, the gratitude of the War Office and especially Lieutenant-General Carrington of Scottish Command. He sketched out the war situation and spent considerable time bringing the staff up to date.

"I'm pleased to tell you that, as of last week, the Army in Britain consists of 26 divisions, plus a number of separate brigades. Only 14 divisions are considered to be fully operational at this time and all are in need of more equipment and training. These forces must defend over 2,000 miles of British coastline, of which at least 800 miles could be attacked from the sea with some degree of success. We have a great deal of work to do to bring all our forces up to a proper state of readiness to repel the invaders.

"You all know that the Nazis are bombing Britain, massive *blitz* attacks to wipe out our RAF bases and other key defensive sites." The room was silent as each member strained to hear every word. Jack continued for several minutes, laying out the key topics. "The situation is grave and every indication is that the Germans will invade before mid-October. They're making feverish preparations just across the Channel. We don't know exactly when or where they'll land, so everyone must be alert at all times. We must train our forces quickly and give them the confidence they can defeat the Nazi forces should they invade. Our Home Guard and Civil Defense forces must be trained for the basic tasks of village, town, and beach defense." A grim silence hung over the room.

Campbell went on, "Now, let's talk about the Home Guard which comprises the only sizable armed force in your sub-district. Until recently, we might have said that the Home Guard isn't much of a military force, but here are some numbers straight from London. The Home Guard now has 1.4 million men enrolled and undergoing training at this time; more are flooding in every day. This is almost as large as the entire British Army! In Glasgow alone, there are over 14,000 men assigned to nine battalions. In my North Highlands District of ten counties, of which your sub-district is a part, I have 22 battalions with some 35,000 Home Guardsmen. Over 30% are veterans: trained, experienced, soldiers with a few Navy and RAF thrown in, like you, Admiral."

Everyone smiled and the Admiral beamed. "The Navy is here to lend dignity to this force," he replied grandly.

Jack continued, "I'd better not respond to that. In any case, let me say that the loyalty of this force is impeccable. They are all British subjects, men between the ages of 17 and 65. Well, officially they are, and they are in reasonably good physical shape. Here in the Highlands, I suspect that our men are in better physical shape than average, as they work outdoors regularly and walk considerably more than city dwellers. Listen carefully now, as this is important. The press is portraying the Home Guardsmen as an elderly force of dowdy old chaps who are a bit too old to fight effectively. This is wrong! Yes, we have veterans from the First War and many of those chaps are in their forties, some even in their fifties. But the age of the average Home Guardsman is under thirty. The average!

"Now, what about their mission? Officially, the War Office had determined that it wanted the Home Guard to be a passive force. They'd conduct guard duties to observe, report, assist the Army, and to watch for parachutists or fifth columnists. They were to be confined to their neighborhoods or villages and, heaven forbid, not shoot a Nazi invader. That's for the regulars to do." Jack let his sarcasm sink in as the others shifted uncomfortably in their chairs. "Let's be realistic. What British subject would sit passively while the Nazis plunder, rape, and murder in the house next door?

"Scottish Command and all subordinate Army commanders publicly have endorsed the passive policy because it has been the Government's official policy until now. The Home Guard commanders themselves, however, have been preparing for mobile warfare. The new mission of beach defense will require a more active force, units that are trained to attack, not just defend. Men are being divided into two categories based on their age and physical condition. Younger men and some veteran leaders may volunteer for what are called 'battle platoons' or 'mobile platoons,' which will conduct mobile warfare against an invader. Watching them train, I'm impressed by their enthusiasm and their training efficiency. They will deploy to wherever the enemy has landed and will attack and destroy them as best they can. The other men are assigned to static platoons whose mission is neighborhood, village, or area defense. They'll perform the original War Office missions and will be able to delay and damage enemy attackers, wear the Nazis down and kill a few more.

"Now, listen to this. Many of the mobile platoons have 125-150 men each, the size of a regular Army company. So, we're talking about some real battle strength. Right here in Fort William, you have a Home Guard company from the 2nd Inverness Battalion with 500-600 men, just in that one company. That's really a battalion. The other three companies of the 2nd Battalion are similar in size, so the 2nd Battalion is really a brigade-sized force of over 2000 men.

"The key principles to remember for the Home Guard are simplicity, flexibility, decentralized control and a minimum of regulations. Platoons, companies, and battalions may each be organized differently based upon the resources available and the fighting requirements for a given area. But, what about weapons?" Jack paused and took another drink of his tea, then continued.

"Weapons, or lack of weapons, are our major weakness. We simply don't have enough Enfield rifles to arm the regulars as well as the Home Guard. The small number of Enfields, which the Army has issued recently for Home Guard training, will probably be recalled within the next few months to equip new regular units now being formed. So, what do we have left to equip our Home Guard units?

"First, we've registered with the Home Guard over 65,000 privately owned rifles and shotguns. These have been turned in by the owners, on loan for the duration of the war. In addition, we believe there are two or three times that number which have not been officially reported, but are being held by their owners. This includes 'unregistered weapons,' mainly rifles, pistols and revolvers, old fowling pieces, plus obsolete or ancient firearms. People are ransacking their attics and local museums to equip themselves with antique weapons of every kind. So, maybe 200,000 men now have a firearm of private ownership, even if on loan to the Home Guard. So, of 1.4 million men right now, 1.2 million are still unarmed, right?" Heads nodded.

"The good news, gentlemen, is that right this minute about 300,000 First War Ross rifles from Canada are at sea and will be distributed to the Home Guard as soon as they arrive. Mr. Churchill has been aggressively buying military weapons, especially from Canada and the United States, and my understanding is he's working on further purchases totaling another 500,000 rifles, plus machine guns and even some First War artillery." Jack beamed as he saw the looks of surprise, then joy go around the table.

"Now, most of the rifles from America, the P-14s, and P-17s, which you will remember from the First War, were not manufactured for our .303 British caliber bullets. Most are 30-06 U.S. caliber. That won't matter much, as we are also buying ammunition in that caliber from the Americans. The Ross rifle, however, has the .303 British caliber. Which rifle will come into your sub-district has not yet been decided, but it won't make much difference. They'll all kill Nazis. Right now, I'm told the rifles will come with 50 rounds per weapon, most of which will be held in district reserve stocks. So, there won't be much rifle training with live rounds until next year. Weapons training will continue with the .22 caliber rifles. But at least we'll have weapons and ammunition to kill the invaders, if they come."

Jack sat back with a look of satisfaction as he let the information sink in. "I expect you'll see these weapons in your sector before very long and you should receive your full share by late-September. Oh yes, Captain Leslie. You should prepare a plan to receive these weapons and distribute them to Home Guard units. The units must get them quickly and prepare them for immediate use. We'll work 24-hours a day and nobody should rest from the time the weapons arrive until they're in the hands of the Home Guardsmen, ready to shoot. You must make arrangements for local weapon and ammunition storage in two categories: immediate use ammo and ammo reserves. If you get the American rifles in the American caliber, a red band is to be painted around the forward hand grip to remind the soldiers to load American ammunition only."

Frank nodded, "I've distributed rifles from storage many times, Brigadier, and I'll find red paint if needed."

"Excellent. Mrs. Ross, I have one small gift for you. Sometime in the next few weeks you will receive a Roneo, an office reproduction machine. It's not a new one, but it will be serviceable. This should speed your work when you produce the multiple copies of documents the Army always requires."

"Now," he continued, "let's talk about other weapons. All Home Guardsmen have been trained on the 'Molotov cocktail' petrol bombs. I'm told that all units now have a store of these. This will be the only anti-tank weapon you'll see for the next few months at least. There are other anti-tank weapons being developed, a couple exclusively for the Home Guard. These will go initially to those sectors which are most threatened by invasion, which isn't your sub-district. Tanks simply don't work well in mountainous areas like the Highlands. In addition, the War Office has indicated that the Home Guard will get a number of Boys rifles within a few months."

Elaine interrupted him. "But Brigadier Campbell, if we are to receive Army rifles and other weapons, why would the Army send us rifles for boys?"

Jack smiled broadly and sat back. "Mrs. Ross, you've just made my day perfectly delightful. Let me explain. The Boys rifle is an anti-tank rifle invented by one, Captain Boys, toward the end of the last war. Unfortunately, it proved to be less effective than expected against the Panzers in France and Belgium. All will be withdrawn from the regular forces as soon as a replacement is found, hopefully quite soon. I expect to get the first few up to you immediately thereafter.

"Also, perhaps even sooner, the Lewis light machine gun will begin to be distributed to the Home Guard. These have been taken out of storage very recently and distributed to the regular forces to replace the Bren and Vickers machine guns, which they lost in France. As production increases, new Vickers and Brens will replace the Lewis guns, which then will be sent out to Home Guard units. I'll ensure some are assigned to your sub-district. There are a few other weapons in the pipeline, although it may be next winter or spring before you begin to see any. It appears that the Americans have also agreed to sell us some of their Browning Automatic Rifles and Tommy guns, perhaps a few thousand, if we're lucky. It may be that some of the Tommy guns were repossessed from Al Capone's gang or other criminals," he joked, "but we won't know which ones. Many of these, perhaps all, will be assigned to the Home Guard.

"Well, gentlemen, that concludes my remarks. I would like each of you to speak briefly about your backgrounds, both civilian and military, and give me your views about your new assignments and any problems you envision. Admiral, please go first." One by one each officer spoke. Jack asked questions of each, then concluded with a general question and answer session.

As the discussion ended, he drew out his pocket watch. "Good Lord, it's almost 2 o'clock. Colonel McKenna and I must meet privately, so I suggest we adjourn."

David and Jack walked to the Argyll. After ordering lunch, Jack said, "I'm impressed with your staff, David. It appears they're solid chaps and well suited to their duties. The Admiral is very impressive, fairly quiet, but he seems to miss nothing and he clearly has the respect of the others. He and CB will make quite a formidable pair. The others are fine and should serve you quite well. I was a bit surprised you added a chaplain to your staff but, after hearing him speak, I think it was a good move. As for Mrs. Ross, well, I'd already heard from Steve Whittaker that she was exceptional, but she's absolutely beautiful, David. Of course I'm sure you already noticed."

"I hired her on trial, Sir, and she's been an excellent employee. I'm sure the staff would all agree with me that she's rock solid."

"Yes, well, let's get on with our discussion and let's speak more softly about some of these subjects. First, are you familiar with the Chain Home Radar Stations?"

"I've heard about them and their role in air defense."

"Right, well you have one in your sub-district now, plus you'll have another on the Isle of Lewis very soon and others on the Hebrides eventually. At Sango Bay, near Durness, you have a Chain Radar station, which has been there for over a year and a half and is being upgraded even as we speak. The new system is more sophisticated than the others and will give Sango Bay both a low and a high altitude capability to detect aircraft. It's the very latest technology. This is most sensitive information.

"These stations are critical to the war effort, David. They must be protected at all costs, and you have only a total of maybe 300-400 people living near Durness and Sango Bay. That might give you a small platoon of Home Guardsmen to protect the station should the Jerries attack. You must work with Lord Sutherland to ensure the 1st Sutherland Home Guard Battalion can provide a rapid response capability to protect that station. Will you visit Durness soon?"

"I've a week of travel in that area next month."

"Good. I hope the Duke of Sutherland has found a good Home Guard commander for Durness. Now, second subject, are you aware that you have a Special Operations Executive training site at Arisaig House, south of Mallaig?"

"No."

"Well, the main SOE training center is at Inverary, not too many miles north of Glasgow, but a smaller facility is being established at Arisaig House. You also will have an Army commando training facility at Auchnacary, the estate of the Camerons of Locheil near Spean Bridge. Lord Locheil is preparing to move out very soon. Auchnacary House will become the headquarters of the commando center, and the Army will lease several dozen other properties in this area. There probably won't be more than a few hundred men assigned even when the center grows to full size, but the Army Commandos and the SOE chaps will conduct training all through the Highlands. The area from Fort William west to the coast has been declared a 'protected area,' with severe restrictions on civilians entering the area."

"What about the people who live or work there?"

"They'll be issued special passes to enter the protected area. I suggest you meet both the SOE commander at Arisaig House soon and the commander of the Commando school as soon as one is assigned. If we're attacked, they may be of some help to you. Otherwise, you may be able to assist them by providing Home Guard units to play the role of aggressors during training exercises. Neither facility is under your command, or mine. Now, have you heard of the 201st Battalion?"

"No."

"Probably just as well." Jack lowered his voice. This is a most secret unit recently organized by the War Office. Mr. Churchill wants a 'stay behind' force in the event of invasion."

"Stay behind?"

"Exactly. If the Jerries invade and conquer territory, small teams of 8-12 men will go into hiding as the German forces sweep over them. Two to four well-camouflaged underground 'hides' are being constructed for every team, each filled with food, weapons and other equipment so that men can hide out for days or weeks. After the Nazi attack force has passed them by, they will come out at night and strike at enemy 'soft' targets: convoys, fuel depots, command posts and so on."

"Won't that lead to German retaliation?"

"Of course, but it will tie down German forces and weaken their attacks elsewhere. The men being recruited for this mission are Home

Guard volunteers who will receive special training on our best equipment. They know their mission may be suicidal, but apparently there's no shortage of volunteers. One or two men are chosen from a unit, and they then select the rest of the team. Nobody else is to know who they are, not even you, me, or the War Office. The 201st Battalion covers all of Scotland. There are several battalions being formed throughout Britain and they also are not under the district commanders."

"Extraordinary."

"Precisely. Now, fourth subject. The aluminum plant north of town here is under the control of Lord Beaverbrook. He's determined to protect his aircraft production plants and all other manufacturing facilities under his supervision. Lord Beaverbrook is a member of the House of Lords who has been appointed Minister of Aircraft Production by Churchill to greatly increase aircraft output. Loud and brash, he has enthusiastically tackled each problem, including factory defense and you'll certainly see the results soon.

"He's gotten hold of both Vickers and Lewis machine guns and is using them for air defense at his plants, including a few which will be assigned to your Lochaber aluminum plant. He's also seized motorcars and sheet metal, Lord knows from where, and is improvising armoured cars for plant defense. He immodestly named them his 'Beaverettes;' impressive to look at, but not terribly effective from a military standpoint. So, you can expect to see some of this activity in Fort William."

David responded, "I met last week with Colonel Laughton, the managing director of the aluminum plant and the commander of the Lochaber Home Guard Company. We toured his plant and he briefed me on Lord Beaverbrook's efforts."

"Then you're well ahead of me, David. Well done!"

As they ate, they exchanged small talk. "By the way, David, I'm sending you a new subaltern."

"What will I do with a new subaltern?"

"That's for you to determine. His name is Jonathan Osborne and he was just commissioned from the Aberdeen University Cadet Corps. He has to take exams in two or three months, and the Army would like to utilize him somewhere while he's studying. I don't want him in my headquarters or even with a Home Guard unit in Aberdeen or Inverness. Too many distractions, so I'm sending him to you. Use him as you see fit and give him some useful experiences. Also, not yet for public discussion, you may get some artillery this autumn."

"Artillery? From where and what kind?"

"You know we lost most of our newer artillery pieces in France and Belgium, some 1200 light and heavy guns. Additionally, we lost over 1300 anti-tank and anti-aircraft guns, 11,000 machine guns, and 75,000 motor vehicles. So, our lads returned from France fairly empty-handed, but at least they returned, or most of them. But, we're not defenseless. We have almost 2000 First War artillery pieces in storage and many of these are the 18-pounder field guns. These are now being taken out of storage and issued to our field artillery units as an interim measure until new production catches up, beginning sometime this autumn. As the new 25-pounders are issued to the regulars, the older 18-pounders will be given to the Home Guard; at least that's the plan.

"I've made a fuss at Scottish Command that your sub-district has no artillery: no regular artillery units and no real coastal or harbour defense artillery except the batteries brought in last year to defend the naval forces temporarily relocated to Loch Ewe on Scotland's west coast.

"You also have no air defense guns and really no artillery whatso-ever. Being mindful of Mr. Churchill's admonition, they've agreed I'll get a supply of older 18-pounders from a regular regiment, as soon as they're replaced with new 25-pounders. Of those 24 guns, I'll give you 10 or 12. I'll distribute the remainder to the Inverness and Aberdeen Sub-Districts. Right now, I've a dozen coastal defense guns in my dis-trict: a couple of which are four-inch guns and the rest are six-inch guns. These are mainly to protect Aberdeen and the Firth of Moray. If attacked, I may have a few more guns mounted on ships in those harbours. I may even be able to use one or two Army artillery regiments if I can get them moved into position in time. You, however, have noth-ing at all.

"You must decide where these guns will be assigned in your sector and how to get the Home Guard gun crews trained. Keep in mind, you may wish to use some for harbour defense, but keep the guns mobile so they can be deployed elsewhere as well. Oh, I almost forgot. I may be able to get you a gunner to help with the artillery training, perhaps a sergeant-major. He would be assigned to your headquarters. I have my eye on one candidate, a good man, but too old and unfit for field duty. I'm not sure he would do well in a training depot. He drinks a bit too much."

"I think I can handle a drinking problem and I certainly would be pleased to have a good sergeant-major, especially a gunner. I'm sure we have a few gunners among the Home Guard veterans, but they'll all need refresher training."

After further discussion, they walked back to the train station in time for Jack to catch the late afternoon train back to Glasgow. David returned to his office through a more crowded High Street as people returned home from work. Elaine was alone in the office and working at her desk. "I believe I'm scheduled to conduct my meetings in Mallaig next week, right?"

"Yes, Sir, a single owernight, with twa meetings beginnin' at noon on Tuesday and three on Wednesday."

"I'll leave early and add another meeting on the way to Mallaig, Tuesday morning. I'll arrange the meeting myself and, if all goes well, I'll tell you more when I return." Elaine looked puzzled, as she had always scheduled David's appointments herself. "It's been a good day, Elaine, and you're free to go home now. I've a few more things to finish."

"I ha' the minutes of our meetin' with Brigadier Campbell finished for your review. Do you think it went weel?"

"Yes, he was quite pleased with our work and I am greatly relieved to know that we've rifles and other weapons coming soon. Would you mind locking the door when you leave?"

Elaine walked to the door, pushed the bolt to lock it, and returned to his office. "I brought some soup and bread I baked last evening. I told me Mum I'd be working late tonight, as she's taking the boys to a youth meeting at church. Will you eat with me? I ha' plenty, really." She brought out two bowls and spoons from her basket and a half loaf of bread. She then went to the stove where the soup was warming. They sat at the table and ate, talking about their work and up-coming events. David soon began to relax.

"Colonel, I want you to know how much I appreciate you givin' me this job. It means verra' much to me to ha' regular work and I feel that I'm contributin' to the war effort."

"Your work is important to the Army and I'm very pleased to have you as my assistant. You are capable of far more responsibilities than I ever envisioned. Fixing my dinner, however, isn't your responsibility and I'll insist on buying the food if we are to do this again."

"Thank you, Sir. I would like to eat wi' you fairly regularly." Elaine paused, swallowed, then looked straight at him and said in a soft voice, "Last night, I told my Mum that my job here would require evenin' work twa or three days each week. I wouldna' be home at suppertime and would take my supper with me. I said I would be boltin' the office door to get some privacy in order to do my work quickly." David listened to her intently as she went on. "I told her I'd turn off most lights so that the office would appear to be closed and nobody would interrupt me. I asked her not to come to the office after hours to see me, nor the boys. She knows I work verra' intensely and she agreed."

David was quite confused, but managed to stammer, "Elaine, I don't know that you should have to work late very often. If you need to go home, please feel free to go at the usual time."

"Colonel, my work here wi' you is the best part of my life. I love bein' with my lads, but they are growing up fast and want to spend more time with their pals. I love my Mum, but she's my Mum and we donna' ha' much to talk about other than the family and the household. Here I can speak with you on any subject and you're so kind to teach me things I donna' know." Her large blue eyes moistened slightly. "I enjoy it when you have a cup of tea with me and we talk about everythin'. You know so much and ha' had so many wonderful experiences. You're also very kind to me and to the others. You're a good person and I love. . . . " She paused, "I enjoy being here with you. I feel happy here with you." She dropped her eyes and fumbled with her hands.

David thought about how much he'd looked forward to seeing her each morning and the many times she'd stayed late to talk over a cup of tea. Several times he'd caught himself thinking, "If she was unmarried and I was ten years younger . . . " Then he would push those foolish thoughts from his mind.

"I've also enjoyed our talks and hope to have many more," he replied. "I feel I can trust you with anything I say. Thank you for telling me this." Elaine smiled and collected the dishes.

"How about a cup of tea?"

9

August 6, 1940

ARISAIG HOUSE, THE NEW SOE TRAINING headquarters, was a foreboding estate stripped of the beauty which had gratified its owners, the Camerons of Locheil, and their guests. Instead of the brilliant colors and contrasts which had radiated from its several gardens and groves, a dull black and brown gloom had descended over the plantings, long deadened after two years of neglect and much in need of replanting with loving care.

Two armed guards stopped David as he drove up the gravel road, still some distance from the main gate. Barbed wire surrounded the estate, and he saw movement in several directions as armed men took up positions to repel the stranger, if necessary. David introduced himself and asked to speak to the station commander. The guard looked at him suspiciously and then called for the corporal of the guard, who called a sergeant, who called a lieutenant, who appeared to be the duty officer.

"Not here, Colonel, and don't know when he'll be back. The Major may be willing to speak with you." David said that would be fine for now.

A few minutes later, the Major appeared, dressed in civilian clothes, walking leisurely down the path. "I'd invite you in, Colonel, but it's not permitted. Would you be willing to talk in the guard shack?" David agreed, and they started toward a newly-built wooden structure just behind the wall. "Mind you not to look around as we walk, Colonel, but keep your eyes fixed on the path." David complied silently.

Inside the shack were several rough wooden chairs. A small wood stove, which sat in the corner, completed the furnishings, mercifully without a fire, as the day promised to be steamy and hot.

"We don't allow uninvited visitors to go up to the big house, Sir, regulations you know."

David explained his mission as the new sub-district commander and suggested that a meeting be arranged with the station commander to see if training cooperation was possible. Perhaps they could work together in the event of invasion.

"Don't know if that's possible, Colonel. Are you aware that this isn't an Army installation? Oh yes, we have Army guards, but this installation is, shall we say, under the War Cabinet. We may be deployed elsewhere, if the Jerries march in. You probably know there will be an Army Commando training facility established somewhere near Fort William, probably several throughout the Highlands, and they may be willing to work with you."

David then suggested that, whenever he returned, the station commander call Fort William to arrange a meeting. The Major nodded. Since they hadn't been introduced, David inquired, "Major, what's your name?"

The Major replied, "We don't use our names with outsiders, Colonel. You can say you spoke with 'The Major.'"

As they left the building, David had the sense he'd intruded onto the sacred ground of a secret fraternity. "I may not be welcome here until the Camerons return," he murmured to himself, "and maybe not even then." David returned to his car and drove north to Mallaig, arriving in time for a bowl of fish stew at a small hotel, before walking to the Town Hall.

MALLAIG WAS THE LARGEST FISHING VILLAGE on the west coast of the Highlands and was a port for small boats sailing to the Isle of Skye and other nearby islands. The village was of modest size, and the whole area held fewer than 700 people. The crescent-shaped harbour was nestled against a high bluff, which rose from the beachfront behind a row of scattered cottages. The village was clustered behind the docking pier. Sitting above the main street was the small railway station, the terminus of the rail line from Glasgow through Fort William.

The Provost and Town Council were beginning to assemble when he arrived and they greeted him warmly. David made a brief presentation and explained the role of his sub-district in supporting the establishment and training of the Home Guard forces and Civil Defense groups throughout his sector. Council members asked many questions and were especially concerned with the threat of a seaborne assault on their small coastal town, located thirty miles across the Sound of Sleat from the southern coast of Skye. They were bereft of any defenses, and the sizable fishing fleet was especially vulnerable. David spoke about the role of the Home Guard, the Air Raid Precautions and other Civil

Defense groups. He noted that the Home Guard Platoon Commander for Mallaig and the surrounding villages was present at the meeting.

Also present were supervisors from the police and fire brigade, plus the local utilities: water, electricity, power, telephone, and representatives of the railway, roads and motorways, the schools, public health, housing and welfare. They'd been meeting weekly with the Town Council for several months, but their meetings had taken on an air of considerable urgency since Dunkirk. A draft emergency plan for Mallaig and the surrounding region was nearing completion and included the role of each government department. David complimented them on their efforts and commitment to protecting the people, using their good sense and the limited resources at hand. He also emphasized it was essential for every village and town to establish firm cooperation between government offices, private businesses, and citizens who had the skills to assist in an emergency. The meeting lasted most of the afternoon.

It was almost five o'clock when the door opened and the provost's secretary escorted in two waitresses from the hotel. They brought trays of sandwiches, biscuits, and water for tea. The provost adjourned the formal meeting, but asked everyone to meet in smaller groups while eating. "At seven o'clock, we must adjourn to the church for our public meeting."

David was pleased to speak with the Home Guard Platoon Commander, a veteran of the First War. "We are splittin' our platoon, now over 35 men, to form a mobile battle section of 15 men who will leave Mallaig and defend wherever the Nazis attack. We should ha' more men, but many of our chaps are fishermen who are part of the Naval Reserve. I also ha' a section of Railway Home Guard to protect our rail line. The older men are being trained to take up positions in and around the town, or around the villages wherever they live. We canna' stop a German attack, Colonel, but we can hurt them. In the meantime, I ha' instituted an eight-hour watch by my soldiers, mainly to stand guard each night near the harbour."

The Air Raid Precautions commander reported that the local Ground Observer personnel had been trained and were on station each day around the clock. He said he had ample wardens to patrol the streets in the event of an emergency and two Explosive Ordinance specialists were in training. The Civil Defense director, an imposing woman in her 50's, was mainly concerned about protecting families, especially the very young and very old.

"I wa' a nurse in the First War, Colonel, and I can tell you 'tis bloody hell when the wounded and injured overwhelm the medical facilities. Our clinic is small, but I'm organizin' the women in town to make their beds available, if needed, for the injured. We must also be prepared to move any injured to safer areas outside of town, when necessary. Until then, everyone ha' a role in helpin' those who canna' help themselves. I'll no' let the good people of Mallaig suffer like those poor people in Poland when the Nazis destroyed their towns." David was extremely impressed.

The public meeting began shortly after seven. David summarized the progress of the war and his observations about war preparedness in the West Highlands. He then heartily congratulated the many organizations with which he'd met earlier on their progress and the on-going efforts to protect the town and its citizens.

"Of all the towns I've visited, Mallaig is by far the best prepared at this time for any emergency. I commend you and your leaders." He then asked for questions and held the floor for another 45 minutes. Questions flowed, ranging from serious to silly.

As they filed out of the church, an elderly woman caught his arm. "Colonel, I think ye are doin' this all wrong!" David was taken aback and asked for an explanation. She continued, "When our young men go out each evenin' to stand guard, donna' ye see tha' this is weakenin' them? They work long hours all day, ha' a bit of supper, then go on guard at night. When do they sleep? It's no' healthy, Colonel, and they're bein' worn doon."

David explained they had no choice, as there was a vital need for a nighttime watch, but she interrupted him. "No, no, I ken we mun ha' guards, but you're usin' the wrong people."

He stammered "Ma'am?"

She replied, "Old folks like me can stand the night watch and let the young people sleep. My Charlie and I are like most old folks. We donna' sleep well at night anyway and we doze durin' the day. We can verra' well go out in the middle of the night and take our turn standin' guard and it wilna' hurt us a bit. Probably be good to ha' somethin' to do, as we're no' sleepin' anyway. If we get tired, we can sit on the hill overlookin' the harbour, where we can see both seaward and landward. Let the young people sleep at night, and we'll wake them up if there's an emergency."

David was almost speechless. "I must say I'd never thought of that." Several others joined the discussion and the provost said he would explore this with the Home Guard and Civil Defense commanders.

98

Within weeks, the idea had spread and several towns were testing the old boys watch.

DAVID AWOKE EARLY THE NEXT MORNING. He had plans to visit two small villages south of Mallaig on his way back to Fort William. After tea and a bun in the hotel, he went to a public phone and asked to be put through to his headquarters. Elaine answered promptly, and he briefed her on his previous day's success. Elaine reported on her day's activities, the mail, and visitors.

David asked, "Is there anything else?"

There was a long pause, then Elaine responded haltingly "I just want you to know that . . . that you're verra' much missed here."

"I miss you . . . all of you, too, I mean. I'll be back this afternoon, maybe before you leave. I really look forward to seeing you."

He hung up the telephone and stood silently for several minutes. "Was she hinting at something?" he wondered. "Was she expressing feelings for me?" His mind went back over the past several weeks when he'd begun to realize he was developing serious feelings for Elaine, an attraction that went well beyond their work. He'd quickly suppressed those thoughts each time with a momentary sense of guilt, as she'd given no hint of interest in him other than as a loyal employee. Or had she? Perhaps her feelings were changing as well.

The day seemed to drag on endlessly, although the two other meetings at Arisaig village and Lochallort went well. Those villages were chosen for their central locations, where people from other villages and farms could drive or walk to participate. Although, they were small hamlets, several dozen people attended each meeting.

As David drove east toward Fort William, his mind again turned from the meetings to Elaine. "What a beautiful woman," he thought, "and working in my headquarters." He thought about her for some time and felt his loneliness returning. He imagined holding her, maybe even kissing her, and then forced himself to put her out of his mind. He must focus on the week's remaining work. "Impure thoughts are the Devil's workshop," his mother would say.

ARRIVING AT HIS OFFICE EARLY EVENING, David saw that the lights were off. Or were they? The door was unlocked and, when he entered, Elaine came over and bolted the door behind him. Only one small light burned near her desk. "Good trip?" she asked softly.

"Yes, very good," he responded. He took off his jacket and tie. She poured him a cup of tea from the simmering pot on the stove and re-filled her own cup. They sat down in his office in the two overstuffed chairs she'd recently acquired. They sat silently for several minutes until she said, "Do you want to tell me about your trip?"

"Not now," he replied. After a few more moments of silence, he put his cup down. He felt his emotions stirring again and nervously decided to bare his soul. "Elaine, I need to share something with you. I don't want to upset you and, if you wish, I promise never to speak of this again." The air was thick with tension as he groped for words, and he could see Elaine's body stiffen as she listened carefully.

"I've enjoyed working with you these past few weeks, but my feelings for you are changing." He paused for another moment, while she stared at him intently. "I guess my feelings for you are . . . are much deeper than before. I find myself thinking about you all the time . . . and my thoughts are not about work."

Elaine's face reddened. She felt her heart beat rapidly. She took a deep breath. "Thank heaven; it's finally out, Colonel. I fell in love with you weeks ago and I'm so pleased that you ha' some feelin's for me."

David felt a rush of relief and went on. "I know you're married and I don't want to interfere with that, but I need to tell you how I feel." He struggled to find more words, but they wouldn't come.

"Sir, I need to tell you about my marriage," she said insistently. "Paul and I met in school and he treated me like royalty. You coulda' said he swept me off my feet and I verra' much looked forward to our marriage. Soon after, though, he turned his attention back to his old pals, and I began to feel neglected. Durin' the early years of our marriage, he never spent much time with our boys or me. When he announced he'd joined the Navy, I was angry, but also relieved. He went off and that was that. I made a new life for myself with my boys, my Mum, and my work.

"He comes home for short visits, maybe, twice each year. He's usually drunk when he gets here, but he grabs me and we go into the bedroom and, well, you know wha'. Then he's gone, out with his old pals again, and I mightn't see him again for two or three days. Then it's time for him to go back to his ship. He's so unfair to our boys, they almost donna' ha' a father. I look at you, livin' apart from your daughters, but you write to them almost everra' day and you call them each week. Sometimes, I hear you speak to them on the phone and I almost weep when I hear the love you give them. My boys ha' never known that from their father and it's not fair!" She calmed down, and then looked up at him again with large, moist eyes.

David sat silently, looking at her as his emotions roiled inside. "I don't know what to do from here."

"Brigadier Campbell said you looked verra' tired and worn and asked me if you took any time off. I said no, you worked long hours each day and ha' taken no days off since you ha' been here. He said tha' you would put yourself in a hospital at tha' rate. He made me promise tha' I'd arrange time off in your schedule."

"I don't see how I can do that. There's so much work to do."

"Maybe, if we work hard tomorrow, we can go on a picnic Friday— Brigadier Campbell's orders."

"It might be better if we went on Saturday or even Sunday."

"No, too many people will be out hikin' on the weekend. We'll go Friday, when people are at work."

August 9

FRIDAY MORNING BURST FORTH with rising sunshine and a cool early morning breeze as David cleaned out his car, dressed in a pair of worsted wool slacks and a shirt cleaned and pressed by Mrs. Donaldson. A few people were already on their way to work, and the streets would be filled in less than an hour. After a few minutes, Elaine arrived wearing a light cotton dress and sandals, and carrying a basket. "I ha' lunch," she chirped.

"I took the liberty of bringing a bottle of wine," he replied, "but not much else."

"We wilna' need much. 'Tis the first time I ha' seen you without your uniform. You look nice."

"It felt strange not to put it on, but if we're off for a hike I shouldn't wear it."

"No, it attracts attention. I want to be the only girl who gives you attention today." They got into the car and, at Elaine's instructions, drove out of town.

"Where are we going?"

"To a place I know. We'll drive toward Glencoe, but we'll no' go tha' far." They were silent as they drove east, then south through Spean Bridge. Each could feel the tension and anticipation rising.

Several miles past the small village of Roy Bridge, Elaine said, "Turn here." David did as instructed, and they drove more slowly for several miles along a dirt road westward toward Ben Nevis and the surrounding mountains. The rolling fields gave way to a lightly wooded area and, after a short time, the woods thickened with evergreens. Soon, the road narrowed into a wagon path, and they were surrounded by dense forest. "Turn right up ahead and stop above those two large trees."

David complied. Getting out, he remarked, "I don't think anyone can see the car from fifty feet away."

"Exactly."

She took her basket and walked up a path through the dense underbrush. He followed silently with the wine and a blanket. Presently, they came to a small clearing covered with moss. A very slight breeze stirred the tops of the trees and rays of sunshine warmed the moss and tiny shoots of grass. "Do you like it?" she asked.

"It's perfect," he responded, "but how would you know about a place like this?"

Elaine smiled. "I wa' young once."

They sat quietly while Elaine unpacked her basket, two sandwiches first. "We'll pretend that we're eating caviar and lobster." David smiled and, after pouring two cups of wine, took his first bite. Elaine watched him as she sipped her wine. Their silence was broken only by the sounds of birds and insects. There was heavy tension between them. Both knew what they wanted, but neither was absolutely sure the other wanted the same. David felt like a schoolboy trying to muster enough courage to steal his first kiss. He looked at her large, beautiful eyes, and then they both looked away, feeling their eyes might betray their inner feelings. His heart was beating hard and he never felt less hungry, but she'd prepared the sandwiches.

David took a second small bite. "You're not eating."

"I'm no' hungry," she paused almost awkwardly, "for food." David could stand the tension no longer. He put his sandwich down and leaned toward her. She didn't pull away, but turned very slightly in his direction. He put his arm behind her and gently kissed her. They looked at each other for a few moments, and then their lips met again, this time a longer, deeper kiss.

"You do that so well, Colonel. I ha' dreamed of this moment for many weeks."

They lay back together and kissed intensely, again and again. Elaine took a quick breath as he touched her breast and then relaxed as he unbuttoned her dress.

She placed her hand gently against his chest. After a moment, she slowly unbuttoned his shirt.

THE SUN SHONE BRIGHTLY as David awoke the next morning. His room looked as drab as ever, but he felt refreshed and eager to get on with his Saturday. He dressed quickly and walked downstairs to his office. As he sat at his desk, his mind flew over yesterday and all that had happened. Then Anne crept into his thoughts for the first time, and he felt a deep sense of remorse. "Anne would be horrified," he thought, "Or would she?" Maybe this was simply meant to be a wonderful, brief interlude in his busy, dreary life.

He vowed to refocus on Anne and the wonderful memories she'd given him. It would be foolish to take up with a much younger woman now, especially a married woman. How old was Elaine? He'd never asked. He walked to the file drawer and brought out her application, neatly typed as always. "Born in May 1909, so she would be thirty-one, thirteen years younger," he mused, "and what a beautiful age. Thirteen years difference, however, is considerable. There's no chance this relationship can last very long." No, it made no sense to get involved further with Elaine. He'd find a way to slowly and gently bring it back to just a good working relationship.

He tried to read through yesterday's correspondence, but his mind kept going back to the forest glen and the passion he'd felt. At least, she'll not be coming to the office today. I can finish my work, then go for a long walk, or maybe even a run, followed by a drive into the mountains to find a stream. A cold swim would be wonderful. He fidgeted at his work for some minutes, and then the door opened and she entered.

"Elaine, you're not supposed to be at work today."

"I know. I wanted to see you." She went to the stove and made two cups of tea. Bringing one to David, she sat down and looked at him silently for several minutes. "Yesterday was the most wonderful day of my life and I wanted to thank you."

David began to mumble something about other days, but she interrupted. "Colonel, I'm so in love with you. I've thought about you for days and weeks. I hardly slept all night thinking about us. I got up early and went for a walk and finally realized tha' this was wha' should be." She paused. "There, now I've said it."

David sat silently, not knowing what to say. They looked at each other for a moment and he finally managed to murmur, "Our time together was wonderful."

"Now," she went on, "I ha' a few things to do." She walked to her desk quietly and picked up some papers. A half hour later she returned.

"Do you ha' the key to your flat?" He nodded. "May I ha' it, please?" She held out her hand. He fumbled in his pocket and drew it out. "Thank you. I'm going upstairs to your room. If I see anyone in the hall, I'll go into the loo. Wait ten minutes, and then you come up, quietly." She rose and went upstairs.

Ten minutes later, David followed. Not surprisingly, there was nobody in the hallway, there hardly ever was, and no sound came from the other flats. He opened his door to find Elaine sitting on his bed.

"Hi," she said softly and slipped off her shoes. She unbuttoned her blouse. "Bolt the door."

August 20

DAVID HEARD THE TRUCK RUMBLING slowly down High Street, not an unusual event, but something caused him to look out the window. The truck stopped right by his front door and he saw a large gun mounted on its back, partially hidden by a canvas tarp. A car pulled up behind the truck, and Colonel Laughton, the British Aluminum factory manager, stepped out.

"Lord Beaverbrook is deliverin' on his promise, Colonel McKenna. I ha' received the first anti-aircraft gun to supplement the machine guns guardin' my factory. 'Tis a Hispano Suiza 20-millimeter cannon complete wi' a half-ton of ammunition. They say it has a range of four or five miles. I ha' no idea where they got it, but I think it was manufactured in Spain. They call it a 'portee'."

"That means it's mounted on a truck, from the French word."

"Yes, well that makes sense. Now, I want to ask your opinion. Where should we best place it to guard my factory? We'll have to train our own gun crew."

David thought for a moment. "Perhaps it would best serve if it were placed on the hill above your factory. That would give it a commanding view of your whole facility and it could be dug in with sandbags to protect the crew. I'd suggest, however, that you take it somewhere to train the crews and actually fire the weapon."

"My Home Guardsmen ha' a large firing range near the smelter at Kinlochleven. We use the range now mainly to train the men on .22 caliber rifles so we don't waste valuable wartime ammunition with our rifle practice. We can shoot straight down Loch Leven toward Loch Linnhe, maybe eight or ten miles of open water. Of course, I'd better tell the Navy first. Wouldn't want to hit a friendly boat, you know."

104

They both smiled at the thought. "Anyway, I thought you'd like to see it."

"Why don't you leave it here for a few hours and let the townspeople see it? It should be a real confidence builder."

"A splendid idea. I'll ha' my lads move it to Kinlochleven this evenin'."

September 7

"CROMWELL!"

"Sir!" David responded.

"Cromwell, David. Do you understand what I mean?" The telephone line made a light buzzing sound, but David heard every word and instantly recognized Brigadier Jack Campbell's voice.

"Yes, Sir, I understand you perfectly. I'll take appropriate actions immediately."

"Good. There's no need to call out your Home Guard or Civil Defense forces just yet, but they should be placed on a high state of alert and be ready to assemble on thirty minutes notice. Have the commanders and staffs report to their designated places, and you should activate your own staff immediately. Turn on BBC and keep at least one phone line open should we need to call you." He paused. "David, this may be it!"

"Can you give me more details?"

"Not at this time, David. You know what has been happening lately. Well, it all seems to be coming to a head. Home Forces issued the Cromwell alert just an hour ago. A summary of recent activities was cabled to Scottish Command and a copy is being forwarded here right now. Steve Whittaker has an officer ready to snatch it and bring it straight here to my office. He'll make copies for you and Richard Sinclair and he'll have your copy sent promptly by motorcar to Fort William. You should have it in two or three hours. We're told it has considerable detail of what has transpired and is classified as 'Most Secret,' so you'd best meet the driver yourself. I can't say more than that over the telephone."

"I understand, Sir, and I'll take appropriate actions." David sat stunned for a moment. Cromwell was the code word for *Invasion imminent and probable within twelve hours.*

He quickly called Elaine to alert the staff and to activate the anti-invasion preparations for which they'd been training. Soon, the telephone rang again. "Colonel, 'twas the Chief Constable. He wanted you to know that they ha' just received the Cromwell alert and he's passin' it along to all civil authorities as well as to the Civil Defense organizations."

David felt sick. Although he was no stranger to war, this was the first time he'd fight on British soil. The previous weeks had been increasingly ominous. On August 11, German troops in Norway embarked on ships for what was expected to be an invasion of either Scotland or Northern England. Instead, they went ashore in Belgium and France, further swelling the forces for the subsequent invasion. Two days later, Austrian mountain divisions arrived across the Channel. They were equipped with mules and other equipment, which could climb the cliffs of Sussex and Kent, behind the presumed invasion beaches. On August 15, the Germans had mounted Operation *Adlerangriff*, or Eagle Attack, an all-out air attack by the *Luftwaffe* on the British Royal Air Force. Some 1800 planes attacked that day, including 500 bombers; the damage to RAF bases was extensive. Seventy-six German aircraft were reported shot down that day, for the loss of half that number by the RAF.

All of Britain was alert and waiting for the dreaded attack. But it did not come. Not that day, nor the next day, nor the day after. Finally, Home Forces Command issued a stand down order. The threat hadn't disappeared, however. It had merely been delayed. The invasion threat was greater than before.

10

September 16, 1940

THE WAR WAS NOT GOING WELL. Hitler tightened his grip on Europe, while the *Luftwaffe* ruthlessly bombed British military installations in what was now being called the Battle of Britain, or the *Blitz*. Public morale was sinking further, and the government was struggling to inject a spirit of optimism into the people. Under the threat of German bombings, the British Government established an evacuation program, whereby thousands of children were removed from threatened urban areas and placed with foster families in rural areas. Some children also were sent to Canada by ship.

"COLONEL, I SEE THE ADMIRAL COMING." Newly commissioned Second Lieutenant Jonathan Osborne was standing by the office window eager to greet Rear-Admiral Christopher Evans-Cooper upon his return. Osborne had started work at the office two weeks earlier, and David's most difficult task was finding work within Osborne's limited capabilities. He'd finally directed the staff to come up with jobs, however small, which could be given to Osborne in the priority of must do, should do, and need not do, but will be done anyway to keep Osborne busy.

The Admiral had given Osborne the responsibility to set up his trip to meet the Lords Lieutenant of Caithness, Sutherland, Ross & Cromarty, and Inverness. He was to arrange all lodging and travel by rail, something Elaine normally would do. As Chief of Staff, CB Foster officially directed Osborne's work, but he'd unofficially turned over much of the responsibility to Elaine. Although only a lower ranking administrative assistant, Elaine's skills, maturity, and self-confidence quickly overwhelmed Osborne. He did whatever she asked and addressed her as "Ma'am." CB was pleased to see the transition in their roles, while he emerged free from the responsibility to wet-nurse the subaltern. Like the other officers, CB had developed enormous respect for Elaine, her work ethic, and her considerable abilities. He told David that, when the war ended, he'd do his best to hire Elaine into his firm.

The Admiral gave a quick greeting to Osborne and Elaine, then went straight into David's office and closed the door.

"Welcome back, Admiral, I trust the trip went well?"

"Splendidly, could hardly have been better. You know, I drove to Perth to catch the train north and also went to Queens Barracks to see if the Black Watch had put up a monument yet in your honor," he said with a smile.

"The only monument I'll get will be a gravestone when my time has come."

"Not this week, we hope. Anyway, Oh! Look at that!" he exclaimed, looking past David's shoulder at a new sign on the wall. It read, "*Keep Calm and Carry On.*"

"Our new motto. I heard about it on BBC this past week."

"Yes," David replied, "apparently it's catching on all over Britain. Elaine made up the sign to surprise me. It's very sensible, and I rather like it."

"Someone in London finally did something useful, which is truly amazing. Anyway, the Lords Lieutenant send you their greetings and were both gracious and cooperative. They look forward to meeting you and want you to know they'll give you every possible support. I needn't tell you they're quite nervous and worried about the coming invasion. In each town I visited, the people were tense and their eyes darted about as they walked, as if a Nazi was about to jump out and pounce on them. People also look rather fatigued, as if they're not getting enough sleep. Perhaps this is because of the long workdays that have evolved since the war began, plus the extra work we all are doing with Home Guard, Civil Defense, and volunteer activities. The Lords are doing their best to help people stay calm, but also to be prepared.

"The Duke of Sutherland is a real politician, as you said, and he's proud as punch to be back in uniform again as the commander of his Home Guard battalion. I spoke with him about the German threat to the radar station at Sango Bay. He agreed that the Durness platoon couldn't protect the station if the Jerries launched a raid. He said he'd have his staff work on a plan to reinforce Durness with mobile battle units."

"If they get sufficient warning in time. How were the other Lords?"

"Excellent. Of course, at your July meeting, you met Colonel Sir Donald Cameron of Lochiel, the Lord Lieutenant of Inverness-shire.

You have a real friend and supporter there. Sir Hector MacKenzie, in Ross & Cromarty, has less of a military background, but he's enthusiastic. And Viscount Archibald Henry MacDonald Sinclair, in Caithness, completed my visits. Next week I'll visit Niall Campbell, the Duke of Argyll."

So, what news did you pick up?"

"Have you heard the latest news about the American mobilization?"

"No."

"You know their Congress last month approved mobilizing their National Guard and other reserves for one year. Apparently, the first four National Guard Infantry Divisions have reported for duty at their mobilization posts this past week, and they will be followed each month by several more divisions until all 18 divisions and smaller units are activated. Of course, they will need a great deal of training and equipment to become fully operational. Together with their 10 regular divisions, however, that will give their army 28 divisions by early 1941. Today, their Congress will vote whether or not to begin a peacetime conscription." He lowered his voice. "President Roosevelt has told Mr. Churchill that he plans to activate many new divisions as well."

"When did they meet?"

"No meetings that I know of. They talk by telephone regularly using a secret underwater cable, but it's all hush-hush. Also, you know about the 50 old First War destroyers that the Americans are transferring to our Navy in exchange for leases on British bases in the North Atlantic, Bermuda, and the West Indies. Well, British crews have already taken possession of several of them. This will provide a real boost to our convoy escort capability."

"We really have given up nothing. We'd welcome their Navy at our bases, right?"

"Exactly, Colonel. It's all a political charade to placate the isolationists in the American Congress, so that Mr. Roosevelt can give us the destroyers. We've suffered enormous losses at sea to German U-boats. The destroyers will be used as convoy escorts to reduce some of these losses."

"Mr. Roosevelt is reading the world situation far better than many other Americans, including members of his own Congress. America may be neutral today, but they're getting better prepared for a war that could come their way."

"Oh, and on a very sad note, David, we lost a ship carrying some of our evacuated children."

"Good Lord, no!"

"Yes, the *City of Benares* was torpedoed, with about 250 deaths, including 77 children bound for Canada. I expect this will curtail or even halt the evacuations to Canada. More children will be kept over here."

"My girls, in St. Albans, probably aren't in danger from the *Blitz* and won't be evacuated. If that changes, I'll bring them and their cousins up here to Fort William."

"Have you been told about the 'Cromwell' incident in Cornwall, David?"

"Oliver?"

"No," the Admiral said, smiling. "The code word 'Cromwell.' There was an incident back on August 8th in Southwest England, some village in Cornwall, I think. Someone mistook the returning fishing fleet for a German invasion force and sounded the invasion alarm. All the church bells were rung as prescribed, and the alarm swept through several counties, thoroughly frightening the population and disrupting everything. The War Office now says an invasion alarm can be issued only by proper authorities and will be preceded by the code word 'Cromwell.' "

"Makes sense."

"But, David, another real 'Cromwell' invasion alert has been issued for Southeast England only. Intelligence has been watching the German reconstruction activity with the river barges, and the RAF has been bombing them. Well, the barges have begun to move toward the Channel, and German fighter squadrons also began to move up closer to bases right across the Channel. German Army forces, the *Wehrmacht*, raised their readiness status, so Mr. Churchill authorized a limited invasion alert."

"I'm aware of some of this. The invasion alert hasn't been extended to other parts of Britain yet, unlike the last time. I've seen nothing further since that alert was issued over a week ago."

"Nor has anyone else. The Defense Ministry is quite puzzled. The Germans seemed to elevate their readiness in preparation for an invasion, and then everything stopped."

"Are the German forces standing down now?"

"Apparently not. That's what so puzzling. What's this all about? Are we going to be invaded or not? Nobody knows, and apparently the German forces also don't know, or so our intelligence tells us."

David and the Admiral spoke for another half-hour before the Admiral rose to leave. "I've a lady I want you to meet soon. Lady Frances Stuart and her husband Sir Robert live not far from here. She's a cousin of Sir Donald Cameron. Sir Robert is a major in the Special Reserve and was called up last year. He's now serving overseas, I think in Cairo; and Lady Frances has thrown herself into the Civil Defense effort. As you can imagine, she commands considerable respect and has proven to be an excellent administrator. I guess even the lesser nobility can be quite competent when they want to be."

"And why would I want to meet her?" David said, tilting his head with suspicion.

"We've no liaison with the Civil Defense authorities, and that was quite apparent during our last invasion alert. I thought she might be an asset for your headquarters, since we're supposed to be in close coordination with Civil Defense forces. Just meet with her and you can say 'no' if you feel I'm wrong."

"I suspected that was your motive, but you've been right most of the time, Admiral. I'm willing to meet her if you feel that's best."

"Right only most of the time?" he said smiling and left the office.

September 18

"AIR RAID! AIR RAID!"

David leaped from his bed, barely having gone to sleep. "Is this a dream?" he wondered.

"German Bombers overhead. Get to your shelters!" The insistent voice continued down High Street, and he heard similar voices elsewhere. Then, the frightening wail of the air raid siren on High Street began, soon followed by two others at a distance. This is definitely not a dream, but German bombers? Here? He quickly pulled on his uniform, holstered his revolver, grabbed his torch and helmet, and ran out to the street. People were rushing about. The police and other volunteers herded them into the air raid shelters. David recognized some as Air Raid Precautions volunteers.

"This is a good test of our ARP system," he thought. The shelters included recently dug underground bunkers, as well as the basements of the larger buildings. Because it was far north of urban areas, Fort William had never been as serious as the larger cities about air raids, and it was unrehearsed in a town-wide evacuation to shelters. There was much confusion.

"This way to the shelter, Sir. Hurry!" A volunteer wearing an ARP armband took his arm.

"No," he replied, shaking himself loose, "my duty station is right here." The man dropped his arm. "Oh, 'tis ye, Colonel, is it? My mistake. Beggin' yer pardon, Sir." He moved on to corral others still on the street.

"'My duty station.' Where did that come from?" David wondered. "Anyway, it worked. Elaine! Must find Elaine." He started toward her house, and then saw her turn the corner running toward him.

"Mum and the boys are in the shelter. Are the Germans really attackin' us?"

"I don't know. Let's go see the Chief Constable." They walked down the streets, patrolled by an occasional constable or ARP volunteer. David stopped. "Listen." It was the unmistakable sound of a large, multi-engine plane overhead to the southwest of town.

"German?"

"I don't know," he replied. "I can't tell how many planes, either. Possibly, more than one, but not a large number."

Chief Constable Angus MacDonald was standing in front of his office with two other officers, peering into the sky with an old pair of binoculars. "Do you know what this is all about, Colonel?"

"No, I was hoping you did."

"Glasgow is bein' bombed. A call reportin' enemy aircraft came in to our ARP monitor at the Fire Brigade from one of the ground observers at Glencoe. At first, they dismissed it, but then other observers called in. One other Fire Brigade also called, so the alarm was sounded. There's definitely somethin' up there. I just don't know if it's ours or the enemy's."

"If they're German bombers, wouldna' there be RAF fighters attackin' them?" Elaine asked.

"The nearest fighter bases are near Inverness or Glasgow. Our fighters don't have the range to pursue the bombers for a great distance," David replied.

The sound of the aircraft grew louder and seemed to be flying just west of the town. "They're flying up Loch Linnhe, probably going for the aluminum plant!" David announced.

"Listen! Gunfire."

They heard a very faint popping sound in the distance, but no large explosions. "Are you sure?" asked Elaine.

"Certainly, I know gunfire," David replied. Then, all quieted down, and the plane was gone. In a moment, the phone rang indoors and a constable came out.

"Sir, 'tis from the Fire Brigade. The aluminum plant ha' been bombed."

"Damn! Get my car," MacDonald ordered. David sent Elaine to the office to alert the staff, make a report to Brigadier Campbell, and monitor the telephone. He got into the car with the Chief Constable, and they drove the short distance to the aluminum factory. A security guard blocked their way until the Chief yelled, "Good God, man, I'm the Chief Constable and I've the Army Commander with me. Get your superior!" The factory was a scene of bedlam, but David saw no evidence of the bombing. Presently, Colonel Laughton, the plant manager, appeared.

"There's a bomb inside, but it hasna' exploded yet. I ha' evacuated everra'one. No serious injuries yet, just a hole in the roof."

"Just one bomb?" asked David.

"There may be others, but 'tis the only one tha' hit the factory. We willna' know 'til daylight."

"It probably has a delayed action fuse and may be set to go off later when it might kill more people."

"If it ha' exploded when it first hit it would ha' kilt many of my workers."

"Do you know how many planes there were?" David asked.

"No, 'twas dark, of course, but probably only one. The gunners fired at somethin', but they're no' sure wha'. I doubt if they hit anythin'. It doesna' make sense tha' this wa' the whole air raid. Why would they come all this way and just drop one bomb, or only a few?"

"I don't know," David replied. "It may have been a special operation to target just this one factory and knock it out. That would certainly slow aircraft production. How long will it take you to get back to work?"

"Get that bomb off my factory floor, Colonel, and I'll be back in production tomorrow, unless it explodes first. The Fire Brigade ha' called for an explosive ordinance unit from Inverness. They should be here within twa hours. My own explosive ordinance teams ha' just begun training, and I'll no' hazard them wi' this bomb. I ha' several Home Guardsmen comin' in to help wi' security 'til the bomb is disarmed."

"Let's have a look at the bomb, Colonel," said David. The three men walked to the factory and cautiously stepped inside. The lights were still on and the manager led them around the furnaces to a place where they could see the fins and a part of the body of the bomb. David took the Chief's binoculars and looked closely. "It could be a 500-pound bomb. If it explodes, it'll wreck this wing of the building and most of the machinery."

As they left the building, Colonel Laughton told his supervisors to send the workers home for the night. However, most employees stayed to watch. After an interminable wait, a red truck and a small trailer arrived with two explosive ordinance specialists. After brief introductions, they went inside with tool bags. They returned in less than five minutes.

"Dunno if 'tis delayed action or no', Colonel, but 'tis a 500-pounder. If it explodes 'twill likely wreck this end of the plant. I need someone to take some of those sandbags from the guard post over there and build a little fort about two feet square inside, with an open top for the fuse. Keep everra'one away. We're goin' back in and remove the fuse before it explodes." He paused, "We hope."

Tension hung thick in the air. The men had taken a large spanner wrench and four stabilizing braces, the latter to hold the bomb in place while they unscrewed the fuse. This was a very dangerous business, as the bomb could explode just from their actions. David and the others paced nervously outside, just beyond the lethal range of an explosion. After twenty minutes, the two men returned, one carrying what looked like a pipe, less than a foot long. He gingerly placed it into the sandbag fort and placed another sandbag on top.

"We're goin' to bring out the bomb next. It's no' dangerous now, but I'll need some help. No' ye, gentlemen, of course, I need some strong workers. Where do ye want me to explode it?"

Laughton looked uncomfortably at David, who said, "About a mile in that direction." He pointed at a large open field just east of the smelter. "Is that alright with you, Colonel?" he asked. Laughton nodded, and the men went to their truck. A foreman chose six workmen to assist.

An hour later, there was a terrific explosion in the distant field, as the bomb and its fuse were blown up by a package of explosives brought by the specialists. After congratulations, they drove off to cheers from the remaining factory workers.

"Back to work." said David stepping into the car, "and a report to my superiors."

It was later learned that the one bomb that struck the aluminum factory probably had been deliberately sabotaged by workers at the German bomb-making factory, many of whom were slave labourers from occupied countries, forced to work for the Germans. Construction soon began on a dummy aluminum plant, several miles to the northeast, at Gleann Domhananaidh. This would be made to look like the real factory in the hope it would deceive enemy bombers and draw them away from the real factory.

It was early morning when David returned to his office to find the Admiral waiting. David had never seen him looking so upset. "The Jerries bombed Glasgow last night and sank the heavy cruiser, *Sussex*. I heard on BBC that the dockyards had been hit, so I called Vice-Admiral James Troup, a friend and former colleague who is the Flag Officer commanding the naval base. He told me *Sussex* had gone into dry-dock at Yorkhill Dock last month, for engine repairs. A German bomber put a bomb right into the engine room and started a fire that swept through the ship and threatened to detonate the powder magazines. To prevent an explosion, they flooded the dry-dock, and the *Sussex* capsized. Fortunately, most of the crew was ashore because of the repairs."

"I'm sorry, Chris. Was *Sussex* one of your ships?"

"No, but I saw her often. She was a beautiful ship, one of only twelve 8-inch gun cruisers in the Navy. I hope they can salvage her."

September 19

THE RIFLES FOR THE HOME GUARD had arrived, over 6,000 P-14's from America for David's sub-district. The day had been a blur of activity, as boxes of weapons were delivered to every village and town throughout the Highlands. Home Guardsmen had been organized everywhere to help unpack the rifles and begin the process of disassembling them. Men and women worked side by side to separate the metal parts from the wooden stock and fore grip. The metal parts were then placed in drums of boiling water to loosen the cosmolene grease in which they'd been packed for two decades to prevent rust. A red band was painted on the forward handgrip of each rifle to avoid a mix-up with ammunition. The staff had been on the telephone regularly during the day, checking the progress and answering questions from young officers and sergeants who were unfamiliar with the rifles. Weapons' training was scheduled for the weekend, including the firing of three live rounds per weapon to familiarize the volunteers with their new weapons and to zero the sights. David was confident the soldiers would be comfortable with their rifles by Sunday evening.

"Any problems?" he asked his Quartermaster, Captain Frank Leslie.

"Nothing serious, Colonel. There's confusion in smaller units that have no company or battalion officers to oversee work and answer questions. They're struggling to understand how the rifles are assembled and disassembled. "It'll all work out quickly. I think the men are quite excited to have real weapons and even a few rounds of ammunition. Now they feel like real soldiers."

"How is the redistribution of the privately-owned weapons coming along?"

"That was pretty well resolved several days ago. We told the commanders the new rifles would go first to the fighting men, especially those assigned to the mobile battle platoons. Other platoons would get the remaining rifles. Most support troops and village defenders would then be assigned the privately owned weapons. Up 'til now they had nothing, Colonel, so 'tis a big improvement."

"Scottish Command has told us to expect a small number of revolvers within a month. Do you have a plan for those?"

"Yes, sir, we'll follow the same principle. The lower the rank of the officers and sergeants authorized revolvers, the more likely they are to get them, with the privately-owned revolvers and pistols flowing up to higher ranks. I want the weapons assigned to those most likely to face actual combat, not to people far behind the lines. If all goes well, I'll be the last officer in our sub-district to get a revolver."

"I'll keep my own revolver," David responded.

"Yes, Sir, of course you will. You infantry officers always want to be in the front lines leading the troops," Frank said, smiling. "While you're up front, I'll be far to the rear keeping you supplied. Quartermaster officers shouldn't need revolvers."

September 21

THE WEEKEND CONTINUED the hectic pace for the Home Guard. All rifles were cleaned, reassembled and working properly by Saturday morning. Each unit went to a safe area outside of its village or town to test-fire the weapons and zero in the sights by carefully expending their allocated three rounds of ammunition per weapon. The guardsmen showed a new sense of pride, becoming armed soldiers who now stood a much better chance of slowing or stopping Nazi invaders.

Sensing this opportunity, David's counterpart at the Northeast Subdistrict, Colonel Matthew Harris, ordered all units to march home from the firing areas and parade through their respective villages and towns with their new rifles. After several months of drill, the soldiers paraded quite well, despite the denim uniforms. There were no bands, of course, but a few units had a piper or two leading the parade. The

Lochaber Company of over 500 men marched down High Street. David and his staff saluted them as they marched past his office. These were not unknown soldiers from distant places. These were husbands, fathers, sons, nephews, and neighbors. Elaine stood with the staff, tears streaming down her face. The parades electrified the people, and there was much cheering and applause.

Although these were their own Home Guardsmen, there were shouts of "the Army's here!"

11

September 23, 1940

THE NAZI BOMBINGS, now a month old, continued uninterrupted. Hundreds of aircraft were shot down on either side, a significant victory for the RAF in the face of massive destruction. The *Luftwaffe* almost brought the RAF to its knees with concentrated raids on bases and radar stations. RAF aircraft were depleted and their aircrews exhausted. In retaliation for a possibly accidental bombing raid on London by a group of German aircraft, Churchill ordered a small bombing attack on Berlin. Hitler was enraged and ordered the *Luftwaffe* to shift targets and bomb London instead, later expanding this to other cities in Britain.

The nightly bombing of London wreaked havoc, but its greatest effect was the shock to ordinary citizens. The sickening wail of the air raid sirens struck fear into Londoners as they rushed to the air raid shelters—precisely Hitler's intent. He'd learned the power of terror as an instrument of war and its unnerving effect upon the nation's armed forces. Terror bombings demoralized the forces as they worried about the safety of their families back home. Never again would civilians be safe from war.

REAR-ADMIRAL EVANS-COOPER ARRIVED at the office mid-morning and introduced David and Elaine to Lady Frances Stuart.

"The Admiral tells me you're the force behind the Civil Defense efforts in Lochaber."

"No, Colonel, the Admiral is being too kind. I'm just another worker. I mostly provide coordination between the various organizations, including the Air Raid Precautions people, the Wardens, the Ground Observers, and the Explosive Ordinance parties. I also work with the Police and Fire Auxiliaries, as well as medical and social service agencies. I serve as a point of contact whenever one of our Lochaber organizations wants to do fund-raising to help our forces. Since the bombings began, I've been very busy with our community protection groups. If we're attacked, we now have staffs who will immediately take charge of our expanded medical services. Our hospital here is simply too small to handle mass casualties.

"We also have volunteers who will augment our sanitation workers, a search and rescue force, expanded utility services, people prepared for dependent care, an emergency feeding staff, and a refugee care organization. Our numbers are growing every day as the bombings continue, and they're receiving training regularly from specialists in each field. We've also started a committee to help war widows and those families whose husbands and fathers are off to war. This afternoon, I'll meet with a group of ladies who are collecting knitted goods and money for the Camerons' Comfort Fund. They send socks, gloves, cigarettes, and sweets to our lads in the forces. It's all quite wonderful what our people are doing for others."

"That's very impressive, m'Lady. I didn't know we'd so many groups taking control of so many civilian needs. The Admiral told me you've the title of Area Coordinator, so I suspect you're being too modest about your role. Did the Admiral explain why I wanted to meet you?"

"Yes, he said you're looking for a liaison person with the Civil Defense organizations to join your staff."

"Correct. Since you said you were just another worker, I wondered if you could recommend someone better qualified than you!"

Lady Frances smiled. "Touché, Colonel. Very well, I'd be happy to assist if you feel I can be of service."

"Thank you. Sometime soon, I'd like you to meet CB Foster, my Chief of Staff. In the meanwhile, I think the Admiral would be willing to explain more about our work here. Since the Admiral only works a few hours most days," he said smiling, "you should also spend some time with my assistant, Elaine Ross."

David continued to work through the noon hour while the Admiral and Lady Frances went out to lunch together. Elaine entered David's office with a cup of tea.

"She's beautiful, isn't she?"

"I really didn't notice," he lied. "Do you know her?"

"No, but I ha' seen her many times and Sir Robert also. They're quite involved in the community and participate in many activities."

"She certainly seems to be extensively involved in the war effort, especially with her husband in Egypt. How old do you think she is?"

"She's somewha' older than me, maybe in her late-thirties. She ha' three boys, but I donna' see them often for they go to public school."

Later that evening, after they'd bolted the office door for the day, David and Elaine quietly went upstairs to his flat. As Elaine removed her dress, she said, "Don't get any ideas of gettin' involved with Lady Frances."

"I would never get involved with the wife of a fellow soldier," he said.

She arched her brow. "Really? Then wha' about me?"

"That's different. Paul is Navy."

October 8

THE PAST FEW WEEKS CONTINUED THE feverish pace. The staff remained busy as the Home Guard, to their great satisfaction, received increased amounts of equipment. Several hundred Mills bombs, the No. 36 hand grenade developed during World War I, were delivered to units in the Northwest Sub-District. Special care was required for these dangerous weapons to ensure their safe delivery, storage, and careful use in training. Sadly, one soldier in the 1st Inverness Battalion was badly injured in a training accident, and several others were killed elsewhere in Britain. Bayonets also were beginning to arrive for the P-14 rifles.

A total of 20,000 automatic weapons, purchased from America, began to arrive. Some weapons would be issued to the regular forces and the remainder would arm the Home Guard, especially the mobile battle platoons. By the end of September, the 1st Sutherland Battalion alone boasted both surplus British Vickers medium machine guns and increasing numbers of Lewis light machine guns. Some Browning Automatic Rifles, the famous BAR, and even some Thompson submachine guns, the Tommy Gun, were also being issued. The Lochaber Company received several BARs and one Vickers machine gun.

In addition, each Home Guard company was to be issued several Boys anti-tank guns as soon as they were released from regular units. They were of limited utility, but significantly improved morale within the units. The Boys rifle had a one-half inch bore, technically a .55 inch caliber, too small to penetrate modern Panzers, but capable of disabling other types of vehicles. More significant was the eagerly anticipated arrival of the first Northover Projectors, an inexpensive, clumsy weapon that could launch anti-tank grenades a distance of 200 yards. It proved to be a useful weapon in Home Guard hands and required little training to fire accurately. CB Foster and Frank Leslie worked tirelessly to coordinate weapons deliveries, ammunition storage, and training on the weapons. Storage facilities were readily available in the larger cities and towns at Territorial Army training centers no longer occupied by mobilized TA units. Smaller villages and towns stored their weapons in private homes or other buildings.

The telephone rang as Elaine arrived to open the office. David came down the stairs and went into his office. "It's Brigadier Campbell for you, Sir."

"David, you and I will attend a conference a week from today with Lieutenant-General Carrington and Major-General Adams at Scottish Command Headquarters. They've asked all district and sub-district commanders to attend. Each commander is to prepare a report on all Home Guard and Civil Defense developments in our commands. Additionally, you should assess any civilian issues that could impact our work, and anything else you believe to be relevant. They specifically want us to evaluate our capabilities to repel parachutists, sea-borne raiders and a full invasion force. Each report should run no more than 15 minutes. You must have specific facts and figures to back up your analysis and you'll provide a one page written summary of your report. I expect they're going to London soon after and will present an overview of all this to the War Office."

"I understand, Sir. I'll start working on my report today."

"Excellent. Since the meeting will begin promptly at 10 a.m., plan to drive here Monday afternoon and stay with me. We can discuss your report that evening. In the morning, we'll take the first train to Edinburgh, together with Matthew Harris. Richard Sinclair will join us at the train station in Perth. I expect we'll be late returning, so plan to spend that night here as well."

David felt comfortable preparing the report, as he'd visited many of the villages and towns, met with the local governments and inspected the local Home Guard units.

October 15

WORKING WITH HIS STAFF, DAVID PUT the finishing remarks on his report to General Carrington. Elaine quickly prepared five copies using her Roneo machine. As he drove to Inverness, he turned his thoughts to his verbal presentation. It was a dull, overcast day, but he barely noticed.

Dinner with Jack was delightful, and they spent the evening discussing the war at length.

As they arrived at Waverley Station the next morning, Edinburgh didn't display its usual colorful beauty. The city seemed clothed in various tones of gray, matching the gloomy sky. A driver met the train and took them to Edinburgh Castle, the location of Scottish Command Headquarters. After enjoying a steaming cup of coffee, a rare treat at this stage of the war, they were ushered into a conference room. A large map of Scotland covered one wall, punctured with numerous pins denoting the various Army units. Several of Carrington's staff officers were already present, and the General soon entered the room, followed by Major-General Adams, the Brigadier General Staff, and other key staff officers. He greeted the thirteen attendees cordially and took his seat at the head of the table.

Carrington welcomed the group and gave a general overview of the war. Using classified information from the War Office, he discussed at length the on-going bombing campaign against Britain, and RAF activities to thwart the bombers.

"Since late September, the number of German bombers in our skies has diminished somewhat, with commensurate reductions in aircraft losses, both ours and theirs. In just a two-week period last month, we lost over 400 RAF fighters and a quarter of our pilots. Fortunately, the Jerries lost several times that number. They've suffered enormous losses during the past few months, and I suspect they're licking their wounds. This is good, as we need time to rebuild our fighter strength. But, they'll be back. The *Blitz* is far from over."

Carrington then discussed naval activities, the British, German, and Italian losses, and the massive naval construction program, which was beginning to launch large numbers of new ships. Turning to the Army, he analyzed German military deployments, their training and battle readiness, equipment levels, activities in the occupied countries, and finally the war in the Western Desert of Egypt. While he spoke, there was no other sound in the room and hardly any movement. The attendees were hungry for war information, very little of a highly classified nature getting to them for the past several months.

After pausing, Carrington announced: "Gentlemen, I'm pleased to tell you the War Office has determined that the threat of invasion has passed for this year. Autumn storms are beginning to cross the Atlantic, what with hurricane season in the Americas. The Channel is too turbulent for the safe passage of the low-freeboard invasion barges. This will be followed, as you know, by winter storms, which are fierce. Intelligence tells us the Germans have halted barge conversions for the time being, and the invading army is standing down from their high level of readiness. You might say they're moving into their 'winter quarters.' I think it's safe to say we've been given the gift of another six months to prepare for the invasion. With luck, we might have a comparatively quiet winter, except for U-boats and bombing raids.

"Let me make this very clear. September was Germany's best hope to invade Britain. We were nose to nose and Hitler blinked. Intelligence believes he postponed the invasion several times in September, right at the height of our 'Cromwell' alerts, and finally postponed any future invasion until spring. By that time, we'll be better prepared and we'll throw them back into the sea!" The announcement electrified the attendees. There were looks of relief as if the doomed had been granted salvation.

"However, that does not mean the Nazis will stop bombing our cities or that they can't stage a raid if they want to. Scotland must continue to be vigilant!"

Carrington continued with a *tour d'horizon,* a general discussion of key events around the world, with a heavy focus on Japan and the Pacific. He spoke about the Indian subcontinent and their enormous contribution to the war effort, which was beginning to bear fruit. After a brief discussion of the dominions and the colonies, Carrington announced that a full Canadian Army division had arrived in England and was positioned as an invasion counter-attack force southeast of London; a second Canadian division was preparing to cross the Atlantic to join the first. An incomplete Austral division of mostly Australian troops, with some New Zealanders, was stationed near Aldershot with the same mission.

All the dominions were feverishly raising forces, of which only the Canadians would continue to be stationed in Britain. The Australians and New Zealanders would leave Britain and join British forces in the Western Desert. Every colony was raising forces within their capabilities, and Carrington was pleased and somewhat surprised so many had enthusiastically joined the war effort. He completed his assessment with a long discussion of developments in America, and Britain's fervent hope that America would soon enter the war. He concluded with new developments in the British Army; 29 divisions and 49 separate brigades now guarding Britain. All were receiving new equipment as soon as it left the factories and were training intensely. Alongside the Regulars, there were over 1.5 million Home Guardsmen.

An hour and a half passed while he spoke. He paused while his batman, a corporal who served as a personal assistant, brought in fresh coffee and tea for everyone. "At this point, I would also serve you biscuits if we had any, but there's a war on, you know." Everyone grinned.

"What I suggest now is that we take a short break and then resume our discussion. Given the time before lunch— no, you'll not be served battle rations— I'd ask Brigadier Campbell and his commanders to make their presentations and answer our questions. After lunch, we'll resume with Brigadier Guthrie and his district, which I expect to take considerably longer, and then we'll have the other districts. I've read all of your monthly reports in detail, so tell us what we don't know."

The commanders reassembled after the break, and Jack led off with a brief overview of the North Highland District. He discussed the possible threats and plans to confront enemy forces. He reviewed local political developments and the expansion or new construction of munitions factories. Royal Navy and RAF activities took several more minutes. He discussed the frenetic shipping activities at Inverness and Aberdeen, with the almost daily arrival and departure of warships, troop transports, and merchantmen. Jack then reviewed the North Highland defenses and noted they were woefully short of harbour defense artillery. He asked Carrington when he could expect to receive the 24 18-pounder World War I howitzers he'd been promised. Carrington deferred to General Adams who said, "In about two weeks, Jack. Actually you'll get 26 guns, as that artillery regiment also has two spare guns. The new 25-pounders are coming into Scotland in good numbers now, and all regular units should have the new howitzers by winter's end."

Jack then introduced Colonel Richard Sinclair of the Aberdeen Sub-District. Though a gregarious talker in small groups, Sinclair was somewhat awkward before the generals, but he covered the main points. He noted his sub-district was enduring periodic attacks from German bombers and the threat of a seaborne invasion from raiders landed by submarine or parachute. Although he had one brigade of the 51st Division in his sub-district plus several home defense battalions, he felt those forces were insufficient to defend the coastline, even when augmented by the Home Guard. "I have adequate Home Guard forces because of the larger population in Aberdeen and I can quickly move a number of Mobile Battle Platoons to threatened areas if needed."

General Adams asked "With what transport?"

Sinclair responded, "In civilian trucks, city buses, and even motorcars if necessary. But, I need more regular forces." He concluded his talk by saying the bombing threat in his area was serious, since much of the population and the munitions factories were concentrated along the coast within easy striking distance of the *Luftwaffe*. "I really need more anti-aircraft and coastal defense artillery, and several brigades of troops."

General Adams snapped back impatiently. "Do you think we don't know that, Colonel Sinclair? Everyone needs more troops, but we have none to give you. Your mission is to defend as best you can with what you have, not with what you want!"

Matthew Harris followed Sinclair and discussed the Inverness Sub-District and the counties to the north of Inverness. He analyzed the threat and discussed his plans to move forces, as needed, to threatened areas whenever intelligence indicated German movements. He finished with a brief discussion of his modest regular and Home Guard forces.

David then rose and began his talk with a discussion of threats to the northwest sector, which he put in the priority of possibilities. "Although Fort William is near the maximum range of German bombers, the large aluminum plant north of the city is a tempting target and, as you know, has incurred three small raids already. There may be other targets that attract attention. Second, I think it's entirely possible a submarine may surface off one of our many coastal communities and shell the town with its deck guns. Submarines also will certainly try to sink our MacBrayne ferries crossing to the Western Isles and as many fishing boats as they can find. Merchant ships, and even the occasional warship that comes down the Minch or sails through the Western Islands, will provide tempting targets. Third, we're preparing for possible raids by parachutists or forces that might be landed from a submarine. We have few valuable targets, but our radar station is vulnerable, as are the various communications facilities. When the new radar station on the Isle of Lewis is completed, it also will become a tempting target. Beyond that I foresee little threat."

David continued with a general discussion of his Home Guard forces and how they were split between the large mobile battle platoons and the village defense forces. "I can tell you that the mobile battle platoons are all well-armed and, each week, are becoming increasingly proficient with their battle drills. We've sufficient privately-owned buses and lorries to move them on two-hour's notice or less."

General Adams asked about the weapons for the village defense units. David responded, "The town and village defense units are armed with some of everything that shoots, cuts, or blows up, including the

P-14 rifles. I've seen many old swords of every description, which previously had hung on the walls of people's homes. People have armed themselves with homemade bombs of various types and with very old firearms gathered from the walls of private homes, museums, and public buildings. The privately owned firearms include deer rifles and fowling pieces, but also old army rifles. I've seen the old Enfield Marks I and II from before the First War, Snyders, Lee-Medfords, Martini rifles, and even Brown Bess muskets from the Napoleonic Wars."

"Good Lord," Carrington interjected. "Are they safe to fire?"

"I gave a talk on Raasay some weeks ago, and many Home Guardsmen brought their weapons. One elderly gentleman sat in front of me holding a Brown Bess, this one converted from flintlock to cap and ball. During my talk, I made an off-hand remark about his use of that weapon against the Nazis. As we adjourned, he approached me and said, 'Colonel, would you come outside with me?' We walked twenty paces from the building and he said, 'See that bird?' Down by the wharf there was a large gull sitting on a post, easily over 100 yards away. The gentleman loaded his musket with a few quick movements, raised it, and fired. The bird disappeared in a cloud of feathers. I was speechless. He simply turned and looked at me. I started to clap my hands when the crowd joined in. I told him many soldiers would not hit a small target at that range with a modern rifle. General, I've seen many dozens of Brown Bess muskets during the past few months and I suspect they number in the hundreds in my command. They've been used regularly over the years and certainly appear safe to fire." He paused and added, "But hazardous to the Jerries!" Everyone laughed.

Adams said, "Tell us about your public meetings. I hear they're quite effective."

David spoke for several minutes, then summarized. "I give each community a three-part mission: (1) defend your village and assist others in their defense. (2) Be self-sufficient in all things. (3) Continue the war effort. It's simple and effective with the public. Each person knows where they fit into the war effort and what they must do if we're to prevail."

Carrington gestured one of his staff to write that down, then complemented David on his efforts and his presentation. "I never would have believed the remote communities in the Highlands could have been brought into the war effort so successfully. And to think we now have almost 7,000 men in your sub-district alone; organized, armed, and increasingly trained to fight. Well, it makes me very proud."

Carrington then asked Jack to summarize the entire North Highland District. Jack rose and spoke for a few minutes, contrasting the more-populated Aberdeen area and all its resources, with the sparse population of David's sub-district. He noted the substantial size of the Home Guard and the modest number of Regular Army units that had been activated in the Highlands. He noted the explosion of activity in the seaports; both the arrival and departure of convoys as well as the small ship building industry that was working around the clock. Munitions factories and smaller arms manufacturing facilities also were operating 24-hours per day. "My district has become a factory for the defense of the Empire and, yes, we certainly are a target for German attacks, mainly bombing raids. A few anti-aircraft defense sites are located in Aberdeen and Inverness, but I'm under no illusions that these will stop the German bombers, even with the best efforts of the RAF."

Carrington and Adams both asked questions, which Jack easily answered. They agreed there was little more that could be done with available resources to defend the North Highlands, but maybe more artillery and aircraft would be available in the future. Carrington looked at his watch and adjourned his meeting for lunch.

The afternoon session began soon after the brief lunch, and the reports from the other Districts were lengthy and followed along similar lines. Each district and sub-district commander facing the North Sea focused on the invasion threat as his first priority. They spoke about the on-going efforts to build concrete pillboxes on every potential landing beach, thousands being built along the entire eastern coastline, and the shortage of concrete. Like the North Highland District, weapons were a major concern, although the South Highland and Edinburgh Districts had a higher priority for weapons distribution. They noted the beginnings of training relationships between Regular and Home Guard forces, cooperation that would raise the standard of readiness of both forces. Each report brought questions from the generals, the staff officers present and, occasionally, from the other officers.

One recurring theme discussed by the Lowland sub-district commanders was the amount of anti-war activism in the urban areas, not from ordinary labourers, but from labour union activists and intellectuals.

"Fools!" snapped Carrington. "Can they not see we're being attacked? We're not the attackers!"

"Damned Communists," one of his staff muttered aloud. "They even collected a 'peace petition' of several thousand signatures in London and tried to present it to the Prime Minister. Mr. Churchill refused to accept it, thank God."

David and other sub-district commanders responded that they'd all dealt with anti-war comments, but the Highland area had experienced less activism than the urban areas, and anti-war speakers at public meetings were usually shouted down by other attendees. Invasion, smaller ground attacks, air raids, attacks from both submarine and surface raiders, fifth column activities, every possible threat to Scotland was addressed. It had been a very long afternoon when General Carrington finally brought the conference to a close. He thanked the attendees for their hard work and informative presentations.

"My staff informs me that I skipped one new development. This isn't yet official and I would like this kept among ourselves, but it appears we may soon begin to receive the standard army wool uniform for the Home Guard. Each volunteer will receive one uniform, plus a Mark I steel helmet, boots, a greatcoat, a haversack and web gear. I'm hopeful every Home Guardsman will be fully uniformed before Christmas. Details will follow from my staff, if we get approval. I'm confident our Home Guard units will soon be indistinguishable from regular units, although I can't tell you exactly when.

"As we have with the denim uniforms, the new wool uniforms, if they're approved by the War Office, will have the Home Guard insignia sewn across the upper left sleeve, an inch below the epaulette. Just below that will be the battalion designation, which will be the county designation, with the battalion number just below. For example, the 1st Battalion from Glasgow will have the letter G and the number 1 just below. The 2d Inverness-shire Battalion will have the letters INV and the number 2 just below. The 3rd City of Aberdeen Battalion will have the letters AB and the number 3, and so on.

"Also, the War Office is studying the use of a metal cap badge for each Home Guard Battalion, one which will reflect the Regular regiment for that county. If authorized, for example, Glasgow battalions would use the Highland Light Infantry badge. I knew you'd like that, Jack." Jack Campbell smiled approvingly. "The Stirling-shire battalions would use the insignia of the Argyll & Sutherland Highlanders, and so on. Each unit will use its own funds to purchase these insignia from a local metal fabrication shop in your district. I think our Home Guardsmen have earned the right to be regarded as soldiers, although they must continue to be called 'volunteers.'"

Colonel Harris asked "Military ranks, General?"

Carrington responded, "The War Office is reviewing the issue of replacing the foolish Home Guard rank system with actual military ranks. There's still plenty of opposition to this in London, but my Home Guard Liaison Officer, Sir John Colville, says Parliament may force this on the War Office. It's my understanding Home Guard officers may soon be granted a King's Commission, just like regular officers.

"Oh, yes," Carrington continued. "Effective very soon, the Home Guard will begin saluting its officers."

After the conference adjourned, staff cars took Jack, David, and the other attendees to Waverley Station. They said little, being lost in their thoughts from the meeting. David spent the night again with Jack before driving back to Fort William.

Elaine saw him walking up the street and met him at the door. "How wa' the meetin'?"

"Fine. The report was very well received, and I owe you dinner at a restaurant tonight for all your hard work helping me to prepare for the conference."

"Thank you, but I'd rather go to the restaurant another time. I brought some soup for supper and I ha' other plans for us afterwards." She brought the soup from the stove where it was warming and fixed bread. They ate in silence for some time until Elaine asked if something was wrong. "You ha' hardly said a word tonight."

David searched for words. "Elaine, you know how I feel about you and I think I know how you feel about me." There was another awkward pause. "I've been thinking about this for a long time and I need to tell you, or I need to ask you. I know this isn't the right time or place for this, but . . . " He stopped.

"Wha' is it?"

"I want to marry you," he blurted out. "Of course, that is if you will marry me."

Elaine paused, a surprised look on her face. "David, I would be honored to be your wife."

"May I take that as a 'yes'?" he said eagerly.

"Maybe, yes. I donna' know. This is all so sudden. I love you and I would love to be your wife, but . . . I'm married."

"You don't love him and you can divorce him. Then we can be married and be happy together forever."

"I donna' know," she repeated, "'tis all so complicated. I need to think about it. Please believe me when I say I want to be with you, but

I want to do wha's right for everyone. Let's no' speak about this now."
She bolted the door, took his hand, and led him up the stairs.

Two hours later, after dressing, Elaine gave him a long goodnight kiss. He was convinced their marriage would happen in a few short months.

12

October 21, 1940

THE AIR WAS CRISP and the morning sky a deepening blue as David drove northwest from Inverness to Ullapool. He met with Colonel Matthew Harris in Inverness and was his guest overnight. They had an early supper with Regimental Sergeant-Major Trevor McNabb, nominated by Brigadier Campbell to take charge of artillery training on David's staff. The twelve 18-pounder howitzers would arrive soon in David's sector, and he needed an experienced gunner to train the gun crews. Fortunately, the Home Guard battalion commanders had identified First War artillery veterans who could serve with each gun crew. Younger men would round out the crews. The veteran gunners needed refresher training, especially with the fire direction system. This would be essential if they were to hit their targets quickly. All would require many days of training as a team to become fully proficient with the weapons.

McNabb was a large man with a protruding stomach, the result of too many years of service in training depots supplied with ample food and drink. Heeding Brigadier Campbell's admonition, David focused on McNabb's drinking problem early in the conversation. "I cannot have a member of my staff who becomes intoxicated. If this ever happens, that individual will be promptly arrested and returned to Brigadier Campbell for disciplinary action. At your age, Sergeant-Major, that would result in dismissal from the Army."

"Oh, yes, Sir. I mean no Sir, no, tha' will no' happen, no' ever," he blurted out. "I've learnt my lesson and I limit my drink to no' ower two or three pints a day, I havna' ha' more. Ye can ask Colonel Harris."

Matthew Harris smiled. "I can report that neither I nor any of my staff have seen the Sergeant Major drunk since he arrived last month. I think his meeting with Brigadier Campbell has helped him understand how much the Army needs him to train our soldiers and how much Scotland is depending upon him."

Harris continued, "I've spoken with the Sergeant-Major about working also for my sub-district after he finishes training your gunners. Brigadier Campbell suggested we could share the Sergeant-Major's talents. If he does his work in a professional manner to our satisfaction, there's the possibility of promotion to the rank of Warrant Officer Class I. Perhaps he could serve as an inspector of artillery for our Home Guard forces and then retire after the war with a suitable decoration and pension. I'm confident the Sergeant-Major understands how generous Brigadier Campbell is in giving him a chance to redeem his career."

"Yes, Sir, verra' generous indeed, yes he is. I willna' let him down." His bushy mustache jumped with every word, and David saw that Jack Campbell had put the fear of God in McNabb. He'd been a fine soldier in his prime and his skills were greatly needed, despite his physical deterioration from age, food, and drink.

Driving northwest past Loch Glascarnoch the next morning, David soon made his first stop at Lochdrum, one of several small villages in the Braemore Forest. The Braemore was actually a series of small forests of various names that were actively managed by the timber industry. He would make several such stops on his way to Ullapool, where he would spend the night. The people of Lochdrum turned out their small section of Home Guard soldiers, standing proudly with their P-14 rifles, newly-arrived from America.

"A few men missin', Colonel, off deep in the forest cuttin' trees for the war effort."

"That's fine, Sergeant, I'm sure they'll return if the Jerries invade."

David conducted a brief inspection of the troops and said a few words of encouragement to the small group of people who'd gathered to meet him. He continued his drive along the dirt road, passing through the long, narrow valley, with towering hills on either side. He stopped again for similar visits at the villages of Inverlael and Leckmelm, along the shore of Loch Broome. The populations of the villages were sparse, but the communities contributed a good platoon of almost forty men to the Home Guard. By the time he reached Ullapool, the sky was darkening. At the Argyll Hotel, the manager greeted him warmly for his second visit.

"When Mrs. Ross called for a room, I thought we might have another meeting with the town folk. She said you were just passing through for one night and planned no special meetings here."

"Correct. I'm heading north for more visits." That evening David ate dinner as usual in the Argyll's small restaurant. He squeezed alongside a group of Scottish Savings Committee members who were celebrating a successful campaign to sell Defense Bonds and Savings Certificates to help fund the war effort. Ullapool was primarily a fishing port, but one which had suffered from over-fishing in the pre-war years. The outbreak of war, however, had reduced competition from North European fishing fleets, located in occupied countries, and Scottish fishermen were now bringing in larger catches of fish. Some of the profits went into the Defense Bonds.

The next morning, David briefly stopped at Drumrunte, Ledmore, and Inchnadamph, villages that were too far from Ullapool for villagers to attend the previous meetings. Each village had a Home Guard section commanded by a sergeant. Some soldiers in each section were located in outlying hamlets or farms, making management a challenge for the section sergeants. Nevertheless, the soldiers looked presentable and were confident that they'd give any invader a good fight. After a brief lunch near the Ardvrech Castle ruins, a 15th Century home of the McCleods set on the shore of Loch Assynt, he conducted two more brief stops at Newton and Kylstrome, before arriving at his destination.

The town of Scourie was nestled in a valley and sat just behind a small beach area bordered on either end by rising hills. These formed an arc around the valley. The hill at the south end of the beach held a cluster of cottages aptly called Minchview. As David drove past Minchview, down the long hill into the village, he was struck by the pastoral beauty of the golden fields, with Highland cows grazing near the road and standing guard against intruders. The road split the town, with a small cluster of nicer homes seaward and more modest cottages lining a small road to the east.

Almost a thousand people lived in the town and the surrounding villages and farms. David planned a joint meeting with the town council and representatives from each nearby village. Council members were quite nervous at the prospect of a German attack on the town and its small fishing fleet, much of which operated out of the fishing harbour of Kinlochbervie, twenty miles to the north. David calmed them with an assessment of the reduced threat during the coming winter.

After a supper at the home of a councilman who was the proprietor of several fishing boats, David spoke to a public gathering at the church. Questions echoed those asked in the council meeting. The public meeting lasted almost two hours, and David was tired when it ended. After shaking many hands, the pastor approached him.

"We're a small village with a hotel filled with transient workers, so I told your Mrs. Ross that we'd find a suitable room for you. Mrs. Lewis has generously offered to host you tonight, a home where we sometimes place visitors." He introduced David to Mrs. Catherine Lewis. "Catherine is our District Nurse. She keeps us healthy," he smiled.

"I share me cottage wi' both visitors and occasional sick children from the village who need watchin' durin' the night," she told David as they walked to her home. "I ha' me own private bedroom which Tom and I added to our cottage several years ago. He wa' handy with tools from his years as a fisherman."

"I didn't see Tom at our meeting tonight. Is he at sea with the fishing fleet, Mrs. Lewis?"

"No," she said quietly. "Tom wa' kilt five years ago. There wa' a storm which swept across the North Atlantic, batterin' the fishin' fleets and scatterin' the boats. All the captains looked for him the next mornin', some for several days, but his boat wa' never found. By the way, ye may call me Catherine. Catherine with a 'c'."

"Like the Empress of Russia," he responded with a smile. "I'm sorry about your husband."

"Thank ye. I guess I'm ower the loss, if one ever gets ower losin' a husband or wife."

They arrived at Catherine's cottage after a short walk. A fire was burning in her stove to ward off the cold of autumn. She lit a lamp, and the soft light revealed a bed against the wall beyond the small dining table and a door that led to her bedroom. "The loo's ower there," she gestured, "mind ye duck when ye enter. The cottage is at least one hun'red year's auld, probably more, and people were shorter then. I'm sorra' the bed is so wee, but 'tis all I ha'. Most overnighters are children, so it doesna' matter to them. It's larger than wha' many ha' at home."

"The bed is fine, Catherine. Thank you for letting me borrow it. I hope Elaine mentioned I plan to stay here tomorrow night when I return from Durness."

"Aye, tha' will be fine." Catherine brought out her tea box and two mugs. "'Tis a cold night, Colonel, wouldna' ye like some medicine in the tea?"

"Medicine?"

"Remember, I'm the District Nurse and I ha' some pure alcohol for me work. Sometimes a wee bit finds its way into me teacup. I also ha' a supply of Scotland's finest, well maybe not the verra' finest, but some pretty decent whisky."

"The whisky will be fine, thank you. How did you come to be the District Nurse way up here?"

"Wait, yer motorcar. Maybe ye should park it out front and bring in yer bag." David walked back and returned five minutes later with his motorcar. He put his bag beside the bed and Catherine passed him a cup, gesturing him to a chair. David found the tea to be warm and soothing and he started to relax. "Where do you park your car, Catherine?"

"I ha' no car. I walk everra where in the village and nearby. When I get a call from another village across the sea loch or south to Badcall, one of the men will take me there by boat or car. Sometimes I mun call a neighbor and catch a ride if the patient is some distance, but normally I walk. It keeps me healthy." David noted that Catherine was quite attractive and trim. She wore her straw-colored hair pulled up and clasped in the back with a barrette, like a younger woman. She maintained a youthful complexion that highlighted her bright blue eyes.

David looked around. "I don't see a telephone here. How do you get calls?"

"People come and fetch me. If the patient is up on Minchview or across the sea loch, someone rings a bell; actually they bang on a long pipe hung from a tree. It makes enough noise to wake the dead or at least to wake someone here in the village, and they come fetch me. Scourie folk are verra' kind to each other and they want to help when someone is hurt or sick."

"You mustn't get much sleep."

"Actually, I do quite well. I'm no' called out verra' often at night. I stay busy at school part of everra' day and work here as well with town folk who are ill or hurt. I help young mothers who are expectin' and I check the new babies several times after they are bairn." As David looked around he saw several wall shelves filled with medicines and other supplies. A cupboard on the floor nearby was full of medical equipment.

"You seem to be better equipped than most nurses' offices I've seen."

"Ha' to be. I'm all there is for some miles around. We ha' a doctor here some years back. When I was a schoolgirl here before the First War, Dr. Howard ha' served this region for decades. He was gettin' on in years and wanted help with his practice. I ha' visited him many times because me Mum and Mrs. Howard were good friends. He said later that he saw somethin' in me and asked me to help out in his office. I even went out on some calls with him, especially if he was deliverin' a baby and needed an extra set of hands. When I finished school, he asked me if I would go to Glasgow to become a nurse. I said 'nae,' as I was verra' 'fraid of leavin' me family. But he ha' spoken with me parents already, and they encouraged me to go and try to make somethin' of meself.

"Dr. Howard arranged for me to live and study at the Royal Infirmary. He paid the fees and I worked when we werna' studyin' to earn me keep. I wa' lonely at first and missed me family and friends terrible. After a few days, I decided to quit and come home, but I ha' no money for train and bus fares. I thought I'd work extra for a month and save me shillings for the trip home. The war was bringin' us patients each week, and I really felt needed. After another month, the loneliness ha' passed and I ha' made friends with other student nurses, so I decided to stay after all. I wa' there three years." She took a long drink of her tea.

"Tom wa' a schoolmate here in Scourie," she continued. "His Dad was a fisherman like mine, and Tom just naturally followed the sea. We spent time together most days 'til I went to Glasgow. I missed him terrible as well, and he managed to come down twa visits each year. The last time was in the middle of the war just before I finished me studies. Well, I sorta' got a little pregnant on that visit, and we married just after I came home." Catherine giggled, gave a mischievous grin, and got up to pour more medicine into each mug.

"I went to work for Dr. Howard straight away and took only a few weeks off at Christmas when Sam was born. He paid me for the work, and we stayed pretty busy, as the war had taken many physicians into the forces. We were servin' a much larger area and some doctors ne'er came back. Tom and I saved our money and we bought an old crofter cottage on the edge of town. Julie was born later tha' year. Arthur and William were born two and three years later. Dr. Howard taught me everythin' I hadna' learned at the Royal Infirmary, and I became a verra' experienced and confident nurse.

"In 1927, Dr. Howard said he wanted me to get further trainin' to become a District Nurse. I said 'nae,' as I couldna' leave me family and the bairns. He then explained that his heart was failin' and he didna' think Scourie would get another doctor when he died. I cried all night and, when Tom's boat came in, I told him what Dr. Howard had said. Tom said I mun go to Glasgow for the course, just a few months long, and he would mind the children with our Mums' help. So, off I went again."

"So, Dr. Howard died and you became his replacement as a District Nurse."

"Yes, in early 1929. It was verra' sad. He wa' like a second father. Me Dad had died and mother was doin' poorly. Mrs. Howard was getting quite old and wa' in failin' health. She offered me Dr. Howard's medical equipment for free. He ha' wanted it that way, if we would buy her home so she could move to Oban to be with her son. The Depression ha' started and money wa' scarce, but Tom said 'aye,' we would find the money somehow. We paid her each month for twa years 'til she died, then this home was ours. It ha' room to do me work, but we needed a proper bedroom and a room for our growin' bairns. So we added space and made repairs. Tom enjoyed workin' with tools, and the men in our families helped. Those were good times."

"Where are the children now?"

"Sam's in the Navy at Leith. Arthur and William are both in the Army. Julie lives here in Scourie with her family. She married a fisherman, too."

They talked well into the night, and David was happy to fall into bed.

October 24

AN EARLY MORNING BREEZE blew briskly off the sea as David drove north on the one-lane dirt road to Durness. "It's bigger than a cow path, but not by much," he thought. As he left Scourie, he drove through a narrow pass between two rocky hillocks. He saw that the Home Guard had already prepared firing positions near the pass, secured by rocks and sandbags. The war had created a shortage of African jute, and sandbags were distributed sparingly to the Home Guard. The trip took well over an hour to drive the thirty miles, plus he needed time for brief visits with the Home Guard sections at Laxford Bridge and Kinlochbervie.

As David approached the small village of Durness, tall stonewalls lined the narrow road. Passing over the brow of a hill, the ocean opened in front of him; the stretch of ocean water along northern Scotland to the west of the Orkney Islands and the Pentland Firth. As the village came into view, he saw several dozen men with rifles forming in a field near the church. It was almost 10 a.m., the designated time to meet Lieutenant Duncan Parker, a local schoolteacher, who also commanded the 1st Sutherland Battalion's Durness Platoon. Parker saluted as David drove up.

"Sir, the Duke of Sutherland sends his compliments and apologizes that he cannot join you during your inspection today. Major Priestley also is unavailable, but he looks forward to meeting you soon." The Duke commanded the 1st Sutherland Battalion and served as Lord Lieutenant of Sutherland. Major Priestley commanded the Home Guard Company that included the Durness Platoon.

"All four sections of my platoon are represented today, including men from the villages of Bettyhill and Tongue. Some men are not available due to work."

"How many men are assigned to your platoon, Lieutenant?"

"Fifty-six at this time, with thirty-eight present. I also have some older men who are beyond enlistment age. I have unofficially assigned them to village defense in Durness and the other villages."

David noticed a bustle of activity a half mile to the west, but the dominant sight was a series of massive towers looming over the bay almost a mile to the east. "The radar site at Sango Bay," he thought. "Lieutenant, if Sango Bay was attacked, how many men could you muster within thirty minutes?"

The lieutenant thought for a moment. "Probably 25 or more. Maybe, 35 to 40 within an hour. I expect it would take two to three hours to assemble the entire platoon here in Durness."

"Have you met with the radar station commander or some of his officers?"

"Oh, yes Sir, many times. They're from the Royal Air Force, not the Army. The RAF operates the entire Chain Home Radar network, part of the system called the Air Defense of Great Britain. We often have lunch or dinner together, very decent chaps, you know, but not very happy being stationed way up here. The base commander is from Chester, Wing Commander Ralph Morton; and Squadron Leader William Connor, his deputy, is from Yorkshire. Commander Morton should be here shortly."

"Let's inspect your platoon, Lieutenant. You can then release the men and we'll visit the radar station facilities with Commander Morton, Cape Wrath first."

The main radar site at Sango Bay sat high on a bluff less than a mile east of Durness village, near the area known as Leirinbeg. Its looming towers and numerous underground installations were still under construction, but the radar was operational. A half-mile west of Durness was the main RAF support base of Balnakiel, sitting two hundred yards from the ocean. Balnakiel was a series of cinder block buildings nearing completion that could house 125 to 150 men. The Balnakiel House, a fine estate home owned by the Duke of Sutherland, sat near the beach at the western corner of the Faraid Head peninsula. The peninsula itself projected north, some two-and a-half miles into the ocean and hosted a small signal station at its tip. Fifteen miles to the west at the northwestern tip of Cape Wrath was the lighthouse and a radio relay station.

The inspection went well, and David found the same enthusiasm that he'd seen elsewhere. The lieutenant proudly showed David the Lewis machine gun and the Boys anti-tank rifle, both of which had recently arrived. "We've very little ammunition for the Boys rifle, Colonel, so my men have not yet test-fired it. Major Priestley says it will probably be January before we get any more, so we'll keep the ammo we have until then, in case of attack."

"Lieutenant, this is the first Boys rifle I've seen with the Home Guard. We don't have any yet in Fort William. I guess the Duke has successfully secured some from an unknown source."

Parker grinned and remained silent. Wing Commander Ralph Morton arrived and saluted David, his RAF rank being one rank below an Army colonel. Morton was not under David's command, nor was any part of the RAF installation, but came under his operational control for defense in the event of attack.

Parker drove David and Wing Commander Morton the half-mile to the Faraid Head wooden jetty. There, they boarded a small motor launch, which took them a dozen miles west to the Navy Jetty on Cape Wrath, so named for the tiny supply boat that would periodically land provisions for the lighthouse. Cape Wrath's northern coast had risen from the ocean eons ago and now stood 200-350 feet above the water, presenting an impassible obstacle to a military assault; the Navy Jetty was the only accessible spot for miles around. There, they boarded an old rough-country vehicle for the remaining three-mile journey to the lighthouse, along a road that was little better than a cow path.

Arriving at the lighthouse, perched near the edge of the bluff overlooking the sea, David was surprised at the roar of surf as it pounded on the rocks below. "You should be here in a storm, Colonel; it sounds like the very earth itself is breaking apart." Across from the lighthouse was the radio relay station operated primarily by civilians, with a recent augmentation from the RAF. A total of 25 men operated the two sites, a few living permanently on Cape Wrath and others being temporarily assigned. After speaking with the RAF site commander, Flight Lieutenant Ken Paterson, and being shown the facility, they returned to Durness in time to speak at the public meeting. Over one hundred attended, and David answered the usual questions he'd been asked in almost every town.

After a brief lunch, David inspected the support base at Balnakeil, and then walked out Faraid Head peninsula to the small signal site. Station commander, Lieutenant Matheson, reported that he had 15 men at his site that were armed with Enfield rifles, a Bren Gun and a Boys rifle, the same as at Cape Wrath.

Commander Morton then suggested they visit the actual Radar Station. The Sango Bay Station was an imposing facility perched atop the Leirinbeg headlands, overlooking the ocean a hundred feet below. The headlands extended out into the ocean to the west of Loch Eriboll, with steep walls on either side dropping to the water. Slicing through the middle of the Headlands was the entrance to the famous Smoo Cave, a natural rock formation that had delighted visitors for centuries. Further west was the beginning of a sand beach that stretched several hundred yards in a gentle arc past Durness to the base of Faraid Head. To the north, interrupted only by the Shetland and Faeroe Island groups, lay empty ocean as far as the North Pole.

Tightly secured against outsiders by barbed wire and guards, the radar site contained eight large towers, four of which were 360 feet tall, with wires crossing between them. "Those are the towers for the Type 7000 high altitude radar, Colonel," said Morton. "The wires send out an electrical pulse across a wide arc. If anything is out there, the pulse bounces off and comes back to the receiver, the shorter towers over there. From that signal, a skilled operator usually can determine the height, direction, and number of aircraft approaching. The smaller towers hold the wires that receive the radar pulses. That circulating iron dish-like apparatus serves as the low-altitude radar.

"I must tell you, Sir, this is all most secret. We have some of the latest technology here."

"If you were attacked by land or sea, Commander, how many armed men could you release from their regular duties?"

Morton thought for a minute. "We could release 100 men at all four locations, Colonel, and maybe a few more, if we reduce our radar activities a bit. However, we still must keep the radar operational at all times."

"Do you have weapons and a defense plan in the event of attack?"

"All my men have rifles or pistols and plenty of ammunition. I have six Boys rifles and eight Lewis machine guns. My plan is to have the men lie down along the fence line and fire on any intruders."

David shook his head. "That won't do, Commander. You would be quickly overrun and your men killed or captured. Let's walk the headwall outside the fence." The four men walked for almost an hour, David stopping regularly to assess possible threats and identify safe fighting positions with commanding views of the ocean. The Headland rose steeply almost one hundred feet above the ocean, itself a good barrier to assault, but not perfect. Persistent attackers could scale the heights. Just to the west of the headland, the sand beach provided an easy landing area, despite several obstacles. The Germans still would have to scale the even steeper headland wall near the Smoo Cave. Raiders, however, could land on the sand beach, make a shorter climb up to the road, and attack the radar site from its west flank. This sector would require 20 or more defenders to block such an attack.

To the eastern front, the headland was breached by a semi-circular gap almost 50 yards in circumference, sitting above a steep ascent some 60 feet above the beach. It encompassed a fairly flat area, behind which a sharp rise of another 50 feet led to the top of the headland.

The best protection of all was out in the bay: rocks and sandbars. A U-boat must avoid the rocks, and then carefully navigate through the ever-shifting sandbars or risk running aground. "Not easy, but not impossible," David thought. "It could be done." David ordered Lieutenant Duncan to work with Wing Commander Morton to develop a better defense plan with the help of Lord Sutherland's staff.

"I will ask Colonel Harris in Inverness to assist you in every way. This must be your top priority and it must be completed soon."

As they continued the inspection, a corporal whispered to the Lieutenant, "Sir, Mrs. McPherson is here to see you." Lieutenant Parker explained that Emma Gordon McPherson was a widow in her seventies with quite an eccentric personality. She lived some 500 yards from the radar site in a small, weather worn crofter's cottage, some 30 feet from the edge of the bluff.

Mrs. McPherson was waiting outside the gate of the radar site. When she saw David, she approached him and said, "I'll ha' ye know tha' I am descended from royalty, Captain."

David executed a deep stage bow, removing his hat. "I'm deeply honored to meet you, Lady Emma."

Emma squealed with delight. "I like ye, Captain!"

"Actually, I'm a Colonel."

As they walked to her cottage, she told David about her marriage to Fred McPherson in 1888, their life as crofters, raising both sheep and children. "My son Robert lives in Durness and is a great help. He brings me groceries every week and a bottle, too. He also helps with any chores I canna' do 'Course I might buy another bottle or twa everra now and then," she chuckled. "Susan lives with her family in Bettyhill, and Thomas lives in Ullapool. Those are the only bairns tha' survived. I ha' eight, ye ken."

"So, you live here alone?"

"Wouldna' ha' it another way. After Fred died in '33, I took ower all the work which I ha' been most doin' anyway, as Fred was failin' toward the end. I ha' a garden, a goat, and seven sheep. Robert brings the groceries when he comes ower, usually on Sundays. I ha' everathin' I need. I even ha' a rifle ower here." She produced an old Martini rifle from Zulu War days. "An' I ha' bullets. I donna' sleep well at night, so I come out here on the porch wi' a bottle and me rifle and I listen to the sea." David looked at the rickety porch roof and a well-worn chair stuffed with a badly stained pillow.

"I guess your life is complete."

"Darned right. The RAF said I mun move when they built the radar station, but I said no amount of money'll get me out of me home. I'd ha' to be kilt first."

As David and Parker walked back to his car, Parker said, "She threatened to shoot the RAF fellows. I've known Emma McPherson all my life and convinced the RAF that she would do no harm, being eccentric and all that, but she could be a 'guard dog' for the radar site. They agreed it wasn't worth a fight, so here she is, still." He shrugged his shoulders.

As they drove the short distance back to Durness village and David's car, Parker asked, "Would it be possible for you to come up and watch our anti-invasion exercise on November 23? It's a Saturday and we'll have everyone participating. Our new defense plan will also be completed, subject to your approval of course. A few of the radar site chaps will play the role of the German attackers, and my platoon will repel them, or we hope they will. The Duke himself will be here."

"I think that's an excellent idea," David responded. "That's precisely the type of training the Home Guard needs, and I'll review your new defense plan at that time. I'll ask Mrs. Ross to put that exercise on my calendar."

The afternoon shadows were lengthening and David returned to Scourie for a second night as Catherine's guest.

"We've fish for supper, David. Some of the boats came in this afternoon, and Charlie Suter, one of Tom's friends, brought me a halibut."

David removed his Army jacket and shoes, breathing in the smell of cooking fish. "How's the medicine supply?"

13

October 25, 1940

AN EARLY MORNING STORM whipped the waves in Scourie Bay as David drove the few miles north to Laxford Bridge, then southeast on a small dirt road through the middle of the Highlands and the Reay Forest. The road took him along the shorelines of Loch Stack, Loch More, and Loch Merklin before opening up to reveal the beautiful valley and waters of Loch Shin. Along the way, David stopped at several more villages, those of Achfary, Kinloch, Corrykinloch, and Arscaig. At each village he spoke with village authorities, the Home Guard section sergeant, and those from nearby hamlets who wanted to meet the Colonel from the Black Watch.

Located many miles from the coast, these small, remote hamlets had been largely ignored by defense planners, and David wanted them to know they were important. The villagers throughout the area, including the Braemore and Reay Forests, had conspired to create a small mobile Home Guard platoon, some thirty men who, when faced with invasion, would board lorries and drive to any threatened site in the Highlands. These were the younger men who worked mainly as lumberjacks in the various forests and were among the strongest men in Scotland. "Not a large force," he mused, "but even small groups of determined men have turned the tide of battles throughout the centuries." As he spoke to each group, he wanted them to know their efforts were important and appreciated by senior commanders all the way to London, perhaps something of an exaggeration.

The sun was slowly setting behind him as David drove out of the valley past Lairg, then south through Bonar Bridge and Alness to Dingwall. David bypassed Inverness and drove west along Loch Ness, arriving at Fort William just before midnight. The office was dark, so he climbed the stairs and fell into his bed.

DAVID AWOKE TO A LIGHT TAPPING at his door. He opened it to find Elaine holding her small basket. "Hi," she said softly, "I brought us some breakfast."

It was mid-morning when David awoke again and found Elaine sleeping beside him. The tea sat cold in the cups and the biscuits were untouched. As Elaine awoke, David realized this was the first time they'd actually been asleep together, the first time he'd actually slept with anyone since Anne died. He felt a sense of remorse, and sadness clouded his face.

"Wha's the matter?" she asked.

"Nothing."

"No, its no' nothin'. Somethin' is botherin' you. Is it me?"

"Good Lord, no. You make me happy. You are the best thing in my life right now." He leaned over and kissed her.

"Then what? 'Tis your work here?"

"No."

They were silent for a few minutes before she asked, "Are you feeling guilty about us?"

David quickly looked at her, and then looked away.

"It's about us, isn't it, David?"

"I don't know. I love you so much and I love being with you, especially this." He gestured toward the rest of the bed.

"I love you and I love 'this' also. But we aren't married and you carry Anne in your heart. I understand that, but she died and we're alive." She paused, searching for words. "Life goes on, David. You ha' nothin' to feel guilty about. Anne ha' cancer and she could fight it no more. You couldna' stop it, nobody can. It just happens." Tears began to well up in David's eyes. Elaine held him. "You did your best, but it wasna' in your hands. You shouldna' feel guilty."

"I am guilty," he blurted out. "I was drunk, I drove too fast, I ran through an intersection, and we were almost killed. Some days I wish we had been killed! It would have been less painful for Anne. She suffered from her injuries that I caused, and then she suffered a painful, lingering death from the cancer. The fault is mine!"

His body began to shake with muffled sobs and he put his head down into his hands. "I'm so sorry, Anne, I'm so sorry." His crying didn't stop for a long time. Elaine tried to comfort him, but to no avail. His tears were unstoppable. Eighteen months of pain burst outward and his agony spilled forth.

"Do you know what happened in the hospital after the accident?"

he asked. His voice trembled between sobs. "The next morning she struggled out of her hospital bed, slipped past the nurse and went looking for me. She came into my room to see me because she needed to know that I was okay. She had bandages around her head and she was limping badly. She was in terrible pain, but she came looking for me!" David broke into sobs again. "I caused the accident, but all she cared about was that I was okay." After a time be began to calm down and slowly sat back to look at Elaine.

"I'm sorry; I hadn't meant to do that." She started to speak, but he interrupted. "I did it, Elaine. I'm responsible. Nothing can change that. I also smashed my hip and ruined my career." More tears streamed down his face. "That, too, was my fault. What was I thinking?"

Elaine sat quietly holding him for several minutes. "So, you've been carryin' this pain inside you ever since, your dreadful feeling of guilt. You were drunk, you ha' an accident and maybe tha' was your fault. But you didna' cause the cancer and you couldna' keep her alive. You're a good man, a good father and I bet you were a verra' good husband."

"I'm not a good father. I haven't seen my girls in months."

"Another guilt, but that also isna' your fault." Her voice began to rise and she grasped his shoulders. "It isna' your fault that Hitler started this damned war, it isna' your fault that France collapsed and it isna' your fault that the Nazi Army is just across the Channel waiting to invade! And you certainly canna' carry all this guilt bottled up inside you. It's wearin' you down and it's no' healthy." Elaine took a breath. She'd almost been yelling. "You are here because you are needed here. You were ordered here because the War Office needed someone with your talents and experiences, and you were the perfect candidate."

"I was the only candidate," he said dourly.

"They could ha' found others, but they stopped lookin' when they found you. They were right. You are indeed the perfect candidate. And you're a good father. You love your daughters, you write to them almost everra' day, you ha' given them a safe home with your family while you are here. Wha' is wrong with tha'? Wha' are your expectations for yourself? To be perfect in all things! Tha's no' realistic. Yes, you smashed your hip. I'm so sorry tha' ruined your career. I would love to see you as a general, but wha's wrong with bein' a colonel, especially one whom people admire and your fellow soldiers respect? Canna' you find some peace tha' you ha' served the King admirably and you wear the decorations to prove it? You are bein' too hard on yourself and you torture yourself whenever you think about it."

David sighed and lay back down. Maybe the pain would subside, but it wouldn't disappear. Elaine lay beside him, nestled against his shoulder. They lay quietly for a very long time until Elaine finally spoke softly.

"Breakfast." She thought for a moment. "Or would you prefer something else?"

November 12

THE WAR CONTINUED UNCHECKED, as had the German bombing raids over Britain. On October 28, Italy invaded Greece, similar to its invasion of Southeast France in June, just four days before France surrendered to Germany. Mussolini wanted to share in the plunder of France and Britain. He was convinced of the impending defeat of Britain and couldn't leave the spoils to the Nazis; Italy declared war on both countries. President Roosevelt called Italy's invasion of France "a stab in the back of its neighbor." Now, however, tiny Greece fought back fiercely and its army pushed the Italian forces back to the Adriatic Sea, foreshadowing further Italian defeats in North Africa.

The American Presidential Election was held on November 5th and President Roosevelt won an unprecedented third term, defeating Republican challenger Wendell Wilkie. Churchill was greatly relieved. His relationship with America, vital to Britain's survival, would remain strong.

As if in response to Roosevelt's victory, the *Luftwaffe* staged another small air raid on the aluminum plant at Lochaber during the evening of November 5. By this time, Lord Beaverbrook had convinced the War Cabinet in London of the seriousness of the threat to the plant and its valuable contribution to the war effort. He ringed the smelter with anti-aircraft guns. Bofors 40 millimeter guns now supplemented the small machine guns, and several large 3-inch guns were located nearby. The Hispano Suiza 20 millimeter gun at the Kinlochleven smelter to the south also had been reinforced with additional guns. The German pilot evidently had mistaken a bonfire started by soldiers standing guard some distance away for his target and dropped a bomb near the fire. There were no casualties and no damage was done to the smelter.

David returned from a six-day trip, visiting many villages and towns on the four large peninsulas west of Ullapool, and then took a Navy launch to Stornoway for a four-day visit to the Western Isles. Returning home in mid-afternoon, he was greeted by the Admiral, who asked "Have you heard the news? The Navy has sunk the Italian fleet at Taranto!" Taranto was the main naval station on the base of the Italian peninsula, the "heel of the boot."

"Sunk them all?"

"Well, they sank or damaged several battleships and other ships. We launched the attack from an aircraft carrier, I suspect the HMS *Invincible.* The Italian Navy won't dare attack our fleet again," he said confidently.

"That's good news, Admiral, let's have dinner, and celebrate. Elaine, would you mind watching the office until I return?" She nodded. Although not yet 4 p.m., David was famished, having skipped lunch on his return trip. He shared the news of his visits over a meal of kidney pie, and the Admiral briefed David on new developments.

"There's a new Director-General for the Home Guard, a Lieutenant-General Eastwood. Do you know him?"

"Yes, he was in the War Office when I was first there," David replied. "I believe he was General Brooke's Chief of Staff during our last incursion into France in June. You remember our second evacuation, that time from Cherbourg? The last I knew he was commanding the 4th Division."

"Will this affect us?"

"Perhaps. He's a protégé of General Brooke who, in his capacity as Commander-in-Chief of Home Forces, can allocate resources for home defense. General Eastwood probably can get equipment for the Home Guard better than most other generals because of that relationship. Time will tell."

"I see. Well, most importantly, your artillery will arrive Friday and Brigadier Campbell wants to see your plan for locating each of the twelve 18-pounders. Otherwise, it's fairly quiet."

"Let's work on that plan tomorrow morning. Maybe CB can join us." They parted after dinner and David walked back to his office alone.

Elaine greeted him with "I canna' believe you left me here alone while you ha' dinner with the Admiral. I wanted so much to see you after almost two weeks."

"The Admiral was here and wanted to talk. If I hadn't gone to the pub with him, he would still be here. Now it's just us."

Elaine went over to the door and bolted it, then turned off the lights. She ran back and threw herself in David's arms. "Welcome home, soldier."

THE NEXT MORNING, David met with the Admiral and CB. "More good news," he told them. "The 18-pounders are modified guns with pneumatic tires. They travel faster, quieter and smoother, even over the bumpy gravel roads of the Highlands."

CB responded, "That'll be a great help, Colonel, our roads up here are in verra' bad shape. Of course you already know that, Sir, wha' with all your travelin'." As they studied the map a plan began to take shape.

"Brigadier Campbell wants some of the guns to be used for harbour defense, where possible, but kept mobile so they can be moved elsewhere quickly, if needed. They shouldn't be bolted down on concrete pads. I think we should have Sergeant-Major McNabb locate the best firing sites in each town, and use the Home Guard to fill sandbags and dig the earthen berms around the guns for protection. He must insure there's an adequate trail behind the guns for a lorry to move them safely to another location. Maybe, Lieutenant Osborne can accompany him so they also can begin gunnery training." The others agreed, especially the part about Osborne leaving with McNabb.

After considerable discussion, David announced, "Let's summarize this. We'll assign the guns in pairs, wherever possible. We'll keep two here in Fort William to protect Loch Linnhe and as a mobile reserve. Of course, the Admiral can say that we're defending our tiny sea loch harbour and the naval training station. Two will go to Mallaig, two to Portree, two to Ullapool, two to the Western Isles, and one gun each to Scourie and Durness."

"Are Scourie and Durness large enough to man a gun each?" CB asked.

"They'll have to do as best they can. We need artillery in the northeast corner in case the Germans attack the radar station."

The Admiral asked, "Are two guns enough for the Western Isles? I would think we need more artillery there."

"We don't have more to give them. The War Office recently allocated a single four-inch gun from the Emergency Batteries to defend Stornoway harbor. We'll let the Inverness Group decide where they want the added 18-pounders placed. At least, they'll have something. I visited all the Home Guard units in the Western Isles last week, and they've made excellent progress. But, they're isolated from the mainland and could easily be attacked by a U-boat firing its deck gun. Now they'll have something to shoot back."

After further discussion, David asked Elaine to prepare a letter to Brigadier Campbell in Inverness telling of his plan and asking for a quick yes or no response. She also was to summon McNabb and Osborne to David's office to receive their new instructions.

"I see you ha' Lady Frances on your calendar this afternoon. Maybe the Admiral should attend also," she said coyly.

The Admiral did not.

LADY FRANCES WAS BRIMMING with enthusiasm. "Civil Defense is coming along splendidly, Colonel. The ladies in the various family support organizations have worked together to prepare a plan for any emergency. We now have a detailed plan that includes all Civil Defense organizations and all the other unofficial groups that want to help. I've a copy here for your file. We had a drill while you were away. They made some mistakes, but fewer than before. At least, there was no bumbling around this time. I've asked the public safety groups also to schedule a drill next week, together with the emergency utility services. They've drilled before as individual units, but I think it's time to have a drill with all of them working together. The Chief Constable has agreed and the Provost will take part with his staff. I'll stay in the background and let them run the show."

"I'm confident, Lady Frances, that you'll quietly control the whole affair."

She smiled. "Of course, but remember: I'm only a woman."

David hadn't closed the door to his office for the meeting, in deference to Elaine, who sat quietly at her desk next to his door. Lady Frances continued, "Would you be available for dinner at the hotel this evening? I would like to review the new plan with you in detail and I must stay in town anyway for a meeting afterward with the Air Raid Precautions staff." David agreed. There was a crash in the outer office as Elaine dropped her cup.

"Sorry."

November 14

DAVID SAT IN HIS OFFICE Friday morning reviewing the summary reports from the Home Guard units in his sub-district. A lengthier report was submitted at the end of each month, but a shorter report, describing any new developments, was submitted mid-month.

Elaine arrived early, as usual, and prepared two cups of tea. She knew that none of the staff would arrive before 9:30 a.m. and perhaps not even then. All, except the Admiral, had regular jobs in addition to their Army work. The Admiral scheduled a golf game each Friday morning. Sergeant-Major McNabb and Lieutenant Osborne had been given the day off, as they would depart for Mallaig the next Monday to begin site selection and the emplacement process for the two 18-pounders. They'd continue north to Portree, Ullapool, Scourie and Durness until all guns were emplaced. Reversing their course, they'd begin gunnery training at each site as they returned. It was expected they'd be gone for three weeks. "Good," she thought, "that lieutenant can be a pest."

As they sat with their tea, she said, "It ha' been a long time since you ha' taken a day off."

David responded, "I took several hours off on the Navy launch, going to the Western Isles and back."

"Oh, sure, you probably were readin' an army report, or somethin' about the status of the war."

"Well, yes, but that's relaxing."

"Its no' enough. Brigadier Campbell gave me strict orders to make you take an occasional day off. It's for your health and I ha' made sure tha' you have nothin' on your schedule for Sunday. You ha' to leave town and ha' a picnic with a certain lady," she said firmly.

"Lady Frances?" Elaine glared at him. "I'm joking. Where are we going?"

"Someplace out in the country and away from civilization, so you can relax."

"It's getting cold outside. Are you sure you want to come with me?"

"I'll bring lunch, you bring something to drink. I'm sure we can find a way to stay warm. You still ha' tha' blanket, don't you?"

FRIDAY AND SATURDAY WERE OCCUPIED with the receipt of the eagerly awaited 18-pounders, two of which arrived in Fort William mid-afternoon and were quickly surrounded by onlookers. Sergeant-Major McNabb inspected each gun and pronounced, "They're in good shape, Colonel. They've been fired recently, but at least the chaps cleaned them afterwards. How much ammunition do we have?"

Captain Frank Leslie replied, "Forty-two rounds, enough to train the crews. We'll get more in about two weeks." The two designated Home Guard crews for the Fort William guns included four veteran gunners from the First War and over twenty younger men who would receive artillery training for the first time. This was sufficient to man the two guns with a few extra men in case of absences. As elsewhere, they were known as the artillery platoon.

Leslie told McNabb to move the guns to the Home Guard training site at Kinlochleven. "Archie MacIntyre has loaned us two lorries to pull the guns whenever they need to be moved. He also had towing hooks welded onto the rear of each lorry. As soon as you've dropped the guns, release the drivers so the lorries can get back to work for Mr. MacIntyre."

Later that afternoon, the first gun thundered its report, soon followed by the second. As the sound traveled back to Fort William, people stopped to listen, and then continued on their way, a look of grim satisfaction on their faces.

As THEY DROVE NORTH early Sunday morning, David said "The Germans bombed Coventry last night, a huge raid which practically leveled the city. BBC said hundreds were killed. It just doesn't make any sense. Coventry has no large military garrison. Why bomb a city like that? It was practically defenseless."

"Maybe that's why they chose Coventry," Elaine replied quietly.

"This isn't war. The Nazis have turned this into murder! It's genocide, pure evil!" he shouted.

"Please calm down and try not to think about the war. Let's enjoy a peaceful day in the country for your day off. Tomorrow you can become the sub-district commander again."

They sat quietly while he drove along a narrow road. "If you turn off up ahead, I know a lovely waterfall where we can picnic."

"You know many pretty places, Elaine. I hope that's because your family came here when you were a child."

"Yes, but Paul and I also came here when we were young." After several more minutes Elaine said, "Stop here."

A short walk took them to a stream and a small waterfall that babbled along its eight-foot drop. David laid out the blanket on the grass. They sat quietly for some time looking at the water and marveling at the gurgling sounds, as crystal clear liquid poured over the smooth, shiny rocks below.

David said, "I'd like to go for a swim, how about you?"

"'Tis cold and I dinna' bring a swimsuit."

"You won't need a swimsuit. There's nobody for miles around and I'll keep you warm."

He stripped off his clothing, and Elaine reluctantly removed her footwear ever so slowly. He waded naked into the water up to his knees and shuddered at the cold. His calves quickly turned blue.

Elaine gradually followed him in. She wrapped her upper body with her jacket, lifted her dress above her knees, and then stopped with the water at her ankles. "I don' know if I can stand this. Freezin' doesna' make me feel romantic." She looked around at the blanket. "Would you consider doing somethin' warmer?" David didn't respond, but continued to wade in the icy water, shivering as he went. "David, please get out of the water now and come hold me under the blanket. I need to be warmed up, and then we can think of somethin' else to do."

He did and they did.

14

November 22, 1940

DAVID DROVE NORTH to Scourie from Portree, where he'd inspected the first battery site of the two new 18-pounder howitzers. Sergeant-Major McNabb had identified two firing positions on the northern bluff overlooking Portree harbour that offered a clear field of fire at any enemy vessel entering the harbor. It was just north of the Folly Tower, built in the 19th Century to look like an old Norman tower.

The Isle of Skye Home Guard Company had furnished McNabb a crew of men who worked tirelessly for two days emplacing the guns behind protective earthen berms. They widened a trail so each gun could be pulled out quickly by a lorry and towed to another firing site. Several sites had been identified around Skye for possible use in defense of threatened beaches. They also dug protective trenches on either side of the firing positions for infantry sections to provide security for the gunners should enemy soldiers actually land near Portree. Finding the battery site to be generally satisfactory, David gave McNabb suggestions on how to better protect the gunners and the infantry sections by creating impediments to ground attacks. He then critiqued the Skye defense plans with the Home Guard officers and helped them devise a better defense scheme for Portree, Skye's most important target.

McNabb and Lieutenant Osborne drove north to Ullapool the next day to begin their ten-day training mission. Osborne, newly commissioned in the infantry, had no field artillery experience. David thought he'd benefit from this mission under McNabb's guidance. Osborne would also provide a check on McNabb's drinking.

David's drive north seemed longer than usual, perhaps an effect of the dull, overcast sky. The mountains to the east showed a light dusting of snow, not uncommon for this time of year. The sea to the west, when he could see it, was wind-tossed and uninviting. Occasional fishing boats fought the waves as they returned to port, and David was gratified he'd conducted his visit to the Western Isles, weeks ago. A boat trip wouldn't be pleasant today.

It was early evening when he arrived at Catherine's cottage in Scourie. Smoke rising from the roof promised a warm welcome. The smell of mutton cooking greeted him upon entering and he saw the stew kettle slowly bubbling on the stove. Catherine smiled when she saw him. "Do ye like onions in yer stew?" He did. Removing his jacket and shoes, he slumped into one of her chairs.

"Tough drive?" she asked.

"Not really; just slow and tiring."

"Maybe ye're no' gettin' enough rest. Tha' will hasten the fatigue and bring on a 'burn-out' syndrome. Ye mun be more careful and take better care of ye'rself. I don' want to hear ye've ha' a motorcar accident, caused by fatigue. Ye ha' best get to bed early tonight. It sounds like ye ha' a busy day tomorrow."

"Yes, nurse."

"Don' be smart with me, David, I'm serious."

They ate silently. David relaxed as he devoured the mutton, potatoes, carrots, and onions. It tasted like the stew his mother often made. The hot tea, with an added shot of whisky, was far better than any tea his mother had served him as a boy. It soothed his raspy throat, the result of yelling instructions to the men at Portree.

"What ha' ye been doin' since I saw ye last?" she asked.

David told her about his travels, the large Civil Defense exercise in Fort William, and the arrival of the artillery.

"I saw our gun when it arrived here," she said. "The whole village turned out, even the school children. 'Tis really verra' impressive, David, and we all feel safer, at least we will when our fellas learn to fire it. Right now, it's stored in Mr. Owen's shed along with some ammunition."

David explained the training plan and McNabb's coming visit with Lieutenant Osborne.

"They willna' be stayin' with me," she said "no' enough room. Mr. Owen is fixin' twa beds in his storeroom. He says they'll be quite comfortable."

"I'm glad I'm not staying in his storeroom tonight."

"Me, too," she smiled.

THE NEXT MORNING, David left early for Durness. Catherine had risen well before dawn to fix an early breakfast. The air had turned

154

colder under a threatening sky, and a fierce wind blew from across the sea. Few cars passed him on the single-lane road.

His mind turned to the war, which was not going well. Victory eluded British forces in North Africa, and U-boats continued their merciless toll on Allied shipping. Japan's belligerent threats were growing and the Pacific seemed destined for greater troubles. Britain had limited capabilities to respond. Former Prime Minister, Neville Chamberlain, died on November 9. He had enjoyed public support because he, like the public, wanted to pay neither the price of war nor of peace. Now, all Britain was paying an unimaginable price. This was discouraging, and David found some solace in returning to his own work of helping his sub-district prepare for invasion.

Arriving in Durness in less than two hours, he was greeted by Lieutenant Duncan Parker, platoon commander of the Durness area Home Guard. Parker took him to meet the Duke of Sutherland, the Home Guard Battalion Commander for Sutherland. With the Duke was Parker's Company Commander, Major Priestley, both of whom had spent the night in Durness.

"A storm coming in tonight, Colonel," said Lieutenant Parker, "but we should be finished with the exercise well before it arrives."

"I've heard a great deal about you, Colonel," said the Duke, himself an Honorary Colonel in the Territorial Army and a veteran of the First War. The Duke's First War service was unusual in that he'd served in both the Army and Navy. They talked for a time, after the Duke's driver brought a tray with cups of hot tea. Parker finally interrupted them and announced that the exercise was about to begin.

Parker raised his revolver skyward and fired a shot. Men soon came running from their houses with rifles and helmets, and then assembled on the main street. Thirty-four soldiers gathered quickly, knowing in advance of the exercise. Today, being Saturday, they'd have assembled for drill anyway. Another group of considerably older men, some armed with fowling pieces and others carrying petrol bombs, stood off to the side. They were the village defenders, officially too old to join the Home Guard, but members nonetheless. They would take up positions in and around the town as the Home Guard platoon moved out to confront the enemy.

And move out they did, driving slowly east about a mile behind Lieutenant Parker's motorcar, five or six men to a vehicle. David, the Duke, and Major Priestley followed in the Duke's large motorcar. The newly assigned 18-pounder was towed behind an old farm lorry, looking impressive, but unable to be fired, as the gun crew wouldn't be trained for several more days.

Arriving at the Sango Bay radar station a few minutes later, they were greeted by four-dozen armed airmen under Wing Commander Ralph Morton, the radar station commander. His men had taken up positions to act as defenders for the exercise.

Parker brought out his new defense plan for the radar station, which he'd prepared under the close guidance of Major Priestley and Colonel Matthew Harris. In the event of an actual raid, the plan called for 60 armed RAF men from the radar station and the Balnakiel support site to take up positions on either side of the bluff, to prevent an enemy flanking attack. Those men would also control the rear area, the road access, and would secure the inner perimeter of the radar site, which would never cease operation. Other Home Guardsmen would reinforce them as needed.

Parker's Home Guard platoon would initially secure the center of the bluff, facing directly seaward. Upon arrival of one or more mobile battle platoons from the Home Guard 1st Sutherland Battalion, the Durness platoon would displace into supporting positions to the west of the bluff, leaving the forward positions to the younger and better trained men of the mobile battle platoons. A small reserve would be established to provide a counter-attack force. Excess RAF men from the Balnakiel support site would reinforce the RAF men at the radar site, possibly bringing the number of RAF personnel to 75-80.

If overwhelmed by the Germans, the critical equipment for the radar and all documents would be blown up, leaving nothing of value for an enemy raiding party. This outcome was considered fairly unlikely, provided the mobile battle platoons were given sufficient warning time to relocate to Sango Bay and take up defensive positions in advance of an actual attack.

A smaller group from Balnakiel would protect that site and also would reinforce the small section that manned the signal station on Faraid Head. At Cape Wrath, the 25 men would be divided, with half taking up positions three miles east to protect the Navy jetty-landing site, the only possible landing site for several miles in any direction. "It's unlikely they'd be attacked," said Parker, "but armed with rifles, the Lewis gun, and a Boys rifle, they would put up a pretty good fight."

When the exercise began, Parker had his men lie down near the edge of the bluff; he then signaled them to attack. They charged the radar station; shouting, "Bang, Bang," and the other side responded likewise, neither side having any blank ammunition for the exercise. After a half-hour of maneuvering, Parker blew a whistle and brought an end to that part of the exercise.

"Not bad," said the Duke, "but they need more practice. They should practice each drill until it becomes automatic. It's easy to charge when the other side is yelling, 'Bang, Bang.' It's quite different when the other side is firing live rounds at you, especially from machine guns. That's when we find out who the real soldiers are. Have the men rest for fifteen minutes, Lieutenant Parker, and then take up a defensive position so the RAF men can attack them. This afternoon, I want the men to perform the attack and defense roles until they get it right."

"No Germans out there today, Captain!" came a voice. They all turned to see Emma McPherson waving at them. "I've been up most o' the night and no one ha' come ashore."

David smiled and waved back. "I'll explain later, Sir," Parker said to the Duke.

The exercise continued all morning and, after a lunch break, into the afternoon, practicing various maneuvers that could be used in the event of attack. The wind had picked up and the surf pounded hard against the rocks below. By mid-afternoon, Parker's men had gone down a rocky path to the sand beach to take up positions for yet another simulated attack directly across the beach. The enormous boulders provided excellent defensive positions, and any sea borne attack would have to come through the rocks and up the steep slope to the road.

"Major Priestley, you take Colonel McKenna down to the waterfront," said the Duke. "I'd better stay here with Commander Morton and not risk a fall. Getting a bit old, I guess." Priestley and David slowly stepped down the steep path, carefully avoiding loose rocks, while the Duke maintained a commanding view from above. Arriving at the water's edge, they watched the men get into position among the boulders.

"Colonel, Major, come see O'Neill's position." Parker had climbed a large, sloping boulder to find O'Neill completely concealed in the rocks above the beach, yet able to fire to his front. "This is the best defensive position I've seen today."

David and Priestly started to climb up the rocks carefully toward O'Neill's position. "If I'd known I'd be rock climbing" said Priestley, "I'd have brought different shoes."

David stepped gingerly up the slick face of the rock, doing his best to remain upright and steady. As he stepped forward cautiously, he suddenly slipped and fell back several feet, hitting his right hip hard on a rock. "Damn!" he cried out in pain.

"Sir, are you all right?" Parker and Priestley both scrambled down to help him. David winced as they helped him up. He clearly had injured his bad hip, but he could move his leg, despite the discomfort.

"No broken bones, only broken dreams," he tried to joke through his pain, quoting from an old movie. "I'll be okay." He grimaced as they helped him slowly climb back up the trail to the top, where the Duke was waiting.

"Was that your bad hip, Colonel?" he asked. "Maybe we should get you to a doctor."

"No, it's just a bruise. I'll be fine. No doctors around here anyway. Since this is the last segment of the exercise today, I think I'll start back to Scourie now, if Major Priestley would drive me back to my motorcar."

As they drove the short distance back to Durness, a few light flakes of snow began to fall. "Why don't you spend the night here, Colonel? The storm's definitely coming across the water and I'm sure we can find you a bed someplace."

"Thank you, Major, I think not." He gingerly stepped into his vehicle, started the engine, and drove out of Durness. As he motored south, the wind increased and the snow began to fall steadily. "If I can get south of this storm fairly quickly, things should get better," he muttered to himself.

David drove carefully at a very moderate speed as the snow blew against his windshield. The storm, however, got worse. Although the first big snow of the season, the ground was still cold from the previous night's frost. The snow soon stopped melting upon contact and began to accumulate. "Good thing I have new tires." As he drove downhill past the stone walls which lined the road, snow built up on his windshield, forcing him to stop and clear it off. "The first snow is a sticky snow," he thought, "but it usually doesn't last long and melts quickly."

Carefully, he followed the winding single-lane road southward over the rolling hills. As the depth of the snow increased, David was forced to go slower and slower. He rolled down his window to reach around and wipe off the snow, but more snow was driven into the car by the wind from the sea. "I wish I was driving north, not south. Then I'd be on the other side, away from the sea, and I could wipe off my windshield without the snow blowing in." He was forced to drive ever slower, under the darkening sky, as the rising snow made it harder to see the road. Every time he cleared the windshield, more snow and cold air blew in. He felt chilled. He'd been an hour on the road and had gone but a third of the way. "Maybe, I should've stayed in Durness after all."

The second hour was worse. The mounting snow reduced his speed to a walking pace. He thought about stopping entirely for the night, or at least until the storm blew over. "No buildings anywhere. Maybe, I could stop on the side of the road and get some sleep." He thought for a moment. "No, that's not a good idea. I couldn't run the engine for heat, as the fumes would kill me. Without heat, I'd freeze to death. And if I stop, there's no safe place to pull off; someone could come along and smash into me."

He'd seen only two vehicles so far on his journey. Toward the end of the second hour, he passed the turnoff to the small fishing port of Kinlochbervie, several miles to the west. "Heavier snow near the ocean," he thought, "and slippery. I'd never make it over the steep ridgelines into Kinlochbervie. Must press on and hope I don't wind up in a ditch." Slowly, he motored on with the pain throbbing in his hip.

During the third hour, he crawled even slower, alternating between clearing his windshield and peering out to search for the direction of the road. The snow had covered the road to a depth of four or five inches; the road and nearby fields blurred together. A few small trees and an occasional hill provided the only clues as to direction. It had become quite dark and his headlights, covered with mandated blackout protectors, had difficulty shining through the snow. "I can see the headlines," he said out loud, "*Army Colonel Dies in Highland Snowstorm.*"

As the time passed, his mind wandered. He began to think of Anne and the children. Maybe he would see Anne soon, he thought, but his children would be orphans. "Stop it!" he shouted out loud, "Wake up!" He felt himself starting to doze, so he opened the window an inch to let in cold air. "Now I'll probably freeze to death." His mind had fallen into a state of despondency, but he could think of no viable alternative other than to press on. The driving snow and total darkness obscured his vision of any familiar roadside features, increasing his anxiety.

Gradually, a large form began to loom out of the darkness ahead. "What is it, a building?' He came to a stop and got out to look. Sandbags! This is a bunker. Where were the bunkers built on this road?" He wracked his brain. "Laxford Bridge! The Home Guard built one here to control traffic where the road narrows to cross the bridge. I turned left here this morning, so now I should turn right to go to Scourie!" He started the car again, and then turned right to cross the bridge, slowly driving south several more miles toward the village. He twice drove off the road into a field, and then back onto the road.

As he entered Scourie village, the depth of the snow had grown to over six inches. He carefully crept up to Catherine's cottage and parked. She greeted him at the door.

"Wha' are ye doin' here? Why didna' ye stay in Durness tonight? Don' ye know how dangerous it is to be out in this storm. I've been so worrit."

He limped in slowly; ignoring her questions, he slumped into a chair and rubbed his hip. He began to shiver.

"Wha's the matter? Wha' ha' ye done to ye'rself?" She rushed over.

"I fell." He paused. "I hurt my hip. It's not broken, but it hurts."

"Go into the bedroom, remove yer clothing, and put this towel around ye. I want to examine that hip."

He slowly did as instructed. Much of his clothing was soaking wet, the rest damp. After modestly wrapping a towel around his midriff, he returned and hung his clothing over two chairs. Catherine put a large log into the stove firebox, and the room temperature soon rose. She prepared a steaming mug of tea and poured in her special medicine, this time much more than usual.

"Lie on the bed here, face down. No, David, turn around so your bad hip is away from the wall." He did as she said, despite the pain. With practiced hands, Catherine gently moved the towel slightly and carefully felt the injured limb. David suddenly took a quick breath.

"Hurt?"

"Yes." She felt other spots. "Still hurts." Then, "Hurts a little there," he said several times, "and there." Finally, "Doesn't hurt."

After a few minutes, Catherine sat back. "I donna' think ye broke anythin', but ye banged the hip pretty hard and a large bruise is beginnin' to show. Donna' rub the bruise. I'll get some ice. Also, yer muscles are all knotted up, probabla' from the tension of the long drive. Let me get some lotion to help them relax. Take a large drink of tea. The 'medicine' should begin to work soon."

David took a long drink while Catherine brought out some ice and a bottle of lotion that she shook into a dish. After wrapping the ice in a towel and laying it against the bruise, she put some lotion on her hands and gently massaged the muscles around the bruise. He winced several times. Taking more lotion, she ran her hand up his back, then down along his leg to his ankle. She continued this for several minutes, pushing deeper into his muscles and moving the towel as necessary, but carefully keeping it in place over his buttocks.

"I thought you were just going to rub around my hip."

"All muscles are interconnected and they all need to relax. I'll stop if ye wish."

"No, don't stop." He started to relax, and the pain slowly subsided. Her hands seemed to work magic on his body. The room was warmer and Catherine's medicine was having an effect. She took more lotion and carefully ran her hands from his left shoulder down his back and left leg, carefully adjusting the towel. She then repeated the procedure along his right side. David felt the stress from the drive slowly evaporate.

After twenty minutes of massage, she said, "Turn over." David did as instructed, modestly placing the towel across his loins. She repositioned the ice pack and repeated the procedure, slowly rubbing from shoulder to ankle on each side; his whole body began to take on a warm glow. David smelled Catherine's musky odor and it started to arouse his thoughts. She was a beautiful woman, but he was committed to Elaine. Catherine showed no sign of anything but a professional interest in David, and her touch was strictly clinical.

Slowly, she pushed her practiced hands ever deeper into his tired muscles, kneading them gently until they loosened. As he lay there dreamily, he felt stirrings welling up in his loins. He urgently tried to think of something else. Maybe reviewing the artillery gun drill for an 18-pounder would distract him. It didn't. Catherine's hands worked magic on his muscles and his mind quickly shifted back to thoughts of the lovely lady standing over him with her hands on his almost naked body. Her work continued to be clinical, but it had an increasingly sensual effect. The towel across his midriff began to elevate and form a small, but noticeable mound. "No, not now, not that," he thought. It was too late.

"I'm sorry," he murmured, as his face reddened, "I cannot help it."

"Don' be silly. 'Tis perfectly natural." She smiled, "Besides, 'tis nice to know a girl can still ha' tha' effect on a man." Catherine continued her massage for several more minutes with a slight smile. "I hope ye feel better," she said softly.

"I feel like a bowl of warm pudding."

"Good. Now lie there for a few minutes while I clean up. Then ye mun get up and stand so I can check the hip further." David lay there and didn't want to get up. Catherine put away the food and dishes, and then returned. "Take me hand and I'll help ye up." He did so reluctantly and rose slowly from the bed. "Stand by the wall facin' me." She sat down on the bed while he complied, holding the towel across his loins.

She rolled her eyes. "David, I canna' see yer hip through the towel." He sighed, and after a moment's thought, tossed the towel aside, standing naked before her. She slowly but firmly gave him instructions. "Turn to your left a quarter turn." He did so, and his bad hip faced her. "Lift up yer right leg. Further. Now stretch yer leg out, higher. Now down, then up again and hold it. Okay, now back down." She carefully monitored the movement of his hip. "Put some weight on it, just a wee bit. Now a wee bit more. Good. Now another quarter turn, so ye face the wall." She repeated the same instructions and he complied. "Another quarter turn, David." He repeated the procedure, and then finally, "Another quarter turn." He faced her again and went through the final movements. "Swing yer right leg outward a few times." He did and there was a long silence. He was facing her totally unclothed for several minutes and he again began to feel the stirrings as Catherine sat on the bed looking carefully at his hip. Or was it his hip?

After a few moments more of her observation and his growing embarrassment, he asked "Is this all a professional examination?"

She looked up at him quickly. "No." She stood up, walked the three steps between them, and put her arms around him. "Yer a beautiful man, David McKenna."

DAVID AWOKE WITH THE MORNING SUN warming his face through the window. He smelled sausage cooking, nearby. He looked around and realized he was in Catherine's bed, alone and still quite naked. Thoughts of the previous evening rushed into his head, but they were confused. He couldn't remember anything after standing naked in front of Catherine. Had they or hadn't they? A strong feeling of guilt swept through him. How would he explain this to Elaine? He loved her devotedly, but last evening his thoughts were muddled and he couldn't remember the outcome. He stood up carefully, as his hip was still tender from the fall. Pulling a blanket around him, he went out into the kitchen to find Catherine standing by the stove wearing only a simple housecoat.

"Good mornin', Sunshine, did ye sleep well?" Her voice brought back the memory of last night, and he felt both awkward and embarrassed.

"Yes, thank you." He didn't know what to say. Finally, "I hope . . . ," he paused, "I hope I didn't do anything inappropriate last night."

She came over and put her arms around him. "Ye were verra' much a gentleman. Thank ye." She kissed him. "It's been a long time since I've been in bed with a man."

"So, we . . . " David began to ask with considerable embarrassment. Sensing his confusion, she interrupted him.

"Nae, nae, we didna'. As I said, ye were a gentleman. Last night I wa' prepared to give meself to ye. I hadna' been willin' to do tha' for any man since Tom died. But ye fell asleep and nothin' happened. We didna' ha' sex. Then, as ye were noddin' off, ye twice murmured, 'Elaine' and I realized ye ha' another lady in yer life and I ha' no right to be thinkin' about sex with ye. When I woke up this mornin' we were still naked. I ha' forgotten to put on me nightclothes. But nothin' happened between us except a kiss."

She dropped several eggs into the sausage pan and swirled them around. "Why don' ye get back in bed and I'll bring yer breakfast there."

A few minutes later, she came in with two plates steaming with food.

"The storm ha' passed and we ha' almost nine inches of snow outside, much more than expected. Ye shouldna' ha' driven home yesterday, David. I think ye were in a state of shock when ye arrived here." She set the plates down, removed her housecoat, and got into the bed naked beside him. "But I'm glad ye did."

They ate silently. Then she said, "Ye probably were plannin' to drive home today, but ye mun not. Yer hip needs to heal more and the roads are impassable. No one is out today, and I havna' even seen anyone walkin'. I think ye should plan to snuggle up someplace warm and rest. 'Tis a fine day to do nothin'." David nodded silently. When they finished, Catherine removed the dishes and refilled their cups, leaving David alone with his thoughts.

When she returned to the bed, David asked "Do you have a boyfriend?"

"Nae." She shook her head.

"Why not? You're a very attractive lady, and I would think you have so much to offer a man. Do you not want to marry again?"

"Getting' a bit nosy, are we?" Then she smiled, "Weel, thank ye for the flattery, but look around. This region doesna' exactly ha' a long list of eligible bachelors in my age bracket. Oh sure, I had a few invitations after Tom died. I even went out with a couple of fella's durin' the next two years, but it wasna' the same. I could quickly see why the unmarried men were . . . well, unmarried. All the good men are married or dead. The others are . . . ," she paused. "Let's just say I'm not interested in any of them. I'd rather be a lonely widow than an unhappy wife."

David nodded. "Maybe you should move elsewhere."

"I'll no' leave Scourie, David 'tis me home and me whole life is here. I ha' me family, friends, me work, really everythin' I need. Oh, I enjoy visitin' new places sometimes, but I canna' wait to come home again. This is where I belong and this is where I'm happy." David was silent for a moment. "David, let me ask ye. Would ye move to Scourie to marry me?" Embarrassed and feeling awkward, he didn't reply. "Of course no'. Ye are a man of the world, a Scotsman who moved out and made a success of himself, elsewhere. Ye ha' even lived abroad several times, as well as in Edinburgh, London, and who knows where else. Ye love the big world and ye thrive on the excitement of large places. If ye were to move to Scourie ye wouldna' be happy and marriage just wouldna' work. I'm the opposite. I just wouldna' be happy anyplace else."

"Are you saying you haven't been with a man since Tom died? I mean, like this?"

Her face dropped. There was a long silence. "Once." Catherine was silent for a few moments and her voice stumbled. "I hadna' meant to. It wasna' right." She paused again. "Ye see, District Nurses in remote areas are visited every two or three months by a salesman from our medical supply company in Glasgow. A young fellow, I'll call him Colin, ha' visited here for two or three years and he wa' verra' helpful. I'd order medicines and supplies, he'd write it all up, then ha' it shipped to me when he got back to Glasgow. He wa' married with children and wa' always a perfect gentleman. I really grew to like him and I looked forward to his visits.

"Every year there's a District Nurses conference in Inverness. We learn new techniques, new medicines, new equipment and supplies, verra' good information. All the medical supply companies are there. That year, Colin said he'd meet the bus, take me to the hotel and we'd ha' dinner. He did and it wa' all quite lovely. He walked me back to my room and said goodnight. The next day, I saw him several times, as all the salesmen had tables to display their medical supplies, between training sessions. When we finished that afternoon, he again offered to take me to dinner and I agreed.

164

"I guess I was tired from the trip and the meetin', but I felt verra' good. At dinner, he ordered wine and kept refillin' me glass. I donna' drink wine much. When we got up to go back to the hotel, I felt tipsy and leaned on him to steady meself while we walked. Me head felt fuzzy and, when we got to my room, I fumbled with the key. He took it and opened the door. I turned to say goodnight, but he pushed me into the room and onto the bed. It wa' all verra' quick, up skirt, down trousers. He was strong and I couldna' make him stop. Then, 'twas over.

"After a few minutes, he wa' still atop me, I regained my senses and screamed, 'Get off!' He leaped up and ran out the door, pullin' up his trousers. I couldna' believe wha' ha' happened. I laid there in a state of shock for a long time, wonderin' wha' ha' I done wrong? When I finally got up, I walked down the hall to the loo and washed myself again and again and again. Then I burst out cryin'. I must ha' cried for hours. I tried to sleep, but tha' wa' no good. I laid in me bed feeling sad, then hurt, then betrayed, then angry with him, then angry at meself, and every other emotion. 'Twas awful." Tears welled up in Catherine's eyes, and she sat stiffly in the bed.

"The next mornin' we ha' a half-day of meetin's. I don' even remember wha' they covered, but he wasna' there. That wa' good, as I donna' know what I would ha' done if I ha' seen him. Mebbe kilt him. I remember gettin' on the bus and the long ride home, starin' out the window for hours. Later, I found out that he ha' been offered a better position with his company in Lanark and would earn more money. His days of bein' the junior salesman, with the worst territory in Scotland and tendin' to the lady nurses of the Highlands, were over."

"Did you ever report him to the authorities?"

"Nae. Wha' good would it ha' done? Mebbe somethin' would ha' been done, but probably nothin'. It could ha' destroyed his marriage, but his family didna' deserve that. In the end I did nothin' but try to forget it all."

"I'm sorry I brought it up."

"No' your fault, David, I shouldna' ha' spoken of it at all. Actually, you're the first person I've ever told. I may never tell it again. Thank you for listenin'." They were silent with their thoughts for several minutes. Then David broke the silence.

"Did you think I was seducing you last evening?"

Catherine thought for a moment and grinned, then began to laugh. "T'was likely the other way around, if anyone was seducin'. Nae, ye were a perfect gentleman and perfectly innocent. I wa' quite attracted to ye from the first moment I saw you speakin' to the townsfolk at the church, last month. Ye were handsome, poised, verra' knowledgeable, and quite confident. Ye spoke well, and I wa' taken how quickly ye captured yer audience. At least, ye quickly captured me. Then, here at my cottage, we talked for hours, and I wa' taken by yer breadth of experience and what a verra' decent fellow ye were. Yer really no' a stuffy army officer; yer verra' kind. I will tell ye tha' I ha' some verra' private and prurient thoughts about ye tha' night, after I went to bed, and several nights, since. But I ne'er thought we'd e'er become intimate. Intimate friends, no' lovers."

"Nor I. You're very attractive to me, Catherine, but I'm in love with Elaine."

"I know and I'll always respect tha'. Weel, the day is still young and ye need more time to heal." Catherine moved closer, and he felt her soft skin against his. "Do ye like books?"

November 25

THE NEXT MORNING, DAVID DROVE HOME to Fort William. The sun had melted most of the snow on the roads, and people were out beginning their week on a pretty Monday. The sky was a deep brilliant blue, as so often happens after a storm. The fields shone a brilliant white, and the trees glistened with all the colors of the rainbow, as the sun shone through their branches. For the first time, he kissed Catherine goodbye, a kiss between special friends only, and he promised to visit again, when the opportunity arose.

15

December 3, 1940

"WHERE'S THE COLONEL?" The Admiral stepped into the office to find CB and Elaine working together on one more report. Ben Douglas also sat with them.

"No' yet returned, Admiral, but I expect him anytime," replied Elaine.

CB looked up, "Uniforms, Admiral!"

"What? We all have uniforms."

"No, Sir, woolen uniforms for the Home Guard. Scottish Command notified us that the army uniforms finally have been approved and we should begin receivin' them this month. The Home Guardsmen will be given one wool army battle dress uniform, a great coat, web gear and a pair of boots. Helmets should arrive soon after. With their rifles and other weapons, they'll look like real soldiers. This should boost morale. Civil Defense workers also will receive some kind o' uniform beginnin' verra' soon."

For several months, as Lord Carrington had noted weeks earlier, a battle had raged between Parliament and the War Office over uniforms for the Home Guard. Wool was scarce, clothiers were busy outfitting the regulars, and the War Office didn't want to spend money to clothe the Home Guard in a real army uniform. It only reluctantly agreed, in June, to provide the denim uniform under pressure from Mr. Churchill. Some said the War Office feared the public would confuse the Home Guard with the regulars. Parliament, however, wanted the Home Guard to be properly uniformed so that, if captured, the Nazis couldn't shoot members of the Home Guard as partisans or irregulars, a clear violation of the Geneva Convention. Now, the issue was resolved, and army wool uniforms would flow to the Home Guard battalions.

"And the ranks, too," added Elaine, "the same as the regulars."

"So, the Home Guard officers will wear pips and crowns and all that?" asked the Admiral.

"Exactly, and sometime soon, Home Guard officers will be granted King's commissions, just like the regulars." Elaine got up and put on her coat. "Must ha' these reports posted promptly to Inverness and Edinburgh."

The Admiral walked to the door. "I've a meeting with the Chief Constable. I'll be back later." As he left, Lieutenant Osborne walked in.

"Good Morning, Sirs." Osborne sat down at the table while CB worked, and Ben looked on. "So, where's Mrs. Ross going?" he asked.

"Out to post a letter to Inverness," said Ben.

"I bet she's going to meet her sweetie, the Colonel. Maybe they'll have a little tryst together."

The room went deadly silent for a moment. CB Foster looked straight ahead, and Ben Douglas froze, as if in shock. Then it erupted.

"You shut your filthy mouth!"

CB slowly rose from his chair, his head turning a dark red; his piercing eyes looked straight through the young subaltern. Osborne was stunned.

"Ye fancy little pretty boy from the big city begged the Colonel for an assignment, so ye might pocket a few shillings while ye study, and he's kind enough to grant ye a position. Now ye slander yer commander and try to start an ugly rumor," CB roared. The color drained from Osborne's face, and he became unsteady, as he tried to stand at attention. CB's voice kept rising as he approached the young officer. "He's a gentleman, a war hero, a distinguished officer and yer commander!"

Osborne began to quiver, as if about to faint.

"Ye are disloyal, useless and the worst officer I ha' ever seen!" CB spat out. "Ye are a disgrace to the uniform and ye wouldna' last one day on a battlefield." CB stepped in front of Osborne, barely an inch from his face. "Let me tell ye something, Mister. If I ever see ye again, I'll personally arrest ye and break ye to the rank o' private. I'll drag yer sorry arse to Clydebank and haul ye up the gangplank of the next ship bound for Egypt. I'll turn ye over to the ship's captain and ha' ye clapped in irons for the voyage. When ye arrive in Alexandria, I'll ha' a truck waiting to haul yer miserable arse out to the Western Desert for assignment to an infantry battalion, as a private soldier. Ye are NOTHING!"

Osborne shook badly, and his face was white.

"Now get out o' here," CB roared, "and donna' come back!" Osborne ran through the door and straight down High Street. CB took several deep breaths, shut the door, slowly calmed down, and went back to his chair and his work. He and Ben sat silently for several minutes, as CB's face drained its florid colour. Finally, Ben broke the silence.

"Can you really do that?"

"Do what?" CB responded brusquely.

"Break Osborne to the rank of private and all that?"

CB let out a long sigh. "I don' know, probably no'." He paused, "But, he doesna' know tha'."

After another minute, Ben said, "I guess one of us should speak to the Colonel, you know, to warn him that people know."

Without looking up, CB replied, "Well, I don' know anythin'. It willna' be me."

Ben sat silently for a minute, and then said, "It sounds like a job for the Chaplain, but not today."

December 6

It was a bitterly cold morning, with snow spitting across Loch Linnhe and onto Fort William. Ben Nevis had been snow-covered and obscured by clouds for days, and winter had begun to hold the Highlands in its icy grip. David had been unable to keep his flat adequately warm, even with a coal fire burning most hours in the small stove; he had bought an extra blanket for the bed at night. Elaine had gone out mid-morning to post a letter and returned with the day's mail, including a personal letter for David. He opened it eagerly and began to read.

"My girls are coming!" he exclaimed. "I asked Anne's sister if it would be agreeable for them to come north by train for Christmas, and she's worked it out for them to come up on the 18th and stay for two weeks."

Elaine rose. "Wonderful! I know you ha' missed them verra' much, and they surely ha' missed their Dad, as well."

"I wonder if Betty Campbell would meet them in Glasgow and take them from Central Station to Queen Street Station. If they catch the early morning train from Kings Cross, they could arrive in Glasgow early enough to get the late afternoon train to Fort William. If delayed, they could spend the night with the Campbells and take the morning train north."

"If you wish, I can call Mrs. Campbell and inquire."

"Yes, thank you. I could give them my bed to share and I'll sleep in the chair."

Later that day, Ben Douglas stopped in the office. Elaine shared the news about David's daughters. "Where will they stay?" Ben asked.

"They'll stay with him in his flat."

"Good Lord, that won't work. Where's the Colonel now?"

"He's at the Provost's office. He'll be back shortly."

A half hour later, David returned. Ben joined him in his office. "Elaine told me about your girls coming for Christmas. Are you really planning to have them stay with you in your flat?"

"Yes, of course."

"Let me make a better suggestion. We've an extra bedroom at the manse and we would be pleased to have the girls stay with us. My children will be thrilled for the company. Really, I insist. At least, your girls will have a warm bed, and Kathleen is surely a better cook than you."

David smiled. "That probably wouldn't be hard. They'll bring their ration books, and I'll pay for food. Well, yes, Ben, thank you for the invitation."

"Good. Now, come to dinner tomorrow evening, and I'll show you the arrangements. Again, I insist."

THE NEXT EVENING, David put on civilian clothes and went to the manse. The smell of Kathleen's cooking filled the house, and David was surprised that, even under rationing, Kathleen was able to prepare a dinner that seemed ample. David had stopped at the bakery that afternoon to find a sweet to bring for dinner.

"Sorry, Colonel," the baker said, "I ha' nothin' sweet, sugar rationin' and all tha'. I ha' only a few loaves of bread left from this mornin'." David bought one and brought it along. Kathleen graciously took it from him.

"Don't apologize, Colonel, I'll warm this in the oven."

The dinner was delightful. David found the girls to be well behaved, their son a bit of an imp, and he enjoyed talking with Kathleen for the first time in a real conversation. As they ate, he found his heart beginning to ache for the many times he and Anne had eaten meals like this with their girls. He missed Anne terribly and yearned for his girls. "Damned war," he thought.

After dinner, Ben announced that he and the Colonel would have some tea in the library. "We have a real library here in the manse, very nice." Kathleen smiled as they departed and turned to fill the tea kettle. The library was fairly small, and the shelves were lined with numerous theological books and old hymnals. "I think every pastor who retired from this church left his books behind. Actually, I find some quite interesting." Ben closed the door.

"Have you read them all, Ben?"

"Good Lord, no, but I use them occasionally to help prepare my sermons, especially when I run out of ideas."

"I don't know how you can prepare a new sermon each week and not repeat yourself."

"Who said I don't repeat myself?" They laughed. "Besides, life in this parish gives me plenty of new material." They talked for several minutes, and then Ben refreshed their teacups. He turned serious.

"Colonel, with your permission, I'm going to shift from being one of your staff officers to being a pastor and I'd like to address you as 'David' for tonight. After all, we could have been childhood friends." David nodded, a bit uncomfortably. David was accustomed to being addressed by his military rank by all but his closest family and friends. Ben was silent while he searched for words, and then sighed.

"People know, David," he said quietly.

David looked puzzled. "Know what?"

"They know about you and Elaine." David's composure changed quickly and he shifted uneasily in his chair. "I'm not saying this to be judgmental, David. I'm telling you this as a loyal staff officer and a friend."

"I didn't know that people knew," he replied grimly.

"I cannot say that many know, but Osborne has figured it out, or at least he was guessing."

"Osborne? Is that why he left?"

"CB threw him out after Osborne made a comment. I was there. It wasn't pretty."

"So, CB also knows?"

"Maybe, but he's fiercely loyal to you. Not only would he never say anything to anyone, but he would squash anyone who mentions it in any way. Witness, Osborne."

They sat silently for a minute while Ben let his message sink in. "This is a small town, David, and things can quickly get out. I don't know if anyone else knows. Possibly the Admiral, as nothing much gets by him. But, he's also your loyal friend, as well as your faithful deputy, and he's a gentleman from the old school. If he ever knew anything, none of us would ever find out. Maybe nobody else knows. I hope not."

David wiped the sweat from his face. "I don't know what to say, Ben. I don't know why this has happened."

"That's not hard, David. Two attractive people are thrown closely together, one a widower, the other with a broken marriage. It happens," he sighed. "But you have too much to lose. What if Scottish Command found out? Would they be gentlemen enough to let it pass?"

"The Army is full of gentlemen, Ben. They let far worse than this go by without comment. I myself have let far worse go by."

"That may be. Someone in the War Office tried to crush you once, or so I've been told, and he almost succeeded. At the very least, if word of this got out, it certainly would erode your position here. People look up to you and they need you. You're their anchor during these terrible times, and they trust you completely. I listen to people speak about you every day. Behind your back, they praise you and are so grateful that you're here. You make them feel safe. The Prime Minister was right. The War Office had indeed neglected the West Highlands, but it wasn't evident until you arrived. Churchill is a skilled politician and he has a far better feel for the people than does the War Office. Your departure now would be a terrible blow to this sub-district and very damaging to our community." Both were silent for a few minutes.

David put his face in his hands. "I cannot leave her, Ben. I love her so much and she loves me."

"I know, but she's married."

"She doesn't love him."

"That doesn't matter, David, you're committing adultery."

"She hasn't seen him in almost two years. He neglects her and the boys."

"There's a war on, David. Many families are separated. It still doesn't matter. It's adultery. You and Elaine aren't married. Elaine is married to Paul."

Tears rolled down David's face, as they sat silently again. Finally, David spoke. "I lost the woman I love, and it was my fault! At least part of it was my fault." Ben looked at David quizzically. David told him the whole story: Anne's cancer, his fight with General Haining, the accident, and his retirement. Ben looked on in disbelief.

"I ruined my career, Ben, and that, too, was my fault. I've been lonely and miserable ever since I lost Anne. I slowly patched over the pain, but it was always there, just underneath." He paused to drink some tea. "And, then, I was given a reprieve. I was given this job and because of this job, I found Elaine. My whole world has changed. I cannot give her up, Ben. I want to marry her."

"Then marry her, David. Have her divorce Paul and marry you." Ben sat back, a feigned look of astonishment on his face. "I can't believe I just said that. The Church of Scotland would defrock me, if they knew I suggested someone break their sacred vows and seek a divorce." He smiled, "But I'm sure I'm not the first pastor to say those words. David, I'm your friend and I want what's best for you and, also, for Elaine. I want to see you happy, both of you. More importantly, I want most what's best for Scotland, and for your sub-district, and for my parish."

Ben paused and glanced around the room. "If I took the long view of all this, I would say this job is your redemption" David looked at him with a puzzled look.

"Redemption, David, the gift of forgiveness from the Lord, and your opportunity to make something new and better of your life. You can believe it or not, just as you can accept it, or not. But it's there. You've been given the chance to redeem yourself, first as an army officer, second as a husband and father, and third as a Christian. You were put on this earth for a purpose. Maybe this assignment is your ultimate purpose, your ultimate chance to give the greatest meaning to your life and the greatest gift to others. You've done this magnificently. I don't know how Elaine fits into all this, but I know what you're doing with her is wrong and very dangerous."

After a few minutes of silence, David sat up straight and looked at Ben. "I can't give her up." He thought for several minutes. "I don't know why God would even care. I'm getting older, I've been injured, and, at age forty-four, I'm not the man I used to be. Is it too much to ask for a little happiness in my life?"

"No, David, it's not too much to ask, but we have no assurance that happiness will be granted. This is all part of redemption. Yes, you're aging and your body is slowly failing, but don't you see that, as we age, we lose all that we were given? Almost from birth, the losses begin. We lose our grandparents, then our parents and other family members, and our friends. Then we lose our careers and other relationships that were important to us. The older we get, the more we lose. We lose that which sustained us and gave our lives meaning, and pride, and a sense of self-worth. We lose our health, sometimes slowly, sometimes quickly. We lose our physical and mental abilities and we certainly lose the respect of others, including those who most owe us some respect. They forget who we were and they often forget the many contributions we made. We lose our talents, our interests, our capabilities, and our self-respect. We may lose our wealth. In the end, we lose everything of value until we lose life itself."

"That's terrible, Ben."

"No, it's not terrible," Ben said shaking his head. "That's the reality of life. And that's where redemption comes in. Despite our many failings and sins, God replaces our losses with redemption. His love and His forgiveness begin to fill our lives when we least expect it and often when we don't even realize it. It's all part of growing old. God's preparing us for death. But He's also preparing us for our own resurrection into His world. We feel the losses, but we may not feel His love and His forgiveness filling our souls. As we grow older, we feel the pain and we feel the anguish of the loss of those we love. We feel the sadness of all our mistakes and failures, but we don't yet feel the resurrection. You do believe in God and His salvation, don't you, David?"

"I don't know."

"I hope you'll come to know Him soon." Ben paused. "David, I don't know what will happen between you and Elaine, just as I don't know what will be the next stage of your career, if you have one. It's all a mystery. I know, however, that you'll be forgiven, if you ask for it."

There was a long silence. Ben let David ponder these ideas and said nothing. Finally, David spoke up.

"You're a powerful preacher, Ben. I didn't realize how good you were. I really should spend more time in church listening to you."

Ben smiled. "You would always be welcome, David."

"I promise to think more about your words, but I can't promise to give up Elaine. In fact, I think I can promise that I'll not give her up. I love her too much and she loves me. We were made for each other, at least I think we were, and I'll marry her, just as soon as she consents."

"Then be more careful! Please be more careful. This mustn't come out."

16

December 12, 1940

DAVID RETURNED TO HIS OFFICE from a long walk along the shore of Loch Linnhe. The exercise felt good, and he always enjoyed watching the ships moving up and down the seaway. Loch Linnhe had become one of several staging areas for the Atlantic convoys bringing vital supplies to Britain. Merchant ships were anchored in the loch to the west of Fort William, while convoys were being assembled for the return voyage across the Atlantic. HMS *St. Christopher*, the small naval training station on the shore of the loch, was abuzz with the activity of small coastal defense craft, as they crisscrossed the loch as part of their training exercises. Hundreds of seamen, some from allied countries, were now billeted throughout Fort William, giving the town the feel of a wartime garrison.

Each week, David visited Commander A.E. Wellman, the naval station commander, at his headquarters in the Highland Hotel. Some visits were more social than business, as the Navy always seemed to have coffee available, despite rationing. He enjoyed speaking with members of Wellman's staff, including a bevy of young women from all over Scotland who provided clerical support to the training center. They always enjoyed attention from the handsome Army sub-district commander.

David also regularly conducted briefings on responsibilities for newly arrived naval officers, in the event of a German invasion or other emergencies. The Navy had assigned several hundred rifles to the station for training use. Most small craft mounted heavy machine guns and, sometimes, even larger weapons. All these would play an important role in the event of attack.

The Army headquarters was slowly being established at the Alexandra Hotel, although David preferred to use his High Street office. A hotel room would be more comfortable than his dismal flat, but it wouldn't provide safe opportunities for Elaine's visits.

David was preoccupied. In three days, his daughters would arrive by train for the holidays. He hadn't seen them for six months and, despite letters and periodic telephone calls, he missed them terribly. "Damned war," he thought, once again.

The war, however, had provided his personal redemption. He had pondered Ben Douglas's counsel many times over the past few days. A burden finally had been lifted. He hadn't recognized it earlier, but now he understood more clearly how guilt had oppressed his inner spirit. Without the war, his life in London as an import-export broker would've continued as before. His two girls would have grown up, and he presumably would've found another lady to love, hopefully one who was not married. That would've been fine, but it wouldn't have brought the joy he now experienced in his work as a sub-district commander and his life with Elaine. "I would happily sacrifice this joy for a quick end to the war," he mused, "and a return to my former life." Walking up High Street, however, forced him to put things in perspective; there would be no quick end to the war. Obviously, "that's not meant to be," as Ben Douglas might put it.

As he entered the office, Elaine interrupted his thoughts.

"Wha's a V-e-r-y Pistol?"

"It's a portable signaling system for nighttime use," he replied.

"Then, why do they call it a pistol? How does it work?"

David explained, "It looks and fires just like a single-shot pistol, but with a short barrel that's an inch or more wide. You put in the signal shell, point it at the sky, and pull the trigger. Different shells give you different coloured lights. You can also fire an illuminating round. The shell goes up and, when it bursts, a burning phosphorous flare floats down on a small parachute to light the area for about thirty seconds. Why do you ask?"

"Lieutenant-Colonel Whittaker called while you were out to tell you the Home Guard would be gettin' some, soon. He didna' know how many or wha' ammunition would be comin'."

"I guess they could be useful. Did he say anything about revolvers?"

"Yes, Colonel, he said they'd continue to arrive in penny packets, as the regular units were re-equipped. The older revolvers will be collected from the Regulars, divided between the sub-districts, and shipped out. Captain Leslie gets a periodic report on all this."

"I see." He went to his desk and began working through another pile of paperwork. A half-hour later, Lady Frances entered.

"Good morning, Colonel, may we talk?"

Without waiting for an answer, she entered his inner office and closed the door. She gave him a summary of activities conducted by the various Civil Defense organizations. David listened politely, admiring, as always, her stately poise, her diction, and her attractiveness. She spoke as one in total command of the Civil Defense forces, yet she always insisted that she was simply helping them in their brave endeavors. David knew it was a disarming ruse, but very effective with the townspeople. They respected Lady Frances because she was a lady, but even more because of her brains and her energy.

"Any news from Sir Robert?"

"Nothing special. I'm sure you know more about the Desert War than I do. Robert writes regularly. He insists that his war is simply an office in Cairo and a hotel room at night, but I know him better. I suspect he gets out to the Western Desert to visit the forces, whenever he can." There was a short knock on the door.

"Tea?"

"That would be lovely, Elaine," Lady Frances replied. David nodded. Elaine returned quickly with two steaming cups, and then closed the door and returned to her desk.

"I think Elaine is very protective of you, Colonel," she said softly, "and I'm not sure she approves of me being in here with the door closed."

"Oh no," David responded, with a small lie, "she's very comfortable with you and she truly admires you for your many accomplishments." At least, the latter was true.

"I think she's a remarkable young woman and one who has come a long way from her very humble origins. And, she's quite beautiful."

"She's extraordinarily efficient and always performs well." He stumbled with his words.

"I'm sure," she replied coyly. "In any case, the real reason for my visit, Colonel. Do you ride?"

"Why, yes, of course, but I've only ridden once since my accident. I must be careful with my hip, so I'm not quite the wild horseman I was in the Punjab."

"Would you have time to ride with me this afternoon? Our horses need exercise and I would appreciate some company and intelligent conversation. Our trails overlook the loch, and it's really quite beautiful."

"I would enjoy that very much, Lady Frances, thank you for asking."

As she rose to leave, she turned to him. "It would really be quite alright for you to address me as Frances. We're good enough friends now, and I'm a member of your staff. Lady Frances seems a bit formal and unnecessary, wouldn't you agree, Colonel?"

"Yes, and I should like you to call me 'David,' but not when others are present."

"Thank you, David, I respect that. I'll see you at two o'clock at our stables."

There was a short silence after Lady Frances left, then, Elaine spoke without looking up. "Ridin'? You're goin' ridin' with her?" She mimicked, "I'll see you at two o'clock at our stables."

"Do I detect a hint of jealousy?" he responded. "Don't be silly, it's nothing but a professional relationship. And a bit of riding will do me some good. Besides, she's a married woman."

"So am I."

DAVID ARRIVED AT THE STUART RESIDENCE promptly at two. As he drove up the long entryway, he admired the large, old country house and the imposing double row of walnut trees lining an expansive lawn. A half-timbered barn sat off to the side. An old wall of cemented field stones surrounded the estate and divided each portion of grounds for its intended purpose. The house overlooked the sea loch with a view that David found captivating. The day was mostly sunny, but a cold wind blew across the water and up the hill, making David glad he'd brought his fleece jacket.

"Good afternoon, David, welcome to our home. Come meet your mount." Lady Frances led him past the barn and the front of the stables to a dark brown mare, which had just been saddled by the stable hand. "Thank you, Harry," she sang out, as she mounted her chestnut stallion, and they walked their horses to the edge of the field.

"Robert and I try to ride almost every day. Of course that has ended for the duration, I suppose, but one fine day, he'll be back to his beloved 'Scamp.' That's the name of the horse you're riding."

"I suspect he'll be even happier to be back to his beloved Frances," David responded. She smiled appreciatively. They rode westward at a slow trot to allow David and Scamp time to get adjusted to each other. They cantered briefly, and then slowed back to a walk. Frances showed David the views whenever the trail broke out into the open. After almost an hour, they came out into a clearing, which led to a large orchard that flowed downhill toward Loch Linnhe. David found the view priceless. They dismounted, to David's relief, as his hip was sore again.

"Do you own all this land?" he inquired.

"Most of it, down to the tree line above the road. Robert sold that strip of land near the road in '32. You can see the three houses there now, all new and several more to be built whenever the war ends. He had to, as we needed the money for taxes and to make major repairs on the house. At least, that's done, and we won't have to sell any more land, I hope."

After several minutes, Frances said, "Let's mount up and go back to the house. The wind is cold, and I suspect I can find something to drink that'll warm us up."

Slowly, they walked the horses back to the stable, where Harry took the mounts inside. They entered the house, and David found that Harry had built a fire in the large fireplace in the great room. The house seemed spacious to David, being a country house, but hardly a great baronial estate. As they sat talking, a lady in her early sixties brought drinks. "David, meet Mary, my housekeeper. She and Harry have been married for many years. Harry's a pensioner from the Navy, and they've been with me for almost fifteen years. They run the house, and Mary is a wonderful cook, especially when we can get some real food. Our other man is Phillip. He does most of the farming and lives in a small cottage a half-mile from here."

The conversation continued for almost an hour, the fire warming both until it became almost too hot. David declined a second drink, then asked "What type of business is Sir Robert engaged in, at least when he's not off to war?"

"Robert has a background in accounting and business management. He entered his family shipping firm right out of the University of Edinburgh, in 1923. He'd joined the forces in 1918, too late to do much fighting, but he was extremely proud of his brief service under Allenby in Palestine. He developed a great love for the Arab people and the desert, and he studied it as a hobby for years. I guess that's why the Army sent him to Cairo last year."

"What was his role in the firm before his Army assignment?"

"He was a director and supervised a great deal of the contracting work. He worked from his office here most days, but would travel to Glasgow each week to the firm's home office. He stayed quite busy, but always had time for our family."

Mary entered the room and whispered something in Lady Frances' ear. "David, will you dine with me tonight?"

"Thank you, no, I must return to my office before closing," he said, glancing at his watch, but perhaps another time." He excused himself and drove back to town as quickly as possible. "Elaine will be waiting," he thought. He parked the motorcar and walked to the front door. But, he found it locked. He walked around to the back entrance. Unlocking the door, he entered the empty office. "She must've left early, but why?"

The next morning, David returned to his office. The clock ticked by the minutes, but no Elaine. He unbolted the front door, something she normally would do, but it was well after the time to open the office and she still wasn't there.

A half-hour later, the door opened, and Elaine entered. She hung up her coat and went straight to her desk, saying nothing. David went out to the office. "Are you alright?"

"Yes, quite," she replied, not looking up.

"I was concerned. You've never been late before." Elaine remained silent. "I was surprised you weren't here when I returned yesterday," he continued. David walked to the stove, fixed two cups of tea, and brought one to Elaine. She ignored it. Sitting across from her, he asked, "Would you like to know what happened yesterday with Lady Frances?" She shot him a fiery glance. "Nothing happened. We rode horses, had a drink, we talked and, then, I returned to see you."

"Humph!"

"Elaine, I would do the same with any member of my staff: CB, the Admiral, Ben, any of them. It makes no difference that she's a woman."

"Yes, it does! She's a very attractive woman whose husband has been a thousand miles away for over a year. She's rich and she has a beautiful home with servants. She married a knight, she went to a university, and she's so very polished." She looked hard at David. "It isna' fair!"

They were silent for a moment while David composed his thoughts. "Fairness is not the issue. She's a good lady who adores her husband. She works hard at running her household alone and still gives countless hours each week to her work with Civil Defense. We work together, that's all."

"Was yesterday afternoon workin'?" Elaine shot back.

"No, not exactly, for riding with her was pleasant. Having a drink afterwards and talking was also pleasant. She could be a good friend. I like her." He paused. "But I don't love her. I love you."

Elaine took a sip of tea. "I left early yesterday because I couldna' bear the thought of you bein' alone with her."

"We weren't alone. The horses were there."

Elaine tried hard to suppress a smile. "I just canna' stand the thought of you bein' with another woman. I know it's silly, but it's the way I am. I'm married to a man who wanders and I donna' like it! I willna' be involved in another relationship like tha' again. Ever!" She looked at her work and slowly began to relax.

"Would you like to know what Lady Frances thinks of you?" She shot him a quick glance. "She thinks you're extremely intelligent, a hard worker, and well organized." He paused. "Oh yes. She also admires you and thinks you're quite beautiful."

Elaine finally managed a slight smile. "That's nice. Thank you."

"Am I fully scheduled this afternoon? Maybe we can find time for me to show you how I really feel."

She looked down at her work. "We'll see."

CHRISTMAS CAME AND WENT all too quickly. The public mood had relaxed somewhat to a mild state of melancholy as the holiday approached. People tried to put a glad face on the festivities, modest as they were, and given the absence of so many husbands and sons. But, there were signs of the war everywhere. The German bombings further south continued at a somewhat slower pace. Despite the bombings, there was little fear of an immediate invasion.

War production continued at a feverish pace, and the expanding military forces continued their intensive training programs, armed with increasing quantities of new equipment. In the West Highlands, as elsewhere, the Home Guard drilled regularly, dressed in their new Army uniforms and armed with rifles, machine guns, and a few anti-tank weapons. Many officers and sergeants attended special weekend schools in Glasgow to develop further their military proficiency. Increasingly, they looked like regular forces and their training included strenuous small unit offensive operations to enable them to attack and expel Nazi invaders. They refused to consider themselves passive defenders.

David stood at the train station the evening of the 15th eagerly awaiting the arrival of the train from Glasgow. The stationmaster told him the train would be delayed just a few minutes, and he impatiently paced the floor, looking out the window at each turn for a sign of its approach. Darkness prevented any sighting of the smoke from the train, but eventually he heard the whistle wailing its impending arrival.

The girls had grown during the past six months and, after many hugs and a few tears, they slowly walked toward the manse. Ben and Kathleen Douglas greeted them at the door, with their three daughters and one son standing behind them. After introductions, Kathleen invited the girls into the kitchen for some biscuits, which were mainly flour and water decorated with cinnamon spots and a tiny bit of sugar left over from the previous week's ration. David and Ben settled into the library, and Ben's son gratefully disappeared upstairs. Within three minutes, there was a commotion as the girls settled onto the floor of the drawing room with a Parcheesi board, talking among themselves as if they'd been friends for years.

"Doesn't take long at that age," Ben commented.

The holidays flew by much too quickly for David. He had arranged his schedule to take some time off each day to be with his girls. He was grateful to Ben and Kathleen for their hospitality and he spent a great deal of time at their home. One side benefit of the sleeping arrangement was that his flat was free, a privilege he shared regularly with Elaine.

The Home Guard and Civil Defense units, now mostly trained to perform their primary missions, also enjoyed some much needed time to relax with their families. The dusk to dawn watch continued. Training would resume in January. Churches were open most days for afternoon and early evening events, and they were surprisingly well attended. Many town folk found time to walk the streets each evening before the blackout descended, with windows covered and lights extinguished to foil enemy bombers. The recent bombing raid, a few weeks earlier, had reinforced the need for caution. To the south, England wasn't so fortunate. Sheffield was badly bombed in mid-December, and London suffered its second great fire from the *Blitz* on December 29th.

On a snowy Sunday morning in January, David said tearful goodbyes to his girls at the train station, and they began their journey back home to St. Albans and the beginning of a new school session. Kathleen and her girls accompanied them to the station, while Ben prepared for services at the church. David thought his heart would break as the train slowly chugged south, his girls waving out the window. He walked slowly to the church with Kathleen and listened sporadically to Ben's service, while the children fidgeted with pencils and paper. Sunday dinner with Ben and Kathleen centered on a leg of mutton, a Christmas gift to Ben from a grateful parishioner. After dinner, David walked to his office, having declined Ben's invitation to remain for the afternoon. He needed time to think and push the loneliness for his girls from his mind.

With the holiday season ending, all thoughts now returned to the war.

17

January 1941

THE YEAR 1941 OPENED QUIETLY in Fort William, as people put their holiday festivities behind them and returned to the grim business of war. Throughout Britain, the Home Guard and Civil Defense forces increased the intensity of their training. They were well aware that, as soon as the winter weather subsided, the Nazi forces would likely launch the long-awaited invasion. The German plans for the coming assault, called *Operation See Lowe*, or Sea Lion, had become known to British intelligence many months earlier. German preparations for such an attack continued, although at a slower pace than earlier.

David used the time to revise the various plans for defense against such an attack, directing his staff to consider all possible German options and determine the best methods to thwart each possibility. The Home Guardsmen had finally received their steel helmets some weeks after acquiring new Army uniforms. Importantly, the War Office granted permission for Home Guard volunteers to wear a battalion insignia that recognized their affiliation with an Army regiment. For several evenings throughout Britain, small metal shops stamped out the cap badges. In Fort William, the men of the Lochaber Company of the 2nd Inverness-shire Battalion proudly displayed their new insignia; denoting affiliation with the Queen's Own Cameron Highland Regiment.

A full battery of 40-millimeter Bofors anti-aircraft guns had been installed near the Aluminum Plant to the great satisfaction of Colonel Laughton. "Now, we'll really give the Jerries a go if they return." On January 14th and 15th the Jerries did indeed return, with a single-plane raid each day. Machine gun fire deflected the *Junkers 88* bomber on the 14th' and its bombs fell harmlessly into a nearby field. The Bofors guns went into action for the first time the next morning, but the bomber evaded fire and dropped its bombs on the factory powerhouse. They didn't explode. "A very great gift, indeed," said Ben Douglas.

Colonel Laughton responded, "If they keep dropping these dud bombs, I'll have to open a scrap metal shop." Listeners were amused, but were grateful the bombs didn't explode. There was little scrap metal remaining after the bomb disposal squads detonated the bombs in distant fields.

With a well-armed and trained Home Guard, supported by better-prepared Civil Defense capabilities, David felt his sub-district had substantially enhanced its capabilities to block parachutists and raiders. They would also provide vastly improved support forces for the coming invasion of Eastern Scotland. His counterpart sub-district commanders felt similarly. They'd also worked hard to train their better-armed forces and to build more fortifications along Scotland's eastern coasts.

The situation in the Middle East and North Africa had occupied much attention of the British Army during the winter. In mid-1940, the Italian invasion and conquest of Ethiopia, previously known as Abyssinia, was pressed forward into Kenya and the Sudan. In late 1940, Churchill appointed Lieutenant-General Alan Cunningham as General Officer Commanding British and Commonwealth Forces in East Africa, with the mission to drive the Axis forces out of East Africa. On January 19, 1941, Cunningham launched his attack against Italian forces in Eritrea, with supporting attacks on Kenya, Italian Somaliland, and the Sudan, all of which successfully drove the Italian Army back into Ethiopia.

On December 9th, 1940, the Western Desert Force under Lieutenant-General Richard O'Connor began its offensive to drive the Italian Army from Egypt. During the next several weeks, the small force pushed the Italians back, capturing city after city along the coastal highway and inflicting severe casualties on Marshal Graziani's Tenth Army. On January 21st, O'Connor attacked the Libyan port city of Tobruk, which the Italians surrendered the following day. Pushing the Italian force further westward along the Mediterranean Coast, British forces captured Benghazi, and soon forced the surrender of all Italian forces at the Battle of Beda Fomm. Ten divisions, comprising 110,000 Italian soldiers, were taken prisoner in the first major British Army victory of the war.

David followed the East African and North African campaigns with great interest, supplementing newspaper and BBC accounts of the battles with information summaries provided by the War Office. He was proud of the forces and their successful battles with Axis troops, but knew that fighting the Germans would be a greater challenge than fighting the Italians. Britain and Italy had been allies since Italy was unified into a single country in 1871, and they'd been allies in World War I. Six British Army divisions had deployed to Italy after the Battle of Capporetto, in 1916, to help defend Italy against the German invasion. The Italians clearly were not united behind Mussolini in his declaration of war against Britain. Despite Mussolini's decision to join Hitler and the Japanese in the Tripartite Pact in 1940, many Italians harbored great resentment toward the Germans and retained friendly feelings toward the British. German feelings toward the British were a different story.

January 21, 1941

DAVID DECIDED TO RETURN to Portree and Mallaig for further review of the Home Guard and the new artillery installations. His concern about renewed threats, when winter ended, caused him to review each detail of the defenses for every village and town, especially those along the coast. He was less concerned about a full-scale German invasion of the West Highlands, as that was the least likely threat of all. Parachutists, seaborne raids, and fifth columnists were greater threats. David wanted to ensure the home defenses were as strong as possible, so as to deter, or defend against smaller German attacks. He especially wanted to review the training of the Mobile Battle Platoons of the Home Guard, which could be deployed to Eastern Scotland in the event of a German invasion across the North Sea. His staff worked to craft a deployment plan for each of those platoons, including transport vehicles, routes to take, petrol, provisions, and destinations.

David and Sergeant-Major McNabb drove to the fishing dock in Mallaig, where they left David's motorcar. They then sailed the short distance to the Isle of Skye and drove north to arrive at Portree by mid-afternoon. McNabb inspected the artillery platoon and the two guns installed in late-November. He reported the crews were "makin' good progress, but still needed more drill to polish their fire control."

David was pleased that the Home Guard Skye Company was approaching 700 strong; "a good battalion," as he put in his report. They'd recently received a Vickers and several Lewis light machine guns, and a few BARs from America. The men looked very professional and spirits were high. This contrasted sharply with the grim views held by the public at large, and their continuing sense of foreboding.

Almost every Home Guard volunteer now carried a firearm of some type, and their simple battle drill, conducted for David, indicated they'd give enemy raiders a tough fight. David spoke to them about the need to remain calm and clear-headed in battle. He reminded them that "excitement causes mistakes." He urged the veterans, now 35-40% of the company, to keep a steady watch over the younger men to ensure they didn't make mistakes. "Drill, repetition and more drill" was essential to survival and success. The veterans fully understood his message.

After two days in Portree, David and McNabb returned to Mallaig for a similar inspection, with good results. Mallaig was a small town with a small Home Guard platoon, but they'd installed their two 18-pounders on a bluff to the west of town, overlooking the fishing harbour. Several of the gunners actually were Navy reservists, but they provided additional hands to man the guns than otherwise would've been available. After visiting with the Civil Defense Coordinator, he met with the Provost and Town Council. His report was favorable and he complimented the community for its concerted efforts to prepare for every eventuality.

On the second day in Mallaig, the Provost interrupted David's meeting with Home Guard leaders to say that a storm was expected later that day, one that could easily drop several inches of snow. "You're welcome to spend another day or two as our guests but, if you need to be in Fort William tomorrow, I suggest you leave promptly and stay ahead of the storm." David chose the latter option.

The Sergeant-Major loaded their bags into David's car, and they left after a late lunch. As they drove south and then east along the coast, they saw the storm clouds approaching.

"We'll be lucky to stay ahead of the storm," he said, "but we should arrive in Fort William before much snow falls."

A few miles further, there was a sharp bump, a lurch to the left and the sound of escaping air; a sharp rock had done its damage. "Damn! This is the first flat tire I've had since I returned to Scotland." The single-lane dirt road from Fort William to Mallaig was considered to be the worst road in Britain and was greatly in need of repair. After rolling slowly to a stop, McNabb got out to remove the spare tire from its rack, while David drew out the tools. A half hour of work installed the good tire, leaving them spattered with mud. Light snow began to fall, as they drove east, and quickly turned to thick, heavy flakes.

"Where are we?" David asked.

"Someplace southeast of Arisaig, Colonel, but we're still some miles from Druimindarroch. Maybe we should stop there for the night, or at least until this storm blows over."

"No, I think we can make it all the way to Fort William. If the storm gets worse, we can stop at Glenfinnan. There should be a small hotel there."

During the next hour, the wind blew harder and the snow mounted up faster than expected. They drove slowly through Druimindarroch without comment, but the storm pummeled them along Loch nan Uamn, a wide sea loch that offered no protection from the strong winds. They were forced to stop several times and wait until the snow lightened. After two more hours, the sky turned dark.

"What's the next town?"

"No' sure, Sir, maybe Arieniskill or Ranochan. We're someplace along Loch Eilt." David already knew that, as the normally placid loch was turbulent, with the wind pushing waves almost to the road. The snow was several inches deep now and blinded David as he tried to drive through it. He remembered all too well his November drive from Durness to Scourie.

"I can't see the road, Sergeant-Major. Maybe we should look for a place to spend the night. There must be cottages or a farmhouse along this road. At this speed, we'll be lucky if we get to Glenfinnan within the hour and we mightn't make it at all."

McNabb kept wiping the windshield with a rag, peering into the storm. "All I see is snow." David drove at a crawl for another ten minutes. "Colonel, there's a light!" McNabb pointed in front of David's face as they rounded a curve.

"Where?"

"Right over there, Sir, to yer left."

Faintly through the storm, David saw an occasional glimmer of light, about a hundred feet away. He stopped the car.

"Must be a cottage, but where's the path?" McNabb got out and, after a brief search, waved David onto a small pathway barely wide enough for the car. David parked and got out. Joining McNabb, he walked through the snow to the door of a dilapidated, thatched roof cottage. He knocked on the door and, when it opened, David introduced himself.

"Come in, come in, too damned cold out there," said a thin, elderly, stooped man.

"What is it, Will?" came a woman's voice.

"Visitors."

David introduced himself and McNabb again, adding the reason for the stop.

"Weel, ye canna' drive in this storm. Best spend the night, but ye'll have to sleep on the floor. Just one bed here for Carol and me." He introduced Carol, adding the name Miller.

"I donna' ha' much for supper, but yer welcome to eat wi' us," she announced. David noticed steam coming from a small pot on the stove.

"Very kind of you, Ma'am, but we shouldn't."

"Nonsense," said Will, "we can share wha' we ha'."

David turned to McNabb. "Would you check the boot of the car? I think I've a tin of fish someplace and a vegetable." McNabb returned shortly with two cans.

"Look, Will, peas and chopped fish!" Carol said excitedly. "We haven't had peas since summer. She opened the cans, dumped the peas into the broth, and patted the fish into small cakes to fry on the stove. "We donna' get food like this verra' often."

The supper, modest but adequate, was served on two plates and two bowls, the only dishes in the cottage. The room was quite bare and evidenced a hardscrabble life. Carol kept apologizing for their ill-furnished home.

"Will hasna' worked in almost five years. We do the best we can, but we havna' much. We farm and tend two goats, but 'tis hard. Will walks to town several times a week. 'Tis quite a trek, over and back, but he says it keeps him fit. Sometimes he can earn a farthing or two if someone needs some help, but most folk ha' nothin' to spare. He fishes the loch and often catches some supper."

She turned to Will. "Please fetch some more wood, dear."

As the door closed, Carol spoke softly. "The past few years ha' been terrible for Will. He's such a hard-workin' man, but there are no jobs. When he lost his job in '33, we thought he'd ha' another soon, but most men were out of work afore long and nothin' opened for Will."

"Could you move to a larger town and find work?" asked McNabb.

"Nae, we couldna' afford the rent and other expenses. We ha' no car. This is our home and we really ha' no other place else to go. It's just verra' hard, especially on Will. We burn peat and some wood, no money for coal. I worrit 'bout him."

The door opened and Will entered with an armload of wood. "I'll try to keep the fire goin' all night, but ye'd best get any clothes you ha' with ye to keep warm. The thatchin' is full o' holes and the cold comes right in."

McNabb went to the car and returned with two heavy wool army great coats. Although only mid-evening, they prepared for bed shortly after the modest supper, David choosing the one large chair and

McNabb taking a place on the floor near the stove. They slept little that night in their cold discomfort, but could hear Will snoring. "At least someone is getting some sleep," David thought.

They rose early the next morning as Carol put a small log into the firebox and placed the pans back on the stove. The storm had passed, leaving a blanket of snow some five inches deep. Breakfast was a pinch of tea in a pot of water and the remains of last night's supper. As they prepared to depart, David suddenly turned to Carol and said, "I almost forgot to pay you."

"No, Colonel, ye donna' ha' to pay us. We're happy to share wha' little we ha'."

"I'm sorry, Mrs. Miller, but Army regulations are very strict. Whenever we stay in a private home, we must pay the stated rate." McNabb looked at him incredulously. "Yes, well the rate is one shilling per night for the Sergeant-Major and two shillings for me, being an officer and all that." He drew out his money. "And we must pay a shilling each for dinner last night and ten-pence each for breakfast. That would be about six shillings." He counted out the money and put it on the table, leaving two thrupence coins in his hand. "Oh, yes, the parking fee." He dropped the remaining coins on the others.

"But, Sir . . . " McNabb started.

"Sergeant-Major, would you inspect the car thoroughly," David interrupted. "I may have left a tin or two of something in the boot."

McNabb went out dumbfounded. A few minutes later, he returned with three tins. "This is all I could find, Colonel."

"Excellent. Well, leave them on the table, no sense in our taking them with us. We'll be resupplied in Fort William." They shook hands and left, the car mercifully starting on the third try. The Millers watched them go, mystified at their good fortune.

As they drove east, McNabb finally spoke up. "Sir, what Army regulations were you speaking of? I never knew we had to pay civilians like that. And who will resupply us in Fort William? I thought you bought those provisions yourself."

"The Millers are poor as church mice, Sergeant-Major. No, there's no regulation and no resupply, but it was the right thing to do." They remained silent until they arrived at Glenfinnan on the north end of Loch Shiel. David looked around, and then turned into a lot in front of a sign: *Williams and Sons, Colliers*.

"Colonel McKenna, I believe!" A voice boomed from the back of the shed.

"Do you know me, Sir?"

"Why certainly, Colonel, I'm John Williams, proprietor here. I'm also a Sergeant in the Home Guard and ye inspected our section several months ago. Of course, I would ha' figured it out anyways. How many colonels of the Black Watch are there in the West Highlands?"

"So you know regimental insignias, Mr. Williams?"

"Aye, Sir. I wa' an Argyll and Sutherland Highlander durin' the First War, 9th Division ye know. I ken all the Highland regiments."

"I'm very pleased to have you in the Home Guard, Sergeant Williams. We need experienced veterans like you to teach the younger chaps."

"Just doin' me bit, Colonel. Now, how can I help ye, since ye ha' honored my establishment?"

"How much would you charge for a half-ton of coal, delivered?"

"A ha'-ton, will be two pounds, twelve."

"Fine," he said taking out his money, "do you know Will Miller, lives about five miles west of here?"

"I do." He checked an old wooden index file. "He and Carol were customers until the Depression hit. Do ye know them?"

"We spent last night there, out of the storm. They're having a tough time. Will hasn't worked in seven years."

"Will did some work for me back in the twenties. Good man, hard worker and verra' reliable." He thought for a minute. "I've been out of touch in that area since my man left me and joined the forces. Me boys are gone to the forces as well, so the wife and I run the business ourselves. Maybe Will could help me twa or three days each week. I'll be out there tomorrow to deliver the coal and I could inquire."

David paid and said their goodbyes. "Don't tell the Millers who paid for the coal."

Three weeks later, David received a letter addressed to Colonel McKenna, Fort William. It was from Carol Miller, "*Thank you for your generous gifts. Mr. Williams finally confessed that you sent the coal. He offered Will a job taking orders and checking on folk's coal supplies. Will is very happy. So am I. Thank you.*"

It was the best letter he'd received in months.

January 28

ARRIVING IN FORT WILLIAM before noon, McNabb took the car to MacIntyre and Sons to be cleaned, serviced, and have the tire

190

repaired. David went to the office and found Elaine working alone. He kissed her briefly, but she didn't respond. "Is something wrong?"

"No, I'm just feelin' a bit off today."

"Have you seen a doctor?"

"No, 'twill pass."

"I thought we might spend some time together. I've missed you terribly, and it appears this is a quiet day."

"Perhaps another time. No' today."

David went to his desk, perplexed. She'd never refused him before.

THE NEXT FEW WEEKS saw the dreary winter weather turn from bad to worse. Heavy, wet snow fell more often, melted into slush during the day and froze again at night. The roads varied from slippery to muddy, and the deep ruts slowed traffic on all unpaved roads. Even when it didn't snow, the sky was cloudy and the mountains totally obscured. One pundit remarked, "if ye couldna' see the Ben, 'twas snowin', but if ye could see the Ben, 'twas about to snow." David found that to be true and, at the urging of his staff, reduced his travel. He made greater use of the post and the telephone, when it worked.

Even worse for David was his relationship with Elaine, as her moods swung from warm and friendly to distant and aloof. She joined him in his flat fewer times than before and usually left quickly after they finished. He simply didn't understand what had changed.

"What am I doing wrong?" he asked her one evening, after the others had left the office.

"Nothin'."

"There must be something. You seem so withdrawn; you hardly ever look at me at the office."

"'Tis no' you, 'tis me."

"Well, what is it?"

"I donna' know. I just feel pulled in all directions. Please bear with me. I know you love me and I love you. But it just isna' the same as before."

"What isn't the same?"

"I don' know."

Feeling frustrated and unsure, David asked, "Would it be better if we just got married right now?"

"No. Please don' put any more pressure on me." She looked away again.

"I'm not trying to pressure you. I love you and I want to help."

"Weel, you're no' helpin'." She looked at the clock and stood up. "I really must leave. Mum and the boys will be waitin' for me."

"But why?"

"Because I must." And she left.

March 5

THE NEXT MORNING, David left early to drive to Glencoe for a meeting with Niall Campbell, the Duke of Argyll, and Lord Lieutenant of Argyll-shire. David was comfortable with his relationship with the Duke, and they seemed to agree completely on the use of the North Argyll Home Guard Battalion that David supervised, in part. His sub-district responsibility extended a short distance into Argyll-shire and he wanted to maintain a close and proper relationship with the Duke. He'd asked Jack Campbell if Jack was related to the Duke.

"Unlikely, David, but maybe at a very far distance."

Previous meetings with the Duke had gone smoothly, and they'd decided to meet again as soon as the Duke planned his next visit to Glencoe. "I try to do as many mid-winter meetings as possible in different communities," he told David. "It's good for the local folks to see the Lord Lieutenant nosing around to make sure everything is running as well as can be expected. It gives them some faith in their government and more confidence for the future. I also like to check the Home Guard chaps and as many Civil Defense volunteers as are available."

Together they inspected units and facilities. They drove from community to community around Loch Awe and its river valley, and met with local authorities at each stop.

"Beautiful country and nice people," the Duke continued, "and we'll be damned before we turn this over to the Jerries."

Returning to Fort William, David found the drive even slower than the morning drive. He'd slept little the night before, turning every thought and memory of Elaine over in his mind. He felt physically ill at the thought of losing her and he simply couldn't understand what was going on. "Why is she pulling away," he asked himself, "what have I done wrong?"

Parking his car and entering the office through the rear door, he found only emptiness. The front door was bolted and the lights were off. The teapot was still on the stove and faint mists of steam rose from the remains of the water. He fixed a cup of warm tea and sat down at his desk, his body feeling as empty as the room. After a short while, he heard a key turning the back door lock.

"Elaine!"

She walked straight to his desk, her eyes never wavering from his face. She stood before him.

"I want you . . . NOW"

18

March 26, 1941

THE TELEPHONE RANG INCESSANTLY and Elaine dashed across the room to answer it. Calling to David, she said, "Colonel, Commander Morton needs to speak with you."

"Commander Morton?"

"Yes, Sir, Wing Commander Ralph Morton, the commander of the radar station at Sango Bay. He had this call patched through from his headquarters. The connection isn't good, but he says it's urgent." David picked up his phone.

"Colonel, this is Ralph Morton. Something strange is going on. Mrs. McPherson is here with her rifle and she insists she must speak to you immediately. I tried to find out the issue, but she won't tell me. She says it's an urgent matter of national security and she insisted I telephone you directly. I'm sorry to bother you, Sir."

"That's fine, Commander. Put Mrs. McPherson on the line."

"Colonel McKenna, is tha' ye?" Her voice came faintly through the crackling on the line.

"Yes, Mrs. McPherson. What's the matter?"

"Can ye hear me, Colonel, 'tis Emma McPherson?" She was yelling now.

"Yes, I can hear you!" he shouted back.

"Colonel, I saw one early this morning. 'Twas huge. Right near me cottage."

"What did you see?"

"A submarine! 'Twas a German submarine, just offshore. 'Twas huge and another one wa' further out in the bay, a regular size one."

"Emma! How do you know it was German?"

"I ken me ships, Colonel, I've been watchin' 'em from my porch all m'life. 'Twas no' British and they were speakin' German."

"What! You could hear them?" David felt a wave of disbelief flow over him. "Impossible," he thought. "Maybe she's been drinking."

"Put the Commander on the phone." In a moment, Morton came back on the line.

"Is she sober?" David asked.

"Yes, Sir, I think so. She came running over just before daybreak and told us to call you. We'd great difficulty getting through to your office. I've never seen her like this, but she seems quite serious. We had no guards posted to watch the ocean and none of my men saw anything; of course, nobody was looking out into the bay. The radar won't pick up anything that low and close. If a submarine surfaced near to shore we wouldn't see it on the radar. I don't know what to say, Colonel, whether it was real or not." In the background David heard Emma yell, "'Twas real!"

"Commander, have her tell you how she could hear the men talking."

Connor returned a few moments later. "She says the large submarine was close inshore, and there were men on the deck with binoculars looking at the bluff. She said she heard the sub's engines, got her rifle, and crawled to the edge of the bluff so as not to be seen." He paused for a moment. "There was moonlight, and she saw five men on the deck of the sub and three in the conning tower. She called it 'the high part in the middle.' She said she could hear a few words between the surf breaking and they were foreign words. She also says they weren't wearing British uniforms."

David turned to Elaine. "Call the Admiral. Tell him it's an emergency." Elaine quickly went to the other phone and rang up the operator.

"Anything else from her, Commander?"

"No, Sir. She just keeps saying it was a huge submarine and it had no big gun, just small guns. I think she means no deck gun."

"OK, Commander. Tell her thank you for the information and we'll evaluate it. Then, place your men on alert and have two men at all times watching the bay. Alert Lieutenant Parker of the Home Guard, and tell him what you told me. I want his men placed on alert all day and night in uniform, armed and ready to move quickly to your site, if called. Better reinforce your radar station with extra men from Balnakiel, and keep your own men armed at all times. Set up observation posts at all your sites to watch the sea. Prepare your demolitions on standby and notify your headquarters. Then notify both the Cape Wrath and Faraid Head stations, and have them do the same. Real or false, we'd better be ready. I'll get back to you when I've further information."

"The Admiral's drivin' here right now," said Elaine, putting down the phone.

"This may be real or a complete false alarm. I just don't know."

Ten minutes later the Admiral arrived. "Do we have a real emergency, Colonel?"

"I don't know. I need your expertise." David repeated the information Emma and Commander Morton had told him and gave the Admiral his assessment of Emma McPherson. "She's an eccentric lady, but I saw no signs that she was daft or would make up the story."

Evans-Cooper thought for a few minutes. "I wonder if she saw a *milchkuh*, but why would it be off Durness? I knew they were working on those boats, but I didn't know they were operational yet. It might be a prototype."

"What's a *milchkuh*?" David asked. Across the room Elaine listened intently.

"The Germans have been working on new methods of resupplying their U-boats at sea, instead of having them return to their bases for refueling and resupply, a very dangerous and time-consuming process. They came up with the *milchkuh*, meaning a 'milk cow'. It's a very large submarine that would carry fuel, ammunition, spare torpedoes, foodstuffs, and other supplies. The *milchkuh* would sail the oceans and rendezvous with the U-boats to re-provision them on the surface at some safe location. The absence of a deck gun would fit in here. The big *milchkuh* does not attack enemy ships, so it would not need torpedo tubes or deck guns. The small guns would be for anti-aircraft protection while they enter or depart a harbour. These supply subs will permit the U-boats to remain on station far longer and would greatly improve the efficiency of the wolf packs."

"Improve their efficiency to sink our ships," responded David grimly.

"Precisely. Leave it to the Germans to come up with an idea like this."

"So, it could've been a very large German submarine, possibly a *milchkuh*?"

"Yes, it's quite possible, but why would a submarine be just offshore at Durness?"

"The radar station, of course!" David exclaimed. "They were conducting a reconnaissance to see if they could land a raiding party to seize the radar equipment. They would want to test the water depth and the sandbars to see how close to the shore the sub could sail, and how far the raiders must paddle. They also would want to scout a path

196

up the bluffs to get to the radar station. They must determine if they would need any special equipment to haul the radar set down to the beach, onto rubber boats and out to the sub. They would require a very large submarine to carry the radar equipment, as it might not fit into a standard U-boat. A large sub could also carry the raiding party. The smaller sub, the standard U-boat, would stand guard while they did their dirty work and could sink any ships that came to the rescue. Last night's reconnaissance would give them all the information they'd need to launch a raid."

"If that's true, when would they likely attack?"

"Tonight. If Emma was correct they'd be underwater just a few miles offshore right now. They could surface after midnight, sneak in very quietly, launch their boats with partial moonlight, and seize the radar station. They'd likely return to the sub with the equipment and be underwater again inside forty-five minutes. Even if gunfire woke up people in Durness, the Home Guard platoon couldn't get down to Sango Bay in time."

"Colonel, we're guessing, of course."

"Yes, but if we're wrong, we'll have conducted a realistic training exercise. If we're right, we can bloody their noses. If we do nothing, however, we may very well give Hitler the priceless gift of our latest radar system."

"What will you do?"

"I'm calling an emergency mobilization of the 1st Sutherland Home Guard Battalion and all supporting organizations. Two Mobile Battle Platoons will deploy to Durness, and the static units in Sutherland and Caithness will come to full alert and go to their anti-invasion stations near their homes. All other units in our sector will just go on alert. All Home Guard volunteers will change into their uniforms, but continue their normal occupations with weapons nearby. Home Guard and Civil Defense commanders and staffs will assemble at their duty stations and await further orders."

"Should you go through Scottish Command first, Colonel?"

"There's no time. Elaine, call the Duke of Sutherland directly at Dornoch and pass on my orders. I want two Mobile Battle Platoons on the road to Durness within ninety minutes. I want two 18-pound artillery pieces sent to Sango Bay promptly, one from Durness and one from Scourie. If I'm wrong, General Carrington will have a piece of my *derriere*. But if the Jerries land and I've done nothing, he'll have my head."

"Yes, Sir. Then what?"

"Then, call Colonel Matthew Harris and tell him what I've done and why. Have him alert other Regular and Home Guard units as he sees fit. If I'm still here, or the Admiral, we can speak to him ourselves. Then, call CB and have him assemble our staff to work on the situation. I'll go to Durness and command the operation, but I'm sure the Duke of Sutherland will be the first man on the road to Durness."

"Colonel," said the Admiral, "you can't get to Durness before midnight, no matter how fast you drive."

"Quite right, I'll fly." He went to the phone in his office and told the operator to get Brigadier Campbell's office on the line. After a few minutes, Lieutenant-Colonel Steve Whittaker answered.

"Brigadier Campbell's not here, Colonel, he's off somewhere with his driver." David briefed Whittaker on the situation at Durness and explained his plan. "Good Lord, Colonel, this sounds serious. I'll call the Chief Constable and have the police find the Brigadier. I'll also call Scottish Command. They can alert the RAF and the Navy."

"Steve, tell them to proceed with extreme caution. I don't want to scare the U-boats away. They'll just lay low and come back another time when our guard is down. I want to catch that submarine and sink it."

"Sir, with all due respect, you have no weapons to sink it."

"I know, Steve, but, if I can punch a hole in that sub, it'll not be able to submerge and will become easy prey for the Navy or the RAF tomorrow. Have them keep their ships and aircraft at a safe distance."

"Roger that, Colonel."

"And Steve, arrange for a light plane to pick me up at the Lochyside airstrip here in Fort William and fly me to Durness. We'll have to land on the dirt road at Sango Bay, so I need a good pilot."

"I'll get right on it, Colonel."

David went up to his flat and put on his cold weather battle dress uniform and packed his helmet, web gear, a torch, a revolver and a side bag. Thinking hard about potential needs, he added several other items, and then returned to the office. Elaine was still busy on the phone, and the Admiral was at the staff table making other calls. Both looked at David in surprise.

"I ha' never seen you before in battle dress, and with your revolver in its holster," said Elaine. "You look fierce and verra' handsome." David did not reply.

"CB will be here in ten minutes, Colonel, and the others very quickly. I'm ready to call Vice-Admiral Jim Troup in Glasgow. Have you any special instructions?"

"Tell the Navy to keep a very low profile today and throughout the night, unless we call them for help. They should be ready to fight at daybreak tomorrow."

"I think it likely the Germans will require only the two U-boats for this mission," said the Admiral, "but I can't guarantee a third one won't be lurking nearby. They also may send out a few E-boats for support, but that's only a possibility."

CB and other staff began to arrive. The Admiral briefed them quickly and set them to work on the operation. Another half-hour passed before the phone rang again. Elaine answered it.

"Colonel, it is Lieutenant-Colonel Whittaker for you."

"Sir, I've just a brief update. We've not yet found the Brigadier, but I've every bobby in Inverness-shire searching for him. Unfortunately, we've bad news from Scottish Command. Every Regular battalion in the Highlands is participating in a big training exercise in East Lothian and they can't get any unit to Durness before tomorrow morning. Also, both the Commando Training Center and the SOE center at Arisaig have their staff and trainees in Lothian, playing aggressors. Major-General Adams says it's in your hands completely until tomorrow, and to use your best judgment. I guess, Colonel, it's up to you and the Home Guard. I'm confident that Brigadier Campbell will support you completely, if we ever find him."

"What about my aircraft?"

"No luck, yet. I called the RAF liaison officer and he said every plane is committed. All the Army cooperation aircraft are in Lothian, not that they have more than a few anyway. So, I called the RAF station commander at Greenock myself and told him that General Carrington had declared this to be an emergency and he'd hold the RAF responsible for failing to support this operation. I know damned well there are aircraft down there."

"General Carrington said that?"

"No, but I'm sure he would if he knew what was going on. In any case, I expect a call back from the RAF fairly soon."

"Thanks for the good work, Steve. I'll wait for your call."

IT WAS ALMOST 1 P.M. when Elaine came into his office. "Colonel, Brigadier Campbell is calling." David jumped for the phone.

"David. Well, it sounds like some excitement in Durness. Yes, I approve all your actions and I'll telephone Major-General Adams and get his concurrence. Steve Whittaker is calling the RAF again. I may go up there with you, if we can ever get an aircraft."

"Sir, it's not necessary for you to be there, really."

"Nonsense, it would be fun! Have you heard anything from Sutherland?"

"Just a follow-up call from the Duke's office saying he was leaving for Durness with the lead Mobile Battle Platoon. Another one will follow soon after; perhaps 110-120 men in all. He's taking an additional 18-pounder from Dornach, manned by his best gun crew. Lieutenant Parker in Durness had called the Duke's office to say that the Durness Platoon had 47 men already standing by. About 40 Durness men will be at the radar station before nightfall with their 18-pounder. The Scourie Platoon is on alert and they're preparing to send at least 30 men to Sango Bay with their 18-pounder."

"Excellent."

"That'll place over 150 of Scotland's best Home Guardsmen at Sango Bay by nightfall, armed with at least a dozen light machine guns and five Boys rifles, plus the three 18-pounders. Other Home Guardsmen will defend the villages. The RAF will have 75-90 well-armed men at their sites, including 50-60 at the radar site.

"I expect the German raiding party, if there is one, will total 30-40 men, but they'll be highly trained and well-armed. The one deck gun on the smaller U-boat and all the anti-aircraft guns will also support them. We'll give them a good fight, if they try to come ashore."

"Yes we will, David, and that's precisely why I'm coming with you."

David hung up and sighed. "I don't need Jack Campbell looking over my shoulder during the battle, or even running the battle himself," he thought.

Fifteen minutes later the phone rang. "Sir, 'tis Lieutenant-Colonel Whittaker."

"Colonel McKenna, I have an aircraft for you. It's a Lysander, a two-seat trainer from Abbotsinch, near Glasgow. Your pilot is an instructor-pilot who was home on leave until the RAF station commander called him. He hopes to pick you up at the Lochyside Airstrip before 4 p.m." In very hushed tones Whittaker said, "It's only a two-seater, Colonel. I guess Brigadier Campbell can't go with you after all." David momentarily felt a surge of relief.

He briefed his staff on the call. CB responded, "Sir, its well over an hour flight from here to Durness, probably more. I hope he has plenty of fuel, but he can drop you off and fly on to Ullapool or Inverness. Both have airstrips with fueling capabilities. Or the RAF station at Wick."

A short while later Elaine interrupted David with another phone call. "'Tis Colonel Harris from Inverness."

"David, this sounds exciting!" Harris began. "May I go in your place?"

"No, Matthew, this is my party. You're my rear area support commander, remember?" They both laughed.

"How can I help? I don't have a single bloody Regular infantry soldier to offer you, but I've several thousand Home Guardsmen who would like to join your party. I've alerted all units in my sub-district, both Home Guard and Civil Defense. I've also notified the Navy and RAF stations, and the Orkney Island garrison will be on alert. We'll stand on alert all night and at least until noon tomorrow."

"Matthew, my best guess is that this will only be a small raid to snatch the new radar equipment. I took the liberty of calling the Duke of Sutherland and ordering his Mobile Battle Platoons to Durness. But, I'd ask that your Caithness Home Guard Battalion keep both of their Mobile Battle Platoons ready to move to Durness or anyplace else along the northern coast, if needed."

"I'm way ahead of you, old chap. The Duke called promptly to tell me of your order. I've arranged that Lieutenant-Colonel Hardy will send two sections of the Thurso Mobile Battle Platoon from the Caithness Battalion to Tongue and Bettyhill, east of Durness, at the Duke's request. The Wick Platoon will reposition to Thurso to act as a general reserve for anything along the coast. Lieutenant-Colonel Dick-Lauer will do the same from his Ross-Shire Battalion, and will cover the northeast coastline up to John o'Groats. He'll position a Mobile Battle Platoon north of Lairg and be prepared to reinforce you within an hour.

"Oh yes, David. Remember those chaps in the Braemore Forest whom you met with last October, the woodsmen? Well, they threatened to mutiny if they didn't get to go with you, being so close to Durness and all that. I've authorized their small Mobile Platoon to go to Durness to serve as a reserve for you. I told them they could send the best thirty men only, just the ones who have been training all year as a mobile force. I want to reward those who met the training requirements faithfully, but not allow the 'hangers-on' to jump on board at the last minute."

"They were good lads, Matthew. I'll find something useful for them to do. I assume you've passed this along to Brigadier Campbell and to Scottish Command?"

"I alerted them immediately I received your message. I'll call them again shortly and apprise them of the situation. Well old chap, good luck!"

IT WAS ALMOST 4 P.M. WHEN David saw the Lysander begin its approach to the Lochyside Airstrip. The plane landed smoothly despite the crosswinds, and the pilot, Flight Lieutenant Wesley Collins, saluted David, as he taxied toward him. "Taxi for hire," he quipped.

"I wish the taxi had been here three hours ago," David responded in a serious tone.

"Sorry, Sir, I came as soon as I was called."

"Do you have enough fuel for the trip? How's the weather?"

"Fuel should be okay, Colonel, at least enough to get you to Durness and me back to a refueling point. It's a bit breezy up there with a stiff headwind. We may get knocked about somewhat, but we should be fine."

The plane taxied to the end of the runway, and David buckled himself into the rear cockpit seat. Collins pushed the throttle forward, and they were airborne within three hundred yards. It had been years since David last flew over the Scottish hills, and he was pleased Collins decided to fly fairly low, turning away from the mountains as he flew westward down Loch Linnhe. After fifteen minutes, he gained sufficient altitude to safely turn north and cross the mountains, flying within easy sight of the coast to the west.

The fields were slowly regaining their spring colors after a hard winter, but the trees were still without leaves. The afternoon sun was beginning to set just above the ocean to the west, and the clouds were tinged with a brilliant orange hue. "I wish I could just admire the views," David mused. The waters of the lochs and rivers sparkled in the wind, little flickers of bright lights. The Lysander bumped repeatedly and swung to the side as the wind hit the craft, sometimes so wildly that Collins was forced to jerk the stick to bring the plane back on course. David was reminded again why he didn't like to fly. "No choice today. Just grit my teeth and get through it."

"How long to Durness?" he asked, shouting above the roar of the engine.

"Something over ninety minutes, Colonel, maybe somewhat more if the winds stay strong." David decided to distract himself. He peered intently over the sides of the craft. They flew for another forty-five minutes of discomfort from the buffeting winds. David thought it had been two hours.

Suddenly Collins shouted, "There are some of your boys, Colonel!" He pointed down to the right. There, on a road that broke out from the wood line, were four civilian lorries. They were driving northwest

202

and filled with soldiers; distinguishable by their helmets and rifles, even from 2000 feet.

"Looks like more than thirty of them," David said out loud. "Those men comprise a small Mobile Battle Platoon of woodsmen from the Braemore Forest area. They're well-trained, shoot like marksmen, and just want to have a go at some Nazis."

"More power to them, Colonel, maybe they'll get their wish to-night." Collins wagged his wings in salute to the lads below.

"We'll see."

The plane flew on for another twenty-five minutes, and then Collins shouted, "There's another bunch, down to the left." From 1500 feet, David saw clearly the platoon from Scourie; three lorries and five motorcars slowly winding their way northwards, just a few miles from Durness.

"That's the Scourie chaps pulling their 18-pounder gun behind that third lorry. They must have taken the whole Scourie platoon with them."

They passed east of Durness. The Lysander descended below 800 feet, and David noticed the bustle of activity at the radar station. Further east, a lengthy convoy was approaching Durness, winding its way around Loch Eriboll, along the coast road. "I wonder if the Duke is leading that convoy," David thought. His question was answered as they approached the radar station and saw the many soldiers unloading equipment and moving toward the bluffs. "There are too many for just the Durness Platoon. The first Mobile Battle Platoon must have already arrived from Dornach."

As they came down low to make their landing on the dirt road, David saw the unmistakable figure of the Duke of Sutherland, standing with feet astride and hands on his hips. Major Priestley was standing nearby. "Just one big party," he thought.

David scrambled out of the Lysander and recovered his bag. The Duke approached and saluted. "Good afternoon, Colonel, the 1st Sutherland Battalion is present in part, and other units are closing in or taking up positions elsewhere." David wondered if he'd ever been saluted before by a Duke and a Lord Lieutenant at that.

He replied, "One unit is approaching from the east and the Scourie Platoon is approaching the village now from the south, M'lord. They should be here in thirty minutes. How are you positioning your forces?" Although militarily senior in rank to the Duke, David was conscious he was speaking to a prominent political figure and member of the nobility.

"My 1st Mobile Battle Platoon is commanded by Captain McCrae and the 2nd by Captain Grant. They both have three sections, each of 18-20 men. The platoons will be side-by-side, facing the ocean, with one section of each platoon covering the front facing the beach landing zone up to the edge of the bluff. They'll tie into the RAF chaps on either flank. When the Braemore boys arrive, they'll take up positions defending the road along the west flank. As you well know, a bluff isn't the best place to position our forces for battle, but we really have no choice. I don't want my men down on the beach where they easily could be killed or captured by the Jerries.

"Initially, I'll have a thin screen watching from the bluff, hunkered down and camouflaged so they'll not be seen. Behind them, each platoon will emplace the other two sections of their soldiers, one ready to reinforce the thin screen up front immediately before the shooting starts; the other will serve as a platoon reserve. My machine guns and Boys rifles will be sited and dug in near the bluff to give them a full range of fire downwards. They can sweep the beach, the Smoo Cave entrance, and the ocean out as far as they can see. I have set up a V-shaped firing zone on my right flank, facing the crescent-shaped approach up from the ocean. It comprises two Lewis guns, and a half-section of riflemen. That zone will control the lower bluff on the right. Extra ammunition boxes are being placed near the front, as are the boxes of Mills Bombs, all directly supervised by a sergeant. I've two Very pistols to fire illumination flares when the shooting begins. Major Priestley will command my front.

"The Scourie Platoon and any extra boys from the Braemore Forest, maybe fifty in all after subtracting the 18-pounder crew, will be my reserve force dug in behind the two forward platoons," he continued. "My reserve will either move forward or to the flanks upon my order. The Durness Platoon will be to the left near the radar station, and will help cover the road and the beach just west of my left flank. Small numbers of older Home Guardsmen remain in Durness itself, Leirinbeg and the other villages. I also told Commander Morton to place his two groups of airmen on the right flank of the radar station, wherever he felt appropriate, and also cover the road from the east. He's not to set off the demolitions except on your order, unless you and I are both killed. Then he's to blow up the whole damn thing. All vehicles will be concealed behind the hill to the south."

"What about the three 18-pounder guns?" David asked.

"All three will be placed forward near the bluff, so they can fire downwards or out to sea. Like the others, they'll be fully dug in and camouflaged."

"Excellent. Now, I want the artillery to concentrate on the submarines. I want the Boys rifles to concentrate initially on the submarine gun crews and be assisted by several machine guns. If the Jerries try to flee, the Boys gunners should fire on the rubber boats, as they will punch right through those boats, even a mile offshore. The riflemen and remaining machine gunners can handle the men in the boats. Nobody is to fire until I give the order. I want the rubber boats to get to within twenty yards of the beach before we open fire. I don't want to scare the Jerries off, M'lord. I want to kill them or capture them. And I want to punch holes in the subs.

"Also, have Lieutenant Parker communicate to his Civil Defense counterparts in Durness that all lights are to be extinguished by 7 p.m. tonight. No exceptions, total darkness, as I don't want any lights to serve as navigation aids for the submarines."

"I understand, Colonel," the Duke responded.

"What about communications?"

"Voice only, Colonel, as we have no radios. I can call out on the telephone in the Radar Station, but it's not terribly reliable." As they spoke, Sergeant-Major McNabb approached and saluted.

"McNabb!" said David, "What are you doing here?"

"I wa' in Ullapool, workin' with the gun crews, when we got word of the alert and movement of the Scourie Platoon to Durness. I got right into me motorcar and drove straight-a-way here, Colonel. I mun be wi' me gunners if we're fixin' to fight. It wa' a quick trip as I didna' have that useless Lieutenant Osborne with me." He suddenly stopped and looked at David uncomfortably. "Beggin' yer pardon, sir."

"I'm glad you're here, McNabb," David responded. "You should report to Major Priestley and go to work with the gun crews." McNabb saluted again and turned to leave. "Sergeant-Major, wait. You must make it clear to the gunners that they're to focus on the submarines. I want holes, at least in the big sub, even if you can't hit the smaller one. Punch holes in it! I'll buy a keg of ale for the first gun crew that puts a solid hole in either sub." McNabb smiled a crooked tooth smile, saluted again and left.

As David walked among the men, he noticed how proudly they wore their uniforms. They carried their weapons comfortably, most having used firearms since childhood. Almost all displayed the SU and the number 1 patches on their upper left sleeves; the symbol of the 1st

Sutherland Battalion. The platoon from the Braemore Forest wore the R and number 1 of the 1st Ross-shire Battalion. Quite a number also displayed a red diamond patch on their lower right sleeves, the Home Guard Proficiency Badge earned when the volunteer passed a series of soldiering tests.

The sun had completely disappeared by now, and Sango Bay was shrouded in darkness. Scattered clouds slowly drifted across the sky and a quarter-moon shone its silver light dimly through the darkness. David looked up at the stars and murmured a quick prayer that the next few hours would bring success to their efforts. It was turning colder, and the breeze had stiffened. As he looked down from the bluff, he saw Emma McPherson's cottage. She was sitting on the porch with her rifle cradled in her lap—"no doubt," thought David, "watching everything with amazement and delight."

Lieutenant Parker approached and saluted. "I hope the Jerries make a try for it tonight. I'd like to have a go at them. My men have trained hard for something like this, and I'd hate to disappoint them."

David asked, "Have you ever had men under you killed, Lieutenant?"

"No, Sir."

"It's not fun. It'll make you sick and you'll never be the same afterward. You'll spend the rest of your life asking, 'Why them and not me? Why did they die and I was allowed to live?' Then you'll ask, 'What could I have done better that would have saved them from death?' Of course, there is no answer, but those thoughts will haunt you for as long as you live and will wake you countless nights. I hope you never experience that, not tonight, not ever." He paused. "Lieutenant Parker, I'd advise you to spend every waking moment with your men tonight, but all of you should get some sleep before midnight."

Parker was silent for a moment, then saluted and walked slowly back to his men.

David walked over to see Sutherland's two reserve platoons. The men from Braemore Forest had dug in soundly and were well protected from enemy fire. They were also well protected from the cold, having worn warm clothing under their uniforms. As he approached the Scourie Platoon, he saw a familiar form.

"Catherine! What are you doing here?"

She stood up, her helmet tipped uncomfortably to the side. She held a blanket around her. "Right now, I think I'm freezin' here, Dav . . . Colonel, I mean. 'Tis bloody cold. How are ye stayin' warm?"

"Plenty of warm clothing under my uniform," he replied, "a warm pair of gloves and a knitted took under my helmet. Why are you here?"

"I'm the District Nurse, remember? I go where the patients are, and tonight I may ha' to treat wounded soldiers, God forbid! 'Tis always was our plan. Doctors and nurses accompany the Home Guard whenever they're deployed. Look around. The Duke has at least one doctor, Major Watson, wi' him here from Dornach, and I've seen twa or three other district nurses tonight. Welcome to me first aid station." She gestured to a few blankets and medical supplies lying on the ground. David noticed her medicine chest and a large box of bandages.

"I really need for you to stay down, if the firing begins. This can be dangerous."

"I'll ha' the protection of 200 fine men out here tonight, so I'm sure I'll be safe," she responded.

"They won't be able to protect you from artillery fire, and one U-boat has a deck gun. Artillery fire drops down and blows people into little pieces. I know. I've been wounded by artillery, nearly killed."

"How 'bout if I set up me first aid station inside the radar station?"

"No," he replied, "that may become a target for the German deck gun if they cannot snatch the radar equipment. You'd best stay out here. It's cold, but it's safer."

"Yes, Sir!" She saluted awkwardly. "Would ye like some 'medicine'?"

"It's tempting, thanks, but I need to stay alert. Maybe, I'll have some tomorrow."

"If we're alive," she said softly.

19

March 27, 1941

IT WAS JUST PAST MIDNIGHT as David looked at the wind-whipped ocean from the edge of the bluff at Sango Bay. The chill of the wind passed just over him. It made him feel almost glad he was lying on the cold ground, peering through binoculars. He'd told the soldiers lying along the edge of the bluff to keep a thin row of grass to their front so as to avoid being seen by the Germans. The U-boats, if they were there at all, could not see clearly through their periscopes in the darkness, but they could easily pick out the silhouettes of the men, if they stood up. The thin row of grass would further conceal the men, their weapons, and their helmets.

Behind him lay 200 Home Guardsmen and 75 airmen, all well dug in and many now asleep. The crew-served weapons, which were the machine guns and the Boys anti-tank rifles, were carefully sighted near the bluff and well-camouflaged to avoid detection. Three 18-pound artillery guns were dug in so well they looked unusually small compared to their normal size. They were loaded with solid shot and could be aimed quickly at an approaching submarine. The gun crews lay just behind, waiting to spring into action. From the low hum of the generators, David could tell the radar system was operating from a building behind him. Not a glimmer of light escaped from the installation.

The Duke of Sutherland, the Home Guard commander, was twenty-five yards behind the bluff, sitting calmly on the ground and speaking with one of his officers. Major Priestley, who commanded the forward platoons along the bluff, crawled continuously from one position to another to check on his men. These Home Guardsmen, members of the two Mobile Battle Platoons, were mostly men in their twenties and thirties, with only a few in their late-teens. Many were veterans of previous military service. They provided an important calming effect on the younger men who had just nine or ten months of Home Guard training, two or three evenings per week and most weekends.

Along the flanks and rear were the Durness, Scourie, and Braemore platoons, which included some men in their forties and a few in their fifties.

Through the darkness, David heard the force of the surf pound the massive boulders below and along the beach. Scotland's northern coastline was mostly bereft of gently sloping sandy beaches. Instead, massive bluffs overlooked thin strips of sand which cradled huge boulders that had broken off over the centuries from the headwalls looming above. They provided a perilous greeting for sailors nearing the shoreline.

Priestley approached David, crawling silently to his location. "Do you see anything, Colonel?"

"No, Major. It's early yet. I think it would be another hour or two before we see them, if they come at all." He turned on his side to face Priestley. "How are the men?"

"They're quite good, Sir. A few cases of jitters among the younger lads, but the veterans will keep them under control."

"Are they staying warm?"

"Yes, Sir, they've been trained on winter warfare and all have suitable, warm clothing under their uniforms. One lad asked if he could light a small fire." He grinned. "His corporal didn't think that was an appropriate question and swatted him before the other lads could jump on him. I think he got his answer." Priestley paused to look around. "I don't think we could've conducted this mission six months ago, Colonel. The men simply weren't trained well enough to handle an operation like this. They wouldn't have had the remotest idea about how to take up defensive positions."

"Six months ago, the War Office was still telling them to observe and report only." David replied. "Don't even fire a shot from your window if the Nazis are killing your neighbor," he said sarcastically. "Well, almost. Six months ago, some of our chaps were just learning which end of the rifle the bullet comes out." He paused as he looked toward the bay. "They've progressed significantly, Major, and I like the new force we've created. I'm very proud of our men. Maybe we'll fight tonight and maybe we won't. Either way, they'll have done their job."

"I hope the Nazis try something tonight. I'd like to see my company in action."

'I know you were a gunner and I see from your ribbons that you were a veteran of the last war. Did you get into battle?"

"No, Sir. I was with a group of replacement gunners sent to France at the end of the war. We were held in the rear for a few days, waiting to be sent forward to an artillery regiment. Then the war ended."

"If the Jerries come ashore tonight, you most likely will lose some soldiers. Killed, maimed, badly injured; they're all our lads, and we're responsible for them." David raised himself on one arm. "I only wanted to see a battle once in my life, during the First War. That was when I first arrived in France and hadn't yet seen action. After I saw my first battle, I never wanted to see another. I did see more battles, however, several more, some lasting weeks and months. I'd be happy never to see another battle, here or anywhere else."

WHEN HE HEARD A RUSTLING SOUND near him and a muffled voice, David realized he'd dozed off briefly. He glanced at his watch: just past 1:30 a.m. The wind had mostly subsided, but the cold persisted. He looked out to sea and saw nothing. Presently, there was tug on his trousers. Startled, he looked back. It was Major Priestly who'd low-crawled to David's position.

"Sir, something's out there."

"Where do you mean?"

"It's about a mile out, in the center of the bay. It might be a periscope."

"I don't see anything," David said squinting seaward. "How could anyone see a periscope in this darkness and with the wind on the water?"

"MacCloskey saw it first, a young man with sharp eyes. I couldn't see it either, but finally got a glimpse of something. It didn't look like a fish."

David rubbed his eyes. "Not as good as they used to be," he thought. Raising his binoculars again, he peered in the direction Priestley pointed. David scanned slowly from right to left. It was difficult to look down the binocular shaft and see anything on the darkened sea, its surface barely lit by a half-moon and stars. Gradually, his eyes focused on occasional whitecaps, smaller than earlier, as the wind had diminished to a mild breeze. The horizon was barely perceptible.

"I don't see anything." He scanned back and forth for over a minute. "I don't see anything, Major. Are you sure you saw something?" He continued to search the open waters without success. Then, a short finger-like object caught his eye, protruding several feet above the surface with the faint hint of a frothy trail falling behind.

"Wait! I see something!" he whispered breathlessly. Adrenaline surged through his body, bringing him to a high state of alert and a mixture of excitement and apprehension. He realized the object was almost certainly a periscope. "Good Lord, a submarine! It's a German raid," he thought. "The Nazi raiders are less than two miles away and coming to snatch the radar. We'll fight tonight." He brought his emotions under control with a few deep breaths. His assessment had been correct, yet he must remain calm in front of his men. The Jerries were poised to strike, but the Army was prepared to stop them. David took several more deep breaths. He slowly turned to Priestley and spoke calmly, almost nonchalantly.

"I guess it could be a periscope, Major, but I'm not absolutely sure."

Priestley looked again. "I think it's moved from where I first saw it. Not much, but I really think it's moved."

"I can't tell," David replied. They both watched the object for several minutes. "Yes, it's definitely moving against the tide. It's not a piece of floating junk and it definitely doesn't behave like a fish. It appears to be wending its way around a sandbar."

"Colonel, I think it's moving in our direction." They looked again.

"You're right. I think we should have twenty to thirty minutes before the sub, if it is a sub, gets close enough to launch its boats. Go back quietly and begin to alert your troops. No noise and no movement! And pass the warning to the Duke. He may alert the others as he sees fit. I'll give the word when the men can load their weapons."

The artillery and crew-served weapons had been loaded since they were set up in their firing positions, but David didn't want individual soldiers loading their rifles. There was too much chance of an accidental firing. Priestley did as instructed, and soon there was a general rustle as men awoke and assumed their battle positions. There was an occasional shush from a corporal to a young soldier, but overall the men were fairly quiet.

The ammunition boxes nearest the troops were opened. Their covers had been removed earlier in the evening and then gently laid on top to permit quick and silent access. Similarly, the boxes of Mills bomb grenades near the edge of the bluff were prepared under a sergeant's supervision. They would be distributed only when the Jerries were paddling ashore in their rubber boats. The grenades would wreak havoc on any Nazi raider who made it to the protection of the boulders on the beach. The Very pistols were loaded, not with signal flares, but with illumination rounds.

David looked back and saw the clusters of helmets flattened toward the ground. The Mark I steel helmet, with its wide brim flaring outward, had been invented before the First War to give protection to its wearer against shrapnel; artillery projectiles which burst overhead and drove shell fragments downward toward the earth and through any unfortunate exposed soul. David often wondered why the British Army hadn't adopted a more modern helmet which would also provide protection for the sides of heads, as had the French, Germans, Russians, Italians and, most recently, the Americans. In the War Office, he found the answer to be the budget-cutting Chancellor of the Exchequer. Tonight, however, the Mark I helmet might prove more beneficial, as the greatest threat could well be the U-boat deck gun firing shells which could explode overhead. He thought about the 18-pounders and turned back toward a nearby soldier. "Crawl back and bring Sergeant-Major McNabb to me. Be very quiet!" he whispered.

A few minutes later McNabb crawled up to David's position. He was breathing very hard, his bulging stomach no longer up to that exercise. He whispered hoarsely, "I'm gettin' too old for this shit, Colonel."

"We're both getting too old for a lot of things," David responded. "With a little luck this could be our last battle."

"I surely hope so, Colonel, but 'pears like we're in for a fight pretty soon. How can I help you?" McNabb looked out toward the bay, but saw nothing.

"In the next fifteen minutes, I want you to speak to each gun crew. I want the Durness and Scourie gunners to concentrate on hitting the big submarine closest to the beach. Knock out the heavy machine guns and punch some holes in the boat. Remember, there's a keg of ale for the first crew that puts a hole in her. If there are two subs, the Dornach gun crew that the Duke brought with him, his 'best gunners,' is to fire on the U-boat farther out. It's smaller and harder to hit. There will be two kegs of ale if they put a hole in that one. Understand?"

"Yes, Sir, verra' good, Sir. That'll motivate 'em."

"The Dornach gun will fire first, the other two guns right after. I'm concerned about that deck gun. It can kill many of our men. You kill them first!"

A HALF-HOUR SLOWLY PASSED, and the men were getting impatient. The young soldiers wanted to take part in some action, and the veterans just wanted it over. To those who'd been in battle, there was no longer glory in war. The glory would be the end of the war, an end they hoped to survive.

A few minutes later, David felt a tug on his trousers. It was MacCloskey. "Sir, Major Priestley sent me here. I'm your runner for messages."

"There'll be no running for some time, MacCloskey. It would alert the sub crews and they might withdraw before we have a go at them. Stay on your belly when you pass messages; until the shooting starts."

"Yes, Sir. Well, may we load our rifles?"

"No. Wait for my command." They were silent for several minutes.

"Colonel, have you ever been shot at before?"

"Yes, many times, but this isn't the time to talk about it."

"I've never been shot at before. This will be the first time."

"MacCloskey, be quiet!" David whispered, in exasperation.

The periscope disappeared again, the submarine captain raising and lowering it periodically to check his distances and look for signs of British forces. David glanced westward toward Leirinbeg and Durness. There were no lights. The Civil Defense wardens had done a good job. The Germans certainly knew that Durness was there, after all, it was on all Scottish road maps, but David wanted no lights which would give them a navigation aid as they came through the sandbars.

After a few moments, the periscope reappeared, having moved to a position only 300 yards offshore. This time there was no movement. The sub had stopped dead in the water. In the dim moonlight, David saw the periscope slowly turning, as the captain scanned the horizon in all directions. Then the periscope disappeared, the captain satisfied that there was no visible threat.

"David turned briefly and whispered, "MacCloskey. Tell Major Priestley that the men may load their rifles quietly, with safety switches set first."

"Yes, Sir. The Major is ten yards behind us with the Duke."

David looked back to see that Major Priestley and the Duke had taken up positions behind him, both lying flat on the ground. Mac-Closkey crawled the distance quickly, and David saw Priestley nod and say something to MacCloskey, who quickly moved off; presumably to pass along the order to the Platoon Commanders. As Priestley crawled up to David's side, they heard the muffled sounds of a hundred rifles being loaded. A few minutes later, they heard the flank and reserve platoons' rifles being loaded as well. By now, every man was awake and alert, with each rifle's safety switch set so they couldn't accidentally fire.

"Major Priestley, nobody is to fire until the artillery has fired their first round. I want those first rounds to surprise the sub commanders, and then everyone may fire."

"Colonel, shouldn't we fire as soon as the sub surfaces, before they can man their guns?"

"No, Major, fire only when I give the order. I want those rubber boats filled with the raiding party and just a few yards off-shore before we fire and divulge our location. That way, the Germans will be committed, and the U-boat can't just dive underwater and escape with the raiding party. I don't want them coming back another time." By now, the Duke also had crawled up alongside David.

A few more minutes passed, and then the periscope appeared again. "This might be their final check."

"Then what?" asked the Duke.

"Then, if we're lucky, they'll surface," David replied.

"Look," said Priestley, "there's the other periscope, maybe a half-mile further out in the bay." They all looked and confirmed Priestley's sighting.

"They're all set to surface."

"Can they communicate while they're underwater?" asked the Duke.

"I don't know. Maybe the Jerries have. . . . "

"It's surfacing!" Priestley interjected excitedly. The sea churned on the surface above the submarine, as the air tanks blew water from its ballast tanks; it slowly began to rise. The sub's captain was surfacing very slowly so as to remain in place without drifting in any direction. Too much movement could force the sub onto a sandbar. He also was trying to make as little commotion as possible with the water and to minimize air bubbles, which might alert someone on shore. The three men watched with astonishment as the periscope slowly rose, followed by the conning tower and finally the hull. The ninety seconds it took to rise to the surface seemed like twenty minutes.

"Good God, look at the size of that thing!" exclaimed the Duke in a loud whisper. "You know, I once served as a naval officer. I've watched ships all my life and that sub is the size of a small cruiser."

"I've never seen anything like it before," David responded. "It's enormous and there's no deck gun; it must be a *milchkuh*. I wish the Admiral was here to see this."

Major Priestley gave a cautionary wave to the forward platoons to stay down. Several officers had moved forward to get a better view and each was quickly followed by several men. Everyone wanted to see the steel monster.

"Not a sound!" Priestley cautioned in a loud whisper, and his words were passed back by the forward soldiers to those further back. He saw the men put their faces down against the ground, gripping their rifles tightly. They were tense and absolutely silent.

A hatch on the sub's conning tower opened as soon as it broke water, and three men quickly appeared, peering intently in all directions. They used their binoculars to examine the bluff and radar station carefully. The Home Guardsmen pushed down into the earth, each man trying to become invisible. Because the bluff was some eighty feet above the sub as it surfaced on the water, its short distance of only 300 yards from the shore didn't give the submariners a view of anything past the edge of the bluff. The sub's engines were fairly quiet, but the crashing surf muffled any noise from the bluff.

A second larger door opened onto the sub's deck, and several men came out carrying large objects. "The rubber boats," David whispered, "They'll inflate them on the deck."

"There's the other sub!" said MacCloskey excitedly. In their preoccupation with the *milchkuh*, they'd forgotten about the smaller U-boat, which was just now surfacing, a half-mile beyond the large one. Men were running out onto the deck to prepare the deck gun for action. Other men on the conning tower were uncovering the anti-aircraft guns. Designed for protection from aircraft, the smaller guns also could be used for surface fire and would have a very nasty impact on men and equipment on the bluff.

Another three minutes passed, and the first rubber boat was set onto the ocean surface and held in place with a rope. Raiders started to board the boats and weapons were passed to them. David counted the boats; five in number, with seven or eight men on each boat. "Maybe forty men in all," he whispered. When all the boats were ready, a wave of the hand by an officer in the lead boat signaled the men to start paddling. They paddled forward slowly and deliberately, conserving energy for the strenuous pull through the surf. Major Priestley looked at David nervously, but knew better than to ask for permission to fire. Another few minutes passed as the raiders struggled to make progress against the surf.

"Get the men ready," David said to Priestley, "and move the second sections forward to take up firing positions alongside the first sections. The artillery will fire first," he reminded them. Priestley passed the order back.

The men of the second sections quickly came forward using a higher crawl, which moved them faster along the ground. They slid alongside the others into previously prepared firing positions, and rifle muzzles began to protrude a few inches forward of the beach grass. The third sections of each forward platoon remained in reserve, ready to move on command. Each of the two platoons now had almost fifty men lying along or near the bluff. David noticed that both the Duke and Priestley had drawn their revolvers.

"Going to shoot someone?" he asked.

"I'd just like to get off a few shots at the Jerries." said the Duke.

David could see Sergeant-Major McNabb hunkered down behind an 18-pounder, whispering to the three gun crews. The guns were about thirty feet apart, and the crews were sighting the guns on the two submarines. McNabb was starting the firing sequence, and David heard a few loudly whispered commands. "Stand by."

David looked seaward. The rubber boats were now about 200 yards away, moving slowly but steadily toward the beach. The soldiers on the bluff whispered excitedly among themselves. "Pipe down!" said Priestley in a whisper. Other officers took up the command. Several sergeants began to pass out Mills bomb grenades to designated soldiers, usually experienced corporals with strong arms. The tension was so high David feared someone would make a premature sound.

The rubber boats were now within one hundred yards of the beach. There were numbers of men on the two subs' decks, some behind the guns and the others watching through binoculars. "Surely they could see something by now,' David thought. But, they gave out no alarm, and the boats continued slowly forward toward the beach. Fifty yards now, then forty.

David turned toward the artillery. "Sergeant-Major," he spoke in a low voice, "make ready."

McNabb began the final commands. David only heard parts of words through the wind. "Remember, lads, load quickly, and fire slowly." He paused, and raised his voice a half-octave, "At my command." Then, he raised his right arm over his head.

David glanced down at the rubber boats. The lead boat was just crossing the imaginary line, which David had calculated at twenty yards from the water's edge. He looked at Major Priestley.

"Are you ready?" Priestley nodded and raised his arm. Then, "Sergeant-Major, you may fire!"

David saw McNabb's hand come down, but his order to fire was drowned out by the roar of the Dornach gun, immediately followed by the other two guns. At that moment, Priestley's hand also came down and the whole bluff exploded into a thunder of fire, as some ninety rifles joined in the cacophony, along with the machine guns and Boys rifles. Two illuminating rounds from the Very pistols flew forward into the sky, and then opened with a distinctive pop and two bright flares lit up the sky and the subs below. As he looked down in the glimmering light, David saw shock on the faces of the raiders as they dropped their paddles and swung their weapons off their shoulders.

"Into the valley of death and into the mouth of hell, you bastards!" he murmured. David looked at the far U-boat in time to see the first round from the Dornach gun splash into the sea a hundred yards behind her. Immediately, he saw two splashes near the large sub, both rounds missing their target. "Dammit!" shouted the Duke.

McNabb was already redirecting the gunners with a mixture of curses and encouragement. All three guns fired again, but the only results again were water splashes. The riflemen were having some success as several German raiders slumped into the bottom of the boats and three fell overboard. The machine guns and Boys rifles firing at the large submarine anti-aircraft gun crews also were having some effect, and two or three submariners had already fallen.

Then, a sudden flash from the bay, followed by a delayed boom, showed that the U-boat's deck gun had been fired. The scream of the shell passing overhead was followed by an explosion several hundred yards to their rear. "Just an open field," David mused. A second round from the deck gun did the same, and a third. "The men will never forget that sound."

The firing from both sides continued and more raiders fell from their boats. The survivors were frantically trying to turn their rubber boats to escape, but the surf was pushing them beach-ward. David saw two Mills bomb grenades fly forward and explode just before hitting the beach, spraying fragments over three raiders. Punctured boats were being twisted and turned by the surf, with uninjured raiders struggling to hang on. More Mills bombs followed. A large explosion suddenly engulfed David and the others, momentarily lifting them off the ground. The deck gun had found its range, and a large chunk of sandy bluff fell over the side onto the rocks below. David saw two men crawling toward an injured gunner.

McNabb's artillery fired again, followed this time by the sound of ripping metal. David saw a hole in the conning tower of the large sub, where an 18-pound shell had entered and passed through the other side without exploding. The hole was less than a foot in diameter, but David hoped it would be enough to keep the sub from submerging. One gun crew had earned a keg of ale, at David's expense.

As he watched, the larger sub began to traverse slowly, turning its bow toward the open sea. The men in the one remaining rubber boat that was still fully afloat, despite a single bullet hole, were desperately trying to get back to the sub. They were over a hundred yards away and were under heavy fire from the Home Guardsmen. David turned back to the artillery, and another volley led to a cheer, "Got her!" A second shell had penetrated the sub's hull and a muffled explosion occurred. "Old ammunition," David thought, "at least it must have done some damage."

Suddenly there was a blinding flash, stunning David momentarily. A shell from the deck gun had hit the artillery position, knocking the Dornach gun onto its side. Several men ran over, and the dazed gunners stumbled back to the remaining two guns and soon continued firing. By now, all machine guns and Boys rifles were firing at the more distant U-boat, and many riflemen had joined in. A rain of steel was now falling onto its deck and into the water nearby; one deck gunner had fallen. The gun crew ran for the hatch, dragging the fallen gunner and they quickly disappeared below. The smaller U-boat slowly traversed and began to sail toward the open sea, followed by the large submarine. After a few minutes, they were beyond the range of the rifles and machine guns.

David finally stood up slowly and watched in stunned silence, surrounded by Priestley, the Duke and several others. His ears were ringing and his heart pounding, as were several hundred others nearby. "It's over."

"And we won," proclaimed the Duke, himself somewhat unsteady on his feet after the blast. "Casualty count, Major Priestley?" he asked.

"I'll find out, M'lord."

David looked around, saying nothing, and soon discovered that two hundred faces were looking at him. Slowly, the men began to stand, some stiffly, others cautious that the fight might not yet be over. He heard sergeants giving orders: "Stay in your places! Safeties on! Check your ammo!" The men hardly heard them, as the firing of over one thousand round of ammunition momentarily had stunned them. Some were in shock from the firing of the heavier weapons, others momentarily deafened. Then, from the far end of the line there began a faint, hoarse cheer, growing louder as it swept up the line until everyone was on their feet cheering wildly. The Duke smiled and waved, then walked down the line of troops shaking hands. "Ever the old politician," David thought fondly, "but he did his job today."

Major Priestley came running up. "Colonel, you'd better come here. It's the Sergeant-Major." They walked quickly to the artillery position where they found the bodies of McNabb and a Dornach gunner, named Melrose, lying motionless. Doctor Watson from Dornach looked up and said simply, "They're gone." David saw a large hole in McNabb's side, torn open by the last explosion from the deck gun. "Massive trauma and loss of blood, Colonel. Couldna' ha' lived twa minutes."

Presently the Duke and Major Priestley approached. "Two dead and six wounded, maybe a few others with scratches, Colonel," reported Priestley.

"Have an officer use the radar station transmitter to alert the Navy and the RAF of the two subs location, and tell them at least one was holed and should be on the surface. Also, take the wounded lads into the radar station's underground facility. Maybe some RAF chaps can give up their beds for tonight. Have the nurses go with them, of course. Later, we'll determine how to get them to a hospital."

"I'll take care of that, Colonel." said the Duke. "By the way, how long did the fighting last? Thirty or forty minutes?"

David looked at his watch. "The shooting lasted less than ten minutes. It just seems longer." He felt no joy at the small victory, for a deep sadness had already overtaken him at the sight of the casualties. "M'lord, call forward all riflemen who have not fired their weapons tonight."

"Certainly, Colonel, but why?"

"They may each fire two rounds at the submarines before they sail out of sight."

"They couldn't possibly hit them, Colonel; it would be a waste of ammunition."

"We can spare the ammunition, M'lord. I don't want these men who worked so hard tonight to have to tell their grandchildren they were at Sango Bay, but never fired their rifles."

"You're right, Colonel. Brilliant." The order was given and almost fifty men came forward and fired their rifles out to sea. They were followed by small groups on the flanks, along with some RAF men. The Duke was so enthused that he drew his revolver and emptied the cylinder into the distant waters. Major Priestley fired two rounds as well, and then turned to David. "It's your turn, Colonel."

"Thank you, Major, but no. I've fired enough for a lifetime."

The three stood silently for several minutes looking out to the wind-whipped sea. "M'lord," David said finally, "we need an armed party to search the beach for any survivors or bodies. I think you should send an experienced officer with a reinforced section down the trail, with at

219

least one Lewis gun, rifles, torches, rope and maybe some tools. Take some canvas to bring up any wounded. Stack the bodies on the beach for the night, and we'll bring them up in the morning."

The Duke relayed the order to Priestley. "Have Captain Grant from 1st Platoon assemble the party. I want an officer at the top of the trail at all times observing them and reporting back. They must use extreme caution not to shine the torches out to sea; no use alerting any more enemy craft." Priestley saluted and left. Fifteen minutes later the soldiers cautiously began the descent to the beach.

The Duke stepped back, crouched down facing away from the sea, and, with some difficulty, lit his pipe. "Do you smoke, Colonel?"

"Not for many years, M'lord."

"It's good for me, calms me down, and helps me appreciate the good times better, like now."

David had to agree that the pipe tobacco smelled good at this moment. A soldier approached them, saluted and asked "May we build fires, Sirs?"

"No," David replied, "the U-boat could return to shell the radar station. Let's not help them." As the soldier left, David said, "When the search party returns, I think we can have the men bed down in their present positions, rifles unloaded, to get some sleep. Post sentinels. I'd like the artillery and the crew-served weapons to remain loaded and pointed seaward just in case a U-boat or an E-boat returns to make mischief."

"Very good, Colonel."

"Major Priestley, have Commander Morton pass the same instructions to his units. Also, Major, have Lieutenant Parker send a runner up to Leirinbeg and Durness. Of all Scots tonight, they deserve to know first that the Nazi raiding party was defeated, and the subs are fleeing out to sea. But, absolutely no lights throughout the night."

They had been standing together talking quietly for almost an hour when Captain Grant made his way back up the bluff to their position. "No survivors, Colonel. Almost three-dozen bodies have come ashore, maybe a few more still out there. Most have multiple wounds from the rifles and machine guns. A few may have drowned."

"We'll decide where to bury them later. For now, the men should get some sleep."

David and the Duke walked back to the Duke's command post and lay down on the canvas. It was past 3 a.m., and sleep came over them quickly.

DAVID AWOKE GROGGILY with the first light of morning and looked at his watch. "Just after 6 a.m." The Duke was sitting beside him looking toward the sea, over clusters of sleeping men.

"Good morning, Colonel, and a good day it will be."

"Good morning, M'lord. How are the wounded men?"

"They came through the night quite well. I've made arrangements for several large private automobiles to collect the wounded and transport them directly to the Royal Northern Infirmary at Inverness. They'll do better at the larger hospital there, rather than Thurso or Wick." He paused. "I've been thinking about the dead Germans. I don't think we should bury them here at Sango Bay. There's a piece of public land east of Tongue, just off the coastal road. We can use that to bury the bodies. I'm going to call my office and have them send out a work party with shovels to dig the trench and set a marker for each grave, to hold the identification tag from each body. Captain Grant can lead another search party down to the shoreline to look for more bodies and have all of them brought up here. I'll have our men search the bodies for identifications and other papers before we load them into the lorries. We'll give the Germans a respectable Christian burial and fire a salute. I'll turn the names over to the Red Cross for notification to their families."

"Thank you, M'lord. That sounds appropriate."

"Would you like some tea, Colonel? I asked Lieutenant Parker to see if he could ask the town folk of Durness to help us with some food. I suspect the mess section at Balnakiel has been on alert all night, possibly out at the end of Faraid Head. I've food enough in our lorries, but it would be good to have it heated up. I think the men deserve a hot breakfast."

The two men walked up to the bluff. Then, satisfied there was nothing amiss out in the bay, they walked among the soldiers, most now being roused by their corporals. The men were groggy, but pleased with their successful and lethal defense. They carried themselves with the pride of combat veterans, despite the very modest skirmish. "The action will grow larger with the retelling," David mused. Every soldier wanted to shake his hand and tell their families they'd fought alongside the Colonel from the Black Watch.

After an hour or more, several motorcars began to drive down the small road from Durness. Villagers came out with pots and pans to help prepare food and to congratulate their soldiers. Emma McPherson joined them carrying her old Martini rifle.

"We whupped them, Colonel."

"Did you fire at the Germans, Emma?" David asked.

"I surely did, Colonel. I'll no' ha' the lot of 'em up here. I ken we sank a submarine."

"Probably not, Emma, but I hope someone sinks one today."

After breakfast, the men loaded the bodies from the shoreline onto lorries. Captain Grant approached David. "I count thirty-eight dead, Colonel. We found three more this morning and we have the remains of four rubber boats and some paddles that washed ashore. I didn't see anything else down there. I think their weapons are offshore underwater."

"We'll leave them there for now." David walked slowly to the radar station to telephone a report to Brigadier Campbell. The connection was poor, but he heard, "Splendid, David. Well done!" He then called his office. Elaine answered.

". . . I mean, we were so worried. Are you alright?"

"Yes, I'm fine, just tired. We lost two men, including the Sergeant-Major, and six were wounded."

"I'm so sorry, Sir. The Admiral wants to speak with you."

David relayed brief details of the action, amidst the static on the line. He then added, "I've no way to get back to Fort William. I'll ride to Dornach with the Duke, then go on to Inverness. Have someone pick me up at the Caledonian Hotel tomorrow morning at 9 a.m."

As he walked back to join the Duke, a convoy of vehicles was forming. Men and equipment were loading and the convoy was soon on its way home, amidst honking horns and cheers. These had been two very long days.

20

March 27, 1941

THE BATTLE WON, David rode back from Durness in a Home Guard convoy with the Duke of Sutherland, a somewhat triumphant drive along the coastal road for the two Sutherland Mobile Battle Platoons. The Scourie and Braemore Forest platoons had driven south on a different road. David and the Duke sat together in the rear seat of the limousine, while the driver and a Home Guard lieutenant, the Duke's aide, rode in the front. David found the Duke's motorcar to be considerably more comfortable than the Lysander.

An hour into the drive and a small distance east of Tongue, the convoy turned off the narrow road and parked alongside a small loch. The burial party, the Duke had ordered out from Dornach, was already at work digging a large trench for the bodies of thirty-eight Nazi raiders killed in the fighting. The Home Guardsmen joined the effort, and the grave was finished within an hour. The bodies were placed alongside each other and an identification tag was nailed to a stake set above each body. The men surrounded the gravesite with hats removed while Captain McCrae, who had brought a small Bible, read a scripture. Six riflemen fired a salute, and the brief burial service was over.

"It could have been us tha' were bein' buried," said Captain Grant laconically. The grave was filled in, and the convoy reversed course before turning south on the road to Dornach.

As they drove along Loch Loyal, a convoy of regular soldiers from the 51st Division passed them driving north. David stopped them, and their commander, a major, said his company of 160 men had been ordered north to Sango Bay, with one platoon detached to Balnakiel. They were to take up positions defending the radar station and the Balnakiel installation until further notice.

All day, David wondered at the fate of the two submarines they had driven off from Sango Bay. The RAF and Naval forces were hunting them feverishly. The *milchkuh* sub had been damaged during the short battle and probably couldn't submerge, making it a much easier target. The smaller U-boat probably was undamaged and could submerge to escape attack.

As the convoy approached Dornach late in the afternoon, groups of people began to assemble along the road. Driving slowly into the town center, the Duke saw his Deputy Lord Lieutenant eagerly pushing his way through the crowd to the car. "M'lord," he shouted through the window, "A Coastal Command patrol plane from Wick sank the submarine, the big one!"

"Good news, splendid!" the Duke replied, clapping David on the shoulder, "What about the small one?"

"Canna' say, M'lord. We got the call a ha'-hour ago from Scottish Command tha' a patrol plane caught the big one on the surface and quickly sank her, just west of Hoy. Later, another plane attacked a smaller U-boat as it was submergin' north of the Orkneys, but there's no report of a sinkin'."

"We'll take a confirmed sinking of the big sub as very good news indeed, right, Colonel?"

David nodded. He wished he felt more enthusiastic, but he was exhausted. Little sleep for two days was part of the problem, but his high state of anxiety during that time had worn him down further. It had been a dozen years since he'd last been in combat, a dozen years since he ordered men to risk their lives for King and Country, and a dozen years since he endured the agony of watching his own soldiers die. The memory of the dead soldiers shook him back to full consciousness.

"What will happen to the bodies of McNabb and Melrose, M'lord?" There were no coffins and no ice. The bodies simply were wrapped in blankets and lay in the rearmost truck in the convoy.

"I'll have one of my officers take them to the morgue immediately. Major Watson will prepare their death certificates, and we'll notify their families promptly. I'll attend Melrose's funeral and, I assume, you'll attend McNabb's."

"Yes, but I don't know where. I know nothing about his family, save his wife died some years back, and he has a daughter somewhere near Glasgow. I'll have Steve Whittaker find her and see about her wishes."

"I know the Melrose family. I think I'll put him in for a Military Medal for bravery, with your concurrence, of course."

"Yes, I concur," David replied wearily. "I'll recommend McNabb for the Distinguished Conduct Medal. He certainly displayed bravery in the face of the enemy."

The Duke's car slowed to a stop at his office. Darkness was falling and David exited the car, the driver holding the door for both. "M'lord, I would be grateful if you would show me where the coach to Inverness departs, or maybe you know of a truck going there tonight."

"Nonsense, Colonel, you'll go in my car, with my driver and my aide. I'll not have a distinguished Army Colonel traveling like a common labourer."

Ten minutes later, David was riding south in comfort, his mind racing with thoughts of Sango Bay. What if the Home Guard had never been formed or armed? Who would have defended the radar station? What if the Germans had landed that first night, when Emma spotted the U-boats, and only the few RAF guards had been present? What would have been the outcome had Emma not seen the U-boats, or he hadn't correctly divined German intentions? Could he have planned the defense better and saved two lives? He would never know. So much could have gone wrong, and his mission could have failed. He had a profound sense of gratitude, however, that the mission had succeeded, and Hitler had been denied Britain's latest radar technology. His thoughts became increasingly blurred by fatigue and he finally put them aside.

An hour later, he entered the Caledonian Hotel and secured lodging for the night. He walked to his room with an aching hip and washed in a basin for the first time in two days. A wave of relief flowed over him and he collapsed into bed for a very long night's sleep.

March 28

THE DRIVE FROM INVERNESS to Fort William was one of the most pleasant David ever experienced. CB Foster picked him up at the hotel, promptly at 9 a.m., and there was little traffic to delay them along the road to the southwest. He felt reinvigorated after ten hours of sleep and a modest, but satisfying, breakfast. CB asked many questions about the battle, and David found it useful to recollect even the smallest events. They would be included in his report to Scottish Command. As they drove along Loch Ness, David felt reassured that no U-boats lurked beneath the surface, the Loch having no natural navigable passage to the sea at either end.

When CB ran out of questions, David asked him what had happened at his own headquarters in Fort William and how the staff performed. CB told him that every staff officer, including Elaine and Lady Frances, had spent the entire night of the battle at the office. David was pleased to learn that the Admiral had kept tight control over their work and that all had gone as well as could be expected. Each officer stayed on top of his area of responsibility, and each was in fairly continuous communication with counterparts at other headquarters.

"As it should be, Colonel, as it should be. Absolutely no problems except tha' we couldna' communicate with you. After your telephone call in the mornin,' the Admiral sent 'em home for some sleep."

"I think we were most fortunate that Wing Commander Morton and Emma McPherson were able to get through to me from Sango Bay that morning." David responded. "Another few hours of telephone disruption and we'd have missed the Jerries entirely." Then he thought about the words "that morning." That morning was just two days ago, yet it felt like a week. As they drove into Fort William, David found himself instinctively looking around to see what had changed. Of course, the answer was nothing in just two days. CB parked at the office.

"I'll get your bag, Sir." He needn't have bothered, as the staff poured out into the street and opened all doors to help. Elaine put more water into the steaming pot, enough to make tea for everyone. Visitors began to flow in as word of David's arrival spread, including the Provost, Chief Constable MacDonald, and Colonel Laughton. Backslapping and congratulations flowed freely. A few minutes later, David noticed Lady Frances sitting quietly in the corner with a smile on her face.

After 45-minutes of well-wishing, the visitors began to depart. David and the staff assembled around the table and he thanked the members for their work. He briefly outlined the key events at Sango Bay.

"Has anything of significance developed today?"

"Just one," answered the Admiral. "We'll have a visitor tomorrow. Brigadier Campbell will arrive to receive a staff briefing on the Sango Bay operation. I suspect he really wants to congratulate you, but there may be more than that." Discussion ensued on staff responsibilities for the next day and any follow-up work to prepare the after-action report, which David would submit through Brigadier Campbell to Scottish Command.

"I want each staff officer to prepare a written summary of activities undertaken during the past three days; be prepared to present them verbally to the Brigadier. Let's plan to rehearse the presentations tomorrow at 8:00 a.m. Brigadier Campbell is an early riser and he could be here by 9:30 a.m. I'll have my remarks prepared, but I'll call on each of you to make your own report. Subject to corrections, you can then commit them to writing and Elaine will type them as appendices to my report.

I think we should get started now, and you're free to leave when you are satisfied that you're ready for tomorrow." David nodded to CB, who took over the meeting. David went to his office to begin his report.

Over the next two hours, the staff worked on their reports, and Ben Douglas was the first to leave. "I won't have much to say tomorrow," he said to CB. One by one, each officer finished and departed. CB was the last to complete his report on operational and administrative aspects of the action. He quietly picked up his papers, nodded a farewell to Elaine and left. A few minutes later Elaine fixed two cups of tea and took them to David's office.

"I wa' so worried about you," she said, as she passed him his tea. "I knew you were in danger and I couldna' bear the thought of losin' you."

"I'm a soldier, Elaine, and sometimes soldiers have to go into dangerous situations. Fortunately, this one was less dangerous, and I never felt threatened. I didn't draw my revolver. There was no requirement to do so, and I doubt the Nazis fired a single shot at me."

"But there wa' artillery, and you told me artillery could kill anyone anytime. The Sergeant-Major wa' killed and the other soldier. Several others were wounded. It mun ha' been awful."

"It's never easy to lose soldiers." They sat silently for a few moments. Elaine got up and walked to the door.

"'Tis time to lock up for the day." She bolted the door and walked back to his office. "You must be tired. Would you like to go upstairs?"

"I would."

March 29

A COLD WIND HIT DAVID AS he walked along High Street, waiting for Brigadier Campbell's arrival. A thin wet blanket of snow had fallen during the night, reminding the Scots that winter had not yet released its grip. Heavier snow had capped the mountaintops like powdered sugar, but the heavily overcast sky clouded the beautiful panorama of white mountaintops against a blue sky. David bought a newspaper and sat down on a bench for a few minutes of quiet. As he browsed through the paper, he was surprised to find no mention of the battle at Sango Bay. Had the War Office censors banned publication of the story? If so, why had they? It seemed to David that even a small British victory over the Germans would be very desirable news and a boost to public morale. Maybe Jack Campbell would know the answer.

Twenty minutes later, he saw Campbell's car coming around The

Parade. After the usual dodging of cars and pedestrians, it came to a halt by the office door. A familiar shape stepped out, spied David, and gave a hearty wave.

"David, how good of you to meet me here. I didn't bother you last night in Inverness, as I knew you would be exhausted." His arrival attracted the usual spectators and a few well-wishers. At the office, Jack greeted each staff member as if they were old friends, and then took his seat at the head of the table. David introduced the Brigadier to Lady Frances, whom he'd not previously met, and gave a brief formal welcome to Campbell and to those assembled.

"I thank you for devoting yet another Saturday to the war effort," Campbell started, "and I want to hear from each of you regarding your role in the splendid victory at Sango Bay. Let me open first with a few quick words about the war progress, but also to show you how your efforts here fit in with the greater war effort. First, the Balkans is a mess as usual. You perhaps have read in the papers that Bulgaria joined the Axis on the first day of this month, giving Hitler a significant boost in his armed forces and other valuable resources. Britain, of course, condemned the move, but there's precious little we can do about it.

"Last week, Yugoslavia also was forced to join the Axis, giving Hitler total control of the Adriatic Sea and potentially placing Axis forces right on the Greek border. Surprisingly, there has been a counter-stroke by the anti-Axis loyalists, mostly the Serbs. The old pro-Nazi ruler, Prince Paul, has been ousted, and the anti-Nazi Prince Peter has been placed on the throne of Yugoslavia. This won't remove the German influence from that country, but at least there'll be some opposition with which they must deal, probably in their usual tender manner! I expect the pro-Nazi Croats will oppose the new government.

"In response, Mr. Churchill has ordered British forces into Greece to help defend their border. Greece has a tough little army, but too small to defend the whole country, even after mobilizing their reserves. Now for some good news," he continued. "Admiral, you should be especially proud. Have you heard of the naval victory two days ago?" The Admiral shook his head. "Well, two days ago, our Mediterranean Fleet smashed the Italian Navy again at Cape Matapan, off Greece's southwest corner, and sank five or more of their ships. Our lads chased them back to their bases. I expect BBC will have a broadcast today after the censors clear it." The Admiral beamed.

"Next, I want to mention North Africa. Lieutenant-General Cunningham's offensive into Italian Somaliland and Ethiopia continues successfully. British and Commonwealth forces have pushed the Italian Army steadily back, and I look forward to a smashing victory sometime soon. Also, Axis forces are beginning to stir in the Western Desert, but I'm confident General Wilson's forces can handle whatever develops." Jack paused as the news sank in. "All in all, we're not doing badly, but we certainly have our challenges ahead. That very day, the German-Italian forces under General Erwin Rommel, the 'Desert Fox,' began their attack against British and Commonwealth forces in the Western Desert, driving them back out of Libya and into Egypt. It was indeed a victory, but not for the British Army.

"Finally, let me mention our own efforts right here in Britain. We continue to be bombed, as you well know, but the raids lack the intensity of last autumn. We've more and more RAF fighter squadrons coming on line, and we're inflicting severe losses on the Nazis with every raid." Jack paused for another drink of tea. "And, the Navy is bringing more escort ships and aircraft into action in the Battle of the Atlantic. Shipping losses, however, are still severe. During the past year we and our allies have lost almost two million tons of shipping, some ten per cent of our entire merchant fleet, and we've lost many naval escort ships, as well. Nevertheless, German U-boat losses also are increasing." He paused and looked around the table at each of them.

"Each of you now has contributed to the loss of a very valuable German U-boat, a *milchkuh*. How many U-boats at sea will not be re-provisioned because of this, I don't know. However, I feel confident in saying that several allied ships which otherwise would have been sunk will now reach British ports because of your actions. On behalf of Lieutenant-General Carrington, I want to extend my heartiest thanks to each of you for a job well done." Jack sat back and beamed.

"On behalf of my staff I thank you for your kind remarks," David replied. "We really were just doing our jobs."

"And doing them exceptionally well, I should say. You realize, of course, that this is the first Home Guard action against the Nazis and the first Home Guard victory. You'll hear more about this later. Now, Colonel, you may begin your staff briefings."

David had his staff present the remarks they'd rehearsed earlier, beginning with the Admiral and going down the table to Ben Douglas and Lady Frances, both of whom had few comments. As David began his own summation, Campbell interrupted him.

"I'd like for Mrs. Ross to give me her impressions as well." Caught unaware, Elaine began her few comments, somewhat awkwardly, but then warmed to her subject, finishing after five minutes of non-stop commentary. "Excellent, Mrs. Ross, that's exactly what I was looking for and very informative." She smiled.

David then spoke for almost a half-hour, giving full credit to The Duke and his men of the 1st Sutherland Battalion. He asked Campbell if he had any questions.

"No, I think I've a full picture of this action. I want to express again how proud I am of all of you, and how proud I am of the Home Guard and Civil Defense workers for their splendid service. Now," looking at his watch, "Colonel McKenna and I must meet on several important subjects, perhaps over an early lunch. I must return to Inverness by mid-afternoon." With that the meeting was adjourned.

LUNCH AT THE OFFICERS CLUB, recently established near Cameron Square off High Street, was even more modest than usual, rationing having cut sharply into the food supplies of restaurants and pubs, as well as private homes. Jack Campbell ordered a piece of sausage with bread and found some pleasure in a tall mug of stout. "At least, I can still have a glass now and then." Jack told David again how proud he was of the work of David's sub-district. "Six months ago, I never would've believed that a company of the Home Guard would be able to defeat and destroy a highly-trained force of Nazi raiders. It's simply astonishing!"

"We were fortunate that we'd sufficient warning to get into position." David responded. "Moreover, we were fortunate the government had gone to such great lengths to get us weapons and equipment, and to insist the forces be properly trained."

"And all that over the objections of many people in the Ministry of Defense and the War Office," Campbell replied. "The fools! Their thinking was completely outdated and out of touch with the new reality of this war."

"You gave a quite favorable view of the war this morning, Sir. Are you really that optimistic?"

Jack sat back for a moment and sighed. "No, not really. We're obviously hanging on, but Hitler still has the upper hand and he's using it relentlessly. Britain is winning in some peripheral areas, but the Nazis are winning in the key areas. We're building our forces at a steady pace, but the Nazis are building their forces by leaps and bounds. I don't know what will happen this spring, but I'm certain Corporal Hitler will strike again somewhere when he's finished gobbling up the Balkans. It well may be at Britain. He may have missed the boat last autumn, but he'll be so much stronger if the Nazis invade during the next three months. Of course, we'll also be stronger, but the Germans still hold most of the advantages."

"At least our regular forces will be better prepared," David replied, "and the Home Guard has proven it can fight, and fight well. Did you know that not a single soldier at Sango Bay left his position to retreat or seek shelter? The units placed in the rear only wanted the chance to move up front and fire on the Jerries. How could so many in the War Office believe the Home Guard would run at the first shot? These are Britons! Give them a weapon and some training and they'll fight to the death before they surrender their families and their country to the tender mercies of the Nazis."

"I know," Jack replied, "they've made all Britons proud, at least they will when the story is released."

"When will that be?"

"Soon. The War Office is concerned we may give away too much information, so they're scrubbing the story of anything of value to the Nazis. I think it would be a tremendous boost to public morale and a great motivator for Home Guard training. But, the news release is in the hands of the Government and not with old soldiers like you and me."

"Sir, I'll be forwarding a nomination for the award of the Distinguished Conduct Medal for Sergeant-Major McNabb. He certainly earned it. I hope you'll endorse it on to the Scottish Command. Also, I'd like to secure a civilian award for Emma McPherson. Our good fortune would never have happened without her warning, even if a few of us thought she was a bit daft."

"Absolutely," Jack responded. "You were the senior commander on the battlefield and your recommendation certainly will be approved by Lord Carrington."

"Thank you."

"Speaking of Lord Carrington, David, rumor has it that he'll retire soon."

"Why? I thought he'd done an excellent job at Scottish Command."

"Perhaps, but that doesn't matter. The War Office is retiring a number of senior generals, if they haven't had battle experience in this war. They're trying to make room for younger colonels and generals with recent battle experience; so they can move up into senior positions. This really is becoming a young man's war, David, which certainly doesn't bode well for soldiers like me."

"Sir, it would be an outrage if you were to be retired."

"Thank you, but worse things happen in war. Now, on a more pleasant subject, I'm nominating you for the Distinguished Service Order. General Carrington already has agreed to endorse it on to the War Office."

David was astonished. The DSO is a very high decoration awarded to officers in the grade of major and above for bravery or very distinguished service. "I hardly think that Sango Bay would justify a DSO."

"Perhaps not," Jack replied, "but you should've been given one in the First War. Perhaps your service in the Punjab justified the DSO or your War Office Service. In any case, your work as Sub-District Commander, especially at Sango Bay, certainly justifies the award and I'll be submitting the paperwork this week."

"Sir, I'm honored."

"Well, don't pin it on yet. It has to go all the way up through channels, and some envious bureaucrat could very well squelch it. Besides, you probably would be required to wait until the Annual List is published at the end of the year. We'll see. The point I'll stress in the nomination is that we saved our very valuable radar technology and beat the Nazi raiders at Sango Bay because you correctly put together the pieces of that puzzle. You accurately determined the Nazi intentions and responded correctly with strong action. Thus, you're a successful battlefield commander and deserve the DSO."

"Thank you, Sir."

"Now, related to all that: you're being called to Edinburgh Castle to make a presentation in seven to ten days. Lord Carrington has directed that you will speak before all the Home Guard Battalion; Group, Zone, and Area Commanders. Also present will be District and Sub-District Commanders, as well as every Regular Battalion, Brigade and Division Commander."

"And, everyone else in Scotland, save the Castle janitor." David responded.

Jack laughed heartily. "Well done, yes, precisely. But seriously, Lord Carrington wants all commanders to understand the lessons learned at this battle, and for you to share your insights with your fellow commanders. You know the drill; have you any secrets which will help our commanders prevail in future battles?"

"Yes, of course, one secret." he replied, "Don't try to come ashore in Scotland with the Home Guard watching." They both burst out laughing.

"Brilliant! Yes, well those are your instructions for now from on

232

high. I'll have Steve Whittaker call you soon with the precise date and time. Oh, and you may bring a staff officer to assist you."

AT THE OFFICE, DAVID BEGAN to compose his report for Scottish Command. Several hours passed, interrupted occasionally by visitors who stopped by to congratulate him on his Sango Bay success. Although the radio and newspapers hadn't yet received the news release from the War Office, the story had spread from Durness and Dornach across the Highlands, sometimes embroidered beyond recognition. As darkness fell, David asked Elaine to bring in tea. "Brigadier Campbell has passed on a directive from Lord Carrington. I'm to journey to Edinburgh sometime soon and make a presentation to assembled commanders about our Sango Bay operation. Colonel Whittaker will call tomorrow with the date and time."

"I think tha's verra' appropriate," she replied.

"He said I could bring a staff officer with me to assist."

"Will you take the Admiral or Colonel Foster?"

"Neither. The Admiral must remain here as acting commander during my absence. CB is quite busy with his construction job responsibilities, especially after he took a half-week from work while I was gone."

"I see."

"I thought you might accompany me. We could leave a day early and spend one or two nights together in a hotel in Edinburgh. I'll show you the city. We certainly deserve some time off."

"I donna' think tha's a good idea." she said, without emotion.

"Why not? It would give us time together. It would be very special."

"I'm not an officer. I'm only your assistant."

"That doesn't matter. You're the equivalent of an officer, and it would be easy for me to justify your presence to handle the maps and paperwork while I speak."

"I would prefer not to."

"Elaine, what's happening? Last evening was wonderful. You said you loved me and you certainly showed it in every way. I don't understand."

"Please bear with me. I do love you and I'll always love you. But I canna' deal with this right now. 'Tis too much for me." She looked downward.

"Would you like to go upstairs now?"

"No." They sat silently for a minute. "I ha' to go now." she said, without looking up. She rose, put on her coat, and left.

April 3

THE PAST FEW DAYS had been difficult for David. He was asked to participate in Sergeant-Major McNabb's funeral in Glasgow. The service was lightly attended in a small church frequented by McNabb's daughter. David was pleased to see that the attendees included McNabb's battery commander. Also attending were a number of warrant and non-commissioned officers from the artillery battery in which McNabb had served for much of his career. They escorted his body to the cemetery. Brigadier Campbell had used his influence to have Scottish Command expedite the award of the Distinguished Conduct Medal, which was displayed beside the coffin with his other medals.

David offered a eulogy for the Sergeant-Major. He touched on the key points of his career and recognized his contributions to the training of the Home Guard artillery platoons and their successful employment at Sango Bay. His battery provided an honor guard, under the command of a lieutenant. It fired a rifle salute over the grave during the interment ceremony. Afterwards, David said goodbye to McNabb's daughter and left with Brigadier and Betty Campbell for a late lunch at a small restaurant near the Queen Street Station. It was mid-afternoon when David departed for the train trip back to Fort William. It hadn't been an enjoyable day.

His relationship with Elaine was deteriorating and he didn't know why. She came to the office each morning as always, worked hard all day, but her dealings with David were more formal and professional. She went home at closing time most days, and rarely stopped to have tea and conversation with him. Whenever he suggested spending some private time together, she declined. He knew he'd fallen deeply in love with her, and the pain seemed more than he could bear. He worked hard during the day to keep thoughts of her from his mind, but the nights were difficult. He lay awake almost every night rethinking each moment he'd been with her. His fatigue began to show.

It was mid-morning when the door opened and Lady Frances entered. "Good morning, Colonel, I hope I'm not interrupting." Without waiting for an answer, she continued. "I'm having a very small gathering at my house this afternoon and I hope you can come. It's nothing formal, of course, just tea. Would 3:30 be convenient?" David mumbled his acceptance, and she left. He decided to take a walk. The office atmosphere had become stifling with Elaine's silence.

"I'm going out for a walk," he announced. Elaine said nothing, nor did she look up. As he went out the door, he almost bumped into Ben Douglas.

"Good morning, Colonel. I'm stopping by to invite you for a brief ride with me. I must deliver some books to Fort Augustus and I thought you might enjoy a brief respite from the office and some fresh air. We may even stop somewhere for a quick lunch." The clouds had cleared after early morning rain, and the sun promised a better day.

"Yes, Ben, thank you, but I must be back by mid-afternoon." Ben nodded his concurrence, and David told Elaine of his change of plans.

As they drove northeast out of Fort William, the newly-risen sun shone on Loch Linnhe to reveal naval small craft darting back and forth in their endless training patterns. Ben drove slowly, partly to enjoy the early spring day, partly to conserve petrol, but also to afford time for talk. They exchanged pleasantries for several minutes.

As the conversation waned, Ben asked "You've been looking rather tired lately. Is everything alright?"

David started to reply affirmatively, and then paused for a moment. "No, I feel awful. Something's wrong with Elaine, at least between Elaine and me, and I don't know why. What have I done wrong?"

Ben sighed. "What have you done wrong? I don't know." He paused. "You know how I feel about you and Elaine, at least your private relationship with her." David nodded. "You also know I'm your friend, David, and I'm on your side in all things. Well, almost all things." He glanced at David. "I'm your loyal staff chaplain and, if I may say so, I'm also your pastor." David nodded again. "You know your relationship with Elaine is built on passion." David started to object.

"Please let me finish, David. Certainly there's something of substance there, an excellent working relationship, mutual respect, even a friendship and perhaps some real love. All of that's fine. But you've added passion to your relationship, an intimacy that may be mutually satisfying, but still is wrong. You're widowed, so it's easier for you to deal with the wrong. But women are different from men."

"And *viva la différence!*" David mumbled. They both smiled.

"Yes, but that's not what I'm talking about," Ben continued. "Women don't process relationships the way men do. Men often look for satisfying relationships, with or without commitment. Women look for commitment in relationships for safety and security. It's part of their nature. They nurture relationships much more than men. They invest more and they certainly get more out of relationships than men, at least I think they do. You and Elaine have a relationship, one that works on several levels, but you've no real commitment. She knows her marriage established a commitment to Paul, despite the lack of fulfillment. I think that's what's deeply troubling Elaine. Her reaction to these feelings within her may be pulling you apart."

"Ben, I'm committed to her. I asked her to marry me."

"And she said?"

"She said 'no'."

"Hmm. Well, I guess I'm not surprised. To you and me, divorce and re-marriage would seem to be the perfect solution. To Elaine, however, it would open a new box of troubles and I suspect she's unable to deal with those troubles, at least right now."

They sat silently for several minutes. Finally David asked, "What should I do, Ben?"

"I don't know, but I think the first thing you should do is ease back from her. Don't put more pressure on her and don't put more pressure on yourself. She needs time to work things through."

"What things?" he asked, in frustration.

"Many things, like Paul, her boys, her mother, her job, and her friends here in Fort William. Really, she's trying to process everything in her life. You came into her life and swept her off her feet. Not intentionally, of course, at least I don't think you intentionally pursued her, but you represented everything that was missing in her life. She fell head over heels. You really can be quite the charming chap, you know." He smiled. "And you fell for her as well and the inevitable happened."

"I don't know what to do, Ben."

"Let me make a suggestion for now. You'll make your presentation in Edinburgh Monday, right?" David nodded. "Tomorrow is Friday. Leave on the first train to Glasgow tomorrow morning and go on to Edinburgh. Spend the weekend there. See Anne's family, if you wish. Get back in touch with your feelings for Anne and try not to think about Elaine. Relax and forget about the war and everything else. Or at least focus on what you'll say to Scottish Command next Monday. Can Elaine finish typing your presentation by tomorrow morning?"

"I think she's finished now. She was preparing the Roneo to make copies when I left."

"Does this make any sense to you?"

"It makes perfect sense. I just don't know if I can forget about Elaine for the weekend."

"You must."

THE WEEKEND IN EDINBURGH WENT WELL. David felt more rested going into the conference than he had in several weeks. The weekend was an opportunity to escape the daily routine in Fort William and to do as he wished. He was confident his headquarters was in capable hands and he'd receive notification if there were problems. There were no messages.

For the first time since Anne's death, David visited her parents, now retired and noticeably older. They welcomed him as the beloved son-in-law he'd always been, and David was happy to spend the entire weekend as their guest. He enjoyed talking with them and to sense again his feelings for Anne. They were proud he'd re-entered the Army, especially since Britain was in such peril. His father-in-law was generous in his praise for David and the loving care he'd provided to Anne before her death. No mention was made of the motorcar accident.

Lieutenant-General Lord Carrington hosted the Monday conference and was quite generous in his introduction of David. "Colonel McKenna has been the very model of what a sub-district commander should be; a versatile officer with demonstrable skills in civil affairs, as well as battlefield proficiency." Carrington praised his efforts in raising the military and civil defense capabilities of "a meagerly populated sector with no active forces. . . ." And, "where our own intelligence gave us no warning. . ." McKenna "used uncommonly sound judgment. He ascertained an impending threat to our national security, and quickly mobilized untested Home Guard and Civil Defense forces in the face of uncertainty, and led them to a brilliant victory against all odds."

'High praise, indeed,' David thought.

David's talk took forty-five minutes. He was careful to include sufficient details of the challenges and his thought process to help fellow commanders understand his subsequent actions. He reviewed each step of the two-day ordeal and weighed both the successful and unsuccessful outcomes.

"I wish I'd maintained better control over the Home Guard firing, as we killed all the raiders, and I'd have preferred taking some prisoners for interrogation." And, "putting a hole in the smaller U-boat would have ensured it's sinking the next day, along with the *milchkuh*. Our artillery platoons need more training with live ammunition when more becomes available." Finally, "Overall it went better than expected, and I'm enormously proud of the bravery of the soldiers of the Home Guard's 1st Sutherland Battalion."

The questions from his fellow commanders took twice as long as his talk, as the commanders wanted every detail clarified or expanded. When he finished, Carrington reclaimed the podium and ended the conference with announcements, including the serious situation in North Africa.

"The German General, Rommel, has smashed through British defenses in the Western Desert and is driving eastward. British and Commonwealth forces are conducting a fighting withdrawal and are falling back on our lines of communication in Egypt. The sad effect of all of this for Scottish Command is that the Battle at Sango Bay has been driven to the back pages of our newspapers and precious little is being said on the radio. But, I expect that Rommel will soon outrun his supply lines and be forced to halt, allowing our lads in the Western Desert to regroup."

Unfortunately, Rommel did no such thing.

THE CONFERENCE CONCLUDED IN TIME for David to board a train to Glasgow, and then quickly catch the mid-afternoon train to Fort William. He knew he'd return home soon after supper. The trip was gratifying, and David found himself relaxing and not thinking of Elaine. His thoughts drifted from the pleasant afternoon tea with Lady Frances and her friends the previous week, to his weekend in Edinburgh, to forthcoming activities at his office, and he slowly dozed off. Upon his arrival in Fort William, he was surprised to see Ben Douglas standing on the platform. Ben came over quickly as David exited the train.

"David, Sir Robert Stuart has been killed."

"Good Lord! How did this happen?"

"It appears he was flying from Cairo to the Western Desert during Rommel's offensive, and the plane was shot down. There were several passengers on board, but there are no survivors."

"When did this happen?"

"Three or four days ago. They just found the wreckage and the bodies yesterday. I've been with Lady Frances and her family much of the day. I think you should go up there immediately."

"Yes, of course. Thank you for telling me, Ben. How is Lady Frances doing?"

"As you would expect, quite distraught, although she's doing her best to hold everything together. Her family is there, although some aren't doing well with the news. I think your presence would be helpful and greatly appreciated."

After taking his luggage to the empty office, David drove to the Stuart residence. Phillip was directing the parking, and Harry met him at the door.

"Thank you for coming, Colonel. Lady Frances is in the drawing room with the others. I shall tell her you're here." He disappeared for a moment, and then returned. "This way, Sir."

Lady Frances was sitting in her usual chair, surrounded by a dozen family members. Her eyes were red from crying, but her face was firm as she struggled to hold herself together. The room was silent as David entered, and Lady Frances stood up to greet him. "Thank you for coming, Colonel." she said in a formal tone. Then she turned to the others and announced, "This is Colonel David McKenna of the Black Watch, the commander of our Sub-District, on whose staff I serve. Colonel McKenna has just returned from Scottish Command headquarters in Edinburgh where he was instructing Army commanders from all over Scotland on his great victory at the recent battle of Sango Bay."

A murmur went through the group, although most had no idea where Sango Bay was located. "Before I present everyone to the Colonel, I must ask you to excuse us for a few minutes, as he's bringing important information from his headquarters. Colonel, would you join me in the library, please?" A bit confused, David followed Lady Frances into the next room, where she closed the massive oak door.

"Important information," he began, but she threw herself into his arms sobbing uncontrollably. This continued for some minutes. As she calmed down, she drew back and wiped her eyes. "Thank you. I just couldn't do that out there in front of them. I've never cried so much as today. It's just so awful, David. What am I to do?" More sobs followed. They sat down until she slowly recovered her composure. After some minutes, she rose. "Wait here. I want to wash my face." She withdrew to her bedroom, returning a few minutes later looking somewhat refreshed and better composed.

"This is the worst day of my life, David. I can't believe he's gone. He was everything to me and I just don't know what to do." She opened the door to the drawing room. "Please stay with us for a while."

21

April 10, 1941

"Sir! Brigadier Campbell died!"

"What?" David couldn't believe Elaine's announcement. "Are you sure?"

"Yes, Sir, 'tis Lieutenant-Colonel Whittaker on the telephone right now. He must speak with you." Tears welled up in Elaine's eyes as David reached for his telephone.

"Steve, what's happened?"

"Colonel McKenna, I'm so sorry to have to tell you this, but Brigadier Campbell died this morning, quite suddenly. They think it was a heart attack."

"Good God, I can't believe it, Steve. He seemed to be in perfect health at Sergeant-Major McNabb's funeral last week. I'd no knowledge his heart was so bad. What happened?"

"As best I can tell, he went to an early breakfast this morning with some officers of the Cameron Highland Regiment. He then went to review an exercise at a coast defense battery site, east of the city, one of the 6-inch gun batteries. The gunners were going through a drill, and they pretty well balled it up while the Brigadier was watching from below. I'm told he yelled up to the firing battery 'Not that way, dammit!' and scrambled up the embankment. He got almost to the top and fell back unconscious. Of course, they rushed him to the Royal Northern Infirmary, but he was dead well before they got there. Possibly, before he hit the ground, a doctor said."

"Good Lord, this is awful, Steve, and such a tragedy. How's Betty taking it?" David asked.

"She doesn't know yet. I just got the call ten minutes ago and I called Scottish Command immediately, Major-General Adams' office, and then I called you. I'm going to call the Glasgow District headquarters now and ask them to send one of their officers to the Campbell house, preferably one that knows the family. I thought it would be better if someone told Betty personally, not over the telephone."

"Quite right, that would be the best thing to do." David slumped into his chair. "Steve, should I drive over to Inverness now or take the next train down to Glasgow and do whatever I can do to help Betty and the family?"

"Sir, you should come here, now. I forgot to tell you that General Adams will arrive today on the first train from Edinburgh. He'll meet with you, Colonel Harris and Colonel Sinclair early this afternoon. Can you be here by noon?"

"Yes, of course."

"May I suggest you also bring your dress uniform and plan to go by train to Glasgow right after your meeting and stay through the funeral? I'll have someone book a room for you at the hotel."

"Okay. I'll see you before noon." David hung up the phone and sat in stunned silence.

Elaine came to the door of his office, tears dripping down her cheeks.

"Should I call the Admiral?"

"Yes, thank you." She went back to her desk and rang the operator.

David felt as though someone had hit him hard in the stomach. "Jack Campbell had a heart condition," he thought, "but he looked the picture of health. How could this be? What a terrible loss for Betty and the family. What a loss for the Army; a brilliant officer and leader who inspired his men to greatness. What a personal loss for me; my commander, mentor, and friend. Someone, who enthusiastically supported me in all things."

Elaine returned to his office. "Mrs. Evans-Cooper said the Admiral is on the golf course, but she'll get him promptly. I took the liberty of tellin' her why you needed him. I hope tha' is alright."

"Yes, that's fine." He put his head in his hands. "I can't believe this has happened. Poor Betty."

Elaine moved over beside him and put her arm around his shoulders. "I'm so sorry, Sir. I know how close you were with Brigadier Campbell." After a minute, David stood up and put his arms around Elaine. They said nothing, but she held him as tightly as he held her, for several minutes.

"I'd best leave within the hour," he finally said, "just time to pack a suitcase and get petrol for the car." He had not worn his dress uniform for two years, but he'd hung it carefully with his other clothes so it wouldn't wrinkle. As he was packing, the Admiral knocked on the door of his flat. Entering, still dressed in his golf clothes, the Admiral looked around.

"Good God! This looks like a perfectly awful Army barracks, not the quarters of a British Army Commander."

"Maybe that's because I don't command a British Army," he replied somberly, "I'm only a sub-district commander."

The Admiral continued to look around, almost incredulously. "But really, David, this is quite terrible. You should find better quarters. Maybe you should move to the Alexandra Hotel."

"It's convenient to the office and suitably located amongst the public. I didn't know I would have my quarters inspected this morning."

The Admiral gave a wry smile. "Sorry, I was out of place. Elaine told me about Brigadier Campbell. I'm so sorry about your loss of a friend. What can I do to help?"

"I want you to take command for several days while I go to Inverness and then to Glasgow. I'll meet with General Adams this afternoon and then take the train to Glasgow. Tomorrow, I'll call on Betty Campbell and do whatever I can to help. I'll stay through the funeral, probably for two or three days, then return. Call me, if anything develops."

"I will. Don't worry about a thing."

"No, I'll not worry while you're in command." He tried to smile, but it wouldn't come.

When David returned to his office, the Admiral excused himself to go home and change into his uniform.

As he came down the stairs, Elaine asked, "Wha' can I do to help you?"

"Not a thing. I think I'm ready to go. Call me if you can." She came over and put her arms around him again.

"Always remember I love you." she whispered, and then kissed him.

As he approached Cameron Barracks, David saw a young captain waiting. David stepped out of his car, and the captain saluted, took David's suitcase, and accompanied him to what had been Brigadier Jack Campbell's office. Matthew Harris was already there, and Richard Sinclair joined them soon after. It was almost two hours later before Major-General Adams arrived with his aide, both somewhat unkempt after the long train ride. After exchanging greetings, General Adams asked the others to step out of the room so he could speak with McKenna in private.

"This is a terrible loss, Colonel, but the war goes on and we must make plans for the continuation of our efforts in Scottish Command."

"I understand, General."

"We knew about Brigadier Campbell's heart condition, of course, and that's why he was barred from holding an active field command, although he certainly deserved one. Command of the North Highland District was the best we could do. Of course nobody wanted this to happen, but you can imagine the outcome had he been in a battle commanding a brigade or a division. It simply wouldn't do. To lose a senior commander during a battle could spell disaster."

"I understand, Sir." The conversation was making David uncomfortable.

"I'd a brief talk with General Carrington this morning right after we received the news. We reviewed our options for an immediate replacement for Brigadier Campbell. There are several retired major-generals and brigadiers in Scotland who would be pleased to return to active duty in any capacity, especially to take a command like this. Of course, there are a number of colonels who would jump at the chance to be promoted to brigadier. Our situation, however, is more complicated than that. We'll begin the warm season very soon, when the Germans again could invade Britain at any time, and they're certainly preparing to do something. This district requires a highly competent commander who can help meet that threat. We also need a commander who understands where we are in the rebuilding of our forces, one who has had extensive experience working with the regular forces, the Home Guard, Civil Defense and with governmental authorities at every level. It's a more difficult task than simply commanding a brigade. In short, we feel that we need a proven commander."

"Yes, Sir, I agree completely. Would Colonel Matthew Harris be a candidate?"

"Yes, Colonel Harris definitely would be a good candidate. He's healed from his injuries in France and certainly has demonstrated his abilities as a sub-district commander. However, and I must ask you not to repeat this, Harris has been selected to take a position in the Middle Eastern Command, under General Wavell. It's an opportunity for him to become a brigadier sometime in the near future. He and Scottish Command were notified of this by the War Office two weeks ago." He paused for a moment.

"Let me come right to the point, Colonel. General Carrington and I have agreed that, under the circumstances, you would be the best choice for this position. You have the background and certainly have demonstrated the skills needed in this assignment."

David was stunned. "Sir, I didn't know I could be considered for a promotion with my injured hip."

"Well, Colonel, your hip didn't seem to bother you at Sango Bay. No, I think this assignment won't be hazarded by your hip."

"I'm honored, General. I don't quite know what to say."

"I'll take that as a 'yes.' Good, now that's settled. You'll be promoted to the rank of Acting Brigadier for now. If all goes well, you likely will be made a permanent Brigadier later this year. As a matter of fact, I brought a pair of brigadier's insignia with me. I think we'll have a brief ceremony shortly and pin them on. We don't ever want to give the enemy the impression we've a command without a commander. I'll do the honors if you don't mind, as we don't have time to arrange a more formal affair. Now, let's talk about your replacement in Fort William."

David's head was spinning. "Sir, if I may suggest, I'd like to sit down and talk about this in a more thoughtful fashion. Would you join me in a whisky or tea if you prefer?"

"Good idea. Whisky would be fine."

"I believe Brigadier Campbell keeps a bottle in his desk just for such occasions, and I know he wouldn't mind if we share a drink. If he were here, I'm sure he would be the first to offer us a glass." With that, David opened the desk drawer and brought out the bottle. After pouring two glasses, they settled into two comfortable chairs.

"General, may I have your permission to share my thoughts, such as they are at this sudden development?"

"Certainly. I want your ideas."

"Obviously, with my promotion, we need one new sub-district commander and a second commander when Matthew Harris departs. But first, how do you view Richard Sinclair?"

"Very weak, frankly, and he's likely to be replaced soon. He's over his head at the rank of Colonel. We'll rely on you for your recommendation."

"My first recommendation, General, is that we leave him where he is for now. Replacing all three sub-district commanders at the same time could be perilous. At least, he knows the people as well as the units in his sub-district. He certainly commands a less-threatened sub-district than those who are further south."

"I agree. Very well, he stays for now."

"Next, I'd recommend reconfiguring the command structure. The

Inverness Sub-District is running well, thanks to Matthew Harris' efforts, as is my sub-district. In order to minimize disruptions, I'd suggest I remain in Fort William in command of the Northwest Sub-District and, for the time being, simply assume command of the North Highland District as well. With a new Inverness Sub-District commander to replace Harris, I could command the District from Fort William, but I'll come over here once or twice each week to review matters and stay as long as necessary. This would avoid another disruption in my district. In time of emergency, I'll arrive here in less than two hours. That's considerably faster than the Jerries can load their boats, let alone sail across the North Sea. Rear-Admiral Evans-Cooper can command the sub-district in my absence."

General Adams was silent for a few moments. "I see your point. That may be the better course. However, the Inverness Sub-district is a significant component in Scottish Command and we must have a proven commander here, one who knows the situation thoroughly. Do you have someone in mind?"

"I do, Lieutenant-Colonel Steve Whittaker. My experience with him this past year has convinced me that he has gained in-depth knowledge of this sub-district while serving as Brigadier Campbell's chief-of-staff for the North Highland District. He knows this sub-district thoroughly, and I've great confidence in him."

"But he's quite young and hasn't served as a battalion commander. He's a very junior lieutenant colonel."

"Yes, Sir, but these are not ordinary times, and many young officers are being pushed up into positions of great responsibility."

"You're right." Adams thought for a minute. "We could make him an acting colonel. If he does not work out, we can reverse the decision. Very well, Colonel, or I should say Brigadier, let me call Lord Carrington right now. We need to move along with this matter fairly quickly." He stepped out to have his aide ring up Edinburgh Castle, and then returned.

"I'll have a bit more whisky while we wait." David poured the General another drink, but chose not to refresh his own. In a few minutes, the aide returned, having reached Lord Carrington on the telephone. The conversation was quick and the recommendation approved. General Adams opened the door again and told his aide to get Steve Whittaker, who was just hanging up his telephone.

"I was speaking with Glasgow District, General. They've delivered the sad news to Mrs. Campbell."

"How did she take the news?" Adams asked Whittaker.

"They said she took it quite hard, General. She called her children and all are returning home right now. I think telling the children was her most difficult task and it took quite some time. The officer stayed until she allowed him to leave, a good friend having arrived." Steve gestured at David. "I think it would be best if Colonel McKenna were to visit her soon."

"I'll leave for Glasgow as soon as we're finished here," David replied. "I'd like a staff car and driver to be available in Glasgow for the next several days." Steve nodded.

Adams told Whittaker of David's new assignment and promotion. Then he suggested that David tell Steve of his promotion and new assignment. David did so, adding that Steve's promotion to colonel would be an acting rank for time being, as was his own promotion to Brigadier. Adams then asked Steve to assemble as many officers as possible for the brief and fairly informal promotion ceremony.

Within five minutes, the office was full, and General Adams announced the two changes in command and the promotions. He placed the new insignia on David, and then placed David's old insignia on Steve Whittaker. Adams added a few complementary words about David and Steve, and then closed with a few encouraging words about the work of the District. After the officers were dismissed, Adams excused himself to wash up before his brief meeting with David, Matthew Harris, and Richard Sinclair. Adams would then depart for the return trip by train to Edinburgh, accompanied by David, who would go on to Glasgow. David and Steve sat down, both somewhat stunned from the unexpected developments.

"I didn't expect this," said Steve.

"Nor I," added David. "I know you'll be a great success in your new assignment. I think we should talk more at another time, as I must go on to Glasgow to see Betty Campbell and help with funeral arrangements. Congratulations."

THE NEXT FEW DAYS WERE TUMULTUOUS for David. His visit with Betty Campbell was emotionally exhausting. The children had arrived, except for the two older boys who were serving with their regiments and couldn't be quickly released. Betty had regained her composure and hugged David when she saw the brigadier's insignia on his shoulders. "Jack would've been so proud of you and absolutely delighted that you're his replacement. I'm just so sorry for the reason you're replacing him." Tears welled up in her eyes. "I knew this would happen someday, I just felt it inside. I'm going to miss him so."

During the next two days, David met with Brigadier Charles Guthrie, the Glasgow District commander, and visited units and garrisons throughout the area. Because of its large population and the vital role of the Clyde Basin, the district housed many active duty formations, as well as several dozen Home Guard battalions. Of particular interest was a visit to the 12th Battalion of the Highland Light Infantry, Jack Campbell's regiment. The 12th Battalion was a recently activated Home Defense formation, created to train new soldiers and provide a temporary home for wounded servicemen. In the event of invasion, it would offer added firepower for defense. Principally, older officers and sergeants led the battalion, most of whom were not physically able to deploy overseas. Scottish Command had chosen the 12th to take part in Jack's funeral. The battalion commander assured David his men would look sharp and march correctly. "They may not have all their fighting skills yet, Brigadier McKenna, but they do know how to march."

The Monday afternoon funeral ceremony went very well. The church was full to overflowing, a tribute to the esteem in which Jack was held. Numerous dignitaries attended, including Lord Provost Patrick Dollan, who headed a delegation from Glasgow City Government. Lieutenant-General Carrington and a number of subordinate commanders and staff officers represented Scottish Command. Many veterans and retirees attended, each proudly displaying their campaign medals from earlier wars.

David, and Steve Whittaker sat with the family, both wearing their dress uniforms with kilts. Over 400 men of the 12th Battalion marched to the church behind the regimental band with pipers, later providing an honor guard that accompanied Jack's casket to the cemetery. When it was over, David congratulated the battalion commander on their excellent presentation, and then conveyed Lord Carrington's favorable comments to the assembled battalion. They proudly marched back to their garrison with the pipers playing *Scotland the Brave,* Jack's favorite.

After a short time, having taken Betty and several family members back to her home, David said his farewells and promised to return within a few weeks. His driver took him to his hotel to change clothes, and then to Queen Street station for the late train back to Fort William.

April 14

HAVING RETURNED FROM GLASGOW, David arrived at his flat just before midnight. After unpacking and a few hours' sleep, he awoke to the early morning noise on High Street. A bright spring sunrise had dawned, but the occasional pain in his right hip continued. It was more of a simple ache than real pain. "Too much time on the train," he surmised. After washing, he dressed and noticed again the new brigadier's rank on his shoulder straps. Whereas the colonel's rank had been a single crown closest to the neck, followed in tandem by two diamond-shaped stars or pips, the brigadier's rank was the crown, and three pips formed a triangle below the crown. It had still not quite sunk in that he was a brigadier now, an acting one to be sure, but in retirement he would forever be addressed as brigadier. "Anne would be so pleased," he thought. "I wonder if Trevor Henry is now a brigadier. Is he still in the War Office? I must drop him a note."

David went downstairs to his office to review the mail. He was heating a pot of hot water when he heard the rear door lock turn. It was Elaine. She glanced at his shoulder straps, flew across the room, and threw her arms around him.

"So 'tis true. You've been promoted."

"I'm only an acting brigadier. If all goes well, I may receive a permanent promotion later this year or early next year."

"Tha' doesna' matter. I'm so proud of you." She hugged him. "In fact, I plan to show you how proud I am this evenin'," she said almost leering at him, "if you are available, of course."

David felt his heart leap. "I'll be available as soon as the door is bolted. I missed you so much." He started to kiss her again.

"Careful. Hold tha' thought until the evenin'. The officers will be here in a few minutes for a staff meetin'. The Admiral called the meetin' to brief you and learn of new developments. I think they already know of your promotion, but they havna' seen you wearin' your new rank."

Within ten minutes, the staff arrived, each congratulating David. The Admiral started the meeting promptly with a congratulatory welcome to David, then an expression of regret on the death of Brigadier Campbell. Then he continued. "Perhaps the Brigadier can explain to this old sea dog how the new command structure will work."

At that moment, the door opened and Lady Frances entered with the usual apologies for being late. The staff all rose as she approached the table, a common courtesy to women, but Elaine remained seated and whispered "good mornin'" as Frances took a seat next to her. Frances reached over and squeezed Elaine's arm. David was pleased that Elaine's resentment seemed to be more muted, perhaps because of Sir Robert's death. Lady Frances wore a black armband on her left arm in recognition of her own loss. David later learned that she'd declined to wear mourning clothes because of the war and the many others who have been lost. She insisted on continuing her Civil Defense work despite her loss, "because I'm needed." She was greatly subdued and not as animated as normal.

David began his discussion, answering the Admiral's question, which he knew was intended for other members of the staff. He traced the new command relationship from the Scottish Command: Lieutenant-General Carrington, temporarily through Major-General Adams and down to David as Commander of the North Highland District. David would command the district, but he also would continue to command the Northwest Highland Sub-District as well.

"I'll rely more heavily than before on each of you, as much of my attention will be devoted to my new responsibilities with the North Highland District. My absences will be more frequent, and the Admiral will assume command of the sub-district in my absence. When the Admiral is unavailable, Lieutenant-Colonel Foster will assume command." CB gave David a quick nod, and then put his head back down to his notes.

The Admiral had each staff officer briefly report on activities within their areas of responsibility; new Home Guard equipment, training, personnel, Civil Defense, and the past week's events. David then spoke for most of an hour, discussing the funeral, the war, the activities of the Glasgow District and the units he'd visited. He also announced that Lord Carrington, having reached the Army's mandatory age limit, would retire and be replaced by Lieutenant-General Andrew Thorne.

Finally, CB spoke up and suggested that "the new Brigadier" should be honored with a ceremony "or something." David started to decline, not wanting to disrupt more important work, but Lady Frances interrupted him, quite to everyone's surprise.

"This may be a time when I can be of help," she said quietly, almost haltingly. "I could host the staff and spouses at my home tomorrow evening. Food is a bit short, so if several of you could donate a ration coupon, Mary could shop and put something together for us to eat."

"Are you sure you're up to this?" David inquired, and then added carefully "at this very difficult time."

"Yes, quite," she responded, her jaw firmly set. There was a long, awkward pause.

"An excellent suggestion!" the Admiral boomed. "I concur."

The matter settled, the Admiral adjourned the meeting. The rest of the day brought extensive paperwork, but no visitors. David was immersed in his work as the evening began to approach, until he heard Elaine bolt the door. She returned to his office.

"I ha' some soup if you are hungry."

"I'm not hungry," he replied.

"Me neither. Let's go upstairs."

THE RECEPTION AT THE HOME of Lady Frances was a quiet but pleasant affair. Elaine declined to attend, her family responsibilities interfering, but the others were present with their spouses. David met both CB Foster's wife and Frank Leslie's wife, both for the first time. He found them to be capable and resilient women, no great surprise given the lives they had lived and the men they'd married. Lady Frances gave a short tour of the house, the first time David had gone beyond the library.

The next two days were busier than before, with David's new responsibilities added to his previous schedule. He made plans to return to Inverness within a week to continue his orientation and visitations to the many units stationed in that sub-district. He would meet with Richard Sinclair the following week and visit units in the Aberdeen Sub-District. He asked Elaine to accompany him, but was met again with a firm "No, I donna' think tha's a good idea." Later that day, he suggested they find time on the weekend to go for a picnic and enjoy the warm spring weather. She again replied "Thank you, but no, I canna' go." David found her responses to be unfathomable and without explanation. He wanted to have a long talk with Elaine to begin establishing a plan that would lead to their marriage. She was evasive, however, and unwilling to stay very long after work.

It was all very perplexing.

22

April 18, 1941

A GRAY, WET MORNING greeted David, a typical Highland soggy spring day. He entered his office. The first batch of official correspondence from Edinburgh, which had heretofore gone to Jack Campbell, had arrived by train the previous afternoon and been placed in the safe. Retrieving it, he was impressed by the bulk of the materials and estimated it would take at least four hours to review and answer the mail. Some twenty minutes into his effort, the door opened and Elaine entered. She put away her coat, placed the pot of water on the stove, and went to her desk without a word.

David stepped from his office. "Good morning."

"Good mornin'," she responded without inflexion. He longed for a sign of feeling in her voice, but there was none. Returning to his desk, he went back to his correspondence with a sinking feeling that bordered on despondency. An hour later, he went to the stove and made two cups of tea, she having ignored the pot, which by now had half-boiled away. He placed a cup on her desk, but there was no recognition on her part. He returned to his desk.

Another hour passed. The front door opened and the Admiral entered briskly, threw off his coat, and strode into David's office. "Elaine, please come in here." The dark look on the Admiral's face alerted David that something was seriously amiss. The Admiral looked at Elaine. "Sit down, please." She complied uncomfortably. He paused for a moment, and then continued.

"Elaine, I've just learned from Glasgow that the HMS *Bonaventure* was torpedoed and sunk several days ago." Her mouth opened as if to speak, but no words came. Her face drained of colour. "I'm sorry I've no more information, other than the ship was part of an escort force bringing a convoy through the Mediterranean when it was attacked by U-boats."

Tears welled up in her eyes and Elaine finally found her voice. "Paul?"

"I've no further information at this time, but I'll receive a call as soon as more information is available." He paused while he sat down. "You should understand there are almost always survivors when a warship is torpedoed, especially when the ship is part of a convoy and surrounded by other vessels. The situation is never hopeless."

"But he works in the engine room, far below decks. How could he get out?"

"Elaine, my dear, this is my profession. I can assure you that thousands of engine room sailors have escaped from sinking ships." The look on her face told the Admiral she wasn't mollified by his assurances. He continued, "I gave Paul's full name to Vice-Admiral Troup and asked that I receive a call as soon as any information is received on survivors. Until then, we can only wait . . . and pray."

As the tears slowly dripped down her face, David said, "If you wish to go home, you certainly may leave now."

She nodded and murmured "Thank you." After a moment she rose, gathered her things and left.

The Admiral looked at David and said, "I'm sorry."

"No," he replied, "you did the right thing. She needed to know. Was Paul really likely to escape the engine room?"

The Admiral sat back with a long sigh. "I don't know. It depends on many factors. Where did the torpedo hit? Was there more than one torpedo? How much warning did they have? How did the captain and crew respond? We really won't know until the casualty list is posted. One of the problems with a torpedo strike in the engine room is the boiler system, especially the hot water pipes. Water under pressure at several hundred degrees temperature scalds and often kills when a pipe breaks or a boiler is holed. Sometimes many escape the engine room. Other times, nobody gets out. We'll just have to wait and see."

"How long must we wait?"

"It's hard to tell, but probably several days at least."

"Hmmm. I think I'd better alert CB Foster that Elaine likely will be unavailable for the indefinite future." David picked up the telephone to ring up the operator. As he left, the Admiral added, "I thought I should stop by to see Ben Douglas. He may be of some help to Elaine and the family."

The next few hours flew by as David tried to complete all unfinished business at the office. Once alerted, Ben Douglas went to Elaine's home to assess her needs. He walked back to the manse, and Kathleen immediately called women in the church that, despite strict rationing, pooled their resources and cooked passable meals.

CB Foster arrived shortly before noon and brought with him Mrs. Allen, his secretary. "She can as well sit in your office and do our typing, Brigadier, as sit in my office. Here she can also answer your telephone and handle inquiries, well at least the simple ones. I'll have her here most of next week."

David was grateful for the help, which gave him the opportunity to get out of the office, even briefly. As the lunch hour passed, Lady Frances stopped in to invite David horseback riding again the next day. As the weeks went by, following her husband's death, she increasingly returned to her wartime activities. David told her about the *Bonaventure* and Elaine's absence from the office.

"I don't know when she'll return."

Lady Frances thought for a moment. "Let me work on this. I'll be back in two or three hours. I wish to invite you to supper at the Alexandra, David, and I won't take no for an answer. We need to talk about this." David reluctantly nodded his consent and she was out the door.

A half hour passed and CB Foster returned, lugging Mrs. Allen's typewriter. "She'll type better on her own machine, rather than on Elaine's."

"CB, could she type some of our office materials? I'm sure you know her well enough to vouch for her security." David was comfortable with the Scots living in Fort William. He had experienced absolutely no 'fifth column' activity.

"Absolutely, Brigadier," he responded, "Mrs. Allen has two sons in the forces, as was her husband during the First War. He works at the aluminum plant." Mrs. Allen was a rather dowdy woman in her early fifties who moved more slowly than Elaine, but who displayed a basic intelligence somewhat above that of her peers. "I've found her to be quite reliable and a loyal subject of the Crown."

Mrs. Allen took instruction well and soon was typing several of David's reports. Although unfamiliar with military affairs, she dutifully gave full attention to David's paperwork, whenever she caught up with her work for CB's engineering firm.

As the workday came to an end and the office was about to close, Lady Frances returned.

"Shall we?" she inquired. "I have several things to report."

While they walked to the Alexandra Hotel, David told her of his discomfort with the responsibility she was shouldering in her time of mourning and suggested someone else take over her duties.

"Would you have me sit home and mourn like a proper widow?" she challenged him. "I've spent days and nights grieving and at times my loss seems more than I can bear. I loved Robert with all my heart and he, me. He was truly a wonderful husband and father, but he's gone and no amount of grieving will bring him back. No thank you, Sir; I can deal with my loss better by keeping busy. There's a war on and there's much to be done. I find it gratifying to work as hard as I can and then fall asleep exhausted at night. Of course, I often wake up in the night full of grief, but I fall back asleep again after an hour or so. My children and my work give me purpose for my life and I take some small satisfaction in that."

David remained silent, thinking of nothing with which to challenge her position. At the hotel, they sat in a dining room mostly full of young naval officers from the training station. All eyes were on them as they entered. David wore no wedding ring, but Lady Frances continued to wear hers, as was the custom for widows. She ordered whisky for both of them and slowly nursed it throughout their very modest dinner.

"I've seen too many widows turn to drink in their sorrow and I'll not be one of them." She told David that several women from her Civil Defense organization had each volunteered to work at his office a few hours each week to keep things running smoothly during Elaine's absence.

"Most have typing skills, and I've found each to be loyal and thoroughly reliable. They want to help." She continued, "I'll visit Elaine to give her some support. Also, I truly hope you'll join me for an afternoon ride tomorrow. My horses need a good workout." He agreed. "Fine, shall we say two o'clock?" He nodded. It was a warm evening for late-April, the rain having lifted before noon. They walked slowly back to her car. As they said goodbye, she took his hand.

"Whatever the outcome with Paul, give Elaine plenty of time and space to work things through. She needs that right now more than anything else you can give her."

THE NEXT MORNING, Saturday, David opened the office after walking to the train station to collect the mail from the evening train, a task normally performed by Elaine. There was little mail, simply notes from Steve Whittaker telling him of a few minor activities in the Inverness Sub-District. He'd been expecting a report from Richard Sinclair on developments in the Aberdeen Sub-District, but again there was nothing. He returned to his office and put the new materials into the safe, then penned a sharp note to Sinclair pointing out his omission. He went out again and posted the note, then walked to Elaine's house. Her mother answered the door.

"How is she?"

"Doin' poorly, I'm afraid. I'll get her." After a few moments Elaine appeared, looking as if she'd been up all night.

"Is there anything I can do?" he inquired.

"I donna' think so, thank you." She gestured to a chair, but David chose to stand. "Lady Frances wa' here a half-hour ago. She brought a pastry, although Lord knows where she got the sugar. She really wa' very kind." Elaine paused for a minute and then continued. "She said the two of you were goin' to ride horses this afternoon."

"Yes, the horses need exercise." David really didn't want to discuss this any further, knowing it might upset Elaine.

"I think tha's a good idea." She looked down. "I hope you ha' a good time."

David was quite surprised at her response, given her previous reactions to his activities with Lady Frances. Finally, he spoke after a lengthy silence. "I'm so sorry for all that you're going through right now. I know it's difficult."

"The waitin' and not knowin' is the hardest," she replied, "and tryin' to comfort the boys, of course. I thought they hardly knew their father, but evidently I was wrong. They're takin' this quite hard." Another long pause followed. "It's all so difficult. I wish I knew wha' to do." Then she looked at David. "I really ha' things to finish now. I hope you ha' a lovely ride."

"Yes, very well." Then he whispered softly, "I love you" and gave her a quick hug. She nodded, but said nothing in reply, nor did she look at him. As he left the house, he felt a sharp ache deep inside his stomach. He wondered what she would do, if Paul Ross drowned.

April 21

THE NEW WEEK BEGAN AS ALWAYS with a brisk early morning run. This was followed by a good wash, putting on a clean shirt and the same uniform as before, and then going downstairs to open the office. He was surprised when Elaine came in with the mail, even if somewhat later than usual. She was dressed in a simple cotton dress, neatly mended along one pocket, but the worn expression on her face revealed another sleepless night. She made tea without her usual enthusiasm and walked quietly to her desk after giving David his cup. David was explaining that CB Foster had arranged for his secretary to help out in the office for the week, when Mrs. Allen entered. After introductions, David asked Elaine to organize the work for Mrs. Allen, and then returned to his office.

He reviewed the weekend again in his mind; his short visit with Elaine Saturday morning and an equally unsatisfying visit on Sunday. She wasn't at home when he first knocked on the door on Sunday, as she'd gone to Church with the boys, not her typical Sunday morning activity. He returned later and found her standing by the door, but she clearly wasn't interested in conversation and he bid goodbye after just a few words.

The horseback ride with Lady Frances on Saturday afternoon had been considerably more enjoyable. The air was clear and a brisk breeze from Loch Linnhe helped refresh his mind. They rode for almost three hours, halting periodically to let the horses rest. Returning to her house, they enjoyed a hot drink with whisky as they sat in front of the warm, crackling fireplace. Their conversation seemed never to stop, and it was well after 7 p.m. when Mary placed some cold meat and cheese on the side table along with slices of freshly baked bread. It was almost 11 p.m. when David said goodbye. Lady Frances took his hand and held it for a long minute while she thanked him for the lovely evening. They promised to ride together more often.

It was shortly after noon the next day when the Admiral rushed in and took Elaine by the hand and led her into David's office.

"Good news. Paul Ross has been rescued!" David thought Elaine was beginning to faint, then she put her arms around the Admiral and said, "thank you" several times.

"But I must tell you, Elaine, Paul was injured. He appears to have broken an arm and some ribs when the engine room crew escaped up the ladder and through the hatch to the main deck. He's now in a hospital at Valletta in Malta, but he's expected to make a full recovery."

She covered her mouth for a brief moment, and then said, "But he's alive. That's what matters." She looked at David. "I must go home and tell Mum and the boys."

"Yes," he replied, "of course." With that she went out the door, practically running down High Street.

They stood silently for a moment. Then David said, "I think I'm losing her."

The Admiral recognized the double entendre and simply said, "Yes."

April 30

NEW WEAPONS FOR THE HOME GUARD were coming to the North Highland District of Scottish Command a month after the other Districts received them. David was notified that Sten guns would be issued to his district beginning in late May or early June. The Sten gun was a sub-machine gun that fired a nine-millimeter pistol bullet on automatic fire. This meant the gunner could squeeze the trigger and the twenty-round magazine would be emptied in less than three seconds. The weapon was cheap to manufacture and simple to use. It would arm many more Home Guardsmen, as well as members of the regular forces.

Two Vickers machine guns would also be issued to the Lochaber Company, two more being allocated to each company in the North Highlands District. These were medium machine guns, also .303 caliber and mounted on a tripod. They were water cooled and capable of more sustained fire than the Lewis machine guns.

New hand grenades were being issued in large quantities to supplement the Mills Bomb grenades. Most significant was the Sticky Bomb, the No. 4 grenade that could be used to attack tanks. In principle it was merely a glass container and detonator covered with an adhesive which, when thrown, caused the grenade to stick to the side of a tank and then explode. Sometimes, it did. Other times, it proved to be a tricky bomb that would stick to anything, including the uniform of the thrower—with disastrous results.

Of greater importance was the promise of the inexpensive Northover Projector, a metal pipe mounted on a tripod. That weapon used a black powder charge to fire a half-pint bottle of chemicals, which were ignited on impact by a phosphorous strip, giving the projector a limited utility on the battlefield. Two other hastily developed weapons, the Smith Gun and the Blacker Bombard, were also of some utility. They were produced in large numbers to give the Home Guard a modest anti-tank capability. As David and his staff planned for the introduction of these weapons into the Home Guard units in his three sub-districts, they confronted the usual problems of weapon delivery, storage, ammunition supply, training, and employment by the commanders. New training schools also were being established to train further the Home Guard units and their leaders. Clearly the Home Guard was proving itself to be a more formidable force than originally envisioned. The War Office planned to use Home Guard units to replace many regular British Army units in Britain, as the latter were being deployed to combat theaters overseas, a concept which David strongly endorsed.

Elaine came to work fitfully during this time. David was grateful for Mrs. Allen's help, and the assistance provided by the women from Civil Defense. In Inverness, newly promoted Colonel Steve Whittaker appointed a young major to his former position as District Chief-of-Staff. The major, soon to become an acting lieutenant-colonel, served as David's right arm in District matters at the Inverness District headquarters. Whittaker continued to provide advice and assistance as needed and reorganized the group of staff officers who worked for David in his capacity as District Commander. They worked more independently than before and handled many routine staff duties in Inverness which otherwise would have fallen to David and his small sub-district staff. Everything seemed to be working smoothly for David, except Elaine.

David was buried in a report when Elaine appeared at his door. "I ha' a telegram! I've no' received a telegram before." Out the door she flew to retrieve it. Ten minutes later she was back. "It's from the Navy," she said excitedly, "It says Paul is goin' to Devonport and will be lodged on arrival at the base hospital." David said nothing. "I must go see him," she announced. She took her purse and left.

Early the next morning, Elaine walked to the train station, stopping briefly at the office. She told David, "'Twill be a day and a half to get there. Mum ha' made lunches and I'll sleep on the train. As a wife of a war wounded, I ha' priority for a ticket and a discount. I've no' been out o' Scotland before and this is so excitin'." She gave him a quick hug and was gone. Minutes later she boarded the train to Glasgow, from whence she'd travel south to Devonport.

David sat silently for several minutes, then walked to the door and bolted it. He turned off the lights and returned to his office. A half hour later, he heard the back door open. He looked up to see Ben Douglas.

"I locked the door for a reason," he murmured.

"I know. I saw Elaine walking to the station and she told me her plans. I thought you might need a friend."

"Aren't you the Chaplain?"

"Not today, just a friend."

David put his head down in his hands for several minutes. Ben got up and brewed some tea, bringing two cups back with him.

"I lost her, Ben."

"Yes. I'm very sorry."

"I just feel terrible. I haven't felt this way since Anne died."

"This is a death of another kind. You're entitled to mourn. You did your best, but. . . . "

"I would've made her the happiest woman in Scotland." David wiped his face.

"Probably."

"Why did this happen, dammit!" David said sharply. "We were so happy."

Ben responded, *"If meant to be, it would have been. If not, it cannot be."*

"Robert Burns?" David asked.

"No, my mother." They both smiled. "She had a way with old doggerel. I'm glad it amused you.

The agony David endured that morning slowly receded as they talked, leaving him hurt and tired. He took a deep draught of tea, wiped his face, and sat back in his chair. "I feel like hell, Ben, let's get out of here."

"Would you like to go for a ride or go for some breakfast?"

"Breakfast, I'm starving."

Mrs. Allen arrived, as they left the building and walked to the Argyll. Over haggis and eggs, David decided to drive to Scourie and visit Catherine Lewis. "Catherine understands these things far better than I. She can give me a woman's perspective on all this. I'd enjoy some hours of conversation with her, but I can't call her, as she has no telephone."

"I can contact the pastor in Scourie to give her the message. Why don't I say you're on another inspection tour as the new district commander?"

"Brilliant. I'll leave this morning. Please tell the Admiral and CB Foster of my absence. And call Steve Whittaker."

Quickly packing a few clothes, David drove northeast along Loch Ness toward Inverness, then northwest through the Braemore Forest region along Loch Shin. Several people recognized him and waved as he passed by, providing an emotional boost. His mind began to push Elaine to the rear and he focused on the beauty of the day and his anticipation of seeing Catherine. It was late in the evening when he arrived at her house. She greeted him as the dear friend he was and one with whom he could safely share intimate conversation. They enjoyed a whisky, then another, and then went to bed, separately.

A blazing sun greeted them as they awoke the next morning, and Catherine suggested they take a holiday and drive a few miles north past Kinlochbervie on the coast. They could park where the road ends and walk two or three miles along the deserted coast where they would likely find a beach all to themselves.

"I'll pack a lunch. You willna' be needin' swim wear, as there'll likely be nobody there to see us." There was no one within miles around.

Two days later, David slowly drove south again feeling more normal. He was grateful for his friendship with Catherine, their long conversations and her hospitality. She helped him recognize that, as he overcame his obsession for Elaine, he'd regain his strength. They maintained their commitment to a non-sexual friendship, as both knew they could never marry. The pain in his stomach subsided and he was ready to return to work. It would be many months before the pain disappeared completely.

May 20

THE WAR CONTINUED TO PROGRESS UNEVENLY, causing a great strain for British and Commonwealth forces, and their nations. The last remnants of the Italian Army in Ethiopia had surrendered, and Emperor Haile Selassie was returned to his throne. Fighting in North Africa see-sawed, as both British and Axis forces received reinforcements and mounted attacks on one another. Casualties in general were mercifully light. German forces completed the conquest of Greece, forcing the British Army to evacuate, many repositioning on the island of Crete where they awaited a German attack. It would come soon and would lead to another evacuation with severe losses.

The *Blitz* continued, somewhat abated because of the strain on the German *Luftwaffe*, but Greenock for the fourth time had been severely bombed over two nights, May 5-6, with heavy damage. This proved to be the last air raid on Scottish cities. Further south, a final large raid targeted London on May 10th, with Parliament itself bombed. The House of Commons chamber was gutted and public morale dropped still further.

The air raids then stopped, bringing an uneasy respite to Britain that lasted a year. U-boats, however, continued to sink an alarming number of ships, and Hitler triumphantly announced that 40% of all supply vessels to Britain had been sunk; the actual figure was much lower, but those losses were still severe. The most positive sign for David McKenna's war was that people were beginning to accommodate themselves to the reality of the war and the public mood in Scotland was slowly beginning to improve.

It was mid-afternoon when the office door opened and Elaine entered. She went straight to David's office. Surprised, he rose to greet her, but she quickly sat down.

"I'm movin' to Devonport," she blurted out excitedly, "I ha' a job at the Royal Navy Headquarters. The boys are movin', too, as I've found a school for them. Mum will stay here for now, but I think she'll move down soon. She'll miss the boys so much it will force her to join us in Devonport. We donna' know what to do with her house, maybe rent it to someone from the Navy Station." She talked so quickly David couldn't respond.

"I really need a letter from you for the Navy." she continued. "You wouldna' mind, would you?"

"No, I'll prepare a letter," he said without enthusiasm. "Where will you live?"

"There's an organization there that helps Navy families. Paul is still in the hospital, but the ladies found us a small flat not too far from the base. I think it's smaller than your flat here, but we'll adjust." She looked around, seeing that little had changed. "If you could draft my letter, I'll type it when I come back. I ha' packin' to do, you know." She rose, then reached across the desk and squeezed David's hand. "Thank you for my letter." She quickly flew out the door.

All the old feelings had come rushing back, and David was unable to think of anything else. She seemed happy, however, even if he was miserable. He drew out a piece of paper and slowly composed some words. As he wrote he thought, 'She really was my best employee in any position I've held over the years.' The words came faster and he soon finished. Turning to a new report from the War Office, he buried himself in a study of lessons learned from the debacle in Greece, where the Nazi armies had easily conquered the small country, after driving out British forces.

Two hours later Elaine returned, took the letter to her old desk, and quickly typed it in finished form. She brought it to David for his signature. "You were verra' generous with your praise. Thank you."

"You earned it," he responded, as he signed the letter. There was a long, awkward pause. She folded the letter and put it into her purse. She started to leave, then turned to him and he saw tears in her eyes.

Glancing at his shoulder boards she said, "You look handsome as a brigadier." A moment passed as she struggled for words. "I may no' see you again," she said softly. "I want to thank you for all . . . " She paused as her voice wavered, "for all you've done for me and . . . " another long pause, "and for all you've meant to me. I will always love you." The tears dripped off her face. David was unable to control his own tears.

Then she straightened herself. "Goodbye."

David started to say "I love you," but the words wouldn't come before she was out the door.

Fifteen minutes later, David threw the bolt to his office door. He picked up the telephone and rang the operator. "May I have the Stuart residence?"

Arriving at the Stuart home soon after, Harry greeted him warmly. He entered and Lady Frances came out of the sewing room and hugged him.

"Welcome, David, what a pleasant surprise."

He responded, "Are you free this afternoon?"

ON JUNE 22, 1941, Hitler invaded the Soviet Union, the *Wehrmacht* pushing forward some 450 miles within a few weeks. Massive forces almost 3,000,000 strong had secretly been assembled along the Soviet border; Northwestern Europe had been emptied of much of its conquering army. Soviet forces, weakened by Stalin's purges of the Soviet high command, surrendered in masses, and German forces triumphantly drove onward to the gates of Leningrad, Moscow, and Stalingrad. There, with the onset of an early winter, they were stopped.

Hitler's megalomania convinced him that the Nazi forces led by his own military genius would swiftly conquer the rest of Europe and force the British Government to surrender to his will. The 1941 invasion of Britain was postponed in the face of five million trained and equipped defenders, almost two million of whom were Home Guardsmen.

For now, Britain was safe from invasion.

Epilogue

ELAINE ROSS SECURED A CLERICAL POSITION at the Royal Navy Headquarters in Devonport in May 1941, from which she rose to become a chief supervisor by war's end. She and her family lived in a nearby flat while Paul recovered from his injuries. He returned to sea in August 1941. In 1942, Elaine divorced Paul. Three months later, she married Lieutenant-Commander Hugh Kinney Chandler, a 1925 graduate of the Royal Naval College at Dartmouth, and who was also assigned to the same headquarters. Promoted Commander in early 1944, Chandler served in a variety of assignments until his retirement as a Captain in 1959. Elaine continued her work with the Navy and, subsequently, with the Ministry of Defense, also retiring in 1959. They then moved to Chichester, where they lived until Hugh's death in 1990. Soon after, Elaine moved in with her eldest son Aaron and his family in Tunbridge Wells, where she lived until her death in 2001 at the age of 93. She always spoke fondly of her work at Scotland's Northwest Sub-District Headquarters and of its commander, Colonel, later Brigadier David McKenna. She insisted they were only friends and professional colleagues, and she never saw him again after moving to Devonport. Her sons remain silently skeptical.

Brigadier David McKenna was seen increasingly in the company of Lady Frances Stuart who, after her husband's death, assumed a larger role as a member of the staff of the Northwest Sub-District. In October 1943, they announced their engagement and were married a month later, the service being conducted by the Reverend (Captain) Ben Douglas. David received his permanent promotion to Brigadier in December 1941 and was appointed to the Distinguished Service Order soon after. David's assignment as North Highland District Commander and other wartime assignments involved considerable travel, some accompanied by his new wife. Beginning in mid-1941, he traveled to other parts of the UK to advise on the proper integration of civil-military authorities and to work on other War Office duties of a classified nature. He retired from the Army in 1945 and, thereafter, became a director for the Stuart family shipping business, with occasional contract work for the War Office and Ministry of Defense. He was urged by colleagues to stand for Parliament as a Conservative candidate in the 1945 elections, but was defeated. David and Frances were socially active in Fort William and enjoyed prosperity in their later lives. In 1983, David died, followed seven years later by Frances. David avowed he'd two great loves in his life, Anne and Frances. Frances was openly skeptical.

Reverend (Captain) Ben Douglas continued his ministry in Fort William until his retirement in 1966. He was greatly saddened by the death of his beloved wife, Kathleen, to throat cancer in 1957. He never remarried, but enjoyed the close company of several widows in his congregation. He remained an intimate friend of David McKenna until his own death in 1982.

Emma McPherson was honored for her role in the Sango Bay battle, being awarded the King's Commendation for Brave Conduct. The Duke of Sutherland presented Emma with the certificate and badge in a small ceremony in Durness in July 1941. Brigadier McKenna and Lady Frances Stuart were also in attendance. Every day for the rest of her life, Emma proudly wore the red and gold badge, which displayed a sword over a wreath topped with a crown. She died in 1953, slumped over in the overstuffed chair on her front porch, her rifle, and empty whisky bottle beside her. She was buried in the garden of her beloved cottage next to her husband. Her children then emptied the cottage of its contents and the building soon crumbled. After twenty years, it was indistinguishable from the surrounding fields.

The British people volunteered in enormous numbers to support the war effort, many joining the armed forces voluntarily or through conscription. Millions joined the Home Guard, the many Civil Defense organizations, or the civic and social organizations that actively supported the war effort. It's estimated over two-thirds of adult Britons were actively engaged in war work, more, if factory, forest, and agricultural workers were counted.

The Home Guard played an increasingly important role in British military strategy. Its proficiency improved throughout the war as the force received better training and increasingly sophisticated weapons. Its numbers peaked at almost two million men and women by late 1943, of which some quarter-million served in Scotland. This permitted many Regular Army divisions and smaller units to be transferred safely overseas. In 1943, women were permitted to enroll in the Home

Guard as 'auxiliaries,' some 32,000 serving by the end of the war. The Home Guard assumed many roles formerly restricted to the regulars, including air defense and coast artillery. The force so impressed Hitler that he copied the British Home Guard when activating a similar force in Germany, the *Volksturm*. Of the 260,000 British wartime deaths, 10% of which were Scots, over 1,200 were Home Guard volunteers. Active training of the Home Guard was suspended in the autumn of 1944, leaving its members subject to recall in an emergency. The Home Guard was reactivated during the Cold War, but gradually atrophied over the years until its official demise in 1957.

Fort William teemed with activity throughout the war. The Coastal Forces Training Base, HMS *St. Christopher,* grew with the addition of hundreds of sailors. Over 55,000 trainees passed through the base and several dozen large motor launches were stationed there, along with various larger support ships. The Army's Northwest Sub-District Headquarters was disestablished in 1942, and its functions absorbed by the Inverness Sub-District. Thereafter, its staff became an adjunct staff for the Inverness Sub-District. The War Office established a large commando training operation in the Fort William area in 1941, with its headquarters located in Spean Bridge at the Achnacary estate, the ancestral home of the Camerons of Lochiel. Its staff and trainees were regular visitors to Fort William, and 2nd Inverness Battalion of the Home Guard regularly trained with the Commandos at Achnacary. As the war drew to a close in 1945, the military forces began to disband and the Home Guard moved into suspended animation. By mid-1946 there was little military activity left in Fort William, and the mobilized Territorial Army battalions returned home to civilian pursuits. Holiday vacationers soon began to arrive, and the town transformed itself once again to its role as a tourist destination.

About the Author

ABBOTT A. BRAYTON holds a Ph.D in International Politics and served in higher education for 26 years as a Professor, Dean, and Vice President at three institutions, and 17 years in finance.

He also served 31 years as an Army officer, much of it as a reservist, and retired as a Colonel. During his career, he served alongside British Forces several times. He commanded a brigade for three years and was Deputy Chief of the Army's Political-Military Division in the Pentagon, which is responsible for all International Policy for the U.S. Army.

Abbott was raised in Massachusetts and Vermont. He lives in retirement in Vermont and Tennessee.

No stranger to publishing, he is the co-author of *The Politics of War and Peace,* chapters in five other books and numerous research articles.

About Celtic Cat Publishing

CELTIC CAT PUBLISHING was founded in 1995 to publish emerging and established writers. The following works are available from Celtic Cat Publishing at *www.celticcatpublishing.com*, Amazon.com, and major bookstores.

Regional   *Appalachian Tales & Heartland Adventures*, Bill Landry

Poetry   *Exile Revisited*, James B. Johnston
Revelations: Poems, Ted Olson
Marginal Notes, Frank Jamison
Rough Ascension and Other Poems of Science, Arthur J. Stewart
Bushido: The Virtues of Rei and Makoto, Arthur J. Stewart
Circle, Turtle, Ashes, Arthur J. Stewart
Ebbing & Flowing Springs: New and Selected Poems and Prose (1976-2001), Jeff Daniel Marion
Gathering Stones, KB Ballentine
Fragments of Light, KB Ballentine
Guardians, Laura Still

Fiction   *The Price of Peace*, James B. Johnston
Outpost Scotland, Abbott Brayton

Humor   *My Barbie Was an Amputee*, Angie Vicars
Life Among the Lilliputians, Judy Lockhart DiGregorio
Memories of a Loose Woman, Judy Lockhart DiGregorio
Jest Judy (CD), Judy Lockhart DiGregorio

Chanukah   *One for Each Night: Chanukah Tales and Recipes*, Marilyn Kallet

Young Adult   *Voyage of Dreams: An Irish Memory*, Kathleen E. Fearing

Children   *Jack the Healing Cat* (English), Marilyn Kallet
Jacques le chat guérisseur (French), Marilyn Kallet
Twins, Tracy Ryder Bradshaw

Memoir   *Being Alive*, Raymond Johnston